W9-CFJ-482

THE CRYSTAL PYRAMID

He was enough to take a girl's breath away. Tall, golden, to-die-for gorgeous. Over one shoulder he'd slung a canvas bag and his beach towel, a leopard-skin print. His hair was long, sun-blond, and through its sea-tossed and windblown waves she caught the glint of one gold earring.

Pia caught her breath sharply. "Hey, I know you. We met before. But where? When?"

He smiled at her, bemused, as she continued to stare in awed silence. "Egypt!" she burst out. "Years ago, in Alexandria. You're my golden Greek—the sailor who gave me half the crystal pyramid."

With a low chuckle, he fished into the beach bag and brought out the other half of the gleaming alabaster. For a long moment, Pia and Darius both stared at the glowing stone in his palm.

He raised his hand until the piece of alabaster was at eye level before Pia's face. Mesmerized, she watched the colors dance. Then the flow of pastels took on definite shapes. Two naked forms, one male, one female, were captured therein like moths in amber. As she watched, the man came to the woman, took her into his arms, drew her close, and kissed her. Then Darius reached out to her. He gathered Pia into his arms and held her, murmuring words she couldn't under-stand. When the crystal pyramid touched his lips, the stone begun to hum. And then he kissed her . . .

Zebra Books by Becky Lee Weyrich:

SANDS OF DESTINY
ALMOST HEAVEN
SPELLBOUND KISSES

Pinnacle Books by Becky Lee Weyrich:

ONCE UPON FOREVER
WHISPERS IN TIME
SWEET FOREVER

SANDS of DESTINY

BECKY LEE WEYRICH

ZEBRA BOOKS
KENSINGTON PUBLISHING CORP.

For all my special *friends,*
members of Southeastern Writers' Association,
with gratitude, fond memories, and hopes for more fun to come!

ZEBRA BOOKS are published by

Kensington Publishing Corp.
850 Third Avenue
New York, NY 10022

Copyright © 1996 by Becky Lee Weyrich

All rights reserved. No part of this book may be reproduced in any form or by any means without the prior written consent of the Publisher, excepting brief quotes used in reviews.

If you purchased this book without a cover you should be aware that this book is stolen property. It was reported as "unsold and destroyed" to the Publisher and neither the Author nor the Publisher has received any payment for this "stripped book."

Zebra and the Z logo Reg. U.S. Pat. & TM Off.

First Printing: May, 1996
10 9 8 7 6 5 4 3 2 1

Printed in the United States of America

Chapter One

Olympia Byrd was born a dreamer, but until one sizzling-hot morning in her sixteenth year, she had always been able to distinguish fantasy from reality. The man she was about to meet and the events soon to unfold would change all that forever.

She spotted the golden Greek the minute she stepped off the tour bus in Alexandria. In a glance, the American teenager sized him up as a guy who could make a girl feel like his queen one minute, his slave the next.

She had spent the morning's rather dull sightseeing excursion pretending that she was Queen Cleopatra touring her domain. After all, Pia mused, her own hair was as black as any Egyptian's and her eyes were the deep blue of the royal gemstone, lapis lazuli. If only her father would let her wear makeup, she could look exactly like that exotic old queen.

Everyone knew, of course, that the Queen of Egypt had required the services of a lover. All the books claimed she was an extremely passionate woman. That was why Pia had picked out her Greek god so quickly. He was the perfect man to enliven her fantasies. Cleopatra's Mark Antony, she told herself. In reality, he was a Greek sailor—twentyish and golden from head to toe. Every time Pia stole a glance at him, which was often, she felt a warm tingle right down to her strappy sandals.

"He's like a date cake dipped in beer," she murmured softly, remembering the words some long-ago Egyptian teenager had written about her sweetheart in one of the ancient tombs at Memphis. When their guide had translated the intricate hieroglyphics, Pia had thought that was a strange way to describe anybody, but the words fit her handsome Greek to a tee. He had the sweet, golden look of a honey-drenched pastry, yet there was a totally male ruggedness about him that hinted of late nights in seamy waterfront taverns spent over tankards of strong, Egyptian corn beer.

She'd shot him her special look at her first opportunity. Cool, but flirtatious. The same glance she used at high school proms when she wanted to slow-dance with a certain football quarterback. The lazy flash of her blue eyes had worked like a charm. For the past half hour, the sailor had been following along, close enough to keep his tiger-eyes on Pia, but not so close as to make himself obvious to her father.

Clearly, the Greek was flirting, as foreign men will. Naturally, Pia was flirting back, as teenage girls must.

"Pia! Don't lag," her father called from up ahead. "I don't want to lose you again as I did at Luxor."

She smiled, remembering Luxor. That day at the famous Temple of Karnak she had pretended to be Nefertari, the most beloved wife of Ramses II. Pia knew that for a fact because in Nefertari's tomb her husband had ordered the inscription: "Possessor of charm, sweetness, and love." She'd been a beauty too. The perfect wife for the great Ramses, Pia figured.

Oh, the fantasies she had spun as she'd gazed up at the colossus of that strong, silent Pharaoh!

"What a hunk! No wonder he fathered ninety children. His wives probably couldn't keep their hands off him," Pia murmured to herself. "But Cleopatra's more fun. Poor Nefertari had to share Ramses. Ole Cleo took her pick. *All those lovers* and a golden barge to boot!"

Pia's mind wandered to romantic nights, cruising the Nile while some great, lusty Roman sat at her gold-sandaled feet, peeling grapes for a start, then later peeling . . .

"Olympia!"

She jumped, startled out of her wicked thoughts. When her father called her by her full name, Pia knew she'd better shape up. She quickened her pace in spite of the fact that she had little desire to stay close to the group of twenty or so sweaty American, European, and Oriental tourists.

"Do we have to go this fast? It's so hot, Dad," Pia complained. She caught up with her tall, husky, Navy commander father, mopping her sweaty brow to make her point. "This is probably the sort of day when ancient Egyptians baked bricks."

"Exactly what they were doing back there at our last stop, Olympia." She was well aware of the reproach in his tone. "But you missed the demonstration because you're being such a slowpoke."

"Sorry, Daddy-o. "I'll try to keep up."

Stephen Byrd gave his daughter *that look*—pulled-down brows and mouth drawn to a hard, straight line. He hated being called Daddy-o and Pia knew it. It had just slipped out. By way of apology, she offered him her sunniest smile and linked her arm through his.

"What's next?" she asked brightly, trying to sound truly interested.

"If you really want to know, check the schedule our guide gave you."

Pia didn't bother. She simply followed along. To be honest, she found Alexandria a big disappointment. She hadn't read her tour handbook as her father had advised the night before. She'd been too busy writing a love sonnet to Ramses. Consequently, this morning she had expected to see the royal palace of the Ptolemies, the Pharos lighthouse, even the tomb of Alexander the Great. But, as the book clearly stated, those marvelous ancient wonders were long gone, struck down eons ago by earthquake, man, and time. Only a single column called Pompey's Pillar and the hilltop ruins of the Temple of Serapis remained from those distant centuries. The rest of Alexandria, though pretty enough with its modern buildings and touches of Victorian architecture, was not what she had hoped for. In fact, the delta city was nothing at all like the other areas of Egypt they had toured in the past ten days. She might have been in a different country, in any of a number of foreign places she had visited in the past with her dad.

This three-week vacation was one of the annual treats the two of them enjoyed. His Navy career kept him on board ship most of the time, so since Pia's mother's death eight years ago, their family life had consisted of summer jaunts to exotic places—Italy, France, Malta, Australia. This was her first trip to Egypt, although her father had been here many times. Most of the year Pia spent in boarding school in Virginia. She would have only these three weeks with her dad before she was packed off to camp with her cousins in Maine. It was a strange life, but Pia had grown used to it over the years. And it almost seemed that she and her father were closer for having so little shared time.

"There's the *agora,* the old market place, just ahead," Stephen Byrd remarked, ending his brief, frosty silence. The return of his smile told Pia that her tacit apology had been accepted. Not a bad time to press her advantage, she decided.

"Can I buy a souvenir?"

Her father laughed and gave her ponytail a tug. "Sure, honey. But I don't know how we'll get the bags closed to fly home if you buy much more." He frowned down at her again, this time playfully. "Absolutely no more marble statues of naked men! Understood?"

"Dad-dy!" Pia groaned. "They aren't just naked men. They're gods."

"They still need some clothes on, if you ask me. Or at the very least, a well-placed fig leaf."

In spite of the fact that their guide, in a droning monotone, was still telling them about points of interest, most of the group broke away to make a dash for the street vendors. The milling shoppers in the market suddenly swelled to mob proportions. There was nothing for Pia and her dad to do but wait for the crowd to thin.

Pia pulled off her wide-brimmed straw hat, hoping to catch a stray breeze off the Mediterranean. She shaded her eyes and glanced up at the unblemished sky. It was the most perfect pale turquoise, reminding her of the delicate color of the ancient Roman glass they had seen earlier in one of the museums. The tint of her sunglasses added the same iridescent sheen to the sky that so enhanced the beauty of that antique shard.

She peered over her shoulder. Her Greek, a few yards away, gave her a quick, golden wink. She smiled and fluttered her dark lashes alluringly. This game, she decided, was far more fun than sightseeing.

She was about to stray from the group when suddenly the tour guide's monotonous voice caught her attention.

"All of this area, right down to the water's edge at the Great Harbor on the east, was once the site of the marble palace of the Ptolemies. Cleopatra, as you will recall, was the final ruler of that line, which descended directly from Alexander the Great. She was the last Queen of Egypt."

Pia stared down at the cobbles beneath her dusty Jesus-sandals. *"She* might have stood on this very spot once!" Pia murmured, awestruck.

"Cleopatra's grave, next to Mark Antony's," the tour guide continued dramatically, "lies somewhere deep below where we now stand. It was the queen's final request, before putting the asp to her breast, that she be laid to rest beside the man who was the greatest love of her life. And near where those two lovers are buried lies the alabaster sarcophagus of Alexander himself. Julius Caesar visited the conqueror's tomb as did many world leaders of ancient times. But the exact location of the royal mausoleum, the *Soma,* has been lost to us for centuries."

Pia's heart gave a little bump of excitement. Lovers buried side by side, and so near Cleopatra's famous ancestor, Alexander. Her mind whirled suddenly with scenes and feelings conjured up by her fantastic imagination. If only she could visit Cleopatra's Alexandria for just one day . . . one hour. She closed her eyes, willing herself to see that fabulous ancient city. But when she opened them again everything was the same. Heat and dust and tourists.

"Come on, Pia," her father insisted. "We're going to the market now."

Pia's driving urge to buy something had deserted her. What was one more souvenir, after all? Another cheap piece of pottery made in an assembly-line factory especially for the purpose of conning rich American tourists. All at once, she felt disgust for all the junk she'd prized so highly and bought so impulsively, at inflated prices. She'd give it all—even her statuettes of naked men—for one brief glimpse of Cleopatra's Egypt.

As her father pushed through the crowd, tugging Pia along with him, she remembered her golden Greek. A quick glance told her that he was no longer trailing the group. She sighed with regret. He had been the most interesting sight in Alexandria. Silly as it seemed, Pia experienced an enormous pang of disappointment.

"Look, Pia, this is nice." Her father picked up a tooled-leather handbag, stamped with gold hieroglyphics.

She barely gave the handsome purse a glance, busy as she was scanning the crowd for her Greek sailor. But he seemed to have vanished entirely.

As they moved through the noisy throng, Pia passed up gold sandals inlaid with plastic "turquoise," heavy brass necklaces in the shapes of ankhs and cartouches, scarabs that really did look old, even an alabaster statuette of Alexander in the buff.

"Shopped out, eh?" Her father laughed. "Well, you look around and I'll go buy us Cokes."

"Great, Dad," Pia answered without enthusiasm.

Her father had no more than left her side when she heard a man's heavily accented voice whispering to her. "Come, miss! Look! I got precious thing here."

Pia glanced at the old peddler. He was dressed in rags, filthy from the skin out. He reminded her of a grave robber.

"You look, miss. You buy."

Curious, Pia moved closer. The object he had for sale was wrapped in a piece of rusty-black velvet. That seemed pretty strange when all the other vendors were waving their wares in the air, shouting for the tourists' attention.

"What do you have there?" she asked. Curious, tempted.

"Come close. I show you, miss."

Pia had no desire to get any closer. The stench of the man took her breath away. But some invisible force seemed to draw her to the object he held in his hand.

The man hunched closer still. Pia noticed that his eyes had a strange, glazed look. She wondered if he was blind. Apparently he was not. He glanced furtively about, checking to make sure no one else was watching before he eased the tattered velvet from his prize.

Pia caught her breath when the cloth slipped away. A perfect pyramid of opalescent crystal rested in his grimy palm. She reached out to touch it, but he quickly drew it away.

"You like? You buy!" he said emphatically. "You got thirty American dollar?"

Pia stared, transfixed, at the gleaming chunk of stone. It seemed to glow with an inner light, giving off a faint, greenish aura. The colors shifted, turning pink, then gold before her eyes.

"I'll give you twenty dollars," Pia—born to haggle—told the vendor.

He shook his turbaned head furiously, then covered the crystal pyramid once more. Quickly, he turned away from her.

"No!" he growled over his shoulder. "This very ancient, very sacred. Broke from tomb of Alexander by Queen Cleopatra herself. Talisman . . . has mysterious powers. You want, you pay *thirty dollar!*"

The tour guide's words came back to Pia suddenly— Alexander the Great, buried in an alabaster sarcophagus. In that instant, she knew she must have the thing. It was a genuine piece of Cleopatra's Alexandria. Pia dug into her purse, fishing for money.

"Oh!" she cried, coming up empty. "I don't have thirty dollars!" Her father had all their American money. She had only a few Egyptian coins.

The dusky merchant shook his head at her and gave her an evil grimace. Convinced she was trying to trick him into selling his prize for less, he moved off, muttering to himself in some ancient tongue.

"Wait!" Pia called frantically. "I'll get the money from my father."

Her heart raced as she searched the crowd, trying to spot her dad. By the time he came up behind her and touched her arm, Pia was almost in tears. Having the crystal pyramid suddenly seemed a matter of life and death.

"Oh, Daddy, thank goodness!" she cried. "I found exactly what I want. I have to have it! But I didn't have the money and now the man's disappeared and we *must* find him before he sells it to someone else. Hurry! Follow me!"

Pulling her father by the arm, Pia barged through the crowd, searching wildly for the vendor. She almost laughed aloud when she spied her Greek sailor. Only a short time ago, she had been frantic to locate him. Now he seemed totally unimportant next to the man with the crystal pyramid.

Suddenly, she gasped and stopped dead in her tracks. There, beside her golden Greek, stood the hunchbacked peddler. She watched, horrified, as the sailor counted out his money and took the glittering chunk of alabaster into his hand.

"Oh, no!" she wailed. "We're too late! He's sold it already."

The sight of tears streaming down his daughter's cheeks totally baffled Stephen Byrd. "Pia, what on earth's gotten into you? Surely, he has another hunk of rock in his bag for sale. If not, you'll find something else you like."

She shook her head furiously. "I don't want anything else. I want that piece of alabaster!"

When she looked up again, she found herself staring right into the amber eyes of the Greek sailor. A shock went through her. He was even more handsome up close than he had seemed from afar. He didn't smile. He only gazed at her, his eyes smoldering like molten gold. His look was caressing, almost intimate. Pia opened her mouth to speak to him, but found herself unable to utter a sound.

As she stood frozen to the spot, the Greek raised his palm toward her. The sun struck the alabaster pyramid and it gave off a blinding, mesmerizing rainbow of color. Pia blinked her eyes shut against the brilliant glare.

In that instantaneous flash, the dusty market and its noisy tourists vanished. When she opened her eyes again, she was inside cool marble walls. In the distance someone was strumming a stringed instrument. Its soft music mingled with the faint murmur of a fountain.

She blinked again and the lovely scene faded. She was still standing in the hot, dirty market. The Greek was still there, his tiger eyes fixed on her face.

"Will you sell that to me?" she pleaded.

The sailor said nothing. Perhaps he spoke no English. But as Pia waited for some reply, he reached down to the path and found a heavy stone. Pia cried out when she saw what he meant to do, but she was too late to stop him. With one sharp whack, he broke the pyramid into two perfect halves. Still without a word, he handed one piece to her.

The alabaster felt warm in Pia's palm. She stared down at it, seeing its colorful aura intensify through the remnants of her tears. The hot wind swirling through the marketplace turned cool and refreshing. Again, she heard the music and the tinkling of the fountain. When she looked around, she found herself once more within the cool, quiet setting she had glimpsed moments before.

"Cleopatra? Cleopatra!" Someone was calling her name.

"Here, my darling." It seemed Pia uttered the words, but how could that be?

She looked down at herself. She was lying on a golden couch, cushioned in purple silk. Her diaphanous gown hid little of her shapely form. A wide gold collar set with gleaming gemstones and a matching girdle provided only token modesty to her exotic costume.

The sound of the man's voice, although she had yet to see him, sent a warm thrill through her blood. She let her fingers trail in the scented pool beside her couch as she gazed out over the silver-blue sea beyond her marble terrace, savoring the moments of anticipation as her lover approached.

The soft slap of sandals on the smooth pebble mosaic of the palace floor made her smile. Her gaze drifted to his and held for long moments. She shifted slightly toward him and sighed, parting her full, carmine-tinted lips. Her heart was racing as it always did when he came to her. With other men, she retained total control. But not with *this* man. Not *ever* with him!

He strode toward her, the muscles in his powerful thighs bulging. He was devouring her with an intimate gaze. Hungry for passion, he made love to her with his eyes before he ever touched her.

She drank in his presence as he crossed the quiet court. He was tall, muscular, and so handsome that only to look at him made her ache and tremble with anticipation. His hair was a tumbled riot of sun-gold curls. His eyes, gone dark now with desire, were the warm, clear color of the finest amber. The wide hammered-gold collar about his strong neck hid nothing of his powerful chest from her longing gaze. The snowy linen of his pleated kilt fell from a golden girdle that hugged his trim waist. He had the face, the form, and— she knew—the passion of a god.

"I prayed to Isis that you would come," she whispered, raising her hand for his kiss.

"You need no prayers to bring me." His voice was deep, husky with emotion. "It would have taken all the powers of your goddess to keep me away."

He took her delicate fingers in his hand—a hand so large and strong it might have crushed her fragile bones. But she showed no fear, only eagerness. Gently, he pressed his mouth to her cool flesh. Kneeling beside her couch, he slipped one hand across her body, stroking a shapely thigh through the folds of her transparent gown. Meanwhile, his mouth traveled up her arm, to her bare shoulder, then on to her waiting lips. Lips that quivered under his and parted with invitation.

She moaned softly. Without the slightest hesitation, she thrust her tongue toward his, hungry for the taste she knew and savored—honey, wine, and desire.

Her nipples peaked and hardened. Her thighs trembled. Her innermost womanly core raged with the fire of her need.

"You torture me with your tenderness," she sighed. "Would you keep your queen waiting? Must I beg you? Please . . ."

"Please, please, please." Pia realized she was repeating the word over and over. But why? Where was she? What had happened?

She opened her eyes to find a circle of curious tourists crowding around her, staring down. Her father's suntanned face came into focus, filled with concern.

"Olympia, can you hear me? Are you all right, honey?"

All around her the sights and sounds of the marketplace swirled in a maddening scene of too-bright color and too much noise. The sun glared down like a brassy disk, making her head pound. In the suffocating heat, her light sundress clung to her body, sticky with sweat. Gone was the cool, marble palace, the tinkling fountain, the golden lover.

Pia sat up slowly, feeling utterly foolish. "Tell me I didn't faint. Did I?"

"You sure did," her dad answered. "Scared the hell out of me! I'm getting you back to the hotel right now. You've had too much sun."

He scooped up his limp, dazed daughter in his arms.

"Wait, Daddy!" she cried.

She hadn't had a chance to thank the Greek sailor. She glanced about, but the gorgeous, golden man—the very one she had seen in her vision—had vanished. To her vast relief, his gift had not. Her half of the crystal pyramid remained clutched tightly in her palm.

"He's probably gone back to his ship," her father commented in a casual tone.

"Who?"

"That young seaman you've been making eyes at all morning." He chuckled and gave her a squeeze. "I guess you're all right if you're still up to flirting."

"I *wasn't* flirting with him, Daddy!"

"Don't try to fool your old man. I'm a sailor, too, remember. I'd know that come-hither look anywhere."

"I was bored, that's all. And he was cute."

"He's probably off that rusty old tanker out there—the *Nile Queen.* I heard it's heading back to Athens today. I'll bet he has a fat wife and a passel of rowdy little Greeks waiting there for him. Just as well, too. At least I won't have to worry about him showing up at our hotel tonight looking for you like that swarthy guide you mesmerized in Cairo."

"Dad-dy!" Pia was too exhausted and too confused to hold up her end of the discussion. Besides, she didn't want to talk, she wanted to think.

She rested her head on her father's shoulder, wondering what all this meant. Had she really returned to Cleopatra's time for a brief visit? Or was her dad right—was the hot Egyptian sun simply playing tricks with her mind?

On the taxi ride back to their hotel, Pia remained silent, her whole attention focused on the deep inner glow of the chunk of alabaster from Alexander's tomb. She didn't know how or when, but someday, Pia vowed, she would return to Cleopatra's Alexandria and her gorgeous, golden lover.

She closed her eyes and, reliving her vision, ran her tongue over her dry lips. The taste of him still lingered—honey, wine, and a soul-deep desire that could span the ages.

*   *   *

Pia's father was right. The Greek sailor was indeed off the *Nile Queen*, and he was late returning to his ship because of the pretty girl with the lapis blue eyes. He knew he'd have to pull extra duty for his tardiness. But the cute American tourist had been worth it, whatever the cost. He only wished he'd had more time to get to know her.

He hurried back on board, took more than what he figured was his share of abuse for being late, then set to work swabbing the oily deck—his punishment for losing track of time.

Hours later and many leagues away from Alexandria, he was still at it, swimming in his own sweat and blistered by the scorching Mediterranean sun, when the ship's alarm sounded. As the flaming sun sank into the burning sea, chaos broke out on the deck of the *Nile Queen*—running feet, screams of terror, sheer panic.

"Fire below!"

The universal cry sent a chill through the young sailor. He dropped his mop and joined the others in a wild scramble to find life vests.

"Abandon ship!" The urgent call came over the horn on deck. He didn't wait for a second command. He jumped for his life, over the starboard side, into the warm, salty water. It was a long, terrifying plunge into the dark sea.

Coughing and gasping, he surfaced at the very instant of the first explosion. All around him, his shipmates were screaming and dying. He had only a brief moment to say a prayer of thanks that he had survived. A second blast, and he lost consciousness—his last vision the smiling face of the pretty American and the beautiful colors of the crystal pyramid glowing in her soft palm.

For days he drifted alone in the water under the burning eye of the sun. Consciousness came and went, but he was aware of little other than his thirst and his agony. Finally, he gave up hope, willing the drift of the great sea to take him where it would.

Alexandria, Egypt—55 B.C.

Heat lay over The City like a shimmering pall, making it waver and gleam before the girl's wide eyes like some great, many-faceted jewel. The marble palace loomed over the Great Port, its cool expanse offering sanctuary. But shunning its comforts, the dark-haired child-woman remained on the wide steps that ran down to the water's edge, determined to watch for the sails of a certain ship.

"He'll come today." Her words sounded more like a command than mere speculation. She shaded her green eyes with one hand and scanned the horizon beyond Pharos once more.

"Lady?" her young servant called anxiously. "The sun . . ."

The dark-haired girl glanced down at her arms, pale olive by inheritance rather than exposure. Iras was right; she should cover herself. She knew the foolishness of allowing Ra's fire to turn her skin as dark as a peasant's. She moved quickly, smoothly, back up the broad stairway to the vermilion silk tent her serving girl had erected.

"Still no sail, my lady?"

Princess Cleopatra shook her head, never shifting her eyes from the aquamarine water. "He will come," she affirmed, "and those Roman barbarians with him. But even as Rome's puppet, it's far better that my father, the Flute Player, should sit the throne than my wicked sister Berenice."

"*You* should be queen!" the servant exclaimed, as always her young mistress's champion.

"Hush, Iras!" Cleopatra scolded. "You'll turn the gods against me with such talk."

The princess lounged in an ebony chair that was inlaid with tiny ivory and gold leopards. A sudden breeze stirred the delicate linen of her loosely draped chiton. How she would love to strip off her gown and take a swim in the cooling waters as she had done when she was a small child.

She laughed aloud suddenly.

"Lady?" her servant asked, startled. Laughter had once come as naturally to her mistress as breathing. But not for a long time had the young princess been anything other than somber. Her motherless childhood, her drunken father, her squabbling brothers and sisters, and the dreaded Roman threat all had taken their toll. Now, at fourteen, Cleopatra seldom had cause for mirth.

"You're thinking the sun has burned away my senses, eh, Iras, that this is no time for gaiety, with the King of Egypt on his way to drive his evil daughter from his own throne? Well, I declare this a holiday from all grim thoughts. I want to swim. I want to laugh. I want to love and be loved in return." Cleopatra paused and sighed. "My last wish, I suppose, is hopeless. But I mean to satisfy my other desires this minute. Come with me, Iras!"

The serving girl followed mutely as Cleopatra kicked off her sandals and tripped lightly down the marble stairs. The diminutive princess followed the bottom step along the water's edge to a small archway where the shoreline took on its natural contour for a few secluded furlongs. "Cleopatra's Beach," her father called the tiny cove, since his liveliest daughter claimed the spot as her private domain.

The eager princess was already tugging at her heavy girdle to be free of her clothes when her servant caught up to her.

"Help me, Iras," she commanded impatiently. "This accursed clasp is caught in back."

Cleopatra turned to see the girl's pale eyes gone wide. Slowly, Iras's hand rose, one finger pointing to the water's edge. "Lady, look!"

The princess turned slowly, her emotions battling. She had waited so long for her father's return from Rome. She must be here to greet him, to support him against her evil sister. But she had so longed for these last few moments as a carefree child. She fully expected to see the sail of his ship when she turned. What she saw instead brought a gasp of surprise. A man's body floated near the beach.

"Some poor wretch executed by your sister, then thrown to the fishes."

"No," Cleopatra answered. "He hasn't the ghastly look of death about him."

Both young women eyed the man with more than casual interest. His hair was a tangle of golden curls and bits of flotsam. His flesh looked raw from the sun and the sea. Cleopatra could tell, though, that once his body had been strong, virile, and as tawny gold as his manly locks. He was naked, covered only by a girdle of seaweed that hid the secrets of his manhood from her innocent eyes. His face, rough with beard, was still almost beautiful.

"Look!" Cleopatra cried. "He's breathing. Help me, Iras. He's all but drowned, yet we might be able to save him."

Cleopatra hiked the back hem of her skirt through her legs and tucked it into her waist. Then the two of them waded out and pulled the man in to shore.

"Are you sure he's alive?" Iras whispered.

"Barely." The word was tinged with excitement and hope. "Help me turn him on his back."

"Oh, Lady, we shouldn't!" Iras protested. "You should never have touched him. You'll taint your flesh. Why, he could be a common slave!"

"A slave . . . he may be. But common?" A smiled curved Cleopatra's full lips as she stared down at the handsome stranger. "I think not!"

Together—over Iras's strong objections—the girls turned him on his back. Then the servant gasped with shock and disapproval as she watched her mistress lean over the man's still form, pry his sunburnt lips apart, and fit her royal mouth to his.

"Your father will have him tortured and killed for this," Iras warned.

Cleopatra said nothing, but kept at her work on the golden stranger. At length, he stirred, then coughed. His eyes—deep amber—shot open. The princess sat back on her heels and smiled down at him.

"Where am I? What's happened?" He spoke some strange Greek dialect, but Cleopatra knew many languages. Both she and Iras understood him.

Iras scowled at the man. "A more proper question might be *who are you?*" she demanded.

"Be still, girl!" Cleopatra ordered harshly. "Let him catch his breath. Run and fetch some wine from the tent. Bring my robe to cover him."

When they were alone, Cleopatra reached out and began plucking bits of seaweed from the man's salty locks. Only to touch him sent a shiver of pleasure through her. It seemed to her that he was a favorable omen—a gift from the gods, cast up from the sea for her alone. As near dead as he had been such a short time before, each moment that passed seemed to renew his vigor and his manliness.

He coughed again and leaned up on one elbow to spit out more sea water. When he turned from her, Cleopatra winced at the sight of his badly burned back.

"You need ointments for your skin, and food. You're all ribs. I'll take you to my rooms and see to your care myself."

He turned back to her and stared. He tried to smile, but his lips were painfully cracked from sun and salt. Looking up at the lovely girl who had saved him, he touched his fingertips to his mouth.

"You kissed me just now."

Cleopatra leaned closer, her long hair forming a dark curtain to shadow her face. "I did no such thing. I only

forced breath into you to make you live. But now . . . " She
placed her mouth gently but firmly over his scorched lips
for an instant. The intimate contact sent a dangerous fire
surging through her. "Now I have kissed you." A whimsical
smile played over her lips as she seemed to consider the
merits of the kiss. "Yes, I liked it quite well."

In spite of the pain it caused, he grinned. "I didn't think
it was so bad either."

"You have a name?" she asked.

Cleopatra watched as his handsome face went dark with
troubled thought. A blank expression filled his amber eyes.

"Everybody's got a name," he stated matter-of-factly. "It's
just that I can't remember mine right now. Something's
happened to me." He glanced about helplessly. "How did I
get here? Where did I come from?"

"The very questions I meant to ask next," Cleopatra told
him gently. "Someone has given you a potion of forgetfulness. But never mind. I've found you and you are mine now,
so I'll choose a name for you." She paused in thought, one
delicate fingertip pressed to her chin. Her eyes glistened
with pleasure. "*Darius!* I like that, don't you?"

"Darius." He tested the name, nodded. "Fine! I'll be
Darius if you like. But who are you?"

She laughed in utter delight. Imagine finding anyone who
didn't know who she was! "My name is Cleopatra Thea
Philopator. I am the third daughter of Auletes, the Flute
Player."

"A musician's daughter, eh?" He grinned again, appeal-
ingly. "And I'll bet you sing, too. You have the voice for
it, so rich with musical tones."

Cleopatra laughed again, but not at his seeming ignorance.
It was simply wonderful to find someone who had no idea
that the royal blood of Egypt and Macedonia ran through
her veins. How she wished she could remain the offspring

of a street performer in this man's eyes. But soon enough he was bound to find out the truth. Sad thought!

"You're right. My father often plays his flute in the streets, but only when he's drunk too much Mareotic, his favorite wine."

Darius frowned suddenly. "What'll he say if you take me home?"

Cleopatra shrugged. "He's not in The City right now. Besides, I'll hide you in my room and no one will know you're there."

"You live in a big house, huh?"

She motioned casually toward the gleaming palace that rambled on for acres, taking up one third of the entire city of Alexandria.

Darius gave a low whistle and shaded his eyes against the glare off the marble walls. "Where in hell am I, anyway?"

Cleopatra shook her head till her dark hair rippled with sunlight. "Nowhere in hell. You're in Egypt."

With a groan of frustration, Darius lay back on the hot sand of the beach. He closed his eyes, trying to force some recall—some name, some face, some hint of his past. But it was as if his whole consciousness were as smooth and blank and white as the walls of the imposing palace where this flute player's daughter claimed that she lived.

Concentrating with all his might, he caught a fleeting memory—or was it only an impression?—of holocaust and fear and pain. Then he glimpsed another young woman smiling at him—lapis blue eyes, fair skin, ebony hair a shade darker than Cleopatra's. But the pretty, young face was gone before he could focus his thoughts.

"What's that you have in your hand?" Cleopatra asked. "You've been clutching it since Iras and I pulled you to shore."

"In my hand?"

Again, he drew a blank. Slowly, he uncurled his cramped fingers. He stared down. It was a shining piece of rock.

Cleopatra's sharp intake of breath brought his gaze back to her.

"Where did you find that?" she demanded. "It's mine! Someone stole it from my room months ago."

"But you stole it first." Darius spoke the words not as an accusation or a question but as a statement of fact. Why he said such a thing, he hadn't the faintest idea. Still, it seemed to be the truth. Cleopatra's cheeks colored and she looked away from him.

"Hey, I'm sorry," he whispered, touching her hand. "I don't know what made me say that."

"It's true," she admitted with a faint smile. "I'm ashamed to say that when I was only a little girl, I slipped into the *Soma* alone and chipped that piece from my ancestor's tomb. I thought it would bring me wisdom and strength to have something of his."

"Who was this ancestor?"

"Why, Alexander the Great, of course." It popped out before Cleopatra stopped to think.

"Of course . . . " Darius did retain some vague memories after all, he realized. He stared hard at the shining stone.

Alexander the Great? Come on! Who did this girl think she was kidding?

Still, she seemed to set great store by the chunk of rock in his hand. He held it out toward her, experiencing a fleeting sense of *déjà vu*.

Cleopatra shook her head and closed his fingers over the piece of alabaster. "No, you keep it. It must have magical powers. It kept you alive and brought you to me, didn't it?"

She leaned down then and kissed him again. Weak as he was, Darius returned her kiss, eagerly and deeply.

May 4, 1979

Two days after Pia's arrival in the city, she got her final glimpse of Alexandria from the air. As the plane banked steeply, the homeward-bound teenager stared down, thinking back over that strange day at the *agora*—the Greek sailor, the crystal pyramid, and the odd sensations she had experienced.

Rubbing her fingers over the smooth surface of the piece of alabaster and closing her eyes, she vowed again to find a way to return to that cool marble palace and her passionate lover. The very thought kindled fire in her blood and made her ache with a strange longing.

When she opened her eyes and stared down again, the hodgepodge of Alexandria had changed. Gone were the tall hotels, the busy traffic, the Cornische, and all that she remembered of the city. In its place sprawled a cool expanse of marble palaces and the gleam of chryselephantine statues. On the island of Pharos stood the magnificent lighthouse, and ships with colorful sails rode at anchor in the harbor.

Pia's cry of amazement elicited her father's concern. "Just an air pocket, honey. We'll be above the turbulence soon."

"I'm okay, Daddy," she answered, trying to sound casual.

She blinked again and the startling scene below vanished. Disappointment flooded through her. She wanted to race to the cockpit and demand that the pilot turn the plane around and take her back to Alexandria—to its marble palaces and towering lighthouse. But what was the use? She was only daydreaming again.

Pia closed the shade at her window and settled back in her seat for the long flight home.

The rest of the trip proved uneventful. Indeed, once she returned to the States and joined her cousins in Maine for summer camp, the very sameness of the days convinced her that the rest of her life would probably be equally uneventful. She would finish high school, go to college, get married, and raise a family with a man who loved and respected her. . . .

"Yes, " she told herself years later on her wedding day, "I am embarking on a normal, uncomplicated, wonderfully uneventful life."

But Olympia Byrd was *very much mistaken!*

Chapter Two

St. Simons Island, Georgia—May 1991

It was near midnight. Olympia Byrd's face took on an eerie, greenish cast in the semidarkness as she glared at her computer screen. It glared back mercilessly. Tonight it appeared to her that Edgar Allan (affectionately named for her own favorite author, Poe) was acting less than user friendly. The electronic monster seemed to be making fun of her extreme case of writer's block. She scowled at its static, glowing face.

"Don't you look at me that way or I'll change your name to Sidney!"

Pia threatened the computer with her ex-husband's name—a dire warning, indeed. Although gone from her life these past seven years, Sidney Rudolph Olney III *and* his blond bimbo were still well remembered, if not well thought of.

"But Sidney's not the problem tonight," Pia reminded

herself. "Cleopatra is! Damned if I can think how to begin this book."

Pia heaved a weary sigh and pushed aside all thoughts of Sidney, his second wife, and her own brief, failed marriage. "Ancient history," she muttered. She sighed again, but for a different reason.

Ancient history was precisely the topic of this evening— ancient *Egyptian* history. Pia was right back where she'd started, staring at her computer and trying to think of the perfect opening sentence for her fictionalized biography of Cleopatra. This novel was meant to be Olympia Byrd's big breakout book after a string of mildly successful historical romances. But how could she hope to see her new title on the bestseller list, how could she dream of raking in a pile of bucks, how could she afford all the bead and sequin gowns she'd need to accept all the awards that were sure to be showered upon her for this "thrilling, spellbinding, totally enthralling" novel, if she couldn't even get page one going?

"Think *cash*, Pia-bird!" she told herself. "You certainly need the money."

Pia was managing to eke out a living from her writing, but just barely. She hoped Cleopatra's story would put her at least even, if not over the top.

A sudden burst of inspiration sent her fingers flying over the keyboard. She typed with lightning speed: *Cleopatra was not beautiful, but men seldom realized it.*

Pia's excitement died in a flash, the moment she reread the familiar words on the screen. "No! No! No!"

She punched the delete key angrily, wiping out her *Gone With the Wind* opening. Margaret Mitchell's words always popped out of her subconscious when she couldn't think how to begin a book, when she had grown weary and frustrated from trying over and over again to find exactly the right words of her own.

"Nine historical novels published," she muttered in anguish, "but it's always the same when I'm facing page one. Like I've never written a word before in my entire twenty-eight years."

She growled a warning at Edgar Allan and ran cramped fingers—their usually manicured nails gnawed naked of Plum Parfait Perle polish—through her black, shoulder-length hair. After a moment, she glanced at the digital clock across her cluttered office, the room that also served as a guest bedroom on rare occasions when the need arose.

"Past midnight, and here you sit like an uninspired lump," she grumped.

Her lapis blue eyes shifted from the clock to the calendar. Although she knew exactly what year and day it was in Cleo's life, she could barely remember the month in her own time. She'd been shut up in her two-bedroom beach cottage for weeks now—no contact with the outside world, no grasp of reality. She'd slipped out only when she needed milk, bread, peanut butter, or when Alexander-the-Cat wailed pitifully for his favorite, tuna-and-egg.

The James Archambeault photo on the calendar she'd purchased last November at the Kentucky Book Fair told her the month in a glance. The brilliantly colored shot of sleek horses and jockeys' bright silks at some previous Kentucky Derby reminded her that it must be May already.

"Thursday, May second, to be exact," she figured aloud. "And last year this time I was right there when Unbridled crossed the finish line. Well, Strike the Gold will just have to win the blanket of roses by himself. No cheers from the Pia-bird to urge him on in the stretch."

Her gaze shifted back to the blank computer screen from which her plagiarized sentence had now disappeared. "Nope! No trip to the Derby for you this year. And it serves you right for letting this deadline slip up on you."

Pia reached down and shoved a stack of research books

out of the way. Then, bracing her bare feet on the floor, she rolled her office chair away from the computer with a growl of disgust. She threw another hostile glance at poor Edgar Allan. Usually, she thought of the machine as her best friend. But on this particular night, it seemed like an enemy as vicious as any who had ever plotted to tumble Queen Cleopatra from her golden throne.

Pia stood and stretched, hearing bones crack, feeling tight muscles strain with fatigue. The crash of waves outside her cottage told her the tide was high. She drew in a deep breath, feeling a renewal of strength with the heady salt-tang of the air. Maybe a walk on the beach would clear her head and help her sleep. She'd had too many cups of coffee, too many cigarettes, which she had promised to give up "one of these days," as soon as the pressure was off.

Yes, escape to the beach! She'd made up her mind. In the morning she could get a fresh start. She'd think about the beginning of her novel just before she closed her eyes, then let her subconscious work on it while she got some rest. Often, to her delight and amazement, that worked. She would wake up in the morning feeling refreshed, with all her questions answered, all her problems solved, the perfect opening sentence blazing in her mind.

She glanced out the window. The moon hung like a gleaming, ghostly vessel over the water, making the restless ocean look like molten silver. A deep calm settled over her. The waves, especially at night, always had this same soothing effect.

"To the beach!" she cried, fishing about the cluttered floor to find her blue rubber flip-flops.

She had located one and was hot on the trail of the other when the phone gave a jarring ring.

"Damn! Who could that be at this hour?" She wrenched the receiver out of the cradle and shouted, "Yes?"

The ear-blasting racket of a rock band in the background all but drowned out the voice on the other end of the line.

"Who is this?" Pia demanded, ready to hang up unless her midnight caller made his or her identity known pronto.

"It's *Sudibeth,* honey," finally oozed through the line with sugary, Southern sweetness. "Whatcha doin'?"

Pia groaned. Sudibeth Callahan was her best friend, the much lauded author of a dozen or more children's books—the Queen of Kiddy Lit, all their writer friends called her. But she was the last person Pia had hoped to hear from tonight. If she'd only gone barefooted, she would have made good her escape to the beach.

"I'm working, Sudibeth." It was only a small lie, after all. She'd been trying.

"Hell's bells! Still? Don't you ever take a break?"

"Still," Pia answered frostily. It galled her at times that Sudibeth's writing seemed to come so effortlessly while Pia herself had to grope and struggle for every damn word.

"Well, you've worked enough for tonight. Throw on some decent clothes and hurry your beauteous bod down here to the King and Prince."

"You mean my best cutoffs and my faded purple tank top aren't good enough for your fancy friends at the K and P?" Pia asked with mild sarcasm.

"Not tonight, Miss Pia-bird! Some of the out of towners, here for the writers' conference, flew in early and we're having us a part-ee, honey chile. They're all just dying to meet the gal who writes those steamy novels and I promised them I'd get you down here."

"The writers' conference?" Panic swept Pia. "That's not till next month."

"Wrong, Sherlock! It's usually in June, but—remember?—we had to change the dates this year on account of that big ministers' meeting at Epworth By-The-Sea next month. Registration's day after tomorrow. And, don't forget, we're having a costume reception Sunday night. We're all supposed to come dressed as one of our favorite characters."

"Oh, God! Please no!" Pia moaned. She hadn't the slightest idea what kind of costume she could come up with this late, and she remembered, too, that she was supposed to teach the fiction class all week. She was, of course, unprepared.

"Shoot, Pia honey, it's gonna be a dandy conference," Sudibeth enthused. Then in a stage whisper she added, "Wait'll you meet this hunk who just flew in from Miami. I figure on fixing the two of you up."

"Oh, no, you don't! Not again," Pia answered emphatically. She had managed to steer clear of dangerous entanglements with men in general since her rotten Sidney experience, and she certainly cast a jaundiced eye toward any more of Sudibeth's fix-up jobs. Her friend's taste in men ran to big, macho, and horny.

"No!" Pia repeated. "I'm still trying to dodge the truck-driving, hound-chasing, snuff-dipping, gun-toting 'hunk from Hahira' you introduced me to last summer, *dear friend.*"

"Never mind about Bubba," Sudibeth snipped. "Just get yourself down here to the K and P. Now!"

"I can't. Really," Pia answered. "My editor's bugging me to finish this book on time. I have most of it roughed out, but I can't seem to get the opening right. Do you ever have that problem?"

"Sure do, hon!" Sudibeth chimed brightly. "And when it happens, I've found that the very best thing to get my juices flowing again is to treat myself to a night out, especially if I'm with a bunch of good-looking, sweet-talking hero types, who just love to dance."

"Forget it, Sudibeth! I'm serious. I've got a big-time case of writer's block. And if I don't shake it off soon, by butt's going to be in a big-time sling. My advance all went into repairs on the MG."

"Lord, Pia, why don't you just push that purple wreck off the end of the pier and put you and it out of your misery?"

"Sudibeth, that's unkind! You know I love that car. And it's not a wreck. It's just temperamental."

"Then hop in it, if it's running, and haul yourself on down here right now. Miami's just having a fit to meet you."

"Can't!" Pia repeated. "Gotta work!"

Sudibeth sighed forlornly into the phone. "You sure can be bullheaded. I give up, Pia-bird. Go back to work. I'll see you Sunday at registration."

"Right . . . Sunday . . . registration . . ."

Pia hung up and reached for the Rolaids. If she'd had a slight case of peanut butter heartburn before, it was now a full-scale attack of raging, gut-eating indigestion. How could she have forgotten the writers' workshop? And how could she teach all week, plus get her own work done?

"Oh, well," she sighed. "Maybe the break will do me good. I usually get all fired up to write when I see other people struggling so hard, trying to get published. If they only knew . . ."

The murmur of the waves was still calling to her. Pia glanced uncertainly at Edgar Allan's greenish glow. He seemed to be casting an accusing look her way. Quickly, she switched him off. Both flip-flops on her feet at last, she slapped across the room and out the door, pausing on the screened porch to take a deep breath.

"Hm-m-m, that smells good!"

The weather had been unseasonably warm and wet for the past month, forcing summer flowers. The night was perfumed with the scents of early blooming Confederate jasmine and oleander. Pia picked a cluster of pink blossoms from the huge bush beside her steps and twirled it beneath her nose as she headed through the sand dunes toward the water.

Once more Sidney crossed her mind, but this time her

thoughts were more charitable than they had been earlier. The one thing they hadn't fought over during the divorce was the beach cottage. Pia wanted it and Sidney had handed over the deed without the slightest hesitation. She loved the creaky old place with its view of the ocean and its sandy front yard. She wondered if she could write anywhere else. Her characters seemed hidden away in the very woodwork, as if they had always lived in the house, waiting for her to come and release them to the world. And that's exactly what she had been doing since her divorce. Sidney had patronizingly approved of her "literary dabbling," as he'd called it, assuring her that it was probably "good therapy."

"Therapy!" She laughed aloud. It was far more than that—her passion, her obsession, her very life. Poor Sidney would never understand.

Before Pia allowed herself to grow too sentimental and soft over her ex simply because he'd allowed her to have their island hideaway, she reminded herself that he had hated the place. Oleander and the other lush vegetation gave him hayfever. His fair skin blistered with the smallest dose of summer sun. He detested the feel of sand beneath his feet. The tiniest bite from a gnat or mosquito gave him hives. And he had lived in mortal fear of a hurricane striking the coast and cutting him off from the highway back to the mainland and his beloved Atlanta with its hectic traffic, power lunches—*plus a certain waiting blonde,* she reminded herself for good measure.

Pia might have gotten the house she wanted, but it hadn't been a bad deal for Sidney and his new love either. Pia got the beach cottage while they got the big house in Buckhead and the lodge in the Blue Ridge Mountains. Pia also got the 1974 purple MG Midget—the love of *her* life, but prone to frequent and expensive mechanical failure—while Sidney kept the BMW and Bimbo drove a new Cadillac every year.

"Stop this!" Pia cried aloud. "You're supposed to be thinking about the book. What was the turning point in Cleopatra's early life? What was ancient Alexandria really like? *Where can I start the story?"*

She kept quizzing herself aloud as she crossed the dunes. Safely through the sandspurs that lurked among the tall sea oats, Pia kicked off her flip-flops. The sand at the high water line felt cool and smooth against the soles of her feet. A silent ghost crab sidled across her path, then scurried sideways into its hole. It seemed only the two of them inhabited the quiet, quicksilver beach.

"No, the three of us," she informed the crab. "You, me, and good ole Cleo."

Music drifted from the King and Prince down the beach. Pia turned and gazed at the lighted palm trees swaying in the breeze on the hotel's manicured lawn. For two cents she'd give up her struggle and join Sudibeth and the others. But when she found herself drifting in that direction, she forced herself to do an about-face and head the other way.

That distraction off her mind—who needed to have fun, anyway?—Pia turned her thoughts back to the summer of 1979, her vacation in Egypt with her dad. She had planned a return trip to do research for this book, but the Gulf War had changed her mind. Now it was too late to go. Her deadline was drawing near. So, the next best thing to do was to dredge up the memory of that visit to Cleopatra's land.

Pia strolled slowly through the edge of the surf, concentrating as hard as she could. She wished now she had paid closer attention to the scenery when she was in Egypt. But how could she have known, all those years ago, that she would someday write about the place? One thing she remembered clearly—she recalled willing herself to see Cleopatra's Alexandria. And she had seen it, if only for moments.

She stopped and focused her attention on a distant point

out over the water, memories flooding back like the incoming waves.

"I did see something," she murmured. "A palace—a woman I thought was Cleopatra, but who seemed to be me and . . ." A smile lit her face. "And the most marvelous, golden lover. Talk about your hunks!"

Suddenly, another memory made her gasp aloud. Why hadn't she thought of it before?

"The crystal pyramid!"

Pia turned back toward the cottage and broke into a trot. She *must* find that piece of alabaster! The dirty old street vendor had called it a talisman. He'd claimed it had powers. Well, she'd tried everything else to get going on this book. Why not a little magic?

"If only I can find it," she said, struggling through the deep sand of the dunes.

She had kept her precious souvenir on display until she married. When she'd left college to become Sidney's bride, she had hastily packed everything, including the chunk of alabaster. During the few months of her ill-fated marriage, she'd never gotten around to unpacking all her belongings. After the divorce, Sidney had shipped her things to St. Simons, but some of the cartons were still packed, stowed away in her tiny attic.

"Yes!" she cried, punching the humid air with a fist as she raced up the porch steps. "It has to be there!"

The attic's fold-down stairs groaned from want of oil and lack of use. Pia climbed them cautiously. The air above was stifling hot, the atmosphere heavy with dust and the musty odors of mothballs and mildew. She looked around, taking stock. Christmas decorations, old clothes that she *might* wear again someday, writers' magazines. Aha! Three unopened cardboard boxes. She attacked them with fierce determination. Naturally, the searched-for item was in the very bottom of the last box.

Pia sat back on her heels, sweating profusely as she lifted the alabaster fragment out of its worn velvet casing. She closed her eyes and begged, "Show me Cleopatra. Tell me her story. Come on now, *please!*"

She waited, holding her breath. Nothing happened. But the cool piece of stone did feel soothing in her palm. Disappointed that it seemed less than magical, she was happy to have it back in her life again. If nothing else, she could put it on her desk beside her computer and tell Edgar Allan and Alexander-the-Cat that it held ancient, mystical secrets.

"Those two are so easily conned." She chuckled as she climbed out of the hot attic, then folded the stairs back into the hallway ceiling.

Pia hurried into her office and cleared a place for her long-lost treasure, wondering as she did if it really was a piece chipped from Alexander the Great's sarcophagus. Happy with the addition of the crystal pyramid to the cozy chaos on her desk, she flipped on the computer. The greenish light from the screen seemed to kindle a pastel flame inside the chunk of alabaster. She watched, mesmerized, as the colors shifted and changed—green, blue, lavender, pink, and finally a shining gold.

All of a sudden, out of nowhere, a full-blown opening sentence popped into Pia's head.

Letting her fingertips dance over the keyboard, she wrote: *Cleopatra had many lovers, but only two men claimed her heart.*

She sat back and stared at the screen, reading the words over and over. Then she grinned.

"Yes! I like it."

For a few minutes she played with her brainstorm, changing a word here, adding a phrase there. Finally, she came back to her original sentence. She leaned back in her chair and reached for the crystal pyramid.

Suddenly, something like thunder shook the whole house.

"Mercy! What was that?" She glanced about the room, her heart racing. Odd, she hadn't seen any lightning.

She lit a cigarette—only to calm her nerves, she assured herself. But when a second shudder boomed through the house, she stubbed out the glowing butt in her overflowing ashtray. She sat frozen in her chair, waiting for a third shock. Was it an earthquake? A sonic boom?

The next jolt she felt came from her heart trying to leap out of her chest. As she focused her eyes on the glowing piece of alabaster, Pia felt a hand grip her shoulder. She gasped and froze, too terrified to turn around. She took several deep breaths, hoping she could make her pulse stop racing.

Okay, she reasoned silently. So you think there's a hand on your shoulder. Well, the joke's on you, Pia-bird. It's only your imagination. You're making up this whole scenario— something new to add to the book. Right? Your subconscious is working on one of the male characters—the golden lover. Now, here he is—all created and ready to be written down.

Her rather twisted logic seemed to be working. Her heart rate slowed. This wasn't such an unusual occurrence after all. She often created a character only to have her creation appear to her in a dream or talk back to her while she was writing dialogue at the computer. She made her characters come alive. Wasn't that what a good writer was supposed to do?

But this was different. *Very different!* She'd never had one of her characters touch her before. Still, the explanation she offered herself seemed the only one possible.

Trying to calm herself and to ignore the hand on her shoulder, she reread her opening sentence aloud.

"That's a lie!"

Pia jumped when the angry male voice boomed right behind her. "Hey, you can't talk to me that way. I created you, and I'll tell you what I want you to say and when to

say it. Who the hell are you, anyway? I need a name—
something that sounds Egyptian, but isn't hard for my readers
to pronounce."

"You need no name. You need only to tell the truth. The
Pia-bird writes false."

"Pia-bird?" A little ray of light flickered on in Pia's
mystified mind. Things were beginning to make sense. Only
one person Pia knew called her by that nickname. Suspicion
began to ease any lingering fear. "Hey, are you one of
Sudibeth's friends? I'll bet she put you up to this. You're
from Miami, aren't you? She sent you down here from the
King and Prince."

"I know nothing of your king or your prince. I have come
here to be certain that you do honor to my queen."

She couldn't think what the man might be talking about.
Her head was spinning. If he was merely a figment of her
imagination, she was thinking up characters who were
mighty weird. On the other hand, if he was really flesh and
blood, how had he gotten in? And what did he mean to do
to her? Maybe he'd followed her home from the beach and
slipped in while she was up in the attic. Some pretty strange
characters had been known to roam the dunes at night.

"Don't hurt me! Okay?" Pia begged. "I'll do whatever
you say. If it's money you want, I don't have much, but
you're welcome to it. There's seventeen dollars and fifty-
three cents in my purse. Or I could write you a check." She
frowned and shook her head. "No, that's not a good idea.
It would probably bounce. You'd better take my money."

A deep, throaty chuckle sounded behind her. "Why would
I want your pitiful coins? My queen pays me well—silver,
gold, jewels."

"Your *queen?*"

"Yes, Pia-bird. You know her—Cleopatra. You must tell
the truth. I refuse to be left out this time. I will have my

place in your history. Write the words I say. Write them this instant!"

"All right! All right!" Better humor him, Pia decided. The guy was obviously playing with less than a full deck.

Pia's hands trembled when she touched the keys. But if all she had to do to get rid of this fruitcake was write, she would gladly do it. She glanced into the screen and saw her own reflection. Her breath caught. Behind her loomed another figure. A muscular man with long, windblown hair. Instead of a shirt, he wore some sort of strap or sling across his wide chest. No doubt a shoulder holster for his gun, she thought with a shiver.

"You are ready?" he asked.

Pia nodded.

"Then write these words: 'Although Queen Cleopatra had many lovers, only *one* man claimed her heart."

Pia forgot her fear; she was too annoyed by this house-breaker editing her work. "What do you mean, *one* man? Which one? Mark Antony or Julius Caesar? Where'd you get this information? Who's your source?"

"I am my own source!" the stranger declared hotly. "As for those two scheming Roman brutes, Cleopatra cared nothing for either of them. She only used them for her own purposes."

"Bull!" Pia exclaimed.

"Ah!" His manner seemed almost friendly now. "You worship Apis, the holy bull, too? We have much in common, then, although you seem so very different. Our scholars, you see, dress in finer garments and live in much grander style at the Museum."

Stung by his scorn of her attire and her abode, Pia snapped, "No, I mean, *bull,* I don't believe a word you're saying about Cleopatra. This is *my* book and I'm not going to write a pack of lies just because some weirdo muscles his way in here and tries to make me. So, you can just get out or shoot me or whatever. But you're not messing around with my writing, mister. As for how I choose to dress and where I choose to live—that's none of your damn business!"

Pia was gasping for breath by the time she finished her tirade. She was scared, too, *really* scared. She could hardly believe she'd had the nerve to yell at this guy. But at two things she drew the line: changing historical facts and giving a good hot-damn about what other people thought of her lifestyle. The chump was bugging her on both counts.

"I do not lie," the intruder answered calmly. "The Pia-bird lies. *Only one love,* I tell you!"

"And who might that have been?" she demanded.

"Myself, of course, as the world shall soon know."

"And you are?"

"Cleopatra's one and only love."

"Prove it!"

Pia heard him utter a sigh of pained resignation. "Very well, if I must."

In the next moment Pia was lifted out of her chair. The intruder pulled her against his hard, bare chest with such force that the metal-studded leather strap bit into her breasts through her thin tank top.

Man, if my subconscious created this guy, it's doing a bang-up job! she thought. Her surprise was instantly replaced by something just as profound, but much more pleasurable.

His hands tangled in her hair, drawing her head back, forcing her face up to his. When his mouth came down on hers, she parted her lips, feeling obliged to protest. But his invasion was swift and total. Pia's objections turned to quick surrender. Her own tongue returned the caresses of his.

He tasted of honey, wine, and desire.

In spite of Pia's best intentions, she found herself unable to fight him. While his mouth still held her prisoner, his big, warm hands slipped beneath her shirt and stroked her bare back, sending wonderful shivers through her whole body.

He pressed hard against her from the thighs up, letting her feel his powerful muscles—his male heat. She felt her nipples pucker and her legs go weak.

It was dark in the room—too dark for Pia to see him clearly. Even if the lights had been on, she found she could not keep her eyes open. A delicious weariness was oozing into the very marrow of her bones. She was sure if he let her go, she'd sink to the floor and puddle up like a blob of melted Jell-O.

She moaned softly, disappointed when he abruptly ended their kiss. She was totally caught up in the delicious eroticism of the moment. But his lips traveled only as far as her ear, where his warm words flowed like some precious, ancient ointment, arousing her anew.

"Now, do you understand? Do you believe? Were you truly my queen, I would go on, for Cleo is never pleased if we stop short of the most perfect pleasure."

"Cleo? My God, you know her well enough to call her *Cleo?*"

"We are *very* close," he confided with a chuckle.

He stepped back, releasing the victim of his passion suddenly. Pia sank into her desk chair, weak, dizzy, burning.

"But you are not a queen, only a little Pia-bird, a slave to your word machine. I meant only to demonstrate for you the truth of my statement. Now, write what I tell you."

Without further argument, Pia typed the sentence he dictated. The moment she finished, she clicked off the computer and turned to the man.

"Happy?" she demanded, annoyed that he had aroused her so thoroughly and then dismissed her so abruptly.

But he was gone. The room was empty and dark. Had she only imagined him?

"No way!" she whispered. "I don't have that much imagination."

Still trembling, Pia dragged herself off to bed. She had

never been so exhausted in her life. She felt drugged, fuzzy, shaken to the very core. Her eyes closed the minute her head hit the pillow, and for the rest of the night hot, throbbing colors swirled through her dreams. He was kissing her again—a kiss that seemed to go on and on and on. He aroused her beyond belief, yet they never quite reached that most perfect pleasure.

The morning sun woke her in less than three hours. Instead of feeling fresh and rested, she was physically and emotionally drained.

Pia shoved her turquoise-eyed cat off her chest and sat up. She yawned and stretched. "What a night!" she groaned. "What a dream!"

She sifted through last night's events in her mind, viewing her amorous intruder from various angles. Then she smiled. In the bright light of day it was easy enough to analyze her bizarre vision. She'd been exhausted, frustrated, and at her wits' end from worrying over the book and her deadline and overdue bills for car repairs and where Xander-the-Cat's next can of tuna-and-egg would come from. It was only natural for her fertile imagination to start playing tricks on her. Then Sudibeth had planted the seed from which her sexy intruder had sprung—no doubt about it—with her talk of the hunk from Miami. Of course, the part about Cleopatra was all too obvious: Pia had had little else on her mind lately.

She got up, washed her face, fed the cat, then sank into her desk chair, fully expecting to read about Cleopatra's two lovers when she flipped the on switch. She was still tired, but too excited to sleep any longer. She would write while the mood was upon her.

Pia studied the screen as it booted up, going from total black to its greenish glow. At first she thought she was imagining things. But no!

"Oh, God!" she moaned, covering her eyes. "I'm losing it!"

She peeked between her fingers, but it was still there: *Cleopatra had many lovers, but only one man claimed her heart.*

"It wasn't a dream," she murmured. "It all happened. That man . . . that kiss . . ." She slumped back in her chair, trying to get her brain to unscramble. "It couldn't be! Could it?"

Pia shifted her gaze from the screen to the crystal pyramid. A familiar warmth stole through her. She watched the piece of alabaster glow softly in the morning sun, the colors swirling before her eyes—a dancing, sparkling rainbow.

Her emotions swirled with the colors. When she leaned her head back and closed her eyes, she could still feel the sweet, hot pressure of his kiss. She smiled. She sighed.

"Man, what a man!"

She had no idea where to look, but she meant to find him again. She and Cleo's lover had unfinished business of the most delicious kind.

Chapter Three

Pia was still sitting at her desk, transfixed by the shifting colors inside the crystal pyramid when the sound of footsteps on her porch roused her from deep thought.

"Pia? You in there? It's me—Sudibeth."

"At *this* hour?" Pia glanced up at the swinging tail and rolling eyes of her cat-clock on the wall. According to Felix, it was just barely six. Sudibeth was known to be a night owl and a late sleeper. Pia would as soon expect a vampire out of his coffin at this time of morning as she would Sudibeth Callahan on her porch in dawn's early light.

"Something must be wrong," she murmured, hurrying to the door.

"Pia? You hear me?" Sudibeth called louder.

"Coming!" Pia answered.

When she opened the door, she could hardly believe the sight that greeted her. The sexy, pin-neat Sudibeth was a sorry mess, her red hair tangled and clotted with too much hairspray, gone sticky with humidity, her carefully applied makeup smeared from here to Kingdom Come, and her white slacks and hot-pink silk shell wrinkled, rumpled, and sandy. She wore no shoes at all.

"What on earth, Sudibeth?" All sorts of horrible possibilities flashed through Pia's mind.

Sudibeth giggled. "Lord, honey, wait till you hear about last night!"

Pia reminded herself that she had quite a tale to tell, too, about last night. But she wasn't sure she wanted to share it with anyone, not even her best friend.

"Come on in," she invited. "I'll make coffee, and maybe some bacon and eggs."

Sudibeth screwed up her face in a grimace of horror. *"Breakfast?"* She pantomimed gagging. "How can you put stuff like that in your stomach this early in the day? I couldn't bear it." Then she smiled and fluttered her long eyelashes. "But now, a Bloody Mary might go down real smooth, honey."

While Pia rummaged about her closet-sized kitchen, searching for vodka, tomato juice, and the rest of the fixings, Sudibeth lounged in the doorway, working up to telling her tale.

"You shoulda come down to the King and Prince when I called you, Pia-bird. You sure missed out on a dandy evening."

Pia glanced over her shoulder and gave her friend a crooked grin. "You mean, I could look like you this morning? No thanks! What on earth happened, Sudibeth?"

"Oh, me and Miami, we just danced the night away. Then when they closed the place, he suggested we take a walk on the beach and look at the moon. It was *gorgeous!"*

"I know. I went for a short stroll, too."

Sudibeth ignored Pia's interruption and continued in a dreamy tone. "I think I'm in love. Lord, that man is something, Pia! Big and tall and golden *all over!"*

"Golden? All over?" Pia's interest piqued.

"That he is! Get the picture?"

Pia handed her friend a Bloody Mary and nodded. "Graphically! But you haven't been at it all night, have you?"

Sudibeth took a long, slow swig of her drink, then giggled. "Would you believe we fell asleep up in the dunes?"

"Are you telling me that's what really happened, or are you just testing your story on me?"

"Honest to God, Pia! Slept right through till the sun came up, both of us."

"And this *golden man,* where is he now? I'd like to meet him."

Sudibeth laughed. "I'll just bet you would. But you had your chance, Pia-bird. He's *mine* now! He went back, looking for my shoes. I took them off somewhere and forgot all about them."

"Other things on your mind, eh?"

"You've got it, hon. Other *big* things!"

They drifted into the living room and flopped down in soft-cushioned wicker chairs that had seen better days.

"How'd your writing go last night?" Sudibeth asked, licking celery salt from her fingers.

"Strangely," Pia admitted, her mind still on Sudibeth's golden hunk from Miami. "Are you sure he was with you *all* night?"

Sudibeth shrugged. "He was right there till I fell asleep, and he was sure there when I woke up." She giggled again and her eyes sparkled merrily. "Why?"

Pia avoided her friend's curious gaze. She felt foolish about what she was going to say, but she knew that it had to be said. "I had a surprise visitor last night. This guy just popped in out of nowhere."

"Good kisser?"

Pia's cheeks flamed. "Uh, yes, as a matter of fact. Your guy from Miami doesn't make house calls, does he?"

"Olympia Byrd, I am shocked!" Sudibeth's indignation

sounded almost genuine. "You just let any old beach bum into your house and then you let him kiss you? What could you be thinking? Why, that's crazy!"

"I didn't exactly let him in," Pia explained. "I didn't show him out either. He was just here one minute, then gone the next. And he knew about my book. You weren't discussing my Cleopatra idea at the King and Prince, were you?"

"Lord, no! I know how superstitious you are. I'd never tell a soul what you're working on." She paused, thinking back over the evening. "Now, I may have let slip a hint or two, but only to Miami."

Pia groaned and rolled her eyes heavenward. "Sudibeth, how could you? I'll bet he hotfooted it right down here the minute you fell asleep."

She narrowed her eyes and studied Sudibeth thoughtfully. This sounded just like something Sudibeth would cook up— send her new boyfriend in to get Pia all stirred up, then arrive on the doorstep first thing in the morning to get her reaction.

"Why are you looking at me that way, Pia? You couldn't possibly think . . ." Sudibeth presented the picture of out-raged innocence. "Oh, I'd never do anything like that, not when I know how hard you're working, when I know you need to keep your mind focused and uncluttered."

"Like hell you wouldn't!"

A slow smile crept over Pia's face. She sat back in her chair and sipped her Bloody Mary.

"All right, Sudibeth, the jig's up. I'm onto you and your golden guy from Miami." She paused and laughed. "Good joke, I have to admit. You really had me going. Why, I thought I was having hallucinations until he kissed me. I'm so relieved to know you were behind the whole thing that I can't even be mad at you. I really thought I was losing my mind."

"Pia, I swear, I didn't—"

Sudibeth's protest was interrupted by a sharp rap at the front door.

"That must be our guy now," Pia said. "I wonder why he bothered to knock. He certainly didn't last night."

"You've got this all wrong, Pia. I swear to you!"

But Pia was at the door already, grinning like a Cheshire, planning to throw herself into the stranger's golden arms and kiss him as passionately as he had kissed her last night. She'd never have had the nerve to do such a thing had she not joined her friend in a breakfast Bloody.

She threw the door wide. "Ah, back for more so soon?" One glance at the man stopped Pia in her tracks. The huge grin on her face quickly died. "Yes?" she inquired in a stunned voice.

"Hi! I'm Carlos Alvarez," the tall, golden-tanned, *black*-haired stranger said.

"But you're not the one!"

He presented Sudibeth's sandy, silver sandals as if to prove his identity. "I'm from Miami," he added, as if that explained everything.

Pia nodded, still staring at him blankly. "Of course," she murmured. "I'm sorry, Carlos. Sudibeth's waiting inside."

Once the three of them had settled into chairs, Pia haltingly explained everything again for Carlos's benefit.

"Are you sure you didn't dream the whole thing, honey?" Sudibeth sounded truly concerned. "You've been working mighty hard lately."

Pia shook her head. "This was no dream. I thought that, too, when I first woke up. But when I went to my computer and checked, the sentence he made me write was still there. Come on. I'll show you."

The three of them rose and went into the next room, where Edgar Allan was still glowing and humming. Sudibeth scanned the lines quickly. "Hey, I like this. Whoever the guy is, he can write."

Pia said nothing. Whatever she'd meant to say remained trapped in her closed throat. She gripped the back of her office chair for support, her wide, blue eyes glued to the screen.

"You all right, honey? You just lost all your suntan."

Pia felt her friend's hand on her arm. No, she wasn't all right! She sank into the chair, still staring at the screen.

"Oh, my God!" she breathed. "This can't be!"

"What, Pia? What's wrong?" Sudibeth begged. "Talk to me, girl!"

"That paragraph," Pia answered, a quiver in her voice.

" 'I, Cleopatra, though I had many lovers, gave my heart to only one man,' " Sudibeth read from the screen. " 'I wish to tell the truth of my story at long last.' Sounds great to me, Pia. I think you've finally hit on the problem you've been having all these months. When did you decide to switch to first person and let Cleopatra tell her own story?"

Pia swallowed several times before she could speak. "I didn't. I never wrote this. I never even saw it before."

"Then who . . .?" Sudibeth glanced about the room as if she might spy the true author. But only Alexander-the-Cat was there, curled up on a windowsill in the sunshine. He blinked his great, turquoise eyes at her, licked his paw, then went back to sleep.

"This is *so* weird," Sudibeth whispered.

"You don't know the half of it. I was sitting right here at the desk when you came up to the door. I'd just reread what I wrote—what he made me write—last night. And this isn't it!"

Pia turned to Sudibeth. "Do you believe in spirit writing?"

The buxom redhead hoisted her nearly empty glass toward her friend. "Hell, I write using spirits all the time."

"Be serious! That's not what I mean and you know it."

Carlos had remained silent all through their discussion. Now he spoke in a deep, quiet voice. "Stranger things have happened. The mind at work is an awesome machine, with mysterious and superhuman powers."

"Stop that, Miami! You're giving me and Pia the creeps. I think somebody's just playing a trick on you, honey."

"I think so, too," Pia said, her gaze still fixed on the screen.

"Ah, but the question is," Carlos put in, "is the trickster from this world or another?"

Sudibeth broke the long, charged silence that followed Miami's question. "I think I could use another Bloody Mary."

After Sudibeth and Carlos left, Pia shut off her computer, closed the door to her office, and vowed not to go back in there until she felt more in control. She would not even think about the book for the rest of the weekend. After all, she had to come up with a costume for Sunday night, get her lessons prepared for the writers' conference, and there was the Kentucky Derby to watch on TV that afternoon. Her dad would be at the race. Maybe she could spot him in the crowd.

"Costume . . . costume," she muttered as she cleared the glasses from the living room and headed into the kitchen to wash up. She was just finishing at the sink when an idea struck her. All those old clothes in the attic. Surely, she could find something up there.

A few minutes later, she was in the stuffy cubbyhole, sorting through miniskirts, maxicoats, tie-dyes, and bell-bottoms, when the gleam of gold lamé caught her eye.

"What in the world? Why, I haven't seen this since high school."

Pia pulled out the length of shining fabric and held it up. No moth holes, no water damage, no faded seams. She'd worn the costume to a Latin banquet in her senior year at

Virginia Girls' Academy, but she'd had no idea it was still around.

"Perfect!" she told herself. "A few minor changes, the right jewelry, and I'll be Cleopatra."

Downstairs again, she gathered up her sewing things and took the old gown into the living room. The prerace Derby show was just beginning. She could watch and sew at the same time. But first, the obligatory julep preparations.

She went outside and picked two long stems of mint. "My Sunday Silence crop," she said, smiling.

Pia had brought home and rooted the garnish from her Derby julep in '89. Her crop this year was large, lushly green. She remembered how her dad had laughed at her for bringing home yet another souvenir, a living one this time. She scanned the TV screen, hoping to catch a glimpse of him. He'd promised her a rose from the winner's blanket this year, since she couldn't be there.

"Right!" she said skeptically. "That's as sure a bet as my thinking I can get back to Cleo's Alexandria."

Settled on her cushioned wicker couch with popcorn, julep in a frosty Derby glass, and her sewing, she listened to all the prerace hype, aching to be there in the crowd. For the first time in weeks—no, *months*—her mind was far away from Cleopatra.

An hour later, her costume was shaping up, her Derby glass was empty, and Strike the Gold was just crossing the finish line when she heard a crash and a shriek from her closed office.

"Good God!" Pia cried. "What now?"

She jumped up and dashed across the hall to the door, threw it open, and gasped. The afternoon sun coming in the window all but blinded her for a moment. She moved away from the bright shimmer of light and shaded her eyes. Edgar Allan's screen glowed softly. Xander-the-Cat, whose angry cry she had heard, stood on tiptoe on the keyboard, fur at full frizz, tail like a bottle brush, back arched.

"Bad cat!" Pia scolded. "What have you done now? Dancing on the keys again?"

Pia tried to blame her cat, but some creeping dread told her that there was no way he could have turned on the machine, put disks in the drive, then entered the Cleopatra document.

She was trembling when she put Xander on the floor. "Maybe I just *imagined* turning it off. With Sudibeth around, who can think straight anyway?"

Still, she was positive she had shut down the computer for the weekend. She glanced back at the screen, her heart in her throat, and read:

> *I, Cleopatra, though I had many lovers, gave my heart to only one man. I wish to tell the truth of my story at long last. I must begin at the beginning. My lonely and terrifying childhood, the shame brought down upon the house of Ptolemy by my drunken father, known to his subjects as Auletes, the Flute Player, and the magnificent burden laid upon me to save the great Alexander's rich Egypt from barbaric Roman rule. Yes, I took Caesar and Antony to my bed, but I never allowed either of them access to my heart, which was held in gentler hands. I did only what I had to do, what any woman would do to save her homeland for her children.*

Pia remained still and silent, mesmerized by the unfamiliar words on the screen. Not until the sun was down and the room shadowed did she come out of her fog.

"This can't be," she whispered, recalling all the times that she had prayed her book would write itself. Glancing overhead, she said, "I didn't mean it. And besides, first person won't do at all."

The darkness made her skin crawl. She switched on the desk lamp. Everything seemed in order. Then she remembered hearing a crash before the cat yowled. What could have fallen? Her eyes quickly focused on a bare spot on the desk.

"The crystal pryamid!" She panicked. "It's gone!"

A hands and knees search of the floor produced the chunk of alabaster, undamaged and still glowing. Pia sank into her chair, feeling the stone grow warm in her hands.

"Bad cat!" she scolded again. "You're lucky you didn't break it."

Xander leaped onto her lap, circled several times, then settled with a loud purr, as if trying to make up for his mischief.

"Okay, okay," she said, scratching behind his sable ears. "Just be more careful from now on."

Pia placed her prized souvenir back on the desk. She spent the next few minutes playing with the big, lazy tomcat.

"If you'd lived in Alexandria with Cleopatra, you'd have been an Egyptian tom-tomb-cat," she told him. "But you probably wouldn't have cared much for that. I hear they used to mummify your sort and stow them in pyramids."

Xander switched his bushy tail as if he understood every word, then leaped out of her lap to prowl the office. The fat, furry distraction removed, Pia turned back to her computer, ready to switch it off again. She barely batted an eye this time when she noticed that another sentence had appeared. This addition mentioned some other guy Cleo had fallen for—a nobody out of nowhere. No such information had come to light in any of her research.

"I don't like that!"

She hit the delete button with a good bit of force. The

sentence disappeared, but even as she watched it vanish, she felt the hair on the back of her neck rise.

Pia checked behind her. No one . . . at least no one she could see. "Whoever you are, leave my book alone!" she yelled.

Quickly, she shut off the computer, scooped up her cat, and exited the office. She slammed the door behind her and made straight for her bedroom.

"Dammit, I deserve better!" the golden Greek raged. "This stubborn Pia-bird will *not* leave me out of her tale."

Darius swigged wine from a bejeweled cup as he stood at the window of the palace at Alexandria, staring out at the Pharos lighthouse. Night was falling. He knew that signal fires would soon replace the reflecting lenses used for illumination during the day. He knew, too, that soon two infamous Romans would come—men who would change Cleopatra's life forever, indeed, change the face of Egypt for all eternity. But she would never love either of them the way she loved him.

Already he had figured a way to open a channel between Cleopatra's palace and the Pia-bird's word machine. He must make her understand and write what he dictated. He could not change the future, but at least he could correct mistaken notions of the past.

"Odd," he reflected, "that I know so much about the future, but nothing about my own past."

Because of his unique "window on tomorrow," as Cleopatra called his curious knowledge of what was to come, he was looked upon as something of a mystic in Egypt. Secretly, he knew that nothing could be farther from the truth. He was simply an ordinary man caught up in extraordinary circumstances.

He had come to Alexandria—to Cleopatra—by a most

curious route. "A shipwreck . . . it must have been," he mused aloud, stroking the crystal pyramid as he strained to remember. All he could recall was floating up to the marble stairs of the Palace of the Ptolemies—half dead from hunger, thirst and the sun's merciless heat—and being fished out of the water by the most beautiful maiden, Cleopatra herself. She had nursed him back to health, her love being the most potent medicine.

"She saved me and now I will save her from the wicked lies of this Pia-bird."

His handsome face took on a fierce look. His dark gold brows drew down. His smooth forehead furrowed. There was one question for which he had no answer.

"Why is the Pia-bird bent on spreading such vicious falsehoods about my love? Why did she spurn the truth that I wrote on her magic word machine?"

With a toss of his leopard-skin cloak and a muttered curse, he vowed to find out the answer before it was too late.

Fumbling with the chunk of alabaster, he tried to remember exactly what he had done before that had transported him into the Pia-bird's untidy lair. Somehow he knew that the magic of the stone Cleopatra had stolen from Alexander's sarcophagus was the key to his returning to the lapis-eyed woman's time and place.

"If only I could remember how I was holding it . . . what I was thinking . . . exactly what I said . . ."

He curled his long fingers around the stone, enclosing it in his palm, and visualized Pia's face. Immediately, he recalled the taste of her lips. Odd that she was the only woman other than Cleo who had ever tempted him. She was such a strange creature, totally alien to anything he knew, unadorned by jewels, no crown on her head, no throne in her house. Yet he remembered well that under her shabby clothes her body was soft, warm, and tempting.

Determined to return to that other time, he muttered several ancient incantations. A sudden, blinding flash of pastel lights colored the wall of the palace chamber, and the golden Greek felt the world move beneath his sandaled feet.

"Sleep," Pia muttered, closing her office door. "I need sleep. Everything will be fine in the morning. You'll see, Xander. We're imagining all of this. If not, then first thing Monday morning, I'll just call a technician to come get the bugs out of Edgar Allan. He's due for a thorough checkup anyway. *Overdue,* I'd say."

Pia dumped the cat on her bed, then went to the tiny bathroom and turned on the shower. A good, soapy scalding, a glass of warm milk, and she'd sleep like a baby.

Quickly, she stripped off her shorts and tank top, remembering suddenly that she'd worn the same clothes for two days and had slept in them last night.

"Phew!" She sniffed and wrinkled her nose. "Good thing the writers' conference starts tomorrow. I'm beginning to forget how to dress."

Naked, and feeling totally grubby, Pia stepped into the tub and pulled the transparent lavender shower curtain closed. The sharp needles of water stabbing at her bare skin came as a shock. But a moment later she was purring like Xander. Her muscles began to relax as the steamy heat scoured her body and layers of sweat washed away.

She had her hand on the curtain, ready to pull it open, when a noise, a sense of *something* stopped her. Goose bumps crawled up her bare arms.

"Is someone out there?" she whispered. "Hello?"

Only silence greeted her nervous query.

"Pia Byrd, you are being ridiculous!" she chided.

She had started to slide the curtain open when a movement

near the door caught her eye and stopped her breath. She froze, cold fingers of terror closing around her heart.

Darius waved a hand before his face, trying to clear the hot steam so he could see. Whatever he had said or done, the crystal pyramid had worked its magic once again. But had he misjudged time and space and landed in Hades?

Then he spied her, there beyond the violet veil. What manner of dress was this? Cleopatra sometimes wore transparent gowns to please him when they were alone and felt the need of each other, but the Pia-bird's garb was far different. She was not wearing it, but was shut away from him inside the thing. Could it be some sort of open-roofed tent?

"Is someone out there?" he heard her call. He didn't answer. He was too taken with the sight of her—her long, shapely limbs, her slender torso, her raven tresses curling damp against her pale, full breasts. She stood very tall and erect, like the statue of an Amazon goddess. Although her features were distorted by the violet veil, he knew that in her own savage way she was nearly as lovely as his Cleopatra.

The heat and steam made him sweat. Uncoupling the clasp of his leopard-skin cloak, he dropped it to the floor. There was no need to glance down at his pleated linen kilt to realize how the sight of the Pia-bird aroused him. He had kissed her the last time he was here and he knew that the tides of passion flowed rampant in her blood.

But that kiss was in the line of duty, he reminded himself silently. His love was pledged to Cleopatra alone. The thought, if not stilled, at least stayed his erotic urge to slip behind the steamy curtain and join the Pia-bird for a watery frolic.

No, Darius told himself, he had come here on an urgent

mission. He must find the magic writing machine and force it to tell the truth.

Pia took a deep breath and screwed up all her courage. Finally, she threw back the shower curtain and yelled at the same time, trying to sound as dangerous as a woman caught naked in the shower could. Her scream died. Relief left her weak. The room was, blessedly, empty.

"No golden man," she murmured. "Thank You, God!"

Only when she stepped out of the tub and felt fur beneath her wet, bare feet did her goose bumps return. She stared down at the vivid black spots on their tawny background.

"A leopard skin?"

With a shriek, Pia fled the bathroom, not even bothering to towel off. She slammed the bedroom door, locked it, then threw herself on the bed with Xander. For a long time, she lay there, hardly daring to breathe. But, exhausted as she was, sleep finally forced her eyes to close.

Through her strange, confused dreams, it seemed that all night long she heard the faint *clickety-clack* of Edgar Allan's keys. And sometime during the night, she dreamed a kiss that seemed so real—so fervently passionate and tender— that she never wanted it to end.

Only with the dawn of a new day did reason return. At least temporarily.

Chapter Four

The minute Pia opened her eyes the next morning, she vowed to ignore her office and whatever surprises might be lurking there for her. Determined to pass right by the closed door without even taking a peek inside, she intended to put both her book and the strange happenings of the past hours out of her thoughts for the week. The writers' conference would serve to get her mind off her problems, clear her head, and hone her skills.

She turned on her back and stretched her arms above her. There was one thing no writers' conference could make her forget—that kiss she'd dreamed during the night. She still went all fluttery inside just thinking about it.

Forcing her mind to other things, Pia glanced at the clock. Eleven, already! She'd overslept. Whipping out of bed, she fed the cat, then dressed in a brightly embroidered Mexican dress and wove her long, dark hair into a single, swinging braid. She hurried about, gathering name tags, welcome packets, schedules, and car keys. After a final glance around to make sure she hadn't forgotten anything, she dashed out, praying that the MG would start on the first try.

"Come on, baby," Pia murmured, stroking the car's leather dash and giving the choke knob an affectionate tug as she turned the key.

The "Purple Bomb" coughed twice, then purred like old Xander hunched over a dish of tuna-and-egg. Pia grinned and shifted her temperamental classic into gear. She slipped her favorite Jimmy Buffett tape into the slot. His hot-beach-and-a-tall-cool-drink tones mingled with birdsong and the distant thrum of the waves, creating exactly the ambiance Pia craved.

A moment later, the oyster shells in her driveway flew out from under her tires as she pointed the Bomb's white racing stripe toward Epworth. Sudibeth and the others would be there already, tapping their sandaled toes expectantly and wondering where in the world Pia was and when she'd show up to help register the conference participants.

Pia experienced a glow of excitement as she whizzed across the narrow ribbon of road that split historic Bloody Marsh, where British troops had won this land from the Spanish in the 1700s. A man and two teenaged boys stood on the bridge over the creek, hauling up their wire, crab baskets. The strangers waved, as men often did when they spotted her sporty car. She grinned and gave them a couple of beeps of the horn, pretending that it wasn't the MG, but the pretty gal driving it that had caught their eye.

The whole world seemed wonderfully fresh and alive today. The appearing and disappearing night visitor seemed like something Pia had dreamed or something she'd made up for one of her novels.

"None of it's real," she assured herself. "It couldn't be." She relaxed for the first time in days.

The approach to Epworth was always a soothing drive— the little-used road tunneling through a cool, dim arch of centuries-old live oaks, their Spanish moss beards drifting low, almost touching the car. She slowed for the narrow entrance gate.

"And the speed bumps!" she reminded herself, recalling the time she'd taken one of them too fast and almost bent the low-slung MG's frame.

Buffett was wailing out of the speaker behind her head. The rhythmic tattoo of his song matched the thump of her tires on the road, creating a natural rap beat. Words, sentences, rhymes began forming in Pia's head. Beating time on the steering wheel, she sang out in jerky, rap-type phrasing:

> *"Nice little road, with oaks overhead.*
> *People out strolling by the marsh in its bed.*
> *Morning at Epworth, quiet and calm.*
> *Look out, folks, here comes the Purple Bomb!*
> *Pia and Buffett just puttin' right along,*
> *Blaring "Margueritaville," loud and strong,*
> *Puffin' that cigarette, brown and long.*
> *Waving to the joggers, tapping out the beat,*
> *Feeling mighty good about the writers' week.*
> *Look out, Pia! Look out, Purple Bomb!*
> *Speed bump! Speed bump! Gonna do you wrong!*
> *Bounce goes Pia. Bounce goes the Purple Bomb.*
> *Bounce goes Jimmy Buffett in the morning calm."*

"Good rap!" Pia giggled. She'd have to write down her lyrics as soon as she got out of the car. Her class would get a kick out of it. So would Larry Lubin, the conference's resident prankster and purveyor of silly poetry. In Pia's opinion, her new piece ranked right up there with the worst of his limericks.

"Larry Lubin, eat your heart out!" She laughed out loud, feeling good all over.

As she eased the car into a shady parking place in front

of the main building, Pia spotted the infamous poet himself coming across the parking lot, briefcase in hand. He was wearing a grin as wide as any kid's on Christmas morning. According to Larry, he lived for this one week each year.

"Lar-ry!" Pia called.

His bright blue eyes swept Pia and the Purple Bomb in one smooth, approving glance. "Still running, eh?" He caressed a hot, waxed fender. "Looking good, too."

"Me or the Bomb?" Pia teased.

Larry winked. "Both! Hey, I hear you've been having some weird stuff happening over at your place. Reminds me of that play I wrote last year, 'Murder at the Old Tabby House.'" He paused, wiped the back of his hand over his mouth as if trying to hide his grin, then burst out laughing. "God, I love my work!"

"We all do, Larry." Pia gave him the response she knew he hoped for. Then she demanded, "Who've you been talking to? How'd you know about my problems?"

He shrugged. "Sudibeth. Who else?"

"I should have figured. At first I thought she was behind the whole thing."

Larry nodded thoughtfully. "Good prank. Sounds like Sudibeth's work, all right. You realize, of course, that I taught that girl everything she knows."

Pia narrowed her eyes suspiciously. "And just how long have *you* been in town, Mr. Lubin?"

Larry backed up a couple of steps and mugged total innocence. "Just got in an hour ago. Haven't even unpacked yet." Then he grinned and his blue eyes twinkled with mischief. "But don't think I wouldn't have done it if I'd been around and thought of it first."

"Pia-bird! *Where* have you been?" Sudibeth's voice shrilled from the door of the main building. "I got a line of folks waiting. You get yourself on in here. Larry, quit pestering her. Go on back to your room and write some dirty limericks or I'll put you to work, too."

Larry opened his mouth to say something, but Sudibeth cut him off. "I know, I know—God, you love your work! We all do, Larry. Now get going so Pia and I can straighten this crowd out and get things moving."

The two hours of registration passed in a busy blur of new faces, but the same old questions: Are you going to teach us how to write a book?, What time is dinner?, and Where's the ice machine?

By the time Pia and Sudibeth finished, fifty-two people had registered from seven different states, and one from Canada. It promised to be an interesting week.

At five o'clock, Sudibeth said, "There'll probably be a few stragglers drifting in late, but I'll take care of them. You run on home, Pia-bird, and slip into your Cleopatra suit for the party. See you at seven-thirty."

Pia almost dreaded going home. What would she find when she got there? She wished suddenly that she'd taken a room at Epworth for the week with everyone else.

"But then who would take care of Xander?"

She sighed and climbed into her car. She was tired, hot, and sweaty. But she was truly looking forward to the costume party, to the whole week. All during the short ride home, she was lost in thought, planning her classes and sightseeing excursions for the out-of-towners to the haunted lighthouse, the old English stronghold of Fort Frederica, the sandy expanse of East Beach, and, of course, the King and Prince Hotel for cocktails on the oceanfront veranda and dancing under the stars.

When she reached the house, everything seemed quiet and normal. The only phone message on her machine was from her dad, who said he had a flower for her from Strike the Gold's blanket of roses.

Pia avoided her office and the contrary Edgar Allan. She

showered, then dressed in her flowing golden gown and jeweled Cleo collar. She'd made herself an asp crown, using old Christmas wrapping. Lots of eye makeup and blood-red lipstick completed her disguise.

Dressed and ready, she stood in front of her full-length mirror to appraise her handiwork. "Cleo, you never looked so good." Then she switched off the lights and headed for the door.

On the way back to Epworth, she got a few strange stares, especially when she caught the red light at the busy airport intersection. But once she reached the party, she looked no odder than the rest of the conferees. Cleopatra mingled at the punch bowl with Scarlett O'Hara, Dracula, several of Janelle Taylor's Indians, the vampire Lestat, and Little Bopeep—Sudibeth, of course, still managing to look hotly sexy in ruffled organdy and painted-on freckles. Larry, in plaid Bermuda shorts and shiny black shoes, came as "everyone's favorite agent," a character he had immortalized as the villain in one of his plays.

After over an hour of answering questions about writing from the newcomers, Pia, feeling drained and hot, stepped out onto the veranda for a cigarette and some air. A storm was brewing. She gazed out over the dark Frederica River. Its calm surface reflected the strange lightning dancing through boiling black clouds overhead. The electrical flashes were odd colors, almost like the rainbow hues of the aurora borealis she had witnessed years ago in Maine. Or like the odd glow inside the crystal pryamid, she realized with a start.

Suddenly, a lightning strike somewhere nearby plunged Epworth into darkness. Pia heard screams and laughter from inside the building. She continued to stare out at the river, enjoying nature's light show. The power would come back on at any second, she was sure. Not to worry, she told herself. She'd just stay put and wait for the emergency generator to kick in.

Pia had been alone on the veranda before the lights went out. Suddenly, in the darkness, she sensed someone nearby. She looked around, but it was so black out that she seemed to be wrapped in inky cotton.

"This must be how a mummy feels." She shivered.

When something brushed her arm, she jumped and cried out.

"So sorry," a male voice said. "I didn't mean to frighten you."

Pia laughed nervously. "Hey, it's all right. I thought I was alone out here, that's all. You startled me."

"I saw you come out before the lights went off. I've been wanting to speak with you, but I haven't been able to work my way through your throng of admirers."

Pia smiled. He had a nice voice—husky, with a hint of a foreign accent. "The fiction instructor is always a popular person. It's not me they want, it's the name, address, and phone number of any agent or editor."

"You are too modest," he replied. "Everyone knows the whole world beats a path to worship at the feet of Cleopatra Thea Philopator."

Pia was taken aback. Not many people knew the Egyptian queen's full name. She herself had learned it only recently.

"I'm afraid I'm only Cleo for the night—more's the pity. My name's Olympia Byrd, but everyone calls me Pia."

She extended her hand in the darkness toward the sound of his voice. He grasped it warmly and held it for longer than the average shake.

"Darius, Pia. I'm pleased we can talk at last."

"I don't remember your name being on the list. We didn't meet at registration?"

"No," he answered. "I arrived late."

"Oh, then Sudibeth took care of you."

He didn't answer. Pia assumed he nodded his head.

"I hear you're writing a book about Cleopatra."

Sudibeth and her big mouth! She had registered Darius all right, and no doubt filled him in on everything about everybody at the conference.

"I'm trying," she said. "It isn't an easy project, though. Before I started work, I had no idea of the problems I'd be facing."

"Perhaps I could help. I know a good deal about Egypt and the ancient history of the land."

Pia sighed. "I've been to Egypt and done enough research for ten books. It's Cleopatra herself who has me stumped. *Who* was she? *What* was she? Every historian seems to have a different opinion. I'm trying to sort things out, form my own picture of her personality. She's hard to get a handle on."

"Yes, Cleopatra was complicated, but then most woman are."

The statement, or perhaps his tone as he spoke, seemed odd to Pia. This man—Darius—sounded as if he had known Cleopatra personally.

"She was more than complicated, it seems to me," Pia said. "I think she must have been a gifted actress. I've about decided that she discovered the secret of fooling all the people all the time."

He chuckled softly—a deep, warm sound. "Only when she felt she had to fool them. Occasionally, she was permitted to let her guard down, be herself. To say that she lived in difficult times is a vast understatement. Most of her Ptolemy ancestors, as I'm sure you know, dealt in murder to gain the throne. Ptolemy the Fourth was the most terrible—far worse than Nero or Caligula. He murdered his father, his mother, an uncle, and his younger brother. He wanted no threat to his supreme reign. This pattern followed down through the ages. It's truly a miracle that Cleopatra survived to sit on the throne. She never knew her mother. Her father was a drunkard and a pawn of Rome. He eventually married his own sister, who bore him two more daughters. Auletes, as Cleopatra's father was known, had a total of six children—that we know of—by several wives. At least three of them tried to kill Cleopatra at one time or another. But she was stronger, smarter, and more cunning than any of her siblings. She knew Rome was the key to her own survival. And the survival of Egypt, above all else, was her goal. If her plan had succeeded, and she'd managed to have herself declared Empress of Rome, the entire world would be different today. Better, I think."

Pia remained silently thoughtful, trying to absorb all that Darius had said. Finally, she asked, "How could such a young woman hold out against such odds? Nowadays, a girl her age would be finishing high school and far more interested in boyfriends and proms than in politics."

The lights flickered on for a bare instant. In that sudden flash, Pia got a glimpse of Darius. He was dressed grandly as an Egyptian pharaoh. The gleam of his golden collar, girdle, and headdress so overwhelmed her that she hardly noticed his face before the lights blinked off again. But before darkness once more enfolded him, she saw that he was tall and had strong, sharp features. She also noticed the leopard skin that hung about his broad shoulders.

"Age had little to do with Cleopatra's skills or intelligence," Darius said. "She seems to me to have been born wise."

His voice was wistful. Once again Pia got the odd feeling that Darius had known Cleopatra personally. She jumped, surprised, when his hand touched her arm.

"You strike me as a similar sort of woman, Pia Byrd. An old soul who came into this life with much knowledge and experience."

A shiver ran through Pia. "Are you talking about reincarnation?"

"I am talking about life," he said matter-of-factly. "Does

it disturb you to think that you might have lived more than once?"

She had to think about that for a minute. "No, I don't suppose it disturbs me. I'm just not sure I believe it."

"You don't need to believe it for it to be true, you know."

"So you think reincarnation is why Cleopatra was so smart?"

"It makes sense to me. Such cunning as she possessed can only be gained through experience."

Pia was still mulling that over when Sudibeth called to her. "Hey, Pia, come on in here and flick your Bic for us. We want to light candles. It'll be just like a hurricane party."

Annoyed by the interruption, Pia nevertheless excused herself. The sooner she turned over her lighter, the sooner she could get back to her discussion with Darius.

She was gone longer than she'd intended. Once the candles were lit, several of the out-of-towners clustered around her, asking the inevitable questions. Finally, she extracted herself from the throng and went back outside. The moment she stepped through the door, she knew that Darius was gone.

"Damn!" she muttered. "I had so many more questions I wanted to ask him."

Oh well, tomorrow she would catch him after class. They could have lunch together in the Epworth dining room or maybe even go over to Emmeline and Hessie's for more privacy. And she might invite him to her place sometime during the week for an afternoon at the beach—just the two of them. She'd swap him an autographed copy of her latest pirate novel, *Love-Starved Savage,* for his help with Cleopatra. They'd have the whole week together, and if she needed more information, she could write to him or phone him later.

So resolved, Pia headed for her car. The party inside sounded as if it might go into the wee hours. She had the early class on Monday, so she needed to organize her notes and get some sleep. The interrogation from the conferees tonight was only a mild sampling of the battery of questions she'd have to face first thing in the morning.

A cool, misty rain fell as she drove home—top down. The night air felt good on her face and bare shoulders. She would sleep well tonight, she was sure of it.

When she opened her door, Xander was waiting for her with a purr of welcome and a yowl of hunger. She opened a can of food, stripped off her Cleo suit, then stuck her head cautiously into her office. Somehow, the soft green glow of her computer screen did not surprise her. She could see from the hallway that another page had been added to her manuscript. She didn't bother to read it. She closed the door, leaving Edgar Allan humming. What was the use of switching it off? It would only turn itself on again.

Forcing all thoughts of weirdness from her mind, she fell into bed and went instantly to sleep. Her final lucid thought was of the kiss she'd dreamed the night before. She hoped she could pick up where she'd left off.

Sure enough, long after midnight, she felt those urgent lips on hers once more. But this time her phantom of the night did not stop at her lips. She turned and tossed in bed, purring like Xander, as his open mouth found her neck, her shoulder, and then her breast. All night long her dream-lover shared her bed.

Pia woke the next morning with the sweet, languid feeling of a woman who has been well loved. She stretched and smiled, letting her body slither deliciously under the sheet. But there was no time this morning to lie about daydreaming. What had happened to her in private, she could analyze later. Right now, her public awaited her.

She was up and moving like a whirlwind. Her drive to

Epworth went faster than usual—no stoplights and, luckily, no cops to check her speed.

Pia sensed a zing of excitement in the air the minute she drove through the Epworth arch that morning. It was always this way on opening day. She remembered her own thrill of anticipation the first time she had attended this conference as an aspiring writer. She'd sensed that she was on the very brink of something glorious and mysterious and wonderful. The instructors knew all about New York and the publishing business and the people—editors and agents—with contracts and deadlines and promises of bestsellerdom to come. They knew the tricks of the trade and the thrill of seeing their own words in print. Pia had known deep in her heart that if she listened and learned, she too would be among "the chosen."

She laughed as she pulled into her regular parking spot. "I've been chosen, all right. The question is, for what?"

"Hey, Pia-bird!" Sudibeth's voice made a lazy wave in the still, morning calm. "Where'd you run off to last night? Everyone was asking for you."

Pia hefted her yellow wicker briefcase out of the back of the MG. "Had to get some sleep. Lots of work to do today."

Sudibeth smoothed the silver-stitched seam down the tight leg of her designer jeans. "Well, you surely did miss some fun, honey. Why, that Miami, I tell you . . ."

Pia was in no mood for the latest details of the kiddy-lit queen's love life. She cut the bouncy redhead off with an uplifted palm.

"Sudibeth, have you seen that guy, Darius, this morning?"

"Who?"

"Darius something, or maybe it's Mr. Darius. I'm not sure. Anyway, he was here last night, dressed like an Egyptian pharaoh."

Sudibeth shook her head, making her shoulder-length earrings jangle. "I didn't see any pharaohs around the punch bowl. And the name doesn't ring a bell." She lifted her over-sized sunglasses and peered at Pia. "Are you *sure* you saw this guy, Pia? You don't reckon he's the same one who dropped in on you the other night? I mean, you have been having some strange experiences lately."

"Don't be ridiculous!" Pia might scoff, but Sudibeth's question made her seriously uneasy. Maybe she hadn't just dreamed all that good stuff last night. "He said he got here late. Maybe he hasn't registered yet. I'll probably see him in class this morning. If not, I'll catch him at lunch."

"Well, right now you best step on it, girl. Your class is packed to the rafters and you're already two minutes late."

Loaded down with books and papers, Pia headed for her classroom, feeling her excitement rise with every step she took. Not until she had settled in at the podium and scanned the forty or so faces beaming expectantly up into hers did she realize she didn't know what Darius looked like. She could eliminate the females and the short, round men, but any one of a dozen guys in the room could be Darius. Not wanting to single him out and give Sudibeth fuel for her gossip machine, Pia decided against simply asking if he was there. Instead, she went down her list of critique sessions, adding Darius's name somewhere in the middle.

When she called out his name but received no response, Pia looked up from her list, scanning faces. "Mr. Darius?" she repeated. Silence. "Has anyone seen Mr. Darius this morning?"

"He could be in the poetry class," one eager soul volunteered.

Of course. Why hadn't she thought of that? The two classes ran simultaneously, and he seemed like the poetic type to her. She would catch him at the end of the hour.

Pia hurried through the rest of her list, then set her reading glasses aside. She began her class as she always did. Leering out at the bright, smiling faces, she asked, "Are you absolutely certain you want to be a writer?"

The class went exceptionally well. Every last one of her eager pupils wanted to write afterward. It took Pia ten minutes to make her way through the eager group and out of the building. Once she got clear, the members of the poetry class had already dispersed.

"Drat!" she fumed. "Missed him again! Oh well, I'll catch him at lunch."

She tossed her books and briefcase in the car, then headed for Sudibeth's room, still scanning the grounds for any sign of her tall, mysterious stranger.

But all five days of the conference proved as disappointing as the first in her search for Darius. No one but Pia had ever seen him, talked to him, or even heard his name.

"I think you dreamed him up," Sudibeth told her on the final night, the night of the awards banquet. "He's just one more character out of your book, Pia-bird. I swear, you've got to quit working so hard. Let up for a time and have some fun. There wasn't any Darius here all week long, and there's no Mr. D on the banquet list either."

Sudibeth handed the list to Pia so she could see for herself. Finally, she had to admit that perhaps Sudibeth was right—that he was simply a figment of her imagination.

"But he certainly seemed real," Pia mused aloud.

"You've got it bad, girl! What you need is a man in your life. A *real* man!"

Pia ignored Sudibeth's final comment. Without answering, she rose and went to the podium to present the fiction awards.

The end of the conference was always a time for mixed emotions. Pia was fired up and ready to write, but she hated the thought of all her friends—old and new—leaving the island until next year. After a farewell breakfast at Epworth on Saturday morning, she headed back toward her beach cottage feeling strangely alone and empty.

"Lord only knows what Edgar Allan has written this week," she muttered as she pulled into her shell drive. She'd avoided even glancing into her office for the past five days. But she couldn't put it off much longer. She had a deadline, after all.

However, she decided she couldn't work just yet. For one more day she would pretend that she was free, unencumbered by work in progress. Today, she would wash clothes, go to the grocery and really stock up, cook herself a decent meal, then hit the beach later.

Later was when things really got stirred up.

By the time Pia finally headed for the beach for that swim she'd been promising herself all day, it was full dark—after nine o'clock. Her silver strip of sand was all but deserted. Far up in the dunes, she spotted the bright glow of a drift-wood fire. Teenagers, she figured. She walked in the opposite direction, wanting to be alone to think. The sand felt warm and soft under her bare feet. The breeze was cool on her face. The tide had just turned, heading out. She walked the damp line at the high water mark, thinking of everything and nothing.

Suddenly, she stopped and turned. Had she heard someone call her name or was the wind playing tricks? She glanced about, but the beach seemed deserted.

"Pia? Pia Byrd!"

The voice came from out over the water. She gazed off in the distance, frowning. After a moment, she spotted him far out in the surf—a light speck in the darkness. He stood up and came toward her. Who on earth would be way out there swimming at this hour? No one she knew.

She turned and headed back toward the cottage at a trot,

suddenly aware of how alone she was on the beach with this man. But her pursuer was out of the water now and gaining on her. Pia tried to run faster. Her heart was pounding in her ears. She reached the dunes at last, but slipped and slid in the deep sand. When a wet hand clamped on her arm, she screamed.

"Pia, it's me—Darius. Don't be frightened."

She turned to him, choking back another cry for help.

"Darius?" she gasped. "*The* Darius? My mystery man?"

She was laughing and crying with relief all at the same time.

"I am so sorry," he said. "I never meant to scare you."

He touched her cheek with his cool, damp hand, sending a little shivery thrill through her.

"What in God's name were you doing out there?" she demanded.

"Swimming."

"I know that. But why? Where have you been all week? Why weren't you at the conference?"

"I'll be happy to answer all your questions, Pia-bird. But might we go up to your cottage? It's turning a bit chilly out here."

Not until that moment did she realize that Darius was stark naked.

Chapter Five

As they trudged through the dunes, Pia hurrying ahead of Darius so she wouldn't be tempted to stare at him, her mind kept replaying the echoing refrain of an old college sorority ditty: "What do you do with a naked sailor? What do you do with a naked sailor? What do you do with a naked sailor, early in the morning?"

Unfortunately, she could remember only the question. The answer escaped her entirely. Her gentle Southern upbringing required that she simply ignore his state of undress, but that was pretty damn hard to do. Then, too, the fable of "The Emperor's New Clothes" had popped into her thoughts. Maybe Darius was testing her in some way. She muffled a sigh. If that was the case, she had failed the test miserably.

What was she supposed to do—invite him in, offer him a drink, then say in her most genteel hostess-voice, "Pardon me, Mr. Darius, but are you aware that you've lost your drawers?"

Yeah, sure!

Then another thought struck her. She suddenly recalled

her trip to the island of Crete with her dad many years ago. They'd gone to a public beach to swim. But before they arrived at the shore, he'd warned her that the islanders never wore bathing suits. They came to the beach fully dressed, then shucked down to the altogether—men and women alike—right in plain view. No bathhouse, no privacy curtain, no nothing. He had told Pia it was considered extremely poor taste to stare. Everyone was expected to look the other way when one of the Cretans started peeling down. She had managed just fine that day. Maybe she could handle Darius the same way, just focus her sights somewhere above the waist. Look him right in the eye and at all times keep her gaze from straying.

Yeah, sure!

All the while her mental wheels were turning she'd been trudging through the dunes, assuming that Darius, in all his glory, was right behind her. But when she turned to speak to him at the steps to her front porch, he was gone.

"Darius? Hey, Darius!" she called. She really didn't expect an answer. This was just a repeat performance of the night at the costume party. The man was as elusive as foxfire. Here one minute, gone the next.

But to her surprise, he replied, "Over here. Give me a minute and I'll be right there."

He emerged from the shadows of the dunes seconds later—dressed. Pia let out a long sigh of relief. At least that problem was solved.

"Come on in," she invited, holding the screen door open for him. "What happened to you at the conference? I looked for you all week."

Pia got her first good look at Darius when he walked into her living room. She stood there, staring at him like a dummy, her mouth open wide enough to catch mosquitoes.

He was enough to take a girl's breath away. Tall, golden, to-die-for gorgeous. He was wearing a skimpy, European-style bikini and a black tank top, cut low in front to expose his smoothly tanned chest. Over one shoulder he'd carelessly slung a canvas bag and his beach towel, which was a leopard-skin print. His hair was long, sun-blond, and through its sea-tossed and windblown waves she caught the glint of one gold earring.

He smiled at her, bemused, as she continued to stare in awed silence. When their gazes met, Pia caught her breath sharply.

"Your eyes . . . they're like amber. Hey, I know you! I'm sure we've met before. But where? When?"

"Do you mean before I came to this island?"

"I mean before *I* came to this island! A long time ago." Pia pressed her index finger to her temple, thinking hard. "It'll come to me. Just give me time. I never forget a face. How about a beer?"

"Corn beer?" He looked at her expectantly.

"I don't think so." She ambled toward the kitchen and opened the fridge. "I've got Bud or Dos Equis. Name your poison."

"The dark one in the bottle, please."

"You got it!" Pia flipped the tops off two Mexican beers with a church key.

As she led the way back to the living room, his mention of corn beer kept tossing around in her head. Where had she heard that before? Somewhere . . . a long time ago. Suddenly, Pia whirled around to face Darius, pointing at him with the long neck of the bottle.

"Egypt! That's it. I saw you years ago in Alexandria. You're my golden Greek—the sailor who gave me half the crystal pyramid."

"I did?"

"Sure! I'm the American kid who kept making eyes at you in the *agora*. Don't you remember? And this smelly old peddler came up to me and offered me that piece of alabaster for thirty dollars, but I didn't have the money. He wandered off and . . ."

Pia couldn't figure why Darius looked so perplexed. How could he not remember that day? Why, she'd never forgotten a moment of what happened. All the rest of that summer she'd dreamed about him. She'd elaborated on their meeting for her cousins, each telling of the tale getting better and better. By the time she'd returned to school in Virginia, she'd expanded the brief episode into a full-blown affair in order to amaze her roommates.

Now, as Pia watched Darius out of the corner of her eye, she saw a slight smile form below his frown. Then, with a low chuckle, he fished into the beach bag slung over his shoulder and brought out the other half of the gleaming alabaster. He held it to the light so that it showered the room with rainbows. "That vendor tried to cheat you. I paid the equivalent in drachma of only ten U.S. dollars."

"Man!" Pia waggled her beer bottle at him. "They try to sock it to Americans every chance they get, don't they? But I guess we ask for it. It sure was nice of you to break your piece in half and give part of it to me."

For long, silent moments, Pia and Darius both stared at the glowing stone in his palm. They seemed hypnotized by its shifting lights.

"All these years," Pia murmured. "All these miles." She shook her head, then tossed her long hair out of her eyes and looked up at him with the cool smile of a temptress. "What a coincidence! I mean, this boggles the mind. Sit down. Tell me what you've been up to all this time. And how'd you wind up on St. Simons?"

Darius didn't answer her. Pia watched him closely as he sank down in a chair, his gaze still focused on the piece of alabaster. Somehow, he seemed far way—too far away to hear her, too far away to answer.

* * *

Darius was, indeed, drifting. His mind wandered old, half-remembered paths, trying to seek out the man he had once been. All these years he had had fleeting visions of a beautiful, young woman with hair as black as a night on the desert and eyes of lapis blue. Could this Pia-bird truly be that girl? Had he really known her before Cleopatra came into his life? If so, she might shed some light on who he had been and what had happened to him.

An old yearning stirred to life deep inside him. He glanced up at the woman across from him. Her mention of the *agora* in Alexandria had opened a crack on his closed memory. Suddenly, when she'd spoken, a scene had shaped itself in his mind. The marketplace, yes. The foul-smelling peddler. And the pretty girl with her flirting eyes and a smile that had drawn him like honey. He had wanted to talk to her, wanted to kiss her. He'd been so young then, so ready to take on any challenge. And she had challenged him. Come and get me, if you can, she had seemed to dare. Had it not been for his ship waiting in the harbor and her father hovering near, Darius knew what would have happened. He had seen it in a vision, there in the marketplace that day. He had seen the girl draped on a golden couch, near a bubbling fountain. He had seen her lover come to her. His own hands had touched her. His own lips had kissed hers.

And then what? He strained to remember more.

"Is anything wrong, Darius?" Pia's voice seemed to come from miles away.

Startled, he looked up. Their gazes met and locked.

"You fainted," he murmured. "It was all too much for one so young."

Pia laughed nervously. "I don't see what my age has to do with my getting heatstroke in that Egyptian inferno."

"It was not the sun's heat that made you swoon."

"What then?"

"It was *our* heat—yours and mine. I felt it. Admit it, you did too."

The heat Pia felt at the moment was a blush creeping into her cheeks. She'd never had a man challenge her so directly. "I thought you were good-looking, sexy, I'll admit that. And I might have had a daydream or two. But I knew it could never go anywhere."

"But you would have liked it to go somewhere, wouldn't you? You and I both wanted what we knew we could not have."

"Are you talking about the crystal pyramid? You think my fainting was a sort of temper tantrum to get that from you?"

Darius shook his head, but continued gazing deep into her eyes. "You and I both know what you wanted that day— what we both wanted. Yes, the heat kept rising, but it was heat that came from within. You know what I'm talking about, Pia-bird. Admit it. If not to me, then to yourself." He frowned at her suddenly. "Have you tried to deny this all these years?"

He was making Pia uncomfortable, but in an odd way, she enjoyed the sensation. Whoever this Darius guy was, he had a sexual power about him that sent her thermostat soaring. The way he looked at her, like he was stripping away her clothes and her skin and her bones to gaze right in at her soul. And the way he'd made her flesh tingle when he'd brushed her hand as she'd handed him his beer. It was almost as if he had some dark, hidden talent that he reserved especially for females.

"I don't believe you made me faint," she told him firmly. "The man hasn't been born yet who could make me swoon."

He chuckled softly. Actually, it was more like a sexy growl from down deep in his gut. "You think not?" Then perhaps I should show you again."

Darius rose and came to her so quickly that she didn't have time to think. One second he was over there, and the next he was over here—beside her on the sofa, drawing her into his arms. She managed to get half his short name out before his mouth blocked all sound except a soft, inner purr.

He slipped his big, hot hands under her shirt and massaged her bare back while his tongue invaded her mouth. She knew this kiss, but not from the marketplace in Alexandria. No, this kisser had planted one on her not so long ago, in the very next room. He'd left her weak and dizzy and ready to beg for more. Yes, even ready to swoon.

When he finally pulled away, leaving Pia on fire, she said, *"You!"*

"Ah, so you do remember me now?"

"You came here and messed with my computer," she accused. "And you kissed me!"

His hands played over her bare arms. He leaned in closer, ready to repeat his erotic performance. "I did that, yes. And there is more I'd like . . ."

Pia pulled away and put some distance between them—not much, but even a few inches allowed her head to clear a little.

"Now, just hold on a minute!"

He neither answered her nor made a move to draw her back into his arms. Instead, he raised his palm until the piece of alabaster was at eye level before Pia's face. Mesmerized, she watched the colors dance, a ballet of pinks, blues, and violets. After a time, it seemed that the flow of pastels took on definite shapes. Two naked forms, one undeniably male, the other sensually female. She watched the pair inside the stone, captured there like prehistoric moths in amber, but able to move about. The man came to the woman, took her into his arms, and swayed with her. He drew her close and held her, then bent her far back and kissed her breasts.

Pia tried to draw her gaze away from the stone, but realized it was no use. Darius was some sort of wizard, and his magical stone was the perfect object to hold her spellbound. As she continued to watch light play through the alabaster, she saw the tiny figures come together. They were no longer dancing, but their movements were clear enough. Lying together, their hips rose and fell in perfect rhythm.

Darius's low voice broke the sexually charged silence. "Tell me what you see in the stone."

Pia shook her head, never taking her eyes from the tiny, copulating figures.

"Nothing? Ah, that surprises me."

"Colors," Pia whispered. "Only colors flowing into each other." She refused to accept what she was watching, and she certainly wasn't going to admit her erotic fantasy to Darius.

"Usually, when gazing into the stone, one sees what one wishes to see. Shall I tell you what I see?"

"No!" Pia all but yelled her reply, afraid that Darius was seeing the couple making love. That was all she needed— for him to describe in his low, sexy voice what she was watching and getting turned on by.

She forced her gaze away and rubbed a damp palm over her eyes. Finally, she demanded, "Who are you? Why are you *really* here?"

"I *thought* I came here to make you tell the truth about Cleopatra."

"Your lover," Pia added with a touch of sarcasm in her voice.

He nodded. "She was and is."

"Is? What the hell do you mean by that?"

He looked directly into her eyes, his own calm, rational, hiding no lies. "We are lovers even now. When the Romans are there, we must simply be more careful about our rendez-vous."

Pia turned and sat back against a pillow, crossing her legs in front of her. "I think you're losing it."

He grinned at her. "You didn't seem to think so a few moments ago . . . when I kissed you."

"I don't mean you're losing *that!* I mean you're losing your blooming mind! Cleopatra's been dead for centuries."

He nodded. "That is exactly why I am here. You are so far ahead in time that the true facts have been lost in the past or distorted beyond all reason. The Roman historians were especially vicious and cruel in writing about Cleopatra. If you must tell her tale, I would have the truth known in your time."

"You mean, you're not from this time?" To herself, Pia was saying, Sure, buddy! How about another beer?

She'd heard a lot of cock-and-bull stories, but this one took the cake. "What about Alexandria?" she demanded. "How could you have been there, if you're some kind of time-traveler who's come here from ancient Egypt?"

For a moment, Darius looked as perplexed as Pia felt. "I'm afraid I can't give you an answer. You see, I don't remember."

"But you said you remembered the afternoon in Alexandria."

"I do now. However, that memory was lost to me before you spoke of it. Then it all came back like a wave breaking over the shore."

"Well, try to think. Let's see if we can piece it together. Where did you go after you left the marketplace?"

He shook his head. "I can't recall."

"Who were you?"

"I don't know. I don't even know my real name. Cleopatra herself gave me the name Darius after she rescued me from the water and brought me back to life by forcing her own breath into my lungs."

"So you almost drowned?"

"I had been in the water for many days."

"Then my dad must have been right," Pia said almost to herself. "We read in the London *Times* just before we returned to the States that a boiler on the *Nile Queen* had exploded. A number of the crew members lost their lives. It happened the very evening the ship got underway from Alexandria, headed back to Athens."

"And you believe I was on that ill-fated vessel?"

"My dad thought so. He said you had the look of a sailing man."

"And do I, Pia-bird?"

Pia glanced at him. He wasn't begging for a kiss, but she was sorely tempted to give him one anyway. Poor bastard! she thought. The explosion must have scrambled his brains.

"I'm not crazy," he said, as if he could read her thoughts. "And I'm telling you the truth, as far as I know it. If I was on board that ship, the sea carried me far back to the past. I have lived for years in Cleopatra's time—as her friend, her advisor, her lover. But now. . . ." He broke off and stared down into the crystal pyramid.

"Yes? Now, what?" Pia urged.

"It has become difficult for us. Even dangerous. When she was young and her father still lived, life was wonderful for the two of us. But queens cannot always afford to do as they please—to love whom they choose. I see her seldom now. And even when we can manage to steal an hour together, there are so many Romans underfoot." He shrugged and sighed. "I understand, of course, but it is difficult to lose one's love."

"I wouldn't know about that," Pia answered with an edge of bitterness in her tone.

"You are fortunate never to have lost the one you loved."

"That's not what I meant. No man's ever loved me the way you seem to love Cleopatra."

He gripped her hand, his eyes beaming amber fire into hers. "It's not possible."

Pia nodded, finding herself on the verge of tears.

"How sad for you," Darius murmured. "Everyone needs to be loved."

Under her breath, Pia said, "Tell me about it!" But aloud, to Darius, she replied, "I'll survive."

"I don't know that I would wish to survive without love."

Pia was no longer looking at Darius. Instead, she was staring out the window at the starry sky. When he touched her shoulder, she jumped.

"Why do you look so sad?" he whispered.

She tried to laugh if off, even though she knew her eyes were filling with tears. All of a sudden, she felt so alone, so at the mercy of the whole universe.

"I'm sorry," Pia said, the words breaking in a sob. "I don't know what's come over me. I'm not a crier. Really! I never cry, but. . . ."

Darius reached out to her. He gathered her into his arms and held her, murmuring words she couldn't understand. But his tone was soothing and sympathetic. He kissed the tears from her cheeks. And soon he found her lips.

Pia realized when he kissed her how hungry she was for closeness, for understanding, for love. All these years, she'd had no one to talk to when things got rough. No one to hold her when she just needed to feel arms around her and someone's heart beating close to hers. She'd spent years living on fantasies alone, identifying with the heroines in her stories to such an extent that she wept when they did, laughed when they laughed, and experienced her own small ecstasy each time one of her fictitious ladies found her hero and her happy ending. But was there any happy ending for Pia herself? Somehow, she doubted it.

Thoughts gave way to feelings, then. Darius leaned over her on the couch, pressing her down to the worn cushions, his hands cupping her face, his mouth still moving over hers. Little licks of flame along her spine gave way to a raging firestorm of longing. All the urges and desires that she had pushed aside since the breakup of her marriage came rushing back, demanding to be satisfied.

When Darius slid his hands down from her face to the thin straps of her tank top, Pia knew exactly what he meant to do. She made no move to stop him. She shivered slightly as his fingers dragged over her flesh, drawing the straps down her arms, pulling the cotton fabric over her erect nipples until the flimsy top was bunched at her waist.

"I should tell you no," she whispered.

"Why?" he murmured against her breasts.

She was almost panting, but she managed a shrug. "You don't love me. You love Cleopatra."

He dragged his tongue lazily across one of her nipples, then raised his head and stared into her eyes. "But don't you understand?" he said. "You *are* Cleopatra. I knew it the first moment I looked into your eyes. I have lost her in her own time. But, the gods be praised, I have found her again in this new incarnation. Pia-bird, this was meant to be. It must have been written in the stars long before the world began."

"Reincarnation again? You can't believe that, Darius," she argued. "If I was once Cleopatra, why am I having so much trouble writing about her? Shouldn't I retain some sort of cosmic memory of her?"

"Deeply buried," he answered. "Perhaps together we can draw it to the surface. If you are truly Cleopatra, you should remember this."

From out of the darkness, Darius produced the crystal pyramid. He touched it to his lips, then to the very tip of Pia's breast. The stone began to hum, sending wonderful vibrations through her. Her entire body was quivering with the high-pitched sound. She thrashed about on the sofa and moaned. As the piece of alabaster, hot to the touch now, continued to sing its sensuous song, Pia saw herself again as Cleopatra, with Darius reclining beside her on a golden couch. In that moment, she felt the young queen's painful longing and the golden Greek's hot desire.

When she came out of her trancelike state, Pia lay sweating and naked on her own chintz-covered couch. Darius remained beside her, the wickedly vibrating stone still in his hand.

"You remembered?"

"God, yes!" she gasped. "She loves you, all right."

"Loved," he corrected. "You must write of that love and the way it was between us. But to understand, you must first learn the way it was for us."

Abruptly, he rose from the couch. Pia saw instantly that now he was truly naked, naked and fully aroused. He disappeared into the hallway. Oh, no! Pia thought. He can't leave me like *this!* Then she heard the refrigerator door open and shut. A moment later, he came back to her, carrying two more beers. He sat down beside her. Pia reached for her bottle, but instead of giving it to her, he touched the cold bottle to her forehead, then to her lips, then to her breasts.

She caught her breath and a shiver ran through her.

"My Cleo loves some playful sport when we make love. Some teasing and taunting before . . ."

"Then I must be your Cleo," Pia gasped as Darius rolled the cold, wet bottle across her belly, spilling a bit of foam over one hip.

He bent down and smoothed his tongue over her beer-flavored flesh. Finally, he handed Pia her bottle, then drank his down in several long, deep swallows.

Pia propped up on one elbow and drank hers more slowly, watching Darius all the while. Once his bottle was empty, he held it up, smiling at its long neck. Then he glanced down at Pia's slightly parted thighs. His next movement was so quick that Pia hardly had time to think, but what she thought he meant to do both shocked and excited her. He didn't do what she had imagined he intended. Instead, he wedged the cold bottle between the very apex of her thighs so that its chill touched her, making her tingle inside. She tightened the muscles in her legs, gripping the cool glass closer. Then, realizing that she was trembling on the very verge of orgasm, she released her grip.

She drank down the rest of her beer, set her own bottle aside. "Are you going to keep this up all night, Darius?"

Pia could see his broad grin even through the darkness. "If you like."

A little whimper escaped her when she saw him kiss the crystal pyramid again. When he touched the humming stone to the neck of the beer bottle between her legs, Pia fell back on the couch with a cry of pure pleasure. The music was flowing into her body again, but now its point of entry was far more sensitive than her breast had been.

As her hips rose and fell in an unmistakable rhythm, Darius plucked the dark bottle from her grasp. The next instant, he covered Pia's body with his own. Then slowly, agonizingly, deliciously, he entered her.

Pia's whole body—inside and out—was suddenly humming with the erotic vibrations of the stone. But no crystal pyramid had caused this sensation. Darius possessed a magic that was far more powerful. It throbbed, it burned, it soothed, it enflamed.

She lost all track of who she was. One minute she was a writer, receiving more good research information than she had ever known existed, and the next she was Queen Cleopatra, handing over her power and her rule to another through the act of love.

When the crashing, star-strewn explosion finally came down on them, it seemed to Pia that she would never return to earth—she wasn't even sure she wanted to—just fly around somewhere in deep space hitting one high after another while meteors zipped past her molten flesh.

As things returned to normal, Pia could almost see herself slowly floating back to earth through a neon spiral of pleasure.

When she could speak again, she stared up at Darius, her eyes wide with wonder. "Damn, you're good!" It was all she could think to say.

He chuckled, that same deep, growling laugh she had heard before. The sound sent a new shiver through her. She realized, awestruck, that she wanted him again—right here, right now.

He leaned down and kissed her softly on the lips. "It's late. I should leave you now, my little queen."

Total panic seized Pia. "Where are you going?"

He shrugged. "Perhaps, after tonight, I should return to the palace at Alexandria and give you time to think things through. My staying here would only prove a distraction."

"Oh, Darius, stay and distract me," she begged, clinging to his hand, kissing his fingers.

"But you have a book to write. Remember?"

"All the more reason for you to stay. I need your help with my research."

He grinned at her and chuckled softly.

"I don't mean that kind of research. I need to know more about Cleopatra. Please stay! Don't leave me alone, wondering where you've gone this time and if I'll ever see you again." She paused, realizing what she was going to say next, but not quite believing what had happened to her in such a short span of time. "Darius, I love you."

The sun was coming up, sending the first pearly fingers of dawn into the dark room. Pia saw his face clearly for the first time in hours. He was aglow, his golden eyes gleaming as if he'd just been given the morning sun as his own personal gift. With the brilliant light accentuating his already strong features, he looked unconquerable, all-knowing, godlike.

"And I love you," he whispered. "More than you shall ever know. I loved you long before the moment you smiled at me in the marketplace in Alexandria, long before you drew my body from the sea and breathed life back into me. You are my one and only passion—the woman who owns my soul."

"Oh, Darius!" Pia drew him close.

He pulled her into a tight embrace and kissed her deeply. Pia's excitement simmered to the boiling point when his body reacted to her nearness. The next moment, he swept her up into his arms and headed for her bedroom.

"You need rest," he told her between a rain of kisses.

"I'll rest," she answered. *"Afterward. . . ."*

Chapter Six

Pia was seldom surprised by anything that happened to her. Normally, the very unpredictability of her day-to-day existence rendered the shock factor impotent. But with Darius around, each hour proved more exotic than the last. She never knew what he might do or say or what kind of mischief or excitement he might scare up. By now Darius had become a fixture in the village—talking philosophy with fishermen on the pier, haunting the used bookstore on Mallory Street in search of ancient volumes, playing miniature golf with spectacular skill, or simply roaming the beach for hours at a time, communing with tourists, locals, nature, and himself.

Two weeks after his unheralded arrival on the island, they were having breakfast one morning when Darius suddenly set aside his blueberry pop-tart and asked if they could go to the lighthouse that stood between Pia's cottage and the pier at the end of Mallory Street. The great, white beacon towered over the picnic area known as Neptune Park, and cast the glow from its Fresnel lens across St. Simons Sound to Jekyll Island and beyond.

"Sure," Pia answered. "It's open to the public. But what's the attraction?"

"Two attractions," Darius answered, nibbling again at his toaster pastry. "I want to see how it differs from the great lighthouse on Pharos."

When he failed to add anything to that, Pia said, "And?"

He looked across and grinned. "I want to see the ghost."

Pia laughed into her coffee mug. "Who have you been talking to? The chamber of commerce? That so-called ghost was invented purely to draw tourists, I'm sure."

"Well?" He cocked one golden eyebrow at her. "I'm a tourist. I came quite a great distance to see this place."

"You can say that again!"

"I'm a tourist. I came quite a—"

Pia shook her head and waved him to silence. "I didn't mean that literally. It was only a comment."

"It sounded like a command. Had Cleopatra said such a thing, it would have been."

Pia had begun clearing the table, but now she sat back down and propped her chin on the heel of her hand. "What's she like, Darius? You promised you'd tell me when the time was right."

"And you think it is the right time now?"

His smile was so devilish that Pia almost told him to forget it so they could go back to bed. It was pouring rain outside—a good day for staying in the sack. Then she sighed. She had other pressing matters to take care of. Like a book that was no longer writing itself now that she was keeping Darius busy at other things.

"Darius, I have to finish my story. I have a deadline. Without your help, I'm not sure I can do it. And you did say you came here to help me."

He reached across the table and stroked her cheek with his fingertips. "But, ah, love, you are such a distraction."

"That goes ditto for you, my dear golden Greek. But the bills have to be paid." She grinned and winked at him. "Even if I were in the line of work to make money doing what we've been doing the past couple of weeks, you came here minus your bankroll, dearie."

"What is this *bankroll?* What is this *dearie?*"

He scowled ominously at Pia, so ominously that it was clear he was teasing her. He knew exactly what she was talking about. The guy was a quick study. He'd picked up on all things modern just from watching TV in his spare time and from observing Pia and the other islanders. Besides, Pia was convinced that Darius really came from this time, if not from this place. He had seemed very much at home in Alexandria's marketplace a few years back.

Lost in thought, Pia felt his hand on her knee under the table. When she looked at Darius, he was smiling his best bedroom smile, lips parted, nostrils flared, and eyelids at half mast.

"I need no bankroll," he said in a husky whisper. "I've never had to pay a woman, Pia-bird."

She laughed a little shakily and moved her leg away from his fondling hand. "You probably have to pay them to leave you alone. Tell me about Cleopatra, Darius. Please!"

"May we have beer on the front porch while I instruct you?"

"Sure!" she answered, rolling her eyes. It crossed her mind that by the time this guy got back to the Court of the Ptolemies, he was going to be sporting a beer gut. Cleo'd probably put him on a diet and cut off his liquor allowance.

She wished instantly that she hadn't allowed herself to think about that. She couldn't imagine life without Darius. She didn't want to imagine such a thing. He was dear and funny and sweet and the best and most imaginative lover

she'd ever had. She realized after being with Darius that
the heroines in her novels had really been missing out.

They settled themselves in rockers on the front porch. A
slight mist of rain was sifting in through the coppery screen.
Beneath the billowing, leaden sky, the sea oats bent against
the wind and waves crashed on the shore, sending spumes
of foam scudding down the beach. The air was damp, salty,
and pleasantly cool. The creak of the porch swing's chain
in the wind added just the right homey touch. Pia was glad
she was here—on *her* porch, in *her* rocker, with *her* man.

She glanced over at Darius. Gazing off into the distance,
he took a long pull at his beer, then let out a sigh. "Ah-h-
h! That's good stuff! Many's the night the queen and I have
lingered over our corn beer in some dockside dive, spinning
tales and telling lies and enjoying every minute of it."

Pia's eyes went wide. "Cleopatra goes to juke joints?"

Darius nodded. "Well, the early Egyptian equivalent of
your 'joint,' minus the juke. Instead of your jukebox, we
would have slaves on double-harp and sistrum, a sort of
musical rattle, and sometimes a veiled dancer to perform.
The queen loves to be entertained, and is always very generous to those who please her."

"Then you must be as rich as Midas," Pia murmured
under her breath, her jealousy showing in spite of her best
intentions.

Darius either didn't hear her words or chose to ignore
them. "Cleopatra needs this sort of contact with the lower
classes," he continued. "You see, she wants to stay in touch
with her subjects. Did you know that she is the first ruler
in Egypt ever to learn the language of her people?"

"Really?" Pia said, astounded. She tried to think what it
would be like to have a U.S. president who spoke only
Spanish or French. Then, thinking aloud, she added, "That's
right. Cleopatra's ancestors were Macedonian. I guess they
spoke Greek."

"A more ancient tongue, Athenian Attic," Darius corrected, "as pure a language as the Spanish of Castile. She rarely needs an interpreter, speaking with Ethiopians, Troglodytes, Jews, Arabs, Syrians, Medes, Parthians, and, of course, Romans with equal ease."

Pia gave a low whistle. "Smart lady!"

"Cleopatra is far more than simply smart. She is gifted," Darius said. "Her predecessors remained at a distance from their subjects, but Cleopatra is determined to know the people she rules. She'll often disguise herself as a man and join her soldiers or the peasants wherever they go to relax. I, of course, usually accompany her in case she needs protection."

"Wow!" Pia breathed. "That's certainly not the picture I'd formed of her."

"Nor is it the picture that time has painted in such vulgar hues. Don't you see now why it is so important I help you with this book? The historians—especially those Roman thugs—have handed down such distorted notions of who and what Cleopatra was."

"Yes," she said with a nod. "Do go on. Tell me more, Darius. I want to know everything. You claim I'm Cleopatra's spirit, reincarnated. If that's so, let me see what she saw and feel what she felt."

Darius turned slightly in his chair and stared at Pia so intensely and for such a long time that she finally had to look away. His searching gaze made the hair on the back of her neck prickle.

"Very well!" he said at length. "Where is your half of the crystal pyramid?"

"In my office."

"Go and get it. Now! You want to see things? I will show you things. I will take you on a magnificent journey. One you will long remember."

Recalling how Darius could make his stone hum and vibrate when they made love, Pia wondered what he might be up to now. Nevertheless, she hurried to do as he instructed. Moments later, she was back in her chair, the piece of alabaster in her hand. Xander-the-cat jumped into her lap, circled, then settled, kneading her leg through her terrycloth robe.

Darius let his eyes lock on hers for a moment, dark amber smoldering and electrifying lapis blue. Pia felt a tingle sizzle down her spine, and the stone grew hot in her hand. The heat spread all through her, leaving in its wake a languid sensation that took possession of her mind as well as her body.

"Now we are ready," Darius said, his whisper almost lost in the sighing of the wind and the purr of the cat. "Close your eyes, Pia-bird. I have fantastic things to show you."

Pia couldn't have kept her eyes open if she'd wanted to. She wondered if the crystal pyramid had hypnotic powers. Or maybe Darius was some sort of magician. The moment her lids drooped shut, all thoughts ceased. She saw a swirl of hot, pastel colors. Out of the whirling rainbow, a picture began to form, like a ruined watercolor putting itself back to rights. A woman's face emerged, and then her magnificently robed figure.

"Darius? Is that you?" Cleopatra called in a voice that had the rich, musical tone of a lyre.

The princess stood alone in what appeared to be her bedchamber. The pebble mosaics on the floor sparkled with gold and silver, turquoise and carnelian. Silk tapestries covering the walls moved sensually in the breeze from the sea. The furniture gleamed—gilt and highly polished ivory and ebony—but Cleopatra herself shone more brightly than anything else in the room. She wore a filmy gown of shining silk, tinted purple from the dye of the sacred murex. Through the sheer bodice, her young breasts stood out in proud relief.

Paper-thin strips of hammered gold draped her shapely hips. Her slender feet were clad in shoes not unlike Pia's flip-flops, except that they were made of precious metal and encrusted with jewels, emeralds and amethysts.

Cleopatra struck a watchful pose, waiting to see who was outside her curtained door. Pia could tell the young princess hoped it was Darius. Her eyes took on a certain sheen, and a tremulous smile curved her berry-tinted lips.

"Lady, we have brought him," came a low, guttural voice from the corridor.

"Then bring him in."

"Are you certain you wish this?" the same male voice asked hesitantly.

"Never question my commands, Apollodorus." Her annoyance at the delay told in her sharp tone. "Do as I say this minute."

The curtains parted silently and two giants, one a black Nubian and the other her own Sicilian bodyguard Apollodorus, entered carrying a litter. A shrunken form lay on the zebra-skin stretcher. His face was all hard, sharp angles. His body was all bones, and burned horribly by the sun.

Pia realized it was Darius, although he looked more like something from a nightmare than a dream.

"Place him on my bed," Cleopatra ordered, her voice soft now with empathy for the man she had saved.

When the two strong servants took hold of Darius to transfer him from the litter, he moaned in agony.

"Gently, damn you! Cause him more pain and I'll make eunuchs of you with my bare hands."

Suddenly, Darius's voice as he sat beside Pia on her front porch intruded into the scene. She listened to his words without opening her eyes so that she saw as well as heard what happened next.

"The wine she'd given me when she fished me out of the sea an hour before had worn off. I was suffering. My skin burned as if flames were eating me alive. Every inch of me roared with pain. More than anything, I wanted to die and be out of my misery. Until I saw her . . . until she touched me . . ."

Iras, Cleopatra's personal servant, entered the chamber without a word. But Pia read the disapproval in her eyes. So did her mistress.

"Don't say it," the princess warned her maid. "Hold your tongue for once and bring me the ointments in the alabaster jars."

Iras moved swiftly, silently across the room and brought back a golden chest filled with alabaster containers carved in the shapes of animal's heads.

Again, Darius spoke to Pia. "She has the gentlest hands. Long, slender fingers with a touch like cool, Sidonian silk. I was lying on my stomach. She whispered encouragement to me as she removed the light length of linen covering my sunburned back. She called to her girl for the 'monkey jar.' A moment later, the room filled with the scent of palm flowers. In the next instant, I tensed as I felt her touch my scalding flesh. 'Relax,' she whispered. 'Have no fear. The palm oil will soothe you, Darius.'"

Her eyes still closed, Pia watched Cleopatra dip her fingers into the monkey jar, then place her hands on Darius's red, tender shoulders. With light, delicate strokes, she spread the aromatic ointment over his burned flesh. She heard Darius first draw in an anxious breath, then sigh with pleasure and relief. For a long time the petite princess stroked his back, repeatedly dipping her fingers into the jar for more of the soothing, milky balm.

When Cleopatra reached to pull the linen lower, to strip it completely away, Iras gasped, "My lady! No!"

The princess shot her serving woman a warning glance. "More ointment," she commanded.

Looking shamed and blushing deeply, Iras held out the

alabaster jar. Then she averted her gaze as Cleopatra let her dripping fingers stray down her patient's back to his red-raw buttocks. His muscles tightened visibly when she touched him there. Then he relaxed and sighed again.

Slowly, carefully, Cleopatra worked the healing ointment into his flesh, down his legs to the soles of his feet. Somewhere during the painstaking process, Darius's sighs of relief turned to moans of pleasure.

Then the whole process was repeated with a creamy concoction from the "elephant jar" that smelled of red poppies and musk.

"What is that?" Darius asked, his voice thin and whispery now he was so soothed, so near sleep.

"The seed of the opium flower mixed with the seed of a bull elephant," she whispered back. "It will kill your pain and leave new strength in its place. I devised this formula myself."

Darius laughed softly. "I think, Cleopatra, that you are giving me more strength than I can safely handle in my condition."

The smiling princess matched his laughter with the musical sound of her own. "I think not," she said. "For that kind of strength, you need ointment from the lion jar, the king of beasts. Only then will we know your true virility." She leaned close to his ear and whispered so that Iras wouldn't hear, "When you're better we'll test my lion formula, just you and I alone."

Again Darius spoke to Pia. "Her words and her touch made me wonder if I had any need to dip into the lion-head jar. She had me more than a bit aroused by this time. I was glad that Iras insisted I be covered when they turned me over. I was in no condition to act on my body's impulses, and I didn't want Cleopatra to guess my frustration. Worse yet would have been for Iras to catch me in such a state."

"Darius, you're embarrassing me," Pia said through her trance.

He chuckled, then she heard him take another pull at his beer. "If you're easily embarrassed, Pia-bird, you shouldn't be writing about Queen Cleopatra. She was a woman who set her own standards, who played by her own rules."

"So I'm learning."

Ignoring Pia's comment, Darius continued in a dreamy voice. "When she had finished with me and put her ointment jars away, she came to sit beside me on the bed. I remember feeling quite euphoric by that time. I couldn't help staring at her breasts, so plainly visible through her purple gown, and thinking that she was such a beautiful young woman she had every right to display her wondrous body."

Darius paused, drank, sighed.

The scene in Pia's mind grew even sharper. She became aware of Darius staring at Cleopatra's breasts as if he were staring at hers. She felt her nipples pucker inside the terrycloth robe.

Cleopatra raised Darius's head ever so slightly, just enough to bring his lips to the rim of a silver cup, brimming with rich, red wine. "Drink!" she said.

"I drank at her soft command," Darius told Pia. "And as my mind drifted ever deeper, it occurred to me that Cleopatra's sweet, drugged potion tasted like mother's milk from the breast of a goddess. I might have been suckling this ambrosia from my princess's softly pulsing nipple."

Darius's voice drifted off as if swept away by the sea wind.

Pia realized that she was holding her breath and her heart was racing madly. She opened her eyes and glanced at Darius. He was again staring out at the crashing waves. For long moments, he remained motionless, then he gave a nervous laugh, winked at Pia, and tipped the beer bottle to his lips, emptying it in one long swallow.

"So, are you beginning to get the picture?" he asked.

Pia frowned, thinking back over everything Darius had shown her and told her. "I got a lot of things wrong," she said at last.

"Like what, love?"

"For one thing, she's so tiny. I've always thought of Cleopatra as an Amazon—big, strapping, imposing."

"Oh, she is imposing. All five feet of her. You simply didn't take into account that everybody was smaller back then. They have me figured for a damn giant since I'm over six feet tall."

"I know that." Pia nodded. "It was just a shock, seeing her for the first time. And what about her hair? I thought it was jet black. But her hair's lighter by far than mine."

Darius chuckled. "She wasn't wearing her wig when you saw her just now. All the royal women wear those black wigs, and most of the men as well."

Pia grinned at him. "I guess Cleo never had to worry about a bad hair day, eh?"

Darius didn't seem to understand this. Pia waved away his puzzlement and laughed. "Don't mind me. Just making a joke."

He reached over and gripped Pia's hand. Their eyes met.

"You get that from her, you know. Cleopatra loved a good joke." He played with her fingers while he talked. "Most of the time, though, she was too caught up in serious matters to have time for laughter."

"Too bad," Pia murmured. "She was so young. She should have had some fun. It doesn't seem fair that she had so much thrust on her at such a tender age."

"She never wished it any other way. She was born to it. She was royalty. Her one driving force was to save Egypt, not just from the Romans but from her own scheming family. Her brothers both wanted it. Her older sister, Berenice, would have killed her whole family to have the throne. And her younger sister, Arsinoë, nearly took everything before she was captured and sent to Rome to walk in shackles behind Caesar's chariot in one of his triumphs. Cleopatra was the only one cunning enough and with passion enough to succeed."

"But she didn't succeed," Pia argued. "She lost everything, even her life. She committed suicide."

Darius nodded, his face solemn. "An honorable death. She gave it her all and she was never conquered."

"That's an odd way of looking at it."

"It's Cleopatra's way," Darius assured her.

Suddenly, a thought struck Pia. "Darius, you and I know Cleopatra's fate—that she died from the bite of an asp. Yet you speak of her as if she's still alive."

"She is. If I go back, she will be there as she was when I left to come here."

"But how can that be possible?"

Darius stared off in the distance, trying to think how to explain all this to Pia. Finally, he said, "Think of time not as days lined up end to end but as layer upon layer. Any given moment of this day—here on your porch on St. Simons Island—has a corresponding moment in Cleopatra's Egypt or any other time you care to mention. The trick is to learn the method to travel through the layers of time."

"And you've figured that out?"

Darius shook his head slowly. "No. I confess, I have not."

"Then how did you get here?"

He touched the glowing stone that Pia still held clutched in her hand. "The crystal pyramid," he answered. "I don't have any idea how it works, I only know that it has the power to cut through those layers of time. If, as you say, I was in a shipwreck in this time, the piece of alabaster from Alexander's tomb somehow carried me back to its origin. And when my need was powerful enough, it brought me back here, to you."

Pia stared at the stone for a moment, then looked up at Darius. "Do you really believe this came from the tomb of Alexander the Great?"

"I know for certain that it did. I've seen the chipped corner. Cleopatra took me there herself. And she admitted to stealing the chunk of stone, hoping it would give her the wisdom and strength of her legendary ancestor."

"Oh, I wish I could see it! They didn't take us there when I visited Alexandria."

"No one knows where it lies today. The tomb's chamber could be in the sea now or, more likely, crushed under tons of rock due to earthquakes of the distant past. But in Cleopatra's day, it was still accessible, too accessible, in fact. Grave robbers, years before Cleopatra's time, broke in and removed the golden sheathing from the coffin. Still, it is an awesome sight."

Pia stared at Darius, begging with her eyes. "Oh, *please!*"

"You want to see it? Then close your eyes and tighten your grip on the crystal pyramid."

Pia did as Darius instructed. Immediately, she saw the swirl of colors again, but this time they appeared in more somber hues—clouds of purple, gray, and deep blue mist. When a scene began taking shape, she saw only shadows and the eerie light of a torch off in the distance. Out of the darkness, she heard someone call.

"Hurry, Darius!" Cleopatra's voice echoed hollowly through the dark tunnel.

"How much farther?" he called ahead to her.

"Not far, but the way is treacherous. Come, take my hand. I know the path by heart."

"I was more than happy to feel a living hand in mine in that place of the dead," Darius admitted to Pia. "Row upon row of ancient coffins, containing the remains of the Ptolemy ancestors, lay on either side of this narrow, cobwebbed way. Dust-covered gold gleamed dully in the light of the torch, and the painted coffin-faces seemed to watch our every move. I asked Cleopatra which sarcophagus was Alexander's."

"He's not here in the outer chamber with the others," she explained. "He has a secret place, a tomb all his own. This way. I'll show you."

"I gripped her hand tighter as we moved ever deeper into the gloomy, musty cavern. So far below the surface, it seemed to me that I could hear the earth itself groaning with the weight of Alexandria high above. Or maybe the sounds I heard were the moans of the dead all around us."

Her eyes still closed, Pia watched every move Cleopatra and Darius made. She strained to see ahead down the corridor, but the darkness was total beyond the reach of their torch. She sensed Darius's nervousness. Cleopatra, however, seemed calm and at home among her mummified ancestors. At a stone wall curtained with cobwebs, the princess paused, searching with her fingertips for the right spot to press. Now Pia too heard the groaning that Darius had mentioned moments before as a great stone turned slowly in the wall, forming a low doorway.

"Come!" Cleopatra motioned with her torch for him to follow her into the crypt.

"I hesitated," Darius told Pia. "Who wouldn't have— entering that dark hole for the first time? When the stone door moved, we were greeted by a rush of cold, dank air. I almost imagined it was the spirit of Alexander himself, escaping his eerie tomb-prison."

"There's nothing to fear," Cleopatra assured him. She was smiling, seemingly happy to be where she was. "When I die," she explained, "I'm going to lie here, as close as possible to Alexander."

"She's right about that," Pia murmured. "She and Antony both. The tour guide said so."

"Quiet, Pia-bird!" Darius whispered. "You'll break the spell."

Pia fell silent again and concentrated on the scene. She caught her breath when she saw Alexander's coffin for the first time. In the light from the torch, the alabaster seemed to glow with strange, colored lights as if foxfire burned within the stone itself. But what made her gasp was the face of Alexander the Great. As she stared at him, he stared back through a face mask of clear glass, his gaze fixed and penetrating. Eyes as blue as the Mediterranean. He wore a crown atop his head, and by some ancient and secret magic of the embalmers, he looked perfectly preserved. His was a strong face, a bold face, a young face.

"He was only thirty-two when he died," Darius said, sensing Pia's shock.

"See, Darius." Cleopatra rubbed her hand over the one flat corner of the sarcophagus. Here's the place from which I chipped the crystal pyramid. I'm sure Alexander knew, but I'm equally sure that he approved. We understand each other." She moved to the glass and smiled down at her long-dead ancestor as if she were greeting an old friend.

"I couldn't bring myself to go that close," Darius told Pia. "I felt such an awesome force within that chamber. I could almost believe that he was there and still alive. Those staring eyes, that grim, set curve of his mouth. In life he must have been a fearsome adversary. I never understood how one so young could conquer the world. But standing there, staring at him, I knew it was possible."

"Don't go," Pia heard Cleopatra beg.

"I can't stay any longer." Darius's answer came in a choked, emotional voice.

Then the gloomy shadows swirled like sooty cobwebs in the wind and the vision faded.

Pia took a deep breath of the cool, salt air and shook her

head. She turned to stare at Darius and opened her mouth to say something, but words wouldn't come.

He nodded his understanding. "You feel the way I did when I left that place. There was a force there, *his* force. Mighty and majestic." Yet Cleopatra was unafraid. She went there often, alone, to commune with Alexander's spirit.

"She must have been brave."

"Brave doesn't begin to describe her."

Pia turned and looked him straight in the eye. "Then how *do* you describe her? That's what I have to know, Darius. I have to understand what made her tick, how her mind worked, why she did the things she did."

He gave Pia an odd look. "You really want to know her that well?"

"I have to, if I'm going to do her justice in this book. You said yourself that no one has ever really told the truth about Cleopatra. I have that chance, finally, because you're here. But I have to know more."

Darius, his expression somber, nodded slightly. "There may be a way."

"What do I have to do?"

He shrugged. "It's simple. You must go back to her time."

"You mean back to the Alexandria that existed before 30 B.C.?"

"Unless you have a better idea."

Pia slumped back in her chair, her enthusiasm fading as quickly as it had come. "You're talking about time-travel."

"Yes." He nodded.

"That's not possible."

"Oh?" Darius smiled. "Then how do you explain my being here?"

She turned and gave him a long, hard stare. "How *did* you get here? You never did tell me."

"The crystal pyramid. And I did tell you. You simply chose not to believe me. But I've been working on some calculations and coordinates. I believe that if we fit the two halves of the chunk of alabaster together, we may both be able to travel back at the same time."

Pia gave a low whistle, then let out a sigh. "I don't know, Darius. I've done a lot of things for the sake of research, but time-travel?"

He shrugged. "I leave it up to you."

"You honestly think it will work?"

"If I can travel back and forth on my half of the stone, then why wouldn't it work as well for you?"

"You've got me there," she answered.

"Do you want to try?"

Pia hesitated for a time before she answered him. "What if something goes wrong?"

"Like what?"

"I don't know."

"If you don't know, then why worry? I'll be with you. I'll hold your hand all the way."

She gave him a crooked smile. "Like a tour guide through time?"

"Exactly!"

"Tell me this first, what's going on back there right now?"

"Much! When I left Cleopatra, she had been driven from the palace by her brother and sister. She is encamped with her army at the edge of the desert, while Ptolemy's armies stand between her and Alexandria. Caesar is on his way to The City."

"You mean *Julius* Caesar?"

Darius nodded. "That very Roman. You must know what Cleopatra has in mind."

Pia laughed. "I sure do!"

"Then you can guess why she sent me away."

Pia heard the anger mixed with hurt in his voice.

"I thought you loved her, Darius. She must need you now.

Why did you leave? You should have stood your ground
and fought for her and beside her."

He stared into Pia's eyes, his own smoldering with desire.
"I am both for her and beside her at this very minute. You
needed me. She did not. At this moment, Cleopatra has one
goal and one goal only on her mind—to save Egypt by
securing the double crown for herself alone. She has made
many sacrifices in the past in order to become queen. Many
more lie ahead of her. I would be no more than an impedi-
ment to her now."

"So you left your lover without the slightest protest?" Pia
stared at him, in disbelief.

Darius smiled a grim smile. "Not exactly. I'm afraid there
was a scene before I agreed to vanish from her life."

Suddenly, the crystal in Pia's hand grew hot. Without any
other warning, she found herself nodding off again. This
time the colors inside her mind were a blaze of orange and
scarlet flames, whipped all through with clouds of angry
black smoke. A moment later, she spied two men in armor
confronting each other inside a tent.

"No! I won't do it!" the taller of the pair snarled through
the face piece of his black metal helmet. Although Pia had
yet to see his face, she recognized Darius's powerful voice.

The smaller warrior, seemingly weighed down by heavy
breastplate, helmet, and weapons, stamped his boot on the
ground and made an angry gesture common to all ages.

"I've come too far, fought too hard, to have emotions
stand in my way. Caesar has sent his messenger, demanding
an audience with me at the palace."

Cleopatra! Pia realized suddenly. She listened more carefully.

"Have you lost your wits?" Darius demanded, disbe-
lieving. "Your brother's forces will kill you before you get
near Alexandria. You'll never make it."

"I will!"

"Not alone. You must let me accompany you."

"What? Put your life in further danger? And for what? Even if the two of us reached the palace unharmed, Caesar would never let you stay. What am I to say to him—'This is my lover, Darius, and I don't want him killed'? A fat lot of good that would do either of us! I might be able to convince the Roman to spare you for a time, but my brother's henchmen would see that poison found its way into your wine, if they didn't murder you in your sleep. No, Darius! You will not return with me."

She whipped off her helmet so that Pia saw her battle-grimy face for the first time. Smoke had turned her fair skin as dark as a Nubian's. Her beautiful hair was bound in thin strips of leather and wound tightly about her head. She looked like a tough, young soldier instead of a beautiful queen.

Darius removed his helmet and stared at her. Although his voice had been harsh, his face softened when he looked into her eyes. His own held a world of pain, as well as fear for the woman he loved.

"You can't go alone," he repeated. "It's far too dangerous unless Caesar has sent an escort."

She shook her head slightly, and for a moment Pia thought she saw a fleeting sign of uncertainty in the young woman's green eyes. But when Cleopatra spoke, her voice was hard. "The Roman brute hasn't granted me that courtesy. I suppose he assumes that if I'm murdered along the way, one of the Flute Player's troublesome offspring would be out of his hair. If the bald adulterer had any hair, that is." Then she threw back her head and laughed, not the trilling laughter of a young woman talking to her lover but the steel-edged, coarse laugh of a warrior who has managed to live through one more battle only to face another, fiercer conflict. "But never fear, my love, I have a plan."

"What plan?"

She shook her head. "I dare not tell it, even to you."

"They could torture me, but I'd never tell," Darius declared.

"They *would* torture you and you *would* tell. I know their methods because they are my own. When I leave, you must go far away from here. Hide yourself. Use your wizard's magic to disappear. Only then will I feel secure to carry on with what I know I must do. Promise me, Darius!"

His face set in grim lines, Darius reached out for Cleopatra, his intent abundantly clear. He pulled her into his arms. The clang of their breastplates striking sounded more like battle than love, but love was unmistakably his intent. He covered her soot-covered lips with his own. Pia heard Cleopatra's moan of need. Still locked in a passionate kiss, they fumbled at the leather thongs that secured their armor, ripping and tearing until the heavy plates clattered to the ground.

A rough rug and some cushions formed Cleopatra's bed in one corner of the military tent. Kissing with a fury, they groped their way to the pallet and fell upon it.

Embarrassment mingled with Pia's own longing when she saw them tearing at each other's clothes, trying to free their bodies of all barriers. Before this was accomplished, the wave of colors washed over them, obliterating the actual sight of their lovemaking.

"I promised her," Darius said quietly as he stared out at the wild surf. "I vowed to go far, far away."

"Did she know you were coming here?"

"Not exactly. She knows that I have a place to which I vanish—a place so distant that no one can find me. You see, because of my knowledge of the future I'm thought of as a wizard in her court. I am known for my exotic powers. She thinks that I have cast one of my spells to carry me away to my own private netherworld to commune with other wise men."

Pia stared hard at Darius, trying to put everything she had seen and heard into perspective. Trying to believe.

"So, if you were to travel back there at this very moment," Darius said, "you would probably find her with Julius Caesar. It's not a good idea. Forget I mentioned such a wild scheme."

Pia gazed fixedly at Darius. She could tell that thinking about Cleopatra with another man disturbed him deeply.

"If she's not with the Roman," he added, "she'll be on her way to him."

"I *should* go back!" Pia said with sudden determination.

"No," he said. "It's too risky. A foolish scheme. You shouldn't drink beer this early in the day, Pia-bird."

"I'm not drinking. And I mean what I say. The only way I can write the true story is to travel back to Cleopatra's time and observe everything firsthand. *You* suggested this in the first place."

He gave her a sidelong glance, his gaze steely. "I hadn't calculated the danger of the moment when I mentioned the possibility. If it would be dangerous for me, for you it would be sheer lunacy to intrude on such delicate, political affairs."

Pia noted his use of the word *political.* Obviously, Darius was willing himself to believe that whatever happened between Cleopatra and Caesar was purely for the sake of diplomacy.

"I need to go, Darius," Pia insisted. "Surely, they have enough serving girls at the place so that I could blend in and never be noticed. My black hair, my suntan—no one will guess. I'll fit right in."

"Pia, this is crazy! I'm not even sure I can send you back."

"You brought yourself through time. You've traveled back and forth using your half of the crystal pyramid. So why shouldn't it work for me? You're not really a wizard, you know. I saw you before you ever went back in time. You're a sailor—a lowly seaman off an old Greek tanker. It's the crystal pyramid that contains the magic. So, if you can go, I should be able to. Tell me how you do it, Darius."

He gripped her hand. "I won't allow you to go alone."

"But for you it would be dangerous." She argued half-heartedly. In truth, the idea of going without Darius terrified her.

He still looked uncertain, but he could see there was no changing Pia's mind. Slowly, he brought his half of the crystal close to hers. They both felt the magnetism, the pull as the stone came closer and closer. The heat building. The light glowing.

"We'll have to be extremely careful," he warned. "We mustn't intrude on Cleopatra and Caesar. Believe me, you wouldn't enjoy an Egyptian prison."

"Don't worry, love. I'll stay completely out of their way. I only want to observe her from a distance so I can see how she looks and how she acts."

"Very well, then. Close your eyes and think, Pia," Darius said hesitantly. "Think exactly what you want. Clear all other thoughts from your mind and think only of your wish."

Eyes squeezed tightly shut, Pia murmured her wish aloud. "I want to go back to ancient Egypt. I want to see Alexandria as it was. I want to write the truth. I want to get inside Cleopatra!"

She heard Darius chanting incantations. Then a fierce gust of wind blew in from the ocean, sending a swirling shower of sand and rain through the screen. Lightning flashed, so close that it seemed to split the sky and light up the whole world. The boom of thunder that followed was deafening. Through it all, Pia heard the shriek of panic from Xander-the-Cat. She felt him leap from her lap. The next moment, she seemed to be weightless, caught up in a whirlwind, with lightning of all colors flashing about her. She screamed for Darius, flailing wildly to grasp his hand, but all she gripped was the cold, fierce wind.

"Darius!" she cried one last time. Then all went black and silent.

Chapter Seven

Following a final, blinding flash of light, then nothingness, Pia came back to her senses. She opened her eyes to total darkness. Panic seized her. Was she blind? And she was suffocating, gasping for breath. Where was she? What the hell had happened?

Hell! she thought. That has to be it! By messing around with the crystals and those strange, muttered incantations, Darius had shot her straight down below. Any minute now the devil himself would step out of the black void to rustle her soul off to fiery eternity.

But she had more immediate problems to worry about. She had to breathe! She had to see!

The weightless, out-of-body sensation she had experienced a short time before had been replaced by a constricting of her five-foot-eight-inch frame. She now felt as if she were squeezed into a body stocking three sizes too small. Even her fingers and toes were cramped. On top of that, she seemed to be trussed up tightly in a sort of heavy, scratchy shroud. Not only was she gasping for air, but the shallow breaths she was able to gulp were hot, dust-filled, and smelled like Xander's litter box.

Struggle as she would, she could not escape. She tried to relax, to think. Only then did she realize that she was still moving, flying through the air. The motion, though slower now, made her stomach queasy. She forced herself to stay calm. She strained to hear the slightest sound that might give her some idea of where she was.

Pia heard something all right—something weird. A voice inside her head. Someone else's voice. But each syllable rang clear in her mind. The words were spoken, not in her own raspy croak, but with a lilting, almost musical quality. Neither was the phrasing nor the cadence Pia's own. Even the language was foreign. It was so foreign that she couldn't identify it, although, oddly enough, she did understand its meaning.

"Soon now," the soft, but determined female voice said. "At any second we shall be before the *great* man himself." This sarcastically. Then the woman added with venom in her tone, "Barbarian!"

Who? Pia wondered. Who was this strange woman and who could she be talking about?

The voice inside Pia's head continued, as if this other female was sorting things out in her mind and summoning courage at the same time. "Everything hangs on this moment," she said emphatically. "You must handle him well. Entrance him with all the feminine wiles you possess. Be calm, be controlled, and, most important of all, be alluring."

Pia had to laugh at those words. "Alluring, ha! That's easy for *you* to say—whoever you are. You aren't trussed up like a Thanksgiving turkey. I think . . ."

Pia's mumbled, half-smothered words broke off, replaced by a shriek as she felt herself suddenly tumbling, being flipped over and over until her head swam dizzily. The whole world was doing somersaults. Then everything came to a sudden, brutal halt. She landed, sprawled facedown, her head still spinning.

For a moment, Pia couldn't move. She still felt as if she were inside something tighter than her own skin, but at least she could breathe again. She gulped for fresh air like a drowning victim. When she opened her eyes this time, she had to shield them from what seemed like a brilliant spotlight after the total blackness inside her shroud. In truth, it was merely a single guttering torch on the wall.

She blinked. She stared. Her mouth gaped open.

"A carpet, you say?" The tall figure before her scowled at the cowering servant who knelt next to her. "Another gift for me?"

Pia realized the carpet he spoke of had been her smelly shroud. She found herself sprawled at the stranger's sandaled feet.

Nice legs! she thought, letting her gaze drift upward to see whose big toe was almost in her mouth.

The man speaking was like a vision out of one of Pia's research books or the Latin text she'd studied in high school. A Roman, by his dress. An important Roman, she judged, by his purple general's cloak. He was tall, middle aged, with imposing features, his balding pate encircled by a crown of gilt laurel leaves. She'd seen that strong profile on ancient coins, on marble busts.

Julius Caesar?

She was half tempted to cry Great Caesar's ghost! Instead, she moaned silently, *Darius! What have you done?*

Silence! the imperious female voice inside her head commanded. The other woman who was sharing her space paused. When she spoke again a moment later, Pia felt from this alter ego a deep sense of regret, of heartbreak, of longing for something that could never be. Her tone was stern as she hissed silently at Pia, *Darius is to be forgotten as of this moment!*

No way, Jose! Pia thought. I'm going to get him for this and get him good once I find him!

She glanced about, but saw no sign of her erstwhile lover. Only four men occupied the chamber—the big servant who seemed to have brought the carpet, two silent Roman body-guards, and the stony-faced, ebony-eyed Caesar glaring down at her. But his cold stare was quickly turning to bemusement. There was a certain light coming into his eyes, one she well remembered seeing in Bubba-from-Hahira's eyes right before he'd invited her to come along with him in his pickup truck to the town dump to "shoot rats." Guys from Hahira called it "shooting rats;" guys from St. Simons called it "watching the submarine races." She wondered what old Romans called it. Slice it anyway you like, lust was lust, and that was what she was reading in Caesar's eyes right then.

Pia lay before Julius Caesar, staring up at him. She still couldn't believe it. She wondered suddenly how one should greet a Roman emperor—Hi, Emp, how's it going?

Another voice, the one she'd been hearing inside her head, took the problem out of her hands. The urge to speak was rising like a wave in Pia's throat. An instant later, soft words with no sharp edges flowed from her lips like honey from the hive.

"My lord, may I humbly welcome you to Egypt. You do me great honor by accepting lodging in my palace."

Caesar cocked one neatly plucked eyebrow. He looked amused. "*Your* palace, lad? And who might you be? I was led to believe that this place, this very chamber belonged to that much touted beauty, Cleopatra. I sent for her, but am brought a boy?"

His question provoked a sense of pure devilment that stole through Pia's veins. Suddenly, she felt wicked, playful, sexy—not at all her usual self. She offered him a languid, openmouthed smile, winked, then let her tongue glide out snakelike to caress her upper lip. Pia heard the deep-throated, female laugh that followed. It was not her own.

Then came the shocking words. "Were I a boy, my lord, would you find me displeasing? Has it not been said of Caesar that he is *'omnium mulierorum vir et omnium virorum mulier'?"*

Pia's high school Latin might have been rusty, but she remembered Curio's quote about Julius Caesar and its translation—"the husband of every woman and the wife of every man."

She knew few red-blooded men and no emperors at all who would take kindly to such a lewd accusation. Her cheeks flamed with embarrassment to think that the insulting words had come out of her own mouth. She held her breath, waiting for Caesar's reaction. She watched his large hand tighten on the hilt of his sword.

He scowled, a muscle twitched at one corner of his sensuous mouth, and his fingers relaxed. "Scamp!" he spat. "Insolent imp! I should have you stripped and thrashed on the spot."

"Whatever pleases you, master," the throaty female voice invited with a hint of mockery in its velvet tone.

Pia knew she had not initiated this shocking conversation, but there was no way that she could consider herself merely an innocent bystander, a third, uninvolved party. She tried desperately to clamp her jaws shut to keep the alien voice bottled up inside. But she sensed the futility of the action.

Suddenly, the force that had spoken for Pia set her body into motion as well. Pia had no idea what her arm meant to do until her hand shot to her head and swept away the peasant's cap covering her hair. She felt the weight of long tresses as their soft waves cascaded to her shoulders. An instant later her fingers, controlled by the same unknown force, fumbled at the metal clasp securing the neck of her rough-woven cloak. The heavy, nondescript garment fell away to settle at her feet in a dusty, formless heap. Pia heard a gasp from Caesar even as she felt cool air caress her body. She glanced down at herself and her reaction matched the emperor's.

Gone were her shorts and terrycloth robe. In their place, a wide gold collar set with glittering stones and one dangling, blood-red pendant suspended, cool as a droplet of ice, between her breasts. Her *bare* breasts!

She stared aghast as her nipples puckered against the chill of the room. Caesar's gaze focused on the same area of her anatomy, the stony disapproval in his black eyes turning instantly to the hot, iridescent sheen of lust.

"Well, my lord?" the woman's sultry voice taunted. "Do you still wish to thrash this insolent imp for speaking a simple truth?"

Never taking his gaze from her naked breasts, he said to the other three men, "Leave us!"

The chamber emptied instantly. Only two people remained—Caesar and Cleopatra. And, of course, Pia. The silence grew so heavy that Pia could hear her own heart beating. Or was it Cleopatra's heart?

With his gaze still trained on her breasts, Caesar took a step closer and reached out to brush her bare shoulder with his fingertips. Pia shivered, yet her face burned.

"I think we can forgo the whipping for now, my pretty."

"Later, then, if it pleases you, Caesar," Cleopatra purred.

God! What next? Pia wondered in a panic. The bitch is crazy!

His fingers continued playing over her shoulder, threatening to venture downward to her breast. He chuckled deep in his throat, and Pia watched his black eyes dance with dark lights.

"I think not, dear child. After all, as you stated, you spoke only the simple truth. Who am I—one who lost his virginity to King Nicomedes of Bithynia—to deny your statement?"

His hand trailed fire down Pia's side. "As for you, my beauty, tell me your secret now that I've told you mine. Who stole your sweet innocence?"

Totally cowed, Pia was about to confess tearfully and for the first time in her life that her husband had been neither her first nor her best, when the voice within purred, "No one as yet, gentle master."

Horrified at both the implication and the invitation in Cleopatra's voice, Pia tried to back away from the hungry look on Caesar's face and the hungrier grasp of his hand at her waist. Her *bare* waist, she realized as his cool fingers stroked her.

She glanced down at the strong, well-shaped hand possessively cupping her right hip, sending a road map of goose bumps over her whole body. The rest of her costume was nearly as shocking as her bodiceless bodice. She wore a girdle that rode low on her hips, plunging in front to bikini depth. A flowing skirt of soft, totally transparent cotton threaded with gold drifted about her bare legs. Her feet were clad in sandals made of gold and encrusted with bright stones.

Wait a damn minute! Pia thought suddenly, stepping away from Caesar's grasp. This isn't me! My belly button's an insy and this one's an outsy.

These breasts, too, belonged to some stranger. Where was the little mole—her "beauty mark," Pia had always called it—just above her right nipple? And her suntan line—what could have become of it? She'd worked hard for months to get the rich, coppery look, spent a fortune on Hawaiian Tropic. This shocking expanse of flesh was as pale and evenly untanned as antique ivory.

Who am I?

Then all that had happened with Darius came rushing back. "Wish your deepest, heartfelt wish," he had told her, and she had done so.

Well, the crystal pyramid had certainly made her wish come true. Pia's whole five-foot-eight-inch frame was scrunched up inside the body of the tiny, sexy Egyptian queen.

This is going a bit to extremes for the sake of research! Pia mused silently, trying to stave off a panic attack.

"Cleopatra," Caesar murmured, his gaze still caressing her. "For so long I have wondered about you, tried to visualize you. Most tales that reach Rome from Alexandria tend to be exaggerated, farfetched, scandalously improved upon. Even though I had been told by numerous travelers who had accepted the hospitality of your palace, I hardly believed that one so young could be ..." He paused, smiled, and shrugged in an imperial manner.

Pia's mind was still reeling. What was she supposed to do now? If only Darius were here.

Forget Darius! the angry voice raged inside Pia's head.

The words were spoken with such force that Pia felt as if she'd been slapped hard across the face. Quickly, she put Darius out of her thoughts, withdrawing her own will totally to allow Cleopatra to take control.

A passive Pia sensed the other woman move closer to the hard-bodied Roman. So close that Pia could feel his heat. She could feel something else too. Something going on inside Cleopatra. The young queen might be playing the innocent virgin to Caesar's seducer, but it was she who held the reins. Unwittingly, Caesar played the fly to Cleo's spider. Every move she made, every word she spoke was calculated, designed to make the powerful Roman her slave.

Clever! Pia mused, but her thoughts were quickly banished by Cleopatra's determined will.

"You were saying, my lord?"

"I was saying far too much," Caesar answered with a cunning laugh. "You are too young to hear what I might have said, had I finished my statement. Besides, your nearness causes my mind to wander to dangerous territory, little queen."

"Dangerous for whom?" she asked in the innocent voice of a child. "For you, Roman, or for me?"

He turned away from her, forcing his gaze to unlock from her witching eyes. He sprawled his lanky frame in a nearby chair, then sighed deeply.

"You know what they say of me. You've already proven that. My own legions call me *'moechus calvus,'* the 'bald adulterer.' They sing dirty little verses about me."

Cleopatra trilled a laugh and broke into a snatch of Latin song. "Home we bring the bald adulterer. Romans lock your wives away . . ."

"Wretched girl!" he snapped, cutting her off in mid verse. But Pia could tell by the hint of a smile on his lips that Cleo's bawdy singing pleased him, aroused him.

"I care nothing for what others might say about you, Caesar," the scheming young queen answered with a toss of her head. "I shall form my own opinion of you, Roman. I ask only that you give me that chance."

At times, Pia lost track of the fact that Cleopatra meant to use the great man. But whenever she called him "Roman," the way she spat out the word made it clear—at least to Pia—that Cleo was directing the scene. Suddenly, Cleopatra swayed toward Caesar's golden chair and strolled behind him, kneading the taut muscles in his broad shoulders and bull-like neck.

"You should stop that," he cautioned unconvincingly. "I am here on serious business."

"And does your serious business require that you should suffer a stiff neck, my lord? I saw how you held it at an awkward angle as if it was paining you. My own father often had this problem. He said my hands were far more skilled and much softer than his physician's."

Caesar groaned with pleasure at her soothing touch and

shifted in his chair. "Witches usually are more skilled at healing, *and killing,* than most physicians."

"I am no witch," Cleopatra protested. "I am queen, according to my father's will."

"Ah, that!" Caesar sat up and shook off Cleopatra's touch. "That, of course, is the reason I sent for you. You and your brother, Ptolemy the Thirteenth, must stop this fighting. You must marry and share the throne, so states your father's will. So shall it be!"

"That worthless pup! I spit on him! And on his three advisors—the soldier Achilles, the rhetorician Theodotus, and the fat eunuch Pothinus!" She spat four times.

Caesar took her hand, drew her down upon his lap, and kissed her full, pouting lips, slowly and wetly.

At this, Pia roused to full awareness once more. She squirmed with discomfort inside Cleopatra's too-petite body. Her own attempts to release herself from the Roman's aggressive embrace made it seem that the queen was fighting him with all her strength.

"Temper, my beauty," he whispered into her tiny, shell ear. "You *will* marry your brother! Rome decrees it and I *am* Rome!"

Pia sensed the slightest loss of control on Cleopatra's part when she heard Caesar's edict.

"That nasty child? Marry him?" she fumed. "After he drove me away? After he tried to have me murdered?"

Were those actually tears Pia felt stinging her eyes— Cleopatra's eyes?

"Those are grave charges," Caesar said, cradling the distraught queen in his muscle-roped arms. "But still, you will do as I command."

Now she was pouting, childlike. "I am twenty-one years old. He is only thirteen. What does he know of pleasing a wife?"

Caesar chuckled and hugged the gloomy beauty to his

hard chest. "You need not worry about that end of the marriage, my dear. I order you to wed the young fool, not to bed him."

Cleopatra sniffed back the remnants of her tears and hugged the Roman's neck. "Then who?" she whispered. "Or am I to remain unloved for the rest of my life?"

"Who?" Pia watched the color rise on the Roman's high cheekbones as a smile curved his lips. "Who, indeed!" he said, glancing heavenward as if he were mulling over possibilities. His hand slipped down to her bare hip and he squeezed gently. "That is a problem, isn't it? You're still a virgin, so you should have a fine master of the art when first you give yourself."

A fleeting glimpse of Darius passed through Pia's mind—Cleopatra's too, no doubt. The young queen was lying about her virginity, Pia realized with a start. What if Caesar put her to the test? It could be that the whipping he'd threatened earlier might yet come to pass. Pia experienced a creeping terror at that thought. Her eagerness to get inside her character did not extend to sharing lashes on her tender back. She tried to block out the conversation between Cleo and old Julius, but, willing or not, she remained part of the scene.

"I feel it's high time I gave up my tiresome virginity."

Caesar laughed. "Tiresome, is it?"

"Quite, after all these years. And if I must marry my loathsome little brother, I think I deserve some special reward for giving up my freedom and consenting to share my throne."

"What sort of reward, my little queen? Pearls from Briton? Jewels from the Orient? Or will you, like your father, ask for more Roman gold?"

She gave him a sexy pout calculated to drive any man wild. Pia could never have managed such a look, not if she'd given up writing and spent all her time practicing sensual facial maneuvers in front of her mirror.

"Do you mean to buy me with your treasures, Caesar?" Cleopatra accused. "Would you make a whore of me when I offer myself freely, wishing only a woman's truest pleasure in return? You wound me, Roman. I will not sell my virginity. But I would give it as a gift, if the right man enticed me."

Oh, God! It's getting deep. Where are my wading boots? Pia groaned. But Cleo clamped her mouth firmly shut, refusing to allow the words to escape to Caesar's ears.

His carefully plucked brows arched upward. "And is there someone upon whom you wish to bestow this great gift, my beautiful little virgin?"

Cleopatra shook her head sadly. Pia felt another tear dribble down her cheek "In all my years, though many have tried, no man has ever been able to arouse me. I fear I am incapable of such feelings, master. I am cold! My heart and my body are untouchable, it seems."

Queenie, you're damn good! Pia's grin was hidden from view by Cleopatra's sad pout.

How perfectly brilliant of the litte minx—to call Caesar "master" at such an opportune moment! Why, how can he resist her? Pia thought.

She felt an odd sort of triumph in the queen's cunning. However, her elation was short-lived. When Caesar swept Cleopatra up in his arms and headed for the curtained cubicle that served as a bedchamber, Pia's heart all but stopped.

Wait! No! she cried silently.

Cleopatra ignored her, snuggling close in Caesar's arms and licking his neck like a happy puppy. He tasted of salt and male musk.

Pia knew Cleopatra could hear her thoughts. The question was, could she be influenced by them? With all her might, Pia concentrated on making the queen change her mind and avoid this disastrous course of action.

What about Darius? Don't you love him anymore? Pia

repeated the questions over and over again, but Cleo ignored her.

Lying on the bed now, watching Caesar remove the loose girdle over his tunic, the queen tossed her head angrily, defying Pia's thoughts. She willed the secret voice of her conscience to be silent.

"You aren't afraid of me, are you?" Caesar asked, noting the sudden change in Cleopatra's expression. "You've probably heard tales that I enjoy rough sport in the bed as well as on the battlefield. But I'll be gentle this time, my tender little queen. I promise to leave no battle scars to mar your perfection. I have much experience with virgins."

"So I've heard," Cleopatra snapped. Then she looked stricken by her own words and quickly covered her mouth with her hand. When she spoke again, her voice was as soft and caressing as silk. "I'm sorry, master. I don't know why I said that."

Pia knew. *She* had said it.

"I'll call for some wine," Caesar offered. "Although I seldom drink spirits, I might join you in a goblet to help us both relax."

Oh, God! Pia thought. Not wine! Please, not wine! Nothing dimmed her wits quicker than a couple of glasses of wine. She needed to be sane and sober right now. Otherwise, this evening could prove as disastrous as that fraternity party at Georgia Tech where she lost her virginity—and not to Sidney.

Sensing Pia's frantic thoughts, Cleopatra smiled and touched the amethyst ring on her finger. A wizard had given her this charm. "Wear it always," the old hag had told her. "It will keep your senses clear from spirits. Drunkenness you will never know." And it had worked. Cleopatra could drink even her soldiers under the table.

Pia experienced a wave of relief. At least she wouldn't have to worry about getting smashed and tossing her cookies all over the illustrious Julius Caesar. Now, if only she could figure a way to keep Cleopatra from sacrificing their combined, nonexistent virginity to the noble Roman cause.

Caesar disappeared from the bedchamber for a moment to call for wine. While he was out of earshot, Pia said, *Just what the hell do you think you're doing, Cleo?*

The queen sat up in bed and glanced about, as angry as she was bewildered. "Who are you? Where are you? Is this some witch's spell—some curse called down on me by my brother? Begone, spirit!"

You listen to me and listen good, girl. There's not much time. Darius sent me.

Cleopatra's angry features softened. "Darius would never curse me. He loves me. He knows that I love him."

There's no time to explain everything to you, even if I could. But take my word, Darius sent me here. Big, good-looking Greek guy? Floated up to your steps half dead and you saved him? Likes anchovies on his pizza and guzzles imported beer? He's got a piece of alabaster from Alexander's tomb that you stole a long time ago.

"Yes," Cleopatra cried softly. "That's Darius—my love."

So you two have been . . . Pia's words trailed off while she searched for an appropriate word or phrase.

"We are lovers, yes!"

Then how do you figure on pulling off this virginity stunt with Caesar? Mind telling me that?

"He will never know. He's besotted. He will believe whatever I tell him."

Pia groaned. *Man, you don't lie to the most powerful man in the world, not and live to tell about it. He'll know. Then he'll probably hand you—us—over to his four thousand legionnaires and let them take turns. There won't be anything left by the time they get through.*

"Calm yourself!" Cleopatra ordered sternly. "I know what I am doing, and this is the only way. I will save Egypt and

I mean to sit on the throne alone. Once I've borne Caesar a son, which his wife cannot do, I will be not only Queen of Egypt but Empress of Rome and the world. Now, I order you out!"

Hey, it's not that easy, Pia replied. *Don't think I wouldn't go if I could. I'm not sure how I got here, so I sure as hell don't know how to leave.*

"Then be still, won't you?"

That was easy for *her* to say, Pia realized moments later when old Julius returned with the wine. First, he poured a golden goblet for Cleopatra, who drank it down like a trooper, then held her cup out for more. "Wonderful!" she said. "So sweet and smooth." Smooth it might be, but to Pia it had the kick of straight vodka out of a paper cup. Her head was spinning. How could Cleo drink that stuff down so fast, then ask for a refill?

To Pia's vast relief, Caesar refused to pour any more wine into Cleo's goblet. Instead, he lay down beside her on the bed, took a long swig from his own cup, then covered the queen's parted lips with his own. It came as a jolt for Pia to realize she was actually being kissed by Julius Caesar. Then, when he let more of that strong wine flow into her mouth from his, her blood started to burn. A second later, his tongue followed the route of the wine.

Cleopatra was purring. Pia was gasping. By the time they all came up for air, Caesar was ready for action. There was no mistaking that rise under his tunic.

"Good wine," Cleo whispered, once more lifting her goblet toward the ewer.

Caesar chuckled, his gaze fastened on Cleopatra's perfect breasts. Pia had to admit that they were better than her own.

"Yes, it is fine stuff," Caesar agreed, pouring a bit more for himself. "But it's a bit tart. I prefer it sweeter, but that can be arranged."

Pia and Cleo let out a collective gasp when the Roman

tilted his cup and dribbled wine all over those snowy breasts. A moment later, Pia cringed into such a tight ball inside the little queen that she didn't even feel cramped any longer. But there was no getting away from the sensation.

Caesar bent low over his "virgin" and began slowly lapping up the wine he had intentionally spilled. With long, tantalizing strokes of his tongue, he cleaned the purple stain from her tender, white flesh. Pia could feel her host's body trembling with pleasure. She had to admit that she was not entirely immune to the sensation. When he sucked one wine-stained nipple into his mouth, they both gasped aloud, causing an echo effect in the quiet chamber.

Partly to arouse the Roman and partly because she simply couldn't help herself, Cleopatra thrashed about on the bed, moaning and murmuring things that only aroused the man more, that only egged him on. "I am your slave, Great Caesar. Conquer my body the way you conquered the Gauls. Give me no quarter. Make me suffer. Make me beg for mercy."

Jesus, God, and Mother Mary! Pia cried. But once again, Cleo sensed what was coming, caught Pia's words, and clamped her mouth tightly shut in time to hold them in. At the same time, she sucked in her breath, constricting her petite body further, so that she gave Pia a painful squeeze of warning.

"Ah, do that again, my little slave," Caesar commanded. "See how your breasts stand at attention before their master when you draw a deep breath."

Cleo held her breath to allow Caesar to suckle her roughly. The temperature was definitely rising inside the sexy, little queen. Pia was getting *hot!*

"More wine?" Caesar offered, refilling Cleo's empty cup.

Once again, the queen drank it right down. But Pia had no tolerance for red wine. Things were beginning to look blurry. Worse yet, Caesar was beginning to look good.

"No more!" Pia begged, and this time her plea escaped Cleo's parted lips.

"You're right, of course," J.C. agreed. "If I allow you to drink yourself senseless, you'll never know the wonder of the great gift I'm about to bestow upon you." He lifted her hair and reached behind Cleopatra's neck to unfasten her heavy collar. A weight vanished from Pia's shoulders. She sighed with relief. But when his hands went to the golden girdle at her hips, Pia stiffened.

"There's no cause for alarm, my little love," Caesar soothed. "Were this not your first time, I would call your maidservant to come and undress you while I sat back and sipped my wine and drank in the sight of you. More pleasing yet would be to have one of my lieutenants perform the task, then stay to watch my prowess. You can never imagine the pleasure I receive from watching another man disrobe my lover. Ah, the look in his eyes, the pain of envy that comes into his hungry gaze as he sees what he knows is mine alone. His to see, but never to touch. Later, when we have grown accustomed to each other, I will bring in one of my legion—some fine young stallion ripe for mating— and let you see what I mean."

Pia was tipsy, but not so drunk she didn't hear every word he said. She cringed at the thought. Next, he'd probably ask one of his soldiers to join them in bed. It only made sense, after all. There were two women here. Why not two men as well?

Suddenly, Pia felt the tight girdle around Cleopatra's shapely hips fall aside. A moment later, Caesar stripped away the sheer fabric that had been the queen's only claim to modesty.

The Roman rose from the side of the bed and tossed the filmy garment onto a cushioned bench. He stood tall and straight over Cleopatra's reclining form, a slow, lazy smile curving his lips.

"And so, at last, all of Egypt lies bare before me, vulnerable to my attack. I have often dreamed of this moment."

Pia didn't have to stare into the powerful Roman's black eyes to see the lusty heat they generated. She could feel his gaze sear the young queen's pale flesh. His possessive stare swept from her beautiful face to her breasts, then down over her belly to the moist warmth between her thighs that awaited him. There was no love in the look he gave her, only the aloof coolness of a triumphant general. Pia felt herself cower before him. But she was aware that Cleopatra's reaction was far different. The foolish young girl was actually exultant. She lay naked and defenseless before this savage conqueror of the world and gloried in the threat of the lust in his gaze. With her whole body, she dared him to take her. She thrust her breasts upward, slid her hips sensually against the shining, sapphire-colored sheets, and parted her thighs in invitation.

You fool! Pia hissed only for Cleo's ears. *Don't egg him on.*

In response to the voice inside her head—the same voice that had pleaded with her to drink no more—Cleopatra reached for the wine and downed two generous cups, one after the other.

Oh, God! Pia groaned silently, her wits awash on a winered sea. She tried to grip the sides of the bed to steady the spinning room, but Cleopatra had better things to do with her hands. Dipping her fingertips into the dregs in her golden goblet, she lazily rubbed her own nipples until they were the color of the grape and standing rigid and ready for Caesar's lips.

"Wanton!" The word ground out between his clenched teeth.

He fell to his knees beside the bed and gripped Cleopatra's shoulders in a bruising grasp. As Pia watched, her vision blurred. She saw two laurel wreaths, two faces with lust-mad eyes, two tongues flicking out to lick at the wine-flavored nipples. And the sensations she experienced were doubled by the wine as well. For the first time, she felt as if she were not some other being trapped inside the queen. Now she was a full-fledged part of Cleopatra—flesh of her flesh and blood of her blood. As Caesar's rough, wet tongue dragged over the queen's thrusting breasts, the sensation kindled fires at Pia's most intimate core. She moaned with Cleopatra. She writhed and burned.

Sometime during this wine- and passion-drugged time, Caesar shed his tunic. He came to them as naked as Cleopatra herself. Never mind that somewhere deep down inside, Pia was still wearing her terrycloth robe. This was bare male flesh pressing bare female flesh—sliding over it, groping it, kissing it, enflaming it.

"Oh, the wicked things I'd love to do to you, my little queen!" Caesar's voice in Cleopatra's ear came as a shock to Pia, but not half the shock brought by his tongue when it darted in after his words. "Have you ever thought what it would be like to be Caesar's true love slave? I would rip down the bed ropes and tie you where you lie. Then slowly, painstakingly, for hours on end, I would torture you with the most exquisite pleasures I could devise."

Caesar was not disappointed by the double moan that answered his words.

"Ah, you'd like that, eh, my pretty little innocent." He sat back for a moment and sighed. "Alas, such loving sport must wait for another time. To deal with a virgin takes special pains."

"Pain, my lord?" Cleopatra said in a whisper that hinted the very thought made her weak with terror. Pia, even in her drunken state, realized that nothing could be farther from the truth. The queen was playing this Roman as skillfully as her father had played his silver flute.

Caesar leaned down and brushed the girl's pouting, red

mouth. "Not so much pain, my dear. Only for a moment and then it will pass."

He swept one wide palm down over her belly. It came to rest, fingers spread, at the junction of her thighs. Gently, he caressed, touched, stroked. Cleopatra responded with a tremulous sigh. He grew bolder, sliding into her, feeling his way.

The shit's about to hit the fan now, Pia grumbled silently, figuring that Cleopatra, at least, deserved whatever they got once Caesar found clear passage and figured out he'd been duped.

But to Pia's total shock, Cleo boldly slithered her body down to meet his touch until his finger had gone a far as her "virgin" body would allow. Pia watched a wide smile spread over his face. His eyes fairly glittered with anticipation. And she watched in fascination and slight horror as his unusually heavy sex grew stronger still. Pia would have cringed away from such a hefty tool, but Cleopatra murmured her delight, urging him on.

"Eager, are you?" Caesar said with a chuckle. "Well, not just yet, my sweet. It is not so often as you think that I have my chance at a virgin. I must gentle you along until you're ready to receive me."

"I have been ready to receive you, Great Caesar, since long before I ever set eyes on you. Stories of your prowess go before you. I knew that someday you and I would come to this. And you've longed for it as much as I. Admit it, master!"

He laughed and slid his palms up the insides of her thighs. "Is my desire written so plain on my face? Had your father not been less than a fool, he would have offered you to me long ago. By now, you would be my empress, and all of Egypt, Rome—the world—would worship at our feet."

A faraway, dreamy look came into his eyes, and his hands went still on Cleopatra's flesh. She prodded him gently with her hip to bring his mind back to his work. "It is not too late for that, Caesar. I am yours now, only for the taking."

"You speak boldly for all your youth and innocence, child."

Pia almost laughed aloud at his words. Cleopatra Thea Philopator was neither innocent nor a child.

"What do you want of me, Caesar? Would you be more pleased if I were afraid, if I cowered and begged and cringed away from such glorious manliness?"

Like me? Pia observed silently.

"A virgin should never appear too eager," he told her. "It lessens the sport, the pleasure. One must always be gentle with an unbroken child. One should never hurry the act."

"Not even to make you a son, Caesar?"

He gave her no answer, but stared at her with pain in his dark eyes. Pia knew as well as Cleopatra that he wanted a son more than anything in the world. But the expression on his face told them both that he had given up hope. He thought himself at fault.

Pia soon found that Caesar was a pillar of patience and restraint. Again with the wine on the breasts, then the fingertips, then the toes. Not an inch of Cleopatra's fair young flesh went untouched by his hands, untasted by his mouth.

Meanwhile, the more they drank, the drunker Pia became. And the drunker she got, the more enflamed she was. Her head spinning, her body burning, she tried to keep her thoughts on Darius. But the things Caesar was doing to Cleopatra—and to her by proxy—made concentration impossible. Finally, she gave in to the luxurious fire consuming her.

When Caesar *finally* assumed the position, ready to make his loving thrust, Pia had already climaxed three times. She felt wrung out, spent, drained. No way would she ever have believed that Cleopatra could hold out this long. When he bored into Cleopatra, ripping through what Pia later learned was a false maidenhead constructed by one of the queen's faithful old nursemaids, the Red Sea parted and the walls of Jericho came tumbling down. Fourth of July fireworks went off all over the universe and every volcano on earth erupted at the same time. Oceans washed in with tsunami force and earthquakes shook the world.

By damn, the old guy knows his business, Pia said to Cleopatra once she could find strength enough to express herself verbally.

Cleo answered with something too foul for print. Pia was about to curse her back when suddenly a bright flash blinded them both. Out of nowhere, Darius, holding Xander-the-Cat, materialized in the room. His eyes held all the pain and rage of the ages. He had loved only two women with all his heart through the centuries, and both of them were here, glowing in the aftermath of love, Julius Caesar still buried to the hilt inside them.

Luckily, Caesar had just passed out from wine and exertion.

Pia shook her head to clear it. She stared hard at Darius, trying to focus.

"Darius?" she whispered. "You're too late."

His scowl deepened at the sound of her voice, but he still seemed dazed from his flight through time.

Realizing suddenly that he hadn't heard her, Pia drew up inside Cleopatra, hoping he wouldn't know she was there. God, how could she ever face him again if he knew?

Chapter Eight

Slowly, the mist cleared from Darius's eyes and the dizziness dissipated. His eyes focused on a scene that sent shock waves of horror and rage all through him. Had he been holding a sword instead of a cat, he probably would have committed murder, then run himself through for good measure.

The room where he and Cleopatra had shared such happy, intimate times was now strewn with quickly discarded garments. His lover lay beneath a sweating, pale-skinned brute, who remained buried deep inside her, snoring loudly.

He could see Cleopatra's face. Her usually bright green eyes seemed dulled with wine, fatigue, and spent passion. Her lips looked puffy and bruised from the Roman's rough kisses. Darius's anger raged hotter still when he spied what appeared to be purple bruises on her limbs, her neck, and her breasts. Then, in disgust, he realized that they were only wine stains. No doubt this hairy barbarian had drenched her in spirits and had licked the droplets from her delicious body. How often he and Cleopatra had indulged in the same playfully passionate game of love!

"How could you?" he growled under his breath, sickened at the thought.

Bile rose in his throat. His groin throbbed with jealousy, with need. He wanted to rage at Cleopatra, to tear her from beneath the Roman and shake her, to demand that she pledge her love for him and him alone. But his limbs seemed paralyzed, his throat frozen. He could only stand and stare as if the end of the world had come. First he'd misplaced Pia somewhere in time; now he'd lost Cleopatra to a Roman.

With a will of iron, he faced her in silence. He reminded himself firmly of his mission: He was here to find Pia. He *must* find her or she would not survive in this dangerous realm. Even now, she could be out there somewhere, being passed through the ranks of Caesar's legionnaires. They were not gentle men. They were more like animals than human beings, and they'd been long without the comforts of their women.

His heart wrenched at the thought. Wherever she was, Pia was in grave danger. This was all his fault!

Burning with guilt Pia assumed from the fierce expression on Darius's face that he knew where she was. At the moment, she was relieved to be hidden. But, she realized, if she *weren't* inside the Egyptian queen, she wouldn't have been a party to this three-way orgy in the first place.

Slowly, carefully, Cleopatra eased from beneath the weight of Caesar's sleeping form. Gingerly, she slid across the bed. It would never do to wake the Roman now. When he was settled and still, snoring evenly, Cleopatra slipped into a robe. Why she bothered, Pia couldn't imagine. The thin fabric added a shimmer of gold to her naked body, but hid none of her sensual curves.

Cleopatra paused a moment, glanced back one final time to make sure Caesar was sleeping soundly, then motioned silently for Darius to follow her into the adjoining chamber.

Pia could feel all the queen's emotions, but she couldn't quite read her mind. She knew that Cleo was stunned by the sudden appearance of her lover. One part of her was angry and wanted to order him away instantly. He had disobeyed her, after all, by returning unannounced at the worst possible moment—a crime that would have been punished by instant death had any other man committed it. But another, softer side of her was deliriously happy to see him and wanted nothing more than to be in his arms again. She had missed Darius, that much was clear to Pia. Cleopatra loved this man, just as Pia did.

If I get a vote in this, Pia declared to her hostess, *I say we hug him to pieces.*

"Silence!" Cleopatra commanded.

"I haven't spoken a word," Darius said, *"yet!"*

"I wasn't talking to you. But now I am going to, and you had better listen and listen well. Had you come a moment sooner, you would be a dead man."

"Had I come armed, *he* would be dead now. Cleopatra, I—"

"Hold your tongue until I finish." There was no hint of warmth in her voice. "You are a fool, Darius! I should never have dragged you out of the sea. I knew then, as young as I was, that I had a higher purpose in life than love."

What higher purpose is there? Pia demanded. The queen ignored her and continued lecturing Darius.

"I saved you in a weak moment. When I allowed myself to love you, I showed even greater weakness. Love is for peasants, for slaves."

Then call me peasant! Pia interjected with silent vehemence. *Call me slave!* Again, Cleo ignored her.

"You should not have come back here, Darius. I have set

my grand scheme into motion this very night. You might have ruined everything."

"I didn't come back to spoil your precious plans." Darius let his anger flare. "I came for an entirely different reason. An urgent *personal* matter."

Cleopatra was actually hurt by his words, Pia realized. She almost felt sorry for the queen.

"What possible reason could you have for invading my private chamber, if not to see me again?"

Darius extended his arms. Xander squirmed and yowled, furious at being restrained by a mere human being. "I came to return this cat to its rightful owner. Have you seen a tall, dark-haired stranger about the palace? She has eyes the color of the finest lapis."

"A blue-eyed Egyptian? That's rather odd." Cleopatra's voice remained level and cool, but Pia sensed a burst of raw jealousy emanating from her host upon learning that Darius was searching for another woman.

"I never said she was Egyptian. She comes from far away."

"A Roman wench?" Cleopatra sneered. "Darius, how low can you stoop?"

Pia could tell from the look on his face that Darius had a ready retort for that, but he wisely held his tongue concerning Julius Caesar, who was still in Cleopatra's bed.

"I believe," he continued, "that she might be disguised as a servant, working here in the palace."

"A slave girl, Darius?" Cleopatra said disdainfully. Pia could feel her lips curl at the very taste of the words.

"She isn't really. In truth, she is a learned scribe."

Pia puffed herself up inside Cleo. How sweet of Darius! "A learned scribe" sounded very grand.

Cleopatra tossed her head in anger. "If that's the case and she's only maquerading as a servant, she must be here spying on me. Have you hired her to watch me? Darius, you know well the fate of any spy that crosses my path. I will, of course, find her. And when I do she will be tortured and killed."

Pia shrank in horror at the thought. She knew Cleopatra to be a woman of her word. But then she relaxed. She'd be safe inside the queen, as long as they steered clear of asps. She realized, though, that somehow she had to let Darius know where she was. She tried repeatedly to speak, but Cleo intercepted her words each time.

Cleopatra eyed the spitting cat suspiciously. "What are you doing with her beast?"

"Trying to return it, I told you. I have no use for cats."

"As I well remember."

Pia felt Cleopatra relax and smile. A gentle euphoria swept over the queen for a moment. Pia tuned in on her thoughts. Cleopatra was remembering those lovely nights when she and Darius had been together and how he would remove every one of her mousers from the chamber before he would make love to her. He'd often said that the only good cat was a mummified cat. He claimed they watched him and envied him when Cleopatra took him to her bed, that they were only awaiting their chance to pounce and do him damage.

"You're thinking of us, aren't you?" Darius said intuitively. "I know that look in your eyes. They've gone their deepest, most passionate color. They have an almost turquoise glow."

Pia felt Cleopatra quickly banish such sentimental thoughts. Once more the queen was all business. Even so, her attitude toward Darius and his sudden appearance had softened. She reached out, touched his arm with a lingering caress.

"Darius, you *must* go! It isn't safe for you here." She motioned with a toss of her head toward her bedchamber. "He could wake at any moment. He would kill you without a second thought." She dabbed at her eye. Were those *real* tears? Pia wondered. "I couldn't bear that, my dearest."

Her soft words were all the encouragement Darius needed. He dumped Xander unceremoniously. Gripping the folds of her shimmering robe, he opened it wide to let his hungry eyes feast on her perfect flesh. He touched her erect nipples with his fingertips. When Cleopatra—and Pia—moaned softly, he drew them into his arms, drew them so close to his bare chest that Cleopatra's cool breasts were crushed to his hot flesh.

"No, Darius!" she warned. "We mustn't!"

"Kiss me!" he commanded. "I won't leave until you do."

His hands were at the small of her back, pressing her body into his heat. She fought him only halfheartedly. After a moment, she closed her eyes and parted her lips. He accepted her sweet surrender.

Pia caught her breath. It felt wonderful to be in her lover's arms again, even if she did have to share him. Actually, that almost made it better. She had noticed something about Cleopatra. The woman had a nature far more passionate than any Pia had ever experienced. Maybe modern women were incapable of such a total lack of inhibition. Or perhaps it came from living under the hot, Egyptian sun or from knowing that her life was always in danger and she must make the most of every moment. Whatever the cause, Cleo put her whole heart and soul and being into love. She gave herself totally and expected no less from her partners. There was no coy flirtation, only all-out loving warfare. No holds barred, no defining rules to the game.

Pia trembled inside Cleo as the two ancient lovers met in an erotic clash. Darius didn't just kiss her, he seemed to want to devour her whole. With his tongue he searched and fondled and stroked. Cleopatra met him thrust for starving thrust. Teeth scraped and grazed lips until the kiss tasted of blood and salt. Darius gripped her soft buttocks to force her closer. Meanwhile, Cleopatra scored his back with her long nails. All the while, Pia felt the dual assault on her senses. She was close to fainting, she was so aroused.

When Darius lifted Cleopatra off her feet she struggled out of his grasp.

"No!" she moaned. "No, we must not! This is madness. You will get us both killed." Pia felt Cleopatra's heart racing, her own as well. "You promised, Darius. You said one kiss and you would go."

Pia could tell Cleopatra was faltering. She wanted him desperately. She truly loved him, just as Darius had said, but this could be the ruin of her. If Cleopatra had one weakness, it was her all-consuming love for this golden Greek.

It was a love Pia shared. She tried again to let Darius know that she was there. She willed him with all her mental powers to recognize something of her in the Egyptian queen.

Darius gripped Cleopatra's shoulders and stared at her, his face a mask of desire. Suddenly, his expression changed to one of awe, then puzzlement.

"Why are you looking at me that way?" the queen demanded.

"Your eyes! What's happened to your eyes, Cleopatra?"

"I don't know what you're talking about. Release me and go. Now! Before he wakes."

"Your eyes really are a different color. They aren't green any longer."

"Of course they are!"

"No. They're brilliant turquoise, like the finest stones from Persia."

"It is only the light," Cleopatra reasoned. "The shadows from the torch change their shade."

Yes! Pia shouted triumphantly. But Cleo kept the word from escaping. Still, Pia had gotten her message through. Her own blue eyes, peering through, had changed the color of Cleopatra's. Darius knew she was there inside the queen. She could tell by the look on his face.

Someone else knew, too. Xander, Pia realized, was rubbing against Cleopatra's legs and yowling his signal that it was time for tuna-and-egg. He knew where his mistress was. Pia saw Darius glance down at the cat, then back to Cleopatra's turquoise eyes. Concern flickered over his face, but he masked it quickly.

"I will leave now, if you insist," he told Cleopatra. Then for Pia's benefit he added, "I won't be far away, though, if you need me. All you have to do is touch the crystal and think of me. Don't worry. I'll figure out something."

"I'll keep Xander-the-Cat," Cleopatra said suddenly. Then she looked stunned by her own words, since Pia had actually spoken them—in her own voice.

Darius chuckled. "You have more powers than you know, my darling. I never told you the cat's name, but you knew it. He fancies fish and eggs at mealtime."

"And what of your spy?" Cleopatra asked when Darius turned to leave.

"Don't worry about her. I have a feeling she's hidden away where no one will find her. Just make sure you see to your own safety, beloved."

"You know, don't you, Darius?" Pia managed to get out another sentence while Cleopatra was puzzling over his words.

He turned and looked Pia straight in the eye. "I'm a wizard," he answered. "I know everything. And what I don't know, I'll figure out."

"Use the secret passage," Cleopatra warned. "The Roman guards mustn't see you."

Darius touched a stone on a far wall. A door opened and he vanished.

Pia let out a sigh of relief. All she had to do now was bide her time and Darius would find a way to get her out of this mess. *Nothing to worry about,* she told herself silently. *No problem! Just hold that thought.*

For the first time in hours, Pia let herself relax. Her respite lasted only moments.

"Cleopatra?" came a husky call from the bedroom. "Where are you? I was only resting, my precious. We haven't yet finished."

Cleopatra stood with her back to the bedchamber drapes. She closed her open robe over her naked body before she turned toward Caesar. By the time she faced him, she was smiling, lips parted, turquoise eyes hooded. She stood perfectly still for a moment. Only her tongue moved, drawing a full, wet line over her lips.

Caesar gave a low groan.

She made no move toward him. As he watched in apparent eagerness, Cleopatra let her robe slip off one shoulder. Slowly, she extended a shapely leg. Next a breast peeked out. Like a modern-day stripper, she exposed her flesh for Caesar one tempting inch at a time. When finally she let the wisp of shining fabric slither to the marble floor, the emperor was beside himself. Face flushed. Eyes wide.

"Harlot," he breathed, letting his tongue curl lustily around the word.

Cleopatra stood her ground, posing for him a bit longer. Teasing him, testing him, enticing him with her whole luscious body.

Never taking his eyes off her, Caesar reached up and yanked at the soft, golden ropes of the bed curtains.

Pia shuddered, realizing his intent.

He snapped the silken rope in his big hands. "Rome is ready to accept Egypt's total surrender," he said in a low, husky whisper of command. "Or force it, should need be. Your lonely nights as a tender virgin are done, my love."

Pia tried her best to shrink away to nothing inside Cleopatra. *No!* she begged for Cleo's ears alone. *You can't let him do this! It's not right. It's barbaric!*

Then the flesh of Rome met that of Egypt and the battle was joined.

Everyone seemed pleased by the outcome. Julius Caesar had never before found himself tied to a woman's bed, subject to her erotic whimsy. The experience of reversed roles excited him enormously. And while Cleopatra had found the idea of bondage as distasteful as Pia had, she had guessed that the emperor would enjoy it. As for Pia, she was so relieved she could have wept. This whole business had given her new insight into the Egyptian queen's character. Delighted as she was not to find herself bound and at the mercy of a man, she helped Cleopatra contrive new ways of exciting their noble Roman captive. In fact, she rather enjoyed herself.

The real shock came afterward. Leaving Caesar asleep, drugged with exhaustion and spent passion, Cleopatra slipped away to lie down alone on a couch. Soon she, too, was deep in slumber. Only Pia remained wide awake and fully alert, her mind bubbling with questions and possibilities.

After some thought, she concentrated all her powers on controlling the queen's body. Sure enough, she found herself looking about the quiet chamber through the sleeping queen's wide eyes. Next she tried to move. Effortlessly, she brought the other woman's hand to her face and brushed her cheek.

"So," Pia said in her own voice, "as long as she's sleeping, I'm in control."

This was no time to lie around talking to herself. She had to find Darius. Pia made the sleeping queen's body rise from the couch. She hurried to the wall through which Darius had vanished. When she placed her hand on the spot he had pressed, the secret door swung open. Ahead of her she saw a long, narrow stairway of rough-hewn stones, leading down. Torches set at intervals lit the way. She glanced back. Caesar was still bound and snoring, smirking happily in his sleep.

For a moment, Pia hesitated. What would Cleopatra think if she woke up? Then she realized it didn't matter. The queen didn't understand that Pia was inside her. She knew something odd was going on, but not exactly what it was. Pia would be safe.

She hurried down the stairs, not daring to let herself think where they might lead. She would face that when she got there.

On and on she went. Darker and darker it got, until she had to clutch at the walls to feel her way down. Then she saw a glimmer of light in the distance. A shadow moved below.

"Darius!" she whispered. She held her breath for his answer.

He heard her coming and turned. She saw the alarm on his face change quickly to recognition.

"By all the gods, I thought my end had come, Cleopatra. I guessed you'd given me away to the Romans."

"Sh-h-h!" Pia cautioned. "Cleopatra's sleeping and we mustn't wake her. This is me, Pia. Oh, Darius, I'm *so* glad to see you! What happened? Why didn't you come with me?"

She wanted desperately to throw herself into his arms and have him comfort her, but she didn't dare. A kiss, a hug, even the slightest touch might wake the sleeping queen.

"The cat," he said, as if that explained everything. "He jumped out of your lap and I knew you'd worry if I left him behind. So I caught him, then came after you. Oh, Pia, I've been so worried!"

"*You've* been worried!" she exclaimed. "You don't know what worried is! I landed here inside a smelly rug and got rolled out, nearly naked, right at Caesar's feet. Do you know what that does to a person's nervous system? And I'll tell you a secret, it's no joy being inside Cleopatra either. She's too little and too mean!"

"Cleopatra? Mean? How can you say that?"

"Listen, buddy, you haven't been inside her when she decides to give you a squeeze."

"Yes, I have," Darius said without thinking.

Pia's anger turned Cleo's face scarlet. "Not *that* kind of squeeze. When I do something that ticks her off, she sucks in her whole body and squashes the hell out of me. Darius, you've got to get me out of here. Fast!"

"What about your book?"

Pia groaned. How well she remembered!

"Get the crystal and we'll be out of here in a flash. Before that Roman brute can get his hands on you again."

Once more Pia's feelings brought a flush to Cleopatra's pale cheeks, but this time she went scarlet with embarrassment.

"I'm sorry about that." She avoided his eyes. "I wouldn't have—you know—but I didn't have any choice. I'm sort of a prisoner in here."

Darius's eyes were blazing now, just thinking about Caesar with Cleopatra—and Pia. "He didn't hurt you, did he?"

"No," Pia said, almost choking on her embarrassment. "Cleo told him she was a virgin so he took it easy."

"A virgin?" Darius exploded. "Like I never existed? No wonder all the history books tell lies."

"Not so loud," Pia warned. "You'll wake her. The only way I can escape is if she's sleeping and I'm in control. And it's okay. Really, Darius! When he tried to tie us to the bed later, we wrestled the rope from him and tied him up instead."

"Rope? My God!" I'll kill the bastard!"

"No, you won't!" Pia cried. "And please, keep your voice down."

"I'm supposed to just stand **by** and keep calm while you two are up there playing kinky sex games with that old lecher? Not on your life, Pia!"

"That's just it, Darius. This is *my life* we're talking about. You heard what Cleo said. If she finds me, it's torture and death games, probably for you and me both. Now just cool it! I'll go up and get the crystal and be right back. We'll be home in time for a walk on the beach before supper."

In spite of the danger, Pia couldn't resist giving Darius a quick but thorough kiss. Then she turned and headed back up the stairs as fast as she could.

Sure enough, that kiss woke Sleeping Beauty. By the time Pia reached the doorway at the top, Cleo was back in full control.

"Sleepwalking?" she pondered aloud. "That could be dangerous, especially now."

She pressed the stones to close the door on Darius—and on Pia's escape to St. Simons. Pia couldn't help whimpering softly, making Cleopatra wonder at the tears in her own eyes. She dismissed her weeping as fatigue.

Caesar was still sleeping. That was a relief.

"I must look like an unmummified corpse," Cleo murmured. "I'll have my bath before he wakes."

She left the chamber for an adjoining room with a wall that opened onto the sea. Reflected light from the water danced on the blue ceiling, giving the entire room the illusion of being under water. In the center of the floor, a pool was hollowed out of the marble. Scented, crystal water gleamed invitingly, and fresh lotus blossoms bobbed on the surface.

Two attendants stood by, the maid Iras and an ebony-skinned Sicilian, dressed only in a golden loincloth, the same guy who had carried Pia and Cleopatra to Caesar in the rug. Pia trembled inside her hostess at the sight of the imposing servant. For reassurance, she reminded herself he must be harmless, a eunuch, or he wouldn't be serving the queen in her bath.

Intercepting that thought, Cleopatra sent her own silent message to this mysterious inner self. *I would not have a castrated nonman serve me. Eunuchs grow fat and soft and disgusting. Apollodorus is my bodyguard. The only one who should fear him is one who would do me harm. If that is your plan, beware!*

Still, Pia found it shocking that Cleopatra dropped her robe without the flicker of an eye with the big guy standing right there, looking on. She said as much to Cleo.

The queen in turn replied, again silently, *Why shouldn't he look at me? I have a magnificent body. Men admire such a wonder, and I enjoy the look of desire and appreciation in their eyes. Were he to turn away, I would take that as an insult and have him killed.*

Apollodorus must know that, Pia figured. He kept watching them, never taking his eyes off his queen's luscious body.

Iras, meanwhile, flitted about the chamber, bringing fragrant oils, scented powders, and more fresh flowers for the pool. She also brought honeyed cakes, figs still damp with dew from the orchard, and—to Pia's dismay—more wine.

Cleopatra stretched out in the cool water, letting herself relax for a time. Yet she kept a listening ear for any sound from Caesar.

"I was so worried, my lady," Iras said. "To think that you were out there somewhere on that desert battlefield all this time and I was here where I could do nothing to help you."

"Apollodorus was with me."

She smiled at the tall servant. He nodded and Pia felt his gaze do homage to his mistress's body from head to toe.

"But it was unsafe," Iras insisted, "and you were gone so

long. Half a year, my lady! And what has it got you? You must still marry your brother and share your throne with him. Did you know that while you and your brother-husband were playing at being warriors your sister Arsinoë has been plotting against you both?"

Cleopatra only smiled. "Caesar is here now. Rome will see to both of them. I will be the one and only Queen of Egypt."

"That Roman," Iras muttered under her breath. "He's only come for our grain and fabrics and amethysts. Our amber and musk and incense. He'll rob the treasury of ten thousand talents in gold and then be on his way without a backward glance. Let the Flute Players murder each other, he's thinking. Then he can come back and claim all of Egypt without lifting a finger."

Again Cleopatra smiled at her servant's vehemence. "You underestimate your queen, Iras. I have a plan, already set in motion."

"Well, it had better develop itself quickly, for all our sakes. I do not trust these Roman brutes and neither should you, my lady."

Cleopatra glanced at her fair-haired handmaiden, concern in her eyes. "The bitterness in your words betrays you, Iras. The Romans. They didn't hurt you before I returned?"

Iras flushed deeply and tried to hide her face. "No, my lady. Hurt would not really apply." Her smile was overbright. "You can see for yourself. I am fine."

Pia felt a kind of cold rage grip the queen. "They used you, then? Tell me which ones and I will see to them."

Iras glanced toward Apollodorus, obviously ashamed to speak of such matters in front of the man. She whispered for Cleopatra's ears alone, "Only one took his pleasure with me."

"The brute!" Cleo spat out. "I'll have him tortured slowly, then feed his corpse to the fish."

"No, mistress. He was young and quite fair. I think I was his first." She laughed nervously. "He fumbled at me so, hardly knowing how to begin. I had to lead the way."

Cleopatra turned on her servant furiously. "You encouraged him? Iras I should have you stripped and flailed!"

Iras took a step back and shot a wary glance at Apollodorus. He held his whip clutched at the ready in his rock-hard fist. A nod from the queen and he would do her bidding instantly.

"I have put it badly," Iras explained in a shaking voice. "The young centurion saved me from the others. A dozen or more were set on having me, each and every one of them. The youngest one, of some rank, ordered the others away. They refused to go more than a short distance. Still, having them watch was less painful, I'm sure, than having them on me would have been. The lad even tried to give me Roman gold in payment afterward."

"Pay you?" Cleopatra half rose from the water in her fury. "As if you were a common whore?"

"Be calm, my lady. I told him I was not a woman who accepted gifts for such favors. I returned his coins."

"And what did he do?" Cleopatra demanded.

Iras smiled and blushed. "He thanked me very sweetly. Then he escorted me back to the palace so that I would be safe from the others. He has kept them away from me since that day."

Without another word, Cleopatra rose from the pool. Iras wrapped her mistress in a soft length of linen, then led her to a table by the window where the cool breezes from the sea fanned her naked body. Cleopatra stretched out with a sigh.

While Iras rubbed scented oils into Cleopatra's perfect skin, Pia felt herself begin to slip away. The fragrance of poppies, lilies, and heliotrope mingled in her senses with the refreshing salt tang of the sea, reminding Pia of her island home. The firm but gentle kneading of Iras's hands soothed her aching muscles and relaxed her. After a short time, Pia slept.

She dreamed of Darius. Darius and love and home.

Chapter Nine

True to his word, Darius kept an eye on both Pia and Cleopatra. He appeared at the royal chamber the next morning, dressed as a palace slave, one of over a hundred anonymous beings whose only reason for existing seemed to be to serve the queen. But Darius meant to serve her far more intimately and thoroughly than any of the others.

Cleopatra had turned over her private quarters to Caesar. Darius waited for her in the luxurious adjoining suite. As she entered that chamber from her bath, her eyes met his familiar golden gaze. She smiled.

Without a flicker of astonishment, she said smoothly to Iras, "You remember my wigmaker Darius, of course. He accompanied me to the eastern desert. As a reward for his bravery, I have decided to give him extra duty as my special bodyguard." In a whisper to her maidservant, she added, "One cannot be too careful with all these foreigners about."

Iras said nothing, but she offered Darius a narrow-eyed, silent threat. She'd guessed on the day young Cleopatra fished him from the sea that he brought danger and evil with him. She had been relieved when he did not return from the battlefield with her mistress. Now her heart clutched with fear—fear that the queen meant to reinstate Darius, not as a wigmaker but as her lover. Such a daring deception could mean Cleopatra's death now that she had shared her bed with the great and all-powerful Julius Caesar.

And why the lie about Darius having been the royal wig-maker? Iras pondered. While she had known the truth about him since she helped her queen fish him from the sea, everyone else in the palace accepted Darius as Cleopatra's astrologer, her wizard. The answer came to Iras in a flash as bright as a signal from the Pharos lighthouse: No servant, other than Iras herself, was allowed to touch the queen on pain of death. It was believed throughout Egypt that the flesh of slaves was tainted, hence they should not make physical contact with members of the royal family. But a *wigmaker!* How else could he do his duty? He *must* touch the queen's royal head in order to fulfill his task.

Iras frowned. How clever Cleopatra was! Perhaps too clever for her own good when it came to matters of the heart.

Still staring at Darius, the queen said, "Iras, go to my room and select a costume for me. I think Caesar would favor my Sidonian silks. Something simple, mind you. Perhaps the purple, to remind the Roman that he is not the only royal under my roof."

Iras bowed, then hurried out. Apollodorus had stationed himself outside the apartment's entrance. Darius was alone with Cleopatra and Pia.

Some of Pia's joy at seeing Darius must have spilled over into the queen. With a smile that was warm and welcoming, Cleopatra raised her arms to him. "Come and kiss me quickly, my darling, while we have this moment to ourselves."

Darius obliged. He drew her close, once more opening

her robe to feel her naked breasts against his hard, bare chest. Their passion, brief as it was, left Pia dizzy and disoriented. What was different about Cleopatra that she could strike such fire with a single kiss?

Darius held them a moment longer. He smiled down into Cleo's turquoise eyes. "A wigmaker, eh? You've set me quite a task. You're likely to start some new and rather bizarre fashions with me styling your hair."

"Never fear, my love. I have enough wigs to prolong our deception for the next dozen floods of the Nile. You need only play the part. It will give us time together."

Smart lady! Pia mused. She might have hugged the queen if she hadn't been locked away inside her.

"You said I should also guard you. Might I suggest that you insist on having me near whenever you sleep?"

Pia went into a full rejoice mode. Darius was setting things up so *they* could be together.

A catlike smile curved Cleopatra's full lips. "I agree. But only when I sleep alone. I know you hate hearing it, my love, but I haven't yet finished with the Roman."

"I understand. You need him for your plans to win the throne." His voice remained calm, but anger lay simmering under his words.

Cleopatra nodded, not meeting those smoldering, golden eyes. "Exactly. But my plan dictates that I marry him, that I give him a son."

Before Darius could respond to that, Iras returned, carrying a filmy gown of lush purple silk. "This should do nicely, my lady."

Pia could feel Cleopatra's uncertainty. She wanted to allow Darius the pleasure of watching her dress as she had done so often before. But knowing the desires that would bloom in both of them—and that there would be no time afterward to quench their fires—she stepped behind a dressing screen painted with gilded lilies and exotic birds the color of saffron threads.

"Iras," she said, "give Darius the key to my wig closet in the dressing room." She turned toward him and smiled. "Choose something sleek and majestic. A wig as dark as the sun-blackened skin of a Nubian."

Taking the key, Darius bowed slightly. "As you wish, my queen."

Pia all but sighed at the soft slither of silk over their body as Iras helped Cleopatra slip into the purple gown. The fabric was fine and sheer, a shimmering shade of heliotrope. It was quite plain. The skirt fell in long folds while one length of fabric draped over the queen's left shoulder and arm, leaving her right arm and breast bare.

Cleopatra and Pia eyed the effect in a mirror Iras held. Although Pia prodded her hostess to cover her breasts completely, the queen nodded and smiled her approval of the daring look.

"Yes, Iras. This should please Caesar while reminding him that I am both a queen and a woman of passion."

Damn straight! Pia blustered. *Caesar'll have at you on the breakfast table when he sees you looking this sexy!* But there was no changing Cleopatra's mind or her scheme to keep the lusty Roman off balance and distracted at all times.

While Iras was applying kohl to Cleopatra's eyes, she suddenly exclaimed, "They've changed color, my lady! They're no longer clear green, but turquoise. The very color of the Nile."

Cleopatra frowned slightly. Darius had said the same thing. "Perhaps that's a good omen," she said, determined not to let Iras know she was perplexed by the new color of her eyes. "Or perhaps it was simply the brightness of the desert all those weeks. No matter. I'll wear strands of turquoise and gold about my neck to enhance the odd shade.

And you might mix a bit of powdered turquoise in the gilt of my nipple rouge, Iras."

The servant did as her queen directed, pounding a small stone into powder with a pestle, then mixing it with finely ground gold and a drop of fragrant oil. She dabbed at the mixture with a sable brush. When the fine bristles stroked Cleopatra's nipple, Pia giggled. It tickled.

Darius walked into the room, carrying the queen's wig, at the very moment that the maidservant was tinting the plump, ripe crest. He drew nearer slowly, tranfixed by the delicate and fascinating work.

"Shouldn't that be the wigmaker's job?" he asked boldly.

Iras gave him a scornful look.

Cleopatra laughed. "I'll have Iras teach you the art, if you'd like?"

"I will *not!*" Iras exclaimed.

Both Cleopatra and Darius laughed.

"What have you chosen for me?" the queen asked. "Bring it closer for me to see." She took the long, straight, jet black wig from Darius. "Ah, perfect! I have seen its likeness in a tomb portrait of Princess Sit-Hat-Hor-Yunet. It dates back centuries. Caesar will be impressed when I tell him its history."

To Pia the wig looked like modern-day cornrows, complete with gold and amethyst beads. A circlet of hammered gold formed a simple crown, with the sacred cobra, Uraeus, rearing its head in the center. Pia shuddered at the thought of wearing a snake, even a fake one.

"You may leave us now, Iras," Cleopatra commanded.

"But I haven't done your lips, my lady."

"Never mind," the queen answered sharply. "I'll do them myself."

Once they were alone again, Cleopatra turned to Darius, her painted eyes closed, her lips parted for his kiss. He obliged her, thrusting his tongue deeply at her invitation.

Pia found herself wanting more. She longed to feel his body close, his hand on Cleopatra's painted breast. But he was careful not to leave her in disarray.

He drew back and smiled. "Is this part of the wigmaker's job?"

Cleopatra's mind snapped back to business—to Caesar. "No," she said. "Take my combs and fashion my hair close to my head so the wig will fit. Use these ivory pins to hold it in place."

Darius combed and brushed Cleo's thick hair with long, sensual strokes. The queen talked business. Meanwhile, Pia closed her eyes, let her mind wander, and enjoyed. This was the first time in her life a man had ever brushed her hair. She was going to like having Darius as Cleopatra's hairdresser, she could tell.

"Do you know if my brother is in the palace?" Cleo asked Darius.

"He is, and that fat snake, Pothinus, is with him."

"Ah, when has my dear brother ever been far from his chief advisor and mischiefmaker? I should have killed the jackal when I had the chance."

"Listen, Cleopatra," Darius whispered. "The whole city knows about you and Caesar, that you were with him last night."

She turned quickly to stare at him, her turquoise eyes wide with alarm. "How did they find out? No one saw us except you and his own guards."

His expression went grim. "You know I would never spread that tale. I don't know how Pothinus found out— maybe he made it up and only accidentally hit on the truth. But the citizens are up in arms. Pothinus has spread the word that you've thrown in your lot to side with Rome against your brother. He has all of Alexandria whipped to a fury. All-out rebellion could erupt at any time."

"Caesar's troops will put down the uprising." Cleopatra sounded more confident than she felt.

"The odds are against him. He brought four thousand troops in the thirty-five galleys that sailed into the harbor. But your brother's army numbers nearly three times that many."

Pia heard Cleopatra's words, but she also felt her fear.

"Julius Caesar is a great warrior, the greatest since Alexander, while my accursed brother is only a child. The number of troops means far less in battle than the experience of their general."

"For your sake, Cleopatra, I hope you're right. But in case you're wrong, I'm working out a plan to sneak you out of the palace and out of Alexandria, out of harm's way."

She turned on him, a different kind of passion in her eyes. "No, Darius! No matter what transpires, I stand with Caesar. If I were to leave, all would be lost. Egypt would never again accept me as queen. And Caesar would no longer trust me."

Pia sensed Darius's rage, but to his credit, he kept his peace. She did note, though, with a wince of pain, that he stabbed the ivory combs into the queen's hair with more force than was necessary. And, signaling an end to their intimacies, Darius handed her the pot of lip rouge. Their gazes met and clashed for only an instant before she reached for the brush to paint her mouth.

Moments later, her wig in place and her lips as bright as flame, Cleopatra was ready to play her next scene with the Roman.

Pia was scared. Sometime while she'd been sleeping, Cleopatra had taken her half of the crystal pyramid and hidden it. Pia had no idea where it could be. Until she located the crystal, escape would be impossible. She was in for the count now, whether she liked it or not.

* * *

Cleopatra couldn't have been more shocked when she entered the dining hall and found that Caesar was not alone. With him were her despised thirteen-year-old brother-husband, Ptolemy, and his despicable advisor, Pothinus.

When Cleopatra saw the boy's gaze fasten on her undraped breast, she quickly moved her fan of peacock feathers to hide herself. She might have been forced to wed the brat, but she'd die before she'd bed him or even allow him to ogle her in such a wretched way. The gleam of lust in his eyes sickened her.

Caesar motioned Cleopatra to come and sit beside him on the cushioned, thronelike couch. He offered no such invitation to either Ptolemy or Pothinus. His strategy was clear to both Cleo and Pia; the pair would remain standing like common subjects in the presence of royalty. Cleopatra allowed herself a faint smile. So did Caesar when he peeked behind her fan.

Without further ado, Caesar made his announcement. "I have gathered you together here for the official reading of your father's will." He waved a bejeweled hand, and a scribe standing behind the couch read the long, involved document while everyone listened in boredom.

When the learned servant finally fell silent, Caesar said, "In plain Latin, it means that upon your father's death the two of you, Cleopatra the Seventh and Ptolemy the Thirteenth, became husband and wife, as was his desire. As such, you succeed jointly to the throne to govern all of Egypt *in peace.* You have been married these past four years, but Egypt has yet to know peace. Since the Flute Player died owing Rome over ten thousand talents, I mean to see that Egypt survives to pay that debt in spite of the two of you. Do I make myself clear?"

Cleopatra leveled a look of pure hatred at her brother, in

his crown and royal robe. He returned her cold gaze, but she saw a flicker of something else as well. On the battlefield over the past months little Ptolemy had begun to anticipate manhood. He was staring at her now with the expression she'd seen on the bearded faces of rough foot soldiers when she disguised herself and visited the dockside taverns in the seamiest sections of The City. It was a look men reserved for whores.

"Your words are clear enough to me, Caesar," the boy croaked in an angry tone that broke with the uncertainty of adolescence. "Tell *her* she is my wife! Tell *her* a woman's duty to her husband." His lightless eyes narrowed, and his beardless lip curled into a sneer. "Or perhaps she's too busy for her husband . . . too busy lying with all of Rome!"

"Foul-mouthed brat!" Cleopatra shouted, and Pia felt murder in her heart.

The queen's brief outburst ended with Caesar's touch of warning on her arm.

She bit off the venom on the tip of her tongue. She even managed a haughty smile for her little brother.

The tension in the room was as heavy, thick, and menacing as the heavens before a storm. Every nerve in Cleopatra's body tingled. She was coiled, like a snake about to strike. Only Caesar's hand kept her from leaping for a sword and running Ptolemy through. Pia felt dazed by such remorseless rage. She could never harm anyone, much less calculate murder.

After the long, deadly silence, Caesar said, "You may apologize to your wife now, Ptolemy."

The boy's face went all shades of scarlet. Shying from Caesar's hawklike gaze, he fumbled at his robes, shuffled his feet, whimpered softly. Finally, his tears betrayed his fear. In one last outburst of contempt, he tore the golden diadem from his head and smashed it to the marble floor. Sobbing, he ran from the room.

"What now?" Cleopatra asked. "I refuse to be touched by the nasty little beast, you know. I will take my own life before I'll be forced to his bed."

Caesar sighed. "I know." He turned and searched her lovely face with soulful eyes. "Do you think I relish the idea of that simpering young pup pawing and slobbering over you?"

He smudged the turquoise-and-gold that tipped her breast. Pia felt a tremor pass through Cleopatra.

"Still . . ."

"Still *what?*" Cleopatra demanded when he paused.

"You *are* his wife, my dear."

"I am also his sister. Would you sleep with your sister?" Caesar smiled, and Pia wondered.

"Politics makes for strange bedfellows, my little love."

Pia shuddered. *Not that strange, I hope!*

"I refuse!" Cleopatra said in a deadly tone. "So what are your plans for me, Roman?"

He threw back his head and laughed. "You dare much, woman!"

"I expect much," she countered, "of myself and of others. Would you have your noble seed polluted by that of an Egyptian bastard?"

His neatly plucked eyebrows drew down. Cleopatra had hit on the one way to save herself from her brother. If Caesar insisted that their marriage be consummated, and Cleopatra became pregnant, how would he know whose child it was?

A slow, icy smile spread his lips. "Witch!" he accused. He pinched her nipple—hard. "You'll have your way, then. Tomorrow at the *Gymnasion* I will speak to the people of Alexandria. I will read your father's will and declare it to be valid by decree of Rome. The matter will be settled once and for all."

"And my brother?"

Before Caesar could answer, they heard shouts from outside. Ptolemy's supporters were rallying around their young king. They had not fought Cleopatra's ragtag army all these past months to see her thrust upon them by a foreign dictator.

Caesar motioned to a guard for his weapon. "Go to your room now," he told Cleopatra. "I'll set my soldiers to guard you. Do not venture outside or even onto your balcony the rest of the day."

"What are you going to do?"

"I mean to have Ptolemy and his scheming eunuch, Pothinus, brought back to the palace in order to keep an eye on them. They will stand with us tomorrow at the Gymnasion, or by the gods . . ."

He let his words trail off and motioned Cleopatra away.

She paused at the door and turned back to him. "Take care, Roman," she whispered. And then she was gone.

All that long day, Alexandria had the air of a restless animal, hungry for blood. Cleopatra lay in her bedchamber, a prisoner in her own palace. Finally, worn out with worrying over what might happen next, she drifted off to sleep.

"Darius," Pia whispered. "It's me."

He'd been standing by the window for a long while, staring out at the milling mob that surrounded the palace. He turned at the sound of her voice.

"Pia?"

He watched the sleeping queen rise from her couch. Her eyes opened slowly. Blue eyes, as brilliant as lapis.

"Your timing couldn't be better," he said. "There's real trouble brewing out there. I don't know about you, but I'd love that walk on the beach before supper tonight. St. Simons Island would look mighty good about now."

"We can't go," Pia answered almost in a wail.

Misunderstanding, Darius frowned. "This power struggle has nothing to do with you, Pia. Cleopatra can handle it.

You've read the histories. You know she'll come out of it just fine. For the present, at least."

"You don't have to tell me what a rock she is! I think that's the point I missed most in my research. Her strength and her fearlessness. She told Caesar today that she'd kill herself before she'd sleep with her brother. And she *meant* it! Darius, she scared me!"

He came to her and gripped her shoulder. "Forget all that. We'll be out of here before you can blink twice. Get the crystal."

"I can't!"

"Pia, get it," he urged. "It's time for us to leave."

"I don't know where it is. Cleopatra hid it while I was sleeping." Tears gathered in Pia's eyes. "Oh, Darius, I want to go *home!*"

Forgetting their need to let Cleopatra sleep, he drew Pia into his arms. "It's going to be all right," he murmured between kisses.

Pia clung to him, crying away all her fear and frustration. "I'm sorry," she whimpered. "It's just really hard being inside Cleopatra. She's got so many problems to deal with. It drives me crazy, Darius. And it's such a tight squeeze in here. I can barely breathe sometimes. When I do manage a deep breath, I almost choke on all that perfume she wears. What *is* that awful scent?"

"Frankincense."

"Isn't that the same stuff they use to embalm mummies?" Pia shuddered.

"Partly," he confessed. "But forget about all that, Pia. Try to think where Cleopatra could have put the crystal."

"I was asleep. I don't know."

"But you're inside her. Can't you think the way she does?"

"Not while she's sleeping. Maybe once she wakes up I can get her to think about it." She hugged Darius. "That's it! That's what I'll do! We will get to go home. Oh, Darius!"

"Sh-h-h!" he cautioned. "We don't want to wake her just yet."

They were alone in the apartment, except for the sleeping queen. Darius gently lifted Pia into his arms and carried her to a draped couch in the far corner, out of sight of Caesar's guards beyond the door.

As he settled next to her, Pia whispered, "Are you sure this is safe?"

"Does it matter?" he asked. "Caesar's off doing business for the day. I checked on that to make sure. No one will dare disturb the queen while she's napping. The worst that could happen is that we wake her."

"She'd be furious!" Pia cried softly.

He dragged his fingers over the bare, paint-smeared breast. "Do you think so? Even if I told her that I couldn't stand it any longer, that I saw my chance and went crazy to do this to her?"

Darius unwound the silk from her shoulder and kissed her left breast. Pia caught her breath. She felt a fever raging through her.

"Maybe she wouldn't mind so much," Pia admitted breathlessly.

It seemed strange, having Darius make love to her in another woman's body. But it was exciting, too. Cleopatra's nerves were more fine-tuned than Pia's, or so it seemed, and Darius knew both their bodies equally well. While he would have stroked and tickled the back of Pia's neck to arouse her, he concentrated on other zones to enflame the queen to passion.

Pia sighed and cooed, her eyes half closed, as Darius stroked her and fondled her. Inside the flimy, amber-colored curtains, she sensed that she was drifting in liquid gold . . . as if it flowed over her, around her, and all through her. Darius was a far more gentle lover than Caesar. And this time she'd drunk no wine to fog her senses. Inside her mouth, his tongue tasted clean and fresh with mint. When she kissed his neck and shoulders, he was warm and salty and scented with Mediterranean breezes.

Finally, they could wait no longer. Pia was afraid that Cleopatra might wake and steal her precious moment alone with Darius. He entered her. Cleopatra was forgotten and they swam together in a sea of passion, then euphoria.

When Cleopatra woke she was back in her bed alone. She wondered when she had shed her clothes. But often, drugged by weariness and the fierce heat of the afternoon, she would struggle out of her gown to lie naked in the breeze.

"Darius?" she said in a raspy voice. "Is that you?"

The glare from the window made it hard to see. But somehow she knew he was there.

"You slept long," he said. "And well, I hope."

She laughed softly and reached to draw a silk sheet over her body. "I had the most curious dream."

"Really? Tell me."

"You and I," she said softly. "We were together again. Like in the old days."

"Ah, the old days," he said with a sigh. "I miss them, don't you?"

"I've missed *you,*" she admitted. "The dream was lovely."

Darius turned his face from her and smiled. "I wish I could have been there."

Meanwhile, Pia was sending subliminal messages. *Where is the crystal? Go get the crystal. Show Darius the crystal. He wants to see the crystal.*

When Darius turned back, Cleopatra was frowning and rubbing her temple.

"What is it?" he asked.

She shook her head. "It's nothing. A slight hum in my

head. The wig you chose this morning must have been too heavy."

"Are you sure that's it?" He guessed that Pia was trying to get a message through. "You used to get headaches when you forgot something important. Maybe your inner voice is trying to tell you something."

"Yes. Yes, you could be right. I seem to be thinking of crystals suddenly." She was still frowning, trying to figure it out. Then she brightened. "Of course! I know exactly how I'll adorn myself tonight for Caesar. The necklace of polished crystals from Gaul. He'll be pleased. He'll think I do him honor for his victories there."

Pia saw Darius's shoulders slump slightly. Cleopatra had missed the point. Silently, he mouthed, "Keep trying."

Cleopatra thought he was blowing her a kiss. She returned the gesture and smiled. "Fetch Iras for me, won't you, Darius? It's time I bathed and dressed for dinner."

Her spirits buoyed by her afternoon with Darius, but her heart heavy with thoughts of home, Pia tried her best to prepare herself for another evening in the company—and in the bed of—Julius Caesar.

To Pia's vast relief, however, the evening was not another orgy as she had feared. Cleopatra and Caesar shared a quiet dinner in her private dining room. She had gowned herself to please him in turquoise silk, and wore enough gold to make the richest ruler envious. They supped from heavy golden plates and drank sweet red wine from jewel-encrusted goblets.

The Queen of Egypt was none too subtle in ramming her point home. *I am Egypt! See my wealth. Egypt does not need Rome. Rome needs Egypt!*

Cleopatra's grand show went unnoticed. Granted, the Roman's black eyes feasted on her beauty the whole time, but his talk was that of a conqueror, not a servant. Pia felt her hostess's barely controlled rage when Caesar announced that as of the next day Cleopatra would rule with her younger brother and that Rome would oversee their reign so that no outsiders would take advantage of their squabbling to move in. He never asked for her opinion. Indeed, it was all too clear that she would have no real say in governing her nation and no genuine power at all. Rome would preside over everything.

Rome had spoken!

Caesar's edict brought only silence from Cleopatra—a silence that seemed to Pia as dangerous as any murderous fit the young queen might have thrown.

Sensing the tension, Caesar excused himself early. He neither invited nor ordered Cleopatra to his bed that night.

Relieved beyond words, Pia let Cleopatra pace and fume the long night while she slept and dreamed of home.

Chapter Ten

Darius appeared early the next morning. He found Cleopatra alone, her eyes as green as emeralds but flashing a certain fire that he recognized as rage.

"He didn't hurt you?" There was no need for him to mention the man's name.

Cleopatra offered her lover a sad smile. "Rome slept alone last night. And why should he wish to harm me physically when he can destroy me totally with a single word?"

"What's happened?"

The diminuitive queen ran a hand nervously through her long hair. "The worst I could have feared. He means to decree today that the brat and I will share the throne as man and wife." Then she laughed, a bitter sound. "He seems to think that a word from him is all it will take to bring order to the chaos here in Egypt. We're in for a battle, Darius, a bloodbath. You can see that, can't you, with your strange sight of the future?"

Darius knew, all right. History had recorded the fierce war that would rage that winter in and around Alexandria in all its bloody horror. But one thing he didn't know. Would Pia's being here—a part of Cleopatra—make a difference in the outcome? He could see her waking even now. As he stood staring at the queen, her eyes began to change from deep green to brilliant turquoise.

"Did you sleep at all last night, Cleopatra?"

She shook her head. "How could I?"

He took her hand and led her toward her couch. "It's still early. See if you can rest for a while. You'll need your wits about you today, my love."

She sighed wearily as she reclined on the bed. Pia's cat, Xander, hopped up beside her and made several lazy circles before he nestled close and shut his eyes. Cleopatra lazily stroked his silky fur.

"You're right, Darius, as always. There's no way to tell what I'll be forced to face after Caesar makes his oration at the *Gymnasion*. I must try to rest and gather my strength and my wits for whatever's to come."

Darius moved silently to the window and stared out. Even now, in the breaking dawn, he could see the Roman troops forming up to escort Caesar to make his address. The man would soon speak words to enflame all the citizens of The City. Almost half of them backed Cleopatra, but her brother had an even larger number of followers. None of them wanted Rome calling the shots. By the end of the day, all of Alexandria would be rioting. He had to get Pia out of there fast.

"Darius?" Even as he thought of her, she spoke his name.

He turned. Cleopatra was sitting up, her eyes a sleepy blue.

"Pia, thank goodness! When I came in this morning I was afraid something had happened to you."

She stretched and yawned. "No. I just got a good night's sleep for once. Old Julius was too busy talking politics. It's a good thing, too. Cleopatra was as mad as the devil. What's going on, Darius? I'm not sure I follow all this political jockeying. What's the big deal about Cleo having to share her throne with her brother?"

"You know what happens when Egyptian siblings share the rule. Somebody usually gets murdered."

She rose and went to him. Slipping her arms around his neck, she rose up on tiptoe and gave him a kiss. "Don't look so worried, darling. We know Cleo will be okay. This will all blow over before long. The only thing we have to worry about is keeping her away from snakes."

Darius didn't share Pia's amorous mood or her lack of concern. He was worried. He removed her arms from around him and stepped away. "That's the way things *should* be. But now we're dealing with an unknown factor."

"What?"

"*You!* We don't know what will happen with you inside Cleo. Everything could change. And it will be all my fault for coming up with the harebrained time-travel scheme in the first place. I have to get you out of here right now. Have you found the crystal yet?"

Pia shook her head. "I've tried, but she refuses to think about it. Too many other things on her mind."

"Try again, now, while she's sleeping. I have an idea. Maybe we can appeal to her subconscious. Lie down!"

Pia giggled softly. "I think I'm going to like this."

"Stop it, Pia! This is serious and we don't have much time. Close your eyes and try to reach her."

Pia did as Darius instructed. After a few minutes, she sighed and opened her eyes again. "It's no use. She's really out of it. And no wonder. She had a rough night."

"Here, let me try." Darius knelt beside the couch and whispered into Cleopatra's ear. "You need the piece of crystal from Alexander's coffin. It will give you courage and wisdom now. It will give you strength to fight the Roman and Ptolemy."

Cleopatra stirred slightly, as if she meant to rise in her sleep and get the crystal pyramid. But Darius's whispers made Pia giggle.

"Stop that!" he hissed.

"I can't help it. It tickles."

Cleopatra grew still again.

"You messed it up, Pia," Darius accused. "She was about to get the crystal."

"Try again," Pia begged. "I'll stay quiet. I promise."

Darius was leaning down, ready to whisper again, when they heard the tramp of guards in the corridor outside. Quickly, he jumped up and hurried to a curtained area at the far side of the room.

Julius Caesar marched in without so much as a knock. In the morning light, his golden breastplate and helmet flashed blindingly. He looked the warrior ruler that he was, but his hawklike features softened when he gazed at Cleopatra.

After a quick peek to see who it was, Pia lay very still, her eyes closed. What did the bastard want now?"

He stood for several moments, staring down at the sleeping queen. She was still gowned in the shimmering turquoise silk she'd worn the night before, but now her feet were bare of her golden sandals and her jewelry lay in a tangle on an inlaid chest by the windows.

"You look more like a child than a queen," he whispered. "A delicious young thing, ripe for love. Why must we do battle when there are such pleasures for us to share?"

He reached down and stroked her cheek. Pia tried to hold very still, but she was trembling inside the sleeping queen. His fingers brushed down her throat and over her bare breast. Pia held her breath. How far would he go? What would she do if Cleo didn't wake up and she had to deal with him all by herself? She didn't even want to think about it. And all the while, she could feel Darius's angry gaze as he watched from behind the curtain.

Cleo, Pia urged silently. *Wake up! Caesar's here! What are we going to do?*

We're going to ignore him, came the surprising response. *He'll go away if he thinks I'm sleeping.*

Pia relaxed. Leave it to Cleo to know what to do.

Still fondling her breast, Caesar leaned down and kissed her. Then, turning away, he marched out of the chamber. Cleo remained rigid until the sounds of his footsteps echoed off into the distance. Then she sat up and glanced around.

"Darius, are you here?" she called softly.

He stepped out from behind the curtain. "How did you know?"

She rubbed a hand over her forehead. "I'm not sure. I sensed it somehow. One knows when one's lover is watching." Her amorous gaze turned angry. "If he'd caught you here . . ."

"He didn't, love," Darius said softly. He came and sat beside her, kissed her, then took her hand. "What are you going to do?"

"Nothing," she answered. "There's nothing I can do. He will make his announcement, read my father's will to all the citizens, and then the struggle will begin."

"You intend to stand by him, don't you?" Darius's question expressed neither shock nor accusation. He was simply stating what he knew to be the truth.

Cleopatra held herself erect as she answered. "I do! Caesar is my only hope. I'll give him the son he wants, and he'll make me his empress. Nothing has changed, Darius. I will simply have to fight a little harder to get what I want."

"Once *I* was all you wanted," he said in a hurt tone.

She nodded, unable to meet his searching eyes. "When I was young, yes. When I could play at being nothing more than a musician's daughter. But all that's changed now, Darius. I want to rule Egypt *and* Rome. I mean to do everything in my power to accomplish that. I think you should vanish again. I don't want you to stay here. It's far too dangerous."

"You'll be in danger, too."

"There's no help for that. I *must* remain!" She looked at him finally, and her eyes flared with turquoise fire. "Go now!" she ordered. "Go far, far away!"

Darius took her hand and kissed it. "How will I live without you? Knowing that you are in another's arms, loving you and fearing for you as I do?"

Against her better judgment, Cleopatra embraced him. "Please don't say such things now, when we are about to part. Go, and know that you take my heart with you."

"Cleopatra, where is the crystal?" Darius asked. "I can't leave without it."

She stared at him blankly. "I gave it to you. The day Iras and I pulled you from the sea."

"But I found the other half in my travels. I brought it here and left it in your chamber."

She shook her head. "I know nothing of it. Perhaps it's in Caesar's room."

"Ah! That could be. But how will I get it? Guards are posted."

"I'll find it for you. Wait here."

Pia experienced an enormous sense of dread as Cleopatra hurried down the hallway. Sure enough, a fierce-looking guard stopped her at the door.

"No one enters Caesar's private chamber," he growled.

"Do you know to whom you are speaking?" Cleopatra asked imperiously. "I am the Queen of Egypt. I have granted Caesar the use of my quarters, but I must find my looking glass. Step aside!"

The towering Roman let his gaze linger on the queen's naked breast for a time. He was clearly uncertain where his duty lay and obviously half tempted to escort the woman into Caesar's chamber, then have his way with her.

"Shall I have my man remove you, Roman?" Her sharp question snapped him out of his musings.

At Cleopatra's mention of him, Apollodorus materialized from nowhere, looming huge, dark, and menacing. Faced with such a fearsome opponent, the guard quickly moved aside to let Cleopatra enter.

She searched high and low, with Pia offering suggestions all the while—under the bed, behind the curtains, in the potted date palm. The crystal pyramid simply wasn't to be found. Finally, Cleopatra gave up the search.

When she returned to Darius, he knew from her face that she'd found nothing.

"Then I can't go," he said, even before she spoke a word to him.

"You *must!*" she commanded.

"Without the crystal I'm powerless. I'll have to stay here." That wasn't quite the truth. He had the other crystal, but he wasn't going anywhere without Pia. "Don't worry. I'll keep myself well hidden."

"If anything happens to you . . ." Cleopatra's voice was strained with fear.

"It won't, love," he whispered, holding her close for a moment. "Which wig would you like this morning?"

She stepped out of his embrace, the queen again. "Something that will transform me into the loveliest creature on earth. Caesar must have no chance to resist me."

"What man could?" Darius whispered, a sadness in his amber eyes that made Pia want to cry.

In spite of Darius's fears that Pia's presence might change things, history repeated itself to the letter, beginning with the fighting that broke out as soon as Caesar made his announcement in the *Gymnasion*. Pothinus, young Ptolemy's eunuch-henchman, fanned the Alexandrians to flame with his tales that Cleopatra had prostituted herself in the Roman's bed to gain his favor. Caesar found himself set upon by an army five times the size of his own. He held only a quarter of the palace and the harbor. At every turn, he found himself threatened. Had it not been for Cleopatra, he would have been poisoned by palace servants before sunset. Several slaves died from testing his food before he ate.

In a vain attempt to break through to his small fleet in the harbor, Caesar ordered flames to be thrown onto the decks of the Egyptian ships. Ninety burned at the foot of the lighthouse. Cleopatra applauded the success with her cunning lover. Her applause was short-lived, however. A warehouse caught fire. Soon flames were eating their way through The City. Cleopatra wept when the great library burned, destroying thousands of years of knowledge, art, and wisdom. Four hundred thousand priceless scrolls were lost.

For weeks, then months, the battle raged. Each time Caesar thought he might gain the upper hand, Ptolemy's army would threaten on a new front. True to her word, Cleopatra stuck by her Roman lover and lent him aid and understanding along the way.

Near the end of that long, bloody winter, help finally arrived. Caesar was able to surround the Egyptian army— Ptolemy's army—engaging them on all sides. Newly arrived ships with all their lights extinguished put into the swamps at the mouth of the Nile. Battle after confused battle raged. Finally Cleopatra's brother/husband drowned in Lake Moeris, dragged down by the weight of his heavy golden armor. All of his surviving counselors were arrested or killed. Caesar also took as his captives the queen's scheming younger sister Arsinoë and her lover Ganymede.

When Caesar entered The City again, the remaining citizens cheered him. The war was over at last. Spring had arrived, and Cleopatra ruled Egypt alone. She had won the crown with her loyalty to Julius Caesar. During the long days of battle, she had fought by his side, his warrior-queen. At nightfall, she had become a different woman, all softness and tenderness, giving of herself as he required, sometimes surpassing his lust with her own fiery passion.

By the end of the winter war, Julius Caesar had come to look on Cleopatra as both the embodiment of Mars, God of War, and Venus, Goddess of Love. With her by his side, he could conquer the world.

Pia was done in by the time the triumphal procession reached the entrance to The City. She felt a certain pride as the citizens of Alexandria who had fought against Cleopatra now prostrated themselves before their sole ruler, the queen. As one final show of rebellion, they were all dressed in mourning for their dead king, but it was only show, no more. Cleopatra and Caesar were the undisputed champions. Pia sat up a bit straighter inside the queen when that thought crossed her mind.

We won! she said silently to Cleo.

Not yet, the queen replied, accustomed after all these months to hearing and answering this strange voice in her head.

Pia refused to allow her hostess to spoil her good mood. Why, this was better than seeing her name on the cover of a new book, better even than fan mail.

Then a new kind of excitement filled her. Soon she would see Darius again. She'd had little time to fret over his well-being during the past months, but now fear mingled with her joy. Would he be at the palace waiting? Had he survived the intrigues and the murderous battles that had raged throughout Alexandria for so long?

She refused to let herself worry needlessly. Darius would be there. No doubt, he'd found the lost crystal by now, and

tonight they'd both be back on St. Simons, on a beach
blanket with cold beers, snuggling alone under the stars.
Somehow that scene didn't excite her as much as it should
have. With a jolt of surprise, she realized that she'd enjoyed
the past months with the queen and Caesar. The danger and
intrigue had been enthralling. What color and action she'd
be able to put in her book now! She'd never dreamed of
going into battle, much less actually relishing the challenge.
But the fact was, she'd never had a better time in her life.

Caesar leaned from his horse and touched Cleopatra's
arm. "We'll have a feast tonight, my love. A banquet of
delicacies, wine, music, and love. The two of us alone."

Cleopatra smiled at him. "We have much to celebrate,"
she said in a secretive tone. Only Pia realized that there was
something Cleo was keeping from the Roman, something
even Pia herself didn't yet know.

The two rulers parted for the first time in months when
they entered the gleaming palace. They first saluted, then
kissed tenderly.

"Well done!" Caesar said, then in a softer voice, "Until
tonight, my beloved."

Cleopatra went straight to her bedroom. How clean and
bright and welcoming the chamber seemed! Iras, looking
thin and worried, was waiting for her mistress. Weeping and
moaning, the pretty servant helped the queen out of her
armor.

"I never thought to see you again, my lady. And look at
you! Dressed like a soldier, with mud on your cheeks. I'll
have your bath ready instantly. And afterward, you'll rest."

Yes, Pia urged the queen silently, *a nap would be the very
trick.* She was dying to see Darius alone. That couldn't
happen until Cleo took a snooze.

As if on cue, the royal wigmaker stepped into the room.
"Cleopatra," he said softly. "Turn around. Let me look into
your eyes."

Pia felt the flutter of old affection in Cleo's heart at hearing his voice.

"Darius," the queen sighed. "You survived it all."

"To love again," he quipped with a quiet laugh.

The smile on his handsome face broadened as he searched her turquoise eyes. "I see you survived, too." He meant this for Pia, and she knew it; she was fairly bursting to tell him so.

He held Cleopatra in his arms for a moment, making Pia purr with happiness.

Cleo sighed—happy to be back, happy they had won the struggle, happy to feel her true love's arms around her once again. For the first time in months, the queen relaxed.

The moment passed quickly. She stepped away and looked into his amber eyes. "Have you found the other piece of the crystal pyramid, Darius?"

"Yes," he said. "I have it. It was in Caesar's room, as you suspected."

"Then you must use it quickly to leave Alexandria. The war may be over, but other struggles lie ahead. I want you gone from here as soon as possible."

He nodded. "That is my plan. I only waited to make sure of your safe return. I couldn't leave without seeing you once more."

Pia knew he was telling only half the truth. He had waited for *both* his lovers to return so that he could wisk Pia herself away—forward in time—to St. Simons.

"Will you share a glass of wine with me before you go?" the queen asked.

"With pleasure!" Darius answered.

Cleopatra made a slight motion with her hand and Iras hurried to fetch the golden ewer of rich Rhodian wine. They drank in silence, speaking only with their eyes. Even as her lover's gaze made her dizzy, the strong fruit of the wine went straight to Pia's head.

The queen emptied her cup. "Go now, my love. What I have to do is better done alone. It would only pain you to be a witness to my plans."

Darius didn't ask what those were. He knew all too well. Cleopatra's next order of business was to present Julius Caesar with a son.

"I'll watch over you for a time while you sleep. Do you mind?"

She smiled at him and stroked his cheek with her fingertips. "Only be sure that you are far away before I wake. I don't think I could bear another parting."

He nodded and sat back, sipping his wine. Within moments, Cleopatra's eyes closed in sleep.

Pia almost nodded off, too. More than anything, she wanted to rest. The spirits made her head and limbs feel as heavy as Cleo's golden armor. She knew she would drift off if she let herself. But she mustn't. Darius was waiting. With a great deal of willpower, she forced her eyes open.

"Thank goodness," he said, gripping her hand. "I was afraid you'd passed out from that strong wine."

"Almost," Pia admitted. "But I had to be with you. Oh, Darius, I've worried so that you wouldn't be here when we got back. There was so much killing."

He caressed her cheek. "It must have been terrible for you. I never meant for this to happen. But it's all right now, Pia. I have both crystals. We can leave immediately."

Pia was startled by her own reaction. "You mean *this minute?* Oh, I couldn't, Darius!"

"Why on earth not?"

"I promised Caesar I'd be at his banquet tonight. We deserve a celebration. I can't just up and leave. What would he think?"

Darius's eyes went dark with anger. "*You* didn't promise that Roman bastard anything, Pia. Cleopatra is the only one who's invited. Your presence is not required here any longer. And I'm damn tired of that old lecher pawing you!"

The wine was making little fires run through her blood. When she glanced about, all the colors in the chamber seemed to glow with an unearthly light. The golden drapes shimmered. The red stones in the mosaic floor blazed like flames. And the sheer brilliance of the water beyond the window hurt her eyes.

"Maybe I want to stay," she said defensively. "I fought with them. I deserve to celebrate *our* victory! You have no idea what it was like out there in the field, Darius, what we've been through together."

"Pia, you're talking crazy! What about your deadline? You told everybody you'd be gone for a couple of weeks. Pia, it's been *months!* What will your father think? What will your agent and your editor think?"

She turned away from him, tears shimmering in her eyes. She was confused and disoriented. If only she could sleep for a time, maybe she could figure out what she should do. She didn't like to be pressed this way.

Leaning her face down in her hands, she said, "You just don't understand, Darius. These past few months have been a revelation to me. I got to see a side of Cleopatra that I would never have known. I got to see a new side of *myself.*" When she looked up, her blue eyes were blazing. "Do you know what it feels like to ride into battle on horseback, in full armor? To sit in on a war council and have your opinions listened to? Why, I've commanded a ship of war when the captain fell dead at my feet. I've learned to recognize a camel rider coming into camp long before any Greek or Roman could. I can identify ships still far out at sea by the smell of their caulking. I've learned more these past months from Cleopatra than I could have learned in my whole life."

"The only camel riders you'll need to recognize are back home in the deli on Mallory Street."

She shook her head. "You don't get it! You just don't get it, do you?"

"All I know is, I brought you here and I mean to get you home safely. The sooner the better!"

He brought both crystals out of his robe and began muttering incantations.

"Okay, okay, Darius!" She held up her hands, a shield against her lover and his magical stones. "But let me stay for the banquet tonight. Just let me have that and then we'll go back."

By the look on his face, Pia could tell he was far from pleased. But he nodded and agreed.

"One warning, though," he said. "Tonight's sure to turn into another Roman orgy. I'm getting you out of here before Caesar gets his hands on you again. You can stay for the feast, but not for the frolic. Agreed?"

For an instant, Pia's mind flicked back to those frenzied nights of love in the tent on the desert. They never knew how long they'd have alone together before a new battle broke out or a courier arrived with an urgent message. The danger of imminent death had added a certain sweet hysteria to Caesar and Cleopatra's lovemaking these past months. Tonight things would be different . . . slow and lazy and luxurious. Now that they knew each other's bodies so well, tonight's tryst was certain to be spectacular. What a scene she could write for the book!

"Agreed?" Darius repeated stubbornly.

Pia crossed Cleopatra's fingers behind her back. "Agreed," she fibbed.

"All right! That's better. I'll be watching. When the time comes, I'll do what I have to and we'll be gone from here. I'll have you back home before you know what's happened. Why, you can sleep in your own bed tonight, Pia! So can I," he added in a sexy whisper.

Pia simply couldn't hold her eyes open a minute longer.

Leaning back on the cool, silk couch, she joined the queen in her slumber.

By the time Pia woke up, Cleopatra was in her bath. Three maids ran back and forth, bringing scented soaps, fragrant oils, and fresh flowers. Pia had never felt anything so wonderful in her life. Layers of grime and sweat melted away, replaced by a delicious-smelling sheen of soothing unguents. For a long time she luxuriated in the bath, floating among the pure white lilies that drifted on the rippling, silvery surface of the pool.

The servants brought in a parade of gowns so that Cleopatra might make her choice. With a wave of her hand, she dismissed silks of every rainbow hue, gowns fashioned in fabrics from Nubia, Sidon, and China.

"I must wear the perfect costume tonight. Caesar has gazed on me too long in uniform and armor. I must appear regal, yet so feminine he aches to touch me. Something with a golden girdle and clasps, I think." She laughed and murmured for her own ears and Pia's alone, "Yes, a girdle and clasps make a man's fingers itch to undo them. I'll bring all his passion to its boiling point tonight."

Finally, she made her choice. Layers and layers of gossamer fabric as sheer as silken cobwebs. Cleopatra came from her bath and let Iras towel her dry with warm lengths of linen. Then, for an hour or more, the servant massaged sweet oils into her body. Next came the powdering. From head to toe, Cleopatra ordered Iras to dust her with a mixture of rice powder and gold that had been pounded into dust. The effect proved startling. Pia gazed at Cleopatra's form in the looking glass—a pale, curvaceous body that gleamed. She was a gilded goddess. With painstaking care, Iras wielded her sable brush to turn Cleopatra's nipples into auras of purest gold.

When Iras brought the queen's favorite scent bottle, Cleopatra waved it away. "No cedar oil tonight. It reminds me of the desert. I've had too much of that these months. Something sweeter, more exotic."

"The precious myrrh, my lady?" Iras suggested in an excited whisper.

"Yes!" the queen agreed with an affirmative nod. "Only the best for my lover tonight."

Once Cleopatra was properly scented with the sultry musk of myrrh, the process of dressing began. First Iras clad her in a rose-tinted veil called a *mafortes*. This covered the queen's figure loosely and left nothing to the imagination, only adding a faint blush to her lovely, pale flesh. Next came a drape of the finest Milesian silk in royal purple. This Iras arranged carefully over the queen's left shoulder, then wrapped it about her body. The gold of her right nipple shone through. About her waist, Cleo wore a golden girdle of chains and coins, meant as a gift for Caesar—her own personal tribute to Rome. But first she would use it to tantalize him, to stroke his royal fires. Over this went the snow-white robe with its golden clasps.

Pia noted Cleo's smile of mischievous satisfaction as Iras fastened each golden hinge. She was thinking of Caesar's frustration and his eager, rising passion when he'd be forced to free her from the garment later on. Only when he had stripped away all her finery would she present him with another gift—the greatest gift of all. *My secret, my special surprise for him!*

What gift? What secret? Pia demanded, roused out of her euphoric state by the queen's thoughts of private knowledge.

Cleopatra only trilled a laugh in answer.

"Shall I call your wigmaker now, my lady?" said Iras.

"No!" Cleo snapped. Obviously, she thought Darius was long gone and didn't want her servant to know. "I'll wear my hair natural tonight."

"Loose, my lady?" Iras asked, surprised. It was a hairstyle appropriate only for young girls. For virgins.

"Don't act so shocked," the queen chided. "He thinks of me as very young, you know. But I prefer to wear it up, so that Caesar himself can take it down. Men like that, Iras. It fans their flames."

The servant blushed deeply. "As you wish, my queen."

Iras worked the thick, luxuriant hair into soft waves over Cleopatra's forehead, then wound the length of it into a soft coil high at the back of her head.

Cleopatra smiled, pleased with the effect. "Yes, I like it. But it needs something." With her own hands, the queen pulled loose one coquettish curl and let it fall beside the outer edge of her left eye.

"What do you think?" she asked.

"Stunning, my lady."

Pia agreed. If Cleopatra had wanted to enflame Caesar tonight, she had done everything just right. Pia knew the man well—*intimately*. She could imagine his reaction when he saw his lover.

It's going to be quite a night, Pia commented.

Cleopatra smiled. *Quite! Shall we go?*

Julius Caesar had never looked better than when Cleopatra first set eyes on him in the banquet hall that night. He too was scrubbed, powdered, and perfumed. His linens were of the most brilliant white, making his suntanned skin appear darker than ever. The gold laurel crown on his head gleamed with new brilliance, as if his victory over Ptolemy's armies had given it new luster. He looked powerful, sure of himself, almost youthful.

When he first gazed on Cleopatra, his black eyes went wide, then narrowed to what Pia described to herself as a "bedroom look."

"My dearest," he murmured, taking Cleo's hand. "I'd almost forgotten what a beautiful woman you are. Although,

I daresay the sight of you in battle armor did tempt me greatly."

Cleo laughed. "Only because you could imagine then that I was a lad. I know your needs, Roman. *All* of them!"

Pia was shocked. Cleo hadn't taunted Caesar this way since the night she'd arrived at the palace, when he'd first mistaken her for a boy. But why would she bring that up now?

The answer to that question struck Pia almost instantly. By hinting that he might desire her more if she were male, she made herself seem all the more female and alluring.

Playing her role to the hilt, Cleo let her long, tapered fingers stray over the golden clasps that closed her robe. Caesar's gaze went right to the bait. He licked his lips. His face turned ruddy with excitement.

"Shall I help you with those, my dear?"

The queen smiled and lowered her incredibly long lashes. "Not just yet. The air has almost a chill to it this evening."

Caesar had ordered the servants to set up the banquet Roman style, with couches for reclining and later, perhaps, for lovemaking. Low tables were ready with golden plates and goblets filled with sweet, honeyed wine. Taking Cleopatra's hand, he led her to her place, then took his own.

Only the two of them supped tonight, but they were hardly alone. Guards stood at the doors, musicians played their lyres, young Nubians stood about waving great peacock fans, and food and wine stewards moved quickly and silently in and out.

The food the queen had ordered might have fed all of Alexandria, yet she and Caesar barely nibbled at the feast. At Pia's urging, her hostess ate more than she would have of the magnificent repast. Pia, half-starved by the camp rations of the past months, murmured her approval of the hearts of palm in oil, the great ribs of beef, the tiny spiced and pickled quail, the braised tigerfish, the sauteed eel, the pomegranates, the blood oranges, even the locusts, fried crisp and dipped in honey. Great trays of mushrooms were carried in with much pomp and circumstance. In Egypt it was thought that the delicious fungi were too good for the common people. Only royalty were allowed by law to indulge.

Sure beats a peanut butter sandwich, Pia moaned gratefully as Cleo nibbled daintily at a particularly large mushroom cap.

When a servant brought in a great silver trencher, steaming with green cabbage cooked in old wine, flavored deliciously with cumin and mint and garnished with fresh olives, Caesar took a sniff then arched an eyebrow at the queen.

"A Roman dish!"

She nodded and smiled. "My cooks are adept at preparing foreign foods for dignitaries from many lands. This one I thought especially appropriate for tonight. After eating it, we needn't fear the affects of the special wines I've ordered. Priceless vintages from Lesbos, Chios, and even your fine Falernian from Rome."

As she spoke, she played with her great amethyst ring. Pia groaned inwardly. It was going to be another one of *those* nights!

The lyre player struck a chord and three tall, lovely slave dancers entered the chamber—one as golden as honey, one as fair as snow, one as black as night. They were dressed in veils of scarlet, gold, and royal blue—the colors of Egypt itself. They wore bells about their ankles and hips, tiny cymbals on their fingers, and glittering belly-jewels that flashed brilliant rainbows about the room as they moved. Pia's eyes went wide, but not as wide as Caesar's. He stared, awestruck and aroused, when the beautiful slaves began moving their sensuous, oiled bodies to the music. Their well-formed hips gyrated, making their bells tinkle and the belly-jewels spark like fire. By turns the women draped themselves close enough for the Roman ruler to caress their gleaming flesh. Pia watched as his hand smoothed over a pale hip, stroked a golden thigh, and pinched the purple nipple of an ebony breast. Then the slaves whirled away and spun round and round, dancing faster and faster until Pia's head was reeling just watching them. She could tell the dance had a deep effect on Caesar.

Suddenly the queen clapped her hands sharply. The music died. The dancers sank to the mosaic floor, prostrating themselves before the great conqueror. Caesar was sweating profusely, nearly panting with lust.

"Do any of these women take your fancy, my love?" Cleopatra asked sweetly.

Pia could tell from the look on his face that all three did. He laughed nervously. "Certainly not! How could I be tempted by slaves with the most beautiful queen in the world at my side?"

"They don't please you?" Cleo sounded shocked and disappointed, but Pia guessed her game. "In that case, I shall have them killed at once."

Caesar lurched forward on his couch. "No!" he cried. Then, in a less frantic tone, he said, "They dance quite well, my love. But only you can tempt me."

Cleo waved the women away before turning to smile at Caesar. "I'll spare them, should you change your mind."

This was *so* neat! Pia thought. Cleo was something else. She was testing the aging Roman to his limits as she entertained him. She meant to make him prove himself to her—his love and his loyalty—over and over again while they feasted. By the time she allowed him to jerk open those golden clasps on her robe and get to the meat of things, the poor old guy wouldn't know whether he was coming or going. This was certainly a sight to see—to be a part of.

Already too far gone to be cautious, Pia suggested to Cleo, *Why don't we have some more wine?*

The queen raised her jewel-encrusted goblet toward Caesar, then put the cup to her lips and spilled the thick, dark wine down her throat.

Whew! That's a good one! Pia sighed dizzily as the strong vintage from Lesbos hit bottom. *Makes me want to dance like the slaves.*

Cleopatra reached over and touched Caesar's hand. In a voice, husky with wine and passion, she said, "Later, my love, I'll show you how pitifully those slaves performed. I dance myself, you know."

He gripped her soft hand and nibbled at her fingertips, then dragged his tongue across her palm. "If you are as proficient on the dance floor as you are on the battlefield, then I long to witness your skills, my little queen."

Cleopatra withdrew her hand, plucked a lotus blossom from its stem, and tasted its delicate petals.

"I've heard that lotus-eaters suffer from forgetfulness and therefore live wondrously enchanted lives, with lovemaking as their only employment," Caesar whispered hoarsely, never taking his eyes from Cleopatra's teeth and lips as she tore at the fragile bloom.

She smiled, nodded, and offered a blossom to him.

Soon all three of them had a buzz on, from the wine, the lotus flowers, and the heavy, sexy musk in the chamber. Pia found herself wishing that Caesar would undo Cleopatra's clasps. She was turned on!

But the feast continued. Next came the *quand,* as Cleopatra called it. An array of candies, fruits, and sweets. Almond marzipan, baskets of figs and pears, honeyed pastries, and the centerpiece, a towering obelisk of cake, filled with fruit and nuts, oozing with honey, and scented with ambergris.

More wine, more sweets, more music. The night seemed to reel around Pia—a spiral of colored lights, perfumed clouds, and sensual intoxication. Earlier in the evening, she'd thought once or twice about Darius and wondered when he might whisk her away. But now she'd forgotten all that. She no longer was just inside Cleopatra; she felt as if she were the queen.

"Come to me!" Caesar ordered, lifting his right hand to Cleopatra.

A command, Pia realized, was not what Cleo wanted. He would have to beg before she went to him. She would have no master tonight. She was at long last *queen!*

Cleopatra downed another cup of wine. Her smile from behind the goblet was both daring and beguiling. Pia saw Caesar's shiver of desire.

Cleopatra leaned back on her couch and fanned herself for a moment. Closing her eyes, she sighed. "You may help me out of my robe now."

Caesar was at her side instantly, fumbling at the stubborn clasps. He cursed softly as he worked. Cleo offered no help. She merely lay back and let him tend her as if he were a lowly slave. Finally, the robe fell open. He uttered another low curse, but this time in appreciation. The blush-colored veil that only teased at covering her flesh set Caesar's pulses racing. He stared down at her gilded nipple, hypnotized, as if he were gazing into a bewitching golden eye. He touched her breast, which seemed naked, only to draw his hand back with a cry of surprise. He stared, looking stricken, into Cleopatra's half-hooded eyes. A smile of both invitation and amusement curved her bright lips.

Sitting up, she snapped her fingers. Immediately, the musicians began to play. Cleopatra rose from her couch like a serpent raising its body to the sun. She brushed past Caesar and took the floor. He remained sprawled on her couch where she had left him, paralyzed with awe and desire.

Cleopatra moved her body slowly at first, in perfect time with the music. The golden tinkle of the coins on her girdle became louder as she moved her hips in a circular, swaying motion. Slowly, sexily, she raised her arms over her head, never giving up the rhythm of her body. As her fingers entwined, her breasts rose, high and peaked, one gold nipple still gleaming at Caesar. Then she whirled and her purple drape flared wide, giving him a glimpse, a promise of things to come. A moment later, she unclasped her girdle and threw the chains of coins into Caesar's lap.

"My gift to you, Roman!" she called with a throaty laugh.

He flung the precious treasure down. "I desire far more than your gold, woman."

She laughed again and whirled round and round the couch. The purple drape flew from her shoulder and covered him. Caesar, drunk with wine and longing, tried unsuccessfully to fight his way out from under the yards of fabric. Cleopatra advanced upon him and clamped her hands on his shoulders, holding him prisoner under the purple silk. Slowly, she leaned down to his lips and kissed him through the transparent drape. He moaned. She drew away, then lowered her mouth to his once more. With her lips parted, she sucked the silk into her mouth, then stabbed into Caesar's with her draped tongue. He sucked greedily at her silk-clad tongue. A moment later, she freed him, laughing all the while.

His face was nearly the color of her silk by then. His black eyes gleamed with lust. And when he spied Cleopatra, clad now only in her *mafortes,* that transparent veil of blush coloring, Pia knew that it was only a matter of seconds before that, too, would be gone, ripped from the queen's body by the love-starved Roman.

"Cleopatra *please,*" he begged. "I can take no more. I must have you now!"

Pia had never sensed such total triumph in Cleopatra, not even when she'd vanquished her brother's army. She had made this man her slave. She had made him beg. Now she would reward him most generously.

Cleo was slipping the veil from her shoulder when Pia

heard another voice in the room. "Now, my love! This minute!"

It was Darius.

She glanced about frantically, but couldn't see him. "No!" she cried. "Not yet. A few more minutes!"

The words burst from Cleopatra's lips. She was too preoccupied with readying herself for her lover to guard what she said.

"No! Not even another second! I must have you *now!*" Caesar roared. Past all patience, he tore the filmy veil from her body, gripped her by the hips, locked his mouth to her breast, and lowered her none too gently to the couch.

Cleo and Pia moaned in unison. Caesar was half-in, half-out when Pia suddenly felt dizzy and saw swirling colored lights closing in on her.

Darius? Pia moaned silently. *Wait! I can't leave right now.*

Only a wailing whine filled her ears in answer to her plea. Black swirling clouds lifted her and drew her away. She was flying, soaring, being whipped by fierce winds.

Then suddenly all motion stopped. Pia found herself on another couch with another man leaning over her.

She brushed a hand over her eyes. "Darius?" she whispered.

She could see his fierce tiger-eyes even through the twilight shadows.

"How could you?" he demanded. "You really wanted that Roman brute, didn't you?"

"You've got it all wrong. Cleo wanted him, I was just along for the ride." She babbled on, making bad matters worse. "You know how it is, Darius."

"No! Tell me how it is."

"Well, I can't drink wine. It makes me punchy and silly and sex crazed. Then all that dancing and bumping and grinding, and those clothes coming off—the robe and the drape, then when he tore off the veil—"

"You *enjoyed* that?"

She shrugged and tried to avoid his angry gaze. "It sort of gets a girl's temperature up."

"I can do that."

He wrenched the terrycloth robe from her shoulders, the same robe she'd been wearing when she'd left St. Simons. Underneath she had on shorts and a threadbare tank top.

Darius fingered the strap of her top, sending delicious little shivers all through her. "Let's see now, next I believe he just yanked."

Darius yanked and the tank top ripped in his hand. Pia gave a sharp cry of surprise, then another, softer cry when he sucked her left nipple into his mouth. He tormented her with his tongue until she was squirming beneath him. When he released her at last, she moaned in need.

"Isn't that the way old Julius did it?"

Pia was beyond words. She stared up into his wide, golden eyes, licking her dry lips.

"And then what?" Darius glanced up at the ceiling as if trying to think what to do next. In fact, he was only prolonging Pia's delicious agony. "Oh, I know!" he said.

He scooped her up off the sofa and headed for her bedroom.

Pia smiled and leaned her head on his shoulder, kissing his neck. "Don't you want me to dance for you first?"

He answered her with a sexy growl as they tumbled into bed. Pia couldn't be sure what Cleo and Caesar were doing right then, but it couldn't be any better than what occupied her and Darius. By the time he rode her to the top of Mount Olympus to feast with the gods, Pia knew exactly where she belonged—*where* she was—and with whom—*Darius*. Life would be perfect now. She would finish her book, marry her lover, and live happily ever after on her own perfect island.

Near dawn, when they had completely exhausted each other and were lying together almost asleep, Pia suddenly shot up in bed.

"Darius!" she cried, nearly hysterical. "We have to go back! I forgot something!"

Chapter Eleven

"Go to sleep, Pia," Darius mumbled.

"I can't! I forgot something."

"Whatever it is, we'll get you another one."

"No, we can't do that. I forgot Xander, my cat."

"Is that all?" With a weary sigh, Darius turned on his side, away from Pia.

She grabbed his shoulder and shook him. "Darius! Don't you go to sleep on me. I want my cat!"

"Come on, Pia," he begged. "Xander will be fine. Cleopatra loves cats. We'll go back and pick him up later."

"No!" Pia cried. "What if he ends up mummified, like those Egyptian cats I saw on PBS?"

"Take it easy, sweetheart. Cleo would never do that. She's crazy about cats and you know it."

"How can you be so sure he'll be okay? Besides, she has too much else going on right now to worry about taking care of Xander. And he's not used to being just another pet around the palace. He's been raised as an only cat. He must be miserable. I want him back. Now!"

Reluctantly, Darius climbed out of bed. "What time is it?" he asked.

"Search me," Pia answered. "I don't even know what day it is. Turn on the TV. We need some news anyway. For all we know, the whole world could have blown up while we were gone. We could be the only ones left. How long has it been? Six months? Eight?"

Darius clicked on the television set. Harry Smith's gleaming pate came into view, reminding Pia of Julius Caesar's nearly bald head. The morning show host smiled into the carmera and said, "Time for that second cup of coffee. It's seven fifty-eight, July third. And according to our weatherman, it's going to be a scorcher here in New York."

Pia turned to Darius, her eyes wide. "How could that be? We spent all winter in Alexandria."

"Time passes differently on different planes. You told everybody here that you'd be back in a couple of weeks and so you are."

Pia's mind was clicking away. "Then I haven't missed my deadline," she said brightly. Her smile turned into an anxious frown. "Edgar Allan! I wonder what he's been up to while I was gone."

She pulled on her robe and left the room for a few minutes. When she returned from the kitchen she found Darius stretched out on the bed again.

"What are you doing?" she said. "I thought you'd be gone and back by now. You haven't even left yet."

He opened one eye and grinned at her. "Just thought I'd catch a quick catnap before I go."

"It's just as well you're still here. I have something for you to take along."

Pia stalked back to the bed, leaned down, and kissed him softly. Commanding him to leave hadn't worked, so maybe she'd use one of Cleo's techniques. A bit of sweetness and cajolery. While she was kissing him, she stuffed a can of tuna-and-egg into the pocket of his shorts.

"This will make it easier to find Xander, darling. He can smell his food a mile away. He'll come running."

"And how am I supposed to open it? I don't remember any can openers around the palace kitchen."

"No problem!" She kissed him again. "It's a flip top."

He made a grouchy, grumbling sound and closed his eyes again.

"Darling, the sooner you go and come back, the sooner we can relax and enjoy some time off. It won't take you long, will it? While you're gone, I'll fix us a picnic lunch. As soon as you get back with Xander, we can go to the beach. We'll have lunch, then swim and lie around in the sun all afternoon."

"We'll get burned, hanging around on the beach." He was obviously in no mood to be cajoled.

"Well, if you'd rather, after our picnic we can come back to the house and take a nap or something. Whatever you want to do, honey. I'm open to suggestions."

By nine o'clock, Darius was up, but he still hadn't budged. He wanted breakfast, a shower, and a few more of Pia's pleading kisses. All that stopped when the phone rang. Pia dashed into her office to take the call.

"Pia? This is Marel Irving."

"Oh, Marel!" Pia tried to sound surprised yet delighted to hear from her editor. "I was going to call you later today."

"How's the book coming?"

"Great! You're going to love it. I just got back last night from my research trip. I've dug up some wonderful stuff to flesh it out, really add the zing I wanted. Wait till you read it!"

"*When?*" The word sounded steel-edged.

"When?" Pia repeated innocently. "When what?"

"When do I get to read it? You're only a few weeks from

your deadline now. I'd really hoped you would get this manuscript to me early."

Pia laughed nervously. "Well, I know I said I'd try, Marel, but so many unexpected things have come up. I hadn't figured in time for this research trip, and I've had company." She glanced at Darius, lounging against the doorframe and looking so utterly sexy that it made her toes twitch. "And now my cat's missing. I can't write without my cat."

"Exactly how far are you from finishing?"

Pia rolled her eyes. "That's hard to say right this minute."

She held the phone away from her ear while Marel preached about production schedules, jacket design, advance promotion. Darius sidled over and put his ear close to Pia's to listen in. When he wasn't listening, he was blowing softly into Pia's ear, giving her goose bumps. The more Marel talked, the more the muscles in Pia's neck and shoulders tightened. Seeing her tense up, Darius massaged her with long, gentle strokes of his fingers until she sighed into the phone.

"What did you say?" her editor asked.

"Oh, nothing," Pia answered wistfully. She forcibly shook off her languor. "Listen, Marel, why don't you give me a couple of hours to go over everything, then I'll get back to you. Okay?"

"All right, Pia," the woman said hesitantly. "But remember—we have a schedule to keep. Time is money!"

"Right!" Pia answered. "I won't let you down. Talk to you later, Marel."

Pia replaced the receiver gently, then flipped Edgar Allan's on switch. The computer hummed with mysterious internal action for moments before the screen booted up.

"Here goes," Pia said, selecting her document and pressing the proper keys, holding her breath as she did so. Would everything be as she'd left it? Would she find more? Less? Nothing?

She glanced up at Darius. He was grinning, actually enjoying this.

The beginning of the first chapter materialized on the screen. Pia breathed with relief. Page after page of beautiful, glowing words flipped past like swarms of bright fireflies in flight as she quickly scrolled through the chapters. The book was literally writing itself.

"Will you look at this, Darius! Every bit of it's here. It's all written for me."

She looked at Darius, her eyes wide and glittering with amazement. His grin had broadened. He looked like Xander after a tin of tuna-and-egg.

"I hope you like it, sweetheart." He kissed her cheek.

"*You* did this?"

He laughed softly and shrugged. "I didn't have much else to do while you were off with Cleo and J.C. playing war games. I figured I might as well plug in and send some work along. With a few calculations, I managed to open a window through time back to your computer. Edgar Allan's been humming away all the time we were gone. You'll have to fill in the blanks, of course. I didn't even try to guess what was going on while you were away from the palace all those months. I knew you'd want it historically accurate, so I stuck to the facts all the way. I didn't embellish anything."

Pia stopped at a page about Cleopatra's "wigmaker." Her gaze flitted over the lines. She giggled. Then she laughed out loud. "Not much, you didn't! 'The wisest and most skilled lover in all of the ancient world . . . so incredibly handsome that women swooned at the sight of him . . . so clever that he managed to evade the entire Roman army by outwitting the great Julius Caesar himself.' Come on, Darius! Isn't that stretching the truth just the tiniest bit?"

"Edit it, if you must," Darius answered in an injured tone.

Pia reached up and slipped her arms around his neck. His mouth moved over hers, sending familiar fire through her blood. If it weren't for poor Xander, she'd haul this golden Greek right off to bed again and keep him there for the rest of the day.

"At least the lover part is accurate," she whispered.

"But you still want your damn cat," he muttered, reading the pleading look in her eyes.

She nodded.

He sighed. "Okay! Okay! I'm off. But I won't be long. And you'd better be right here waiting when I get back. That flight through time always turns me on."

"I'm not going anywhere," Pia assured him. She smiled, and her hooded gaze spoke volumes about her own desire. "You just be careful, darling. And no fooling around with Cleo while I'm not there. You hear me?"

Darius held his hands up in front of his chest in a defensive pose. "Hey, I'm in, then I'm out of there. Word of honor!"

A thought struck Pia suddenly. "While you're there, Darius, see if you can find out the big secret Cleo was fixing to spring on J.C. when I left. It's driving me crazy. I've got to know."

Darius tried to hide his look of surprise. He knew Cleo's secret. Pia knew it, too, if she'd only stop for a minute and give it some thought. It was right there in all the history books. He'd seen it written in her notes. But he'd just as soon she not know—not ever! To cover, he pretended ignorance and laughed.

"Been keeping things from you, has she? That's Cleo! I'll do my best, sweetheart."

Darius left the room for a moment. When he returned, he was holding the two halves of the crystal in his palms. The colors glowed brighter and brighter until the whole room swam in brilliant light.

When he began mumbling his mysterious incantations, Pia experienced a moment of fear, a panic attack at the thought of Darius returning to Egypt without her. She reached out and gripped his arm, ready to beg him not to go. But even as her fingers closed around his wrist, she realized she was too late. She found herself holding only air and her half of the crystal pyramid. Darius by now was far, far away. She focused her gaze on the shifting fires inside the stone, her ticket back to Egypt if Darius didn't return soon. There was no doubt in her mind that she would make the trip alone, if he failed to come back to her.

If only she could remember the right words, she would follow him this minute. But he had refused to teach her his magical chant. "Too dangerous!" he had said.

"Too dangerous for me, Darius?" she whispered. "Can it be any less dangerous for you?"

Trembling at that thought, Pia crossed her arms on the desk and rested her head on them. She had to get a grip. She couldn't allow herself to go to pieces now that he was gone. After all, she was the one who had insisted he go back. If she hadn't made such a fuss about Xander, Darius would still be right here.

"I shouldn't have made him go," she murmured. "After all, cats have nine lives."

She got up and paced her office, glancing every few minutes at the clock. An hour passed, then two. She knew she should work, but she couldn't. She was too unnerved, too anxious for Darius's safety. The sun was streaming in her windows. Little motes of dust swam in the yellow light.

"That's it!" she cried. "The house could use a good cleaning, a midsummer-spring cleaning. I'll tackle that while Darius is gone. He'll be so surprised to come home to a spotless cottage."

An enormous load of guilt assailed her before she could begin. She glanced at Edgar Allan—a big mistake. His glow looked positively accusing.

"Oh, lighten up!" she snapped at the computer. "I'll be

right there. Just give me another minute or two to get my thoughts together."

Pia turned away from the offending screen. She gazed out the front windows at the softly undulating waves. The tide was low. The air was still. A walk on the beach now would provide hours of entertainment and discovery as she searched each tidal pool for fascinating creatures—sand dollars, starfish, moon snails, spider crabs, sea robins, needlefish. Once she'd even found a tiny squid that squirted his ink when she touched him with one finger.

"A whole fantastic world out there to be explored and I'm tied to this damn computer." She *hoped* Edgar Allan was listening.

She watched the beach a moment longer. The air was still. Not even a seagull stirred as the mid-morning heat climbed steadily toward the burning eye of noon. Finally, she sighed and turned away.

She edged toward the computer. Maybe she'd try to get some writing done after all. "He'll be back before lunchtime," she assured herself.

It never failed. The moment she got settled in her office chair with her fingers poised on Edgar Allan's keys, the phone rang. Sudibeth!

She thanked goodness it was Sudibeth and not her dad! She had yet to figure out what she was going to tell him about where she'd been for the past two weeks.

Her friend had returned only an hour before from a vacation trip to Miami with Carlos from the writers' conference. The bubbly redhead was so full of her own news that she asked only a few vague questions about where Pia had been, then only half listened to her friend's equally vague answers. Pia knew she would have to do a better job when she talked to her dad.

After Sudibeth wound down and hung up—feigning fatigue, not so much from the drive home as from her Latin lover's overdeveloped sex drive—Pia gave some serious thought to what she'd say to her father. She didn't want to lie to him. Still, there was no way she could tell him the whole truth. Carefully, painstakingly, she constructed a story that was almost true without mentioning anything about time-travel or having fought the army of Ptolemy or having slept with Julius Caesar. Satisfied with her tale, Pia dialed Stephen Byrd's number at the Navy base in Key West. It rang only twice before he answered.

"Yes? Captain Byrd here."

"Pia-bird here!" she replied in a deep, official-sounding tone, mocking him affectionately.

"How's my girl? It's good to hear your voice. Where have you been, Pia? I called several times this week and always got the the same message on your machine. Just that that you were going out of town and would be back in a couple of weeks. You're lucky a burglar didn't call. Your place would have been fair game, honey."

"I got home late last night, Dad. I've been off doing more research. What have you been up to while I was gone?"

"Big inspection on base last week. Otherwise, the usual. How did your research go?"

"Fantastic! I have so much great stuff for the Egyptian book now."

"Where were you?"

Now came the tricky part. Pia thought every word through before she spoke. If she told him she'd been in Alexandria, digging in the big library, that would be true. After all, she *had* been in Alexandria and she *had* been in the palace where the great library had been housed before Julius Caesar accidentally set fire to it. Pia herself certainly couldn't be blamed if her dad assumed she meant Alexandria, Virginia, or if he figured she had been digging in the D.C. area—the Library of Congress and the Smithsonian.

She took a deep breath. "Alexandria," she said smoothly.

"And I had some wonderful help with my research. A Greek Egyptologist named Darius. Dad, I wish you could meet him. He knows everything about Cleopatra."

Only after she paused did it dawn on Pia that Stephen Byrd had met Darius. At least her dad had seen him that day in the *agora* in modern day Alexandria.

"Sounds like a productive trip, honey."

Pia only half heard her father's next words. Just speaking Darius's name had made her think of him, wonder where he was this very minute. Was he with Cleopatra?

"I'm sorry. What was that you said, Dad? There's some static on the line." There was static all right, but it was in Pia's mind, not on the line.

"I guess you've got that book about squared away since your trip was so productive."

Productive? Productive!

"That's it!" Pia cried excitedly into the phone. Had she not been so taken by surprise, she would have kept it to herself. However, that single word from her father hit her like the proverbial ton of bricks.

"What's that you say, Pia?"

"Oh, nothing, Dad. Just muttering to myself. Something you said sparked an idea."

Captain Byrd chuckled. "You'd better go write it down fast before you lose it. I'll talk to you later, honey. Glad you're home. I love you, sweetheart."

"Me, too, Dad. 'Bye now."

Pia hung up, but didn't move from the spot. "By damn! If that doesn't beat all," she muttered. "We did it! Me and Cleo! *That's* what her big secret was. She was fixing to tell old Julius when I left."

Pia rose and went to the full-length mirror on the back of her office door. She pulled her shirt taut across her flat belly, turned sideways to see if she could spot even the slightest bulge. Then she threw back her head and laughed.

"Doesn't matter if you can see it or not. It's there, all right. Me and Cleo have us one in the oven. We're smuggling a watermelon. We're knocked up, preggers, in a family way. Whatever you call it, we're *pregnant!*"

She glanced again into the mirror, grinning from ear to ear, speaking to Cleopatra's unborn child. "And you aren't any ordinary baby, are you? No siree! You're the kid who's going to be joint ruler of both the Roman and Egyptian empires. Wow!"

Spreading her fingers across her stomach, she stared down. "Hey, Little Caesar, you in there? Can you hear me? This is your other mother talking to you. You can rest easy, baby. I won't let you down. I know your daddy's going to have to go back to Rome soon and your real mom's always got her hands full running Egypt. But I'll always be there for you. I love kids! You and I will have a great time, just the two of us. Wait and see. I'll teach you nursery rhymes and read you neat books like *The Cat in the Hat.* We'll rent all the Disney videos and watch them together."

Pia frowned in thought. "Wonder if Darius can figure out a way to transport the television set and the VCR?"

Darius! Where could he be? Pia glanced at the clock. He'd been gone quite a while. She began to having a creeping suspicion that he wouldn't be back in time for their picnic lunch.

The trip back to ancient Egypt was rough. Darius got the words to his incantation mixed up. He missed his mark and landed too soon. After the clouds and ancient dust cleared he found himself plastered to the side of the capstone at the very top of the great pyramid of Khufu at Giza. He held on for dear life, gasping for breath. One slip now and he'd be a goner.

Far below he spotted a group of men in uniform scurrying

about like ants. He yelled down at them for help. It was no use. They all appeared to be busy at some important task that involved a large black object. He squinted in the bright sunlight trying to make it out. A cannon? But how could that be?

A moment later, he realized who they were and what was going on. He watched in horror as Napoleon's drunken French troops fired their big gun and blew the nose off the Sphinx.

"You dumb bastards!" he yelled, shaking his fist at the soldiers. "Don't you have any respect for history?"

That move nearly cost Darius his life. His other hand slipped and he found himself sliding down the rocky face of the pyramid, caroming off sharp edges and bouncing off hard surfaces. Quickly, in mid fall, he revised his incantation, screaming the words aloud as he hurtled toward certain doom. An instant before he would have met his death on the desert floor four hundred and eighty feet below, he found himself once more soaring through time and space. His whole body ached with bruises and abrasions, but what a relief to be airborne again!

By the activity Darius spied in the Great Harbor as he flew into Cleopatra's Egypt, he could pinpoint the year exactly. Shipbuilders and laborers far more numerous than Napoleon's bunch of vandals swarmed like bees along the shore. He spotted a great, golden barge and knew immediately that the year was 48 B.C. and that Cleo was getting ready to take Caesar on the cruise of a lifetime up the Nile.

Without further mishap, Darius made a smooth landing inside the palace, in the very chamber that had been his quarters before the Romans arrived. His room was high in one of the towers, from which he could see out over Pharos and both harbors. All of his things were undisturbed. Even the ewer of his favorite wine from Lesbos had been filled by Cleopatra's servants. He went straight for it.

The looking glass over his carved onyx basin showed clearly the damage done by flight, fall, and pyramid. He winced at the sight of himself. He had a black eye with a deep gash over it. His arms and hands were crisscrossed with scrapes. His chest, bare when he'd left St. Simons, looked like so much raw meat. Carefully, he washed the desert dust from his wounds, sipping wine all the while to dull the pain.

Having bathed, he donned his old costume—white linen kilt and leopard-skin cape. If he did run into Cleo, his pride dictated that he look presentable.

He grinned at his battered, but svelte, image in the mirror. "Hell! Who are you kidding? You want to look so good you'll make her wish she never met that Roman bastard! Eat your heart out, Cleo! Your *real* lover's back!"

A sudden stab of guilt shot through him. He was here to retrieve Pia's cat, nothing more. Pia was the love of his life now. It didn't matter that she was nearly two thousand years away. He'd promised to be faithful and he would be.

"Get the damn cat, then head home," he reminded himself sternly as he strode out of his chamber.

He paused in the corridor long enough to open the can of tuna-and-egg. "Yuck! This stuff stinks."

Holding the open tin far away from him and calling softly, "Here, kitty, kitty," Darius skulked through the halls of the palace, trying to avoid human contact. Before long his bait began to work. Like stealthy shadows, long, elegant felines fell in behind him, yowling impatiently, demanding to be fed.

He turned and tried to shoo them. "Scat! Go 'way. This isn't for you. Go find a crocodile to munch on." Then louder, "Xander? Where are you? Kitty, kitty? Here, cat!"

The odd behavior of the palace cats soon drew human attention. Cleopatra had been enjoying her afternoon nap with Xander stretched out beside her and a dozen other palace pets purring on her couch. As one, the animals rose, pricked their ears, twitched their whiskers, then departed her chamber.

A shiver went through Cleopatra. The odd behavior of animals—especially cats—often presaged disaster. Earthquake, flood, tempest—cats sensed catastrophe coming before any human could guess. She rose from her couch, slipped a silk robe over her nakedness, and followed.

Even over the meowing of three dozen cats, Darius heard footsteps coming his way. He hurried around a corner, hoping to hide from whoever was approaching. The cats, however, followed him step for step, giving him away.

"Scat!" he whispered angrily. "Get out of here!"

Just then, with the footsteps drawing ever nearer, Darius spotted Xander in the squirming mass of buff and brown fur. Quickly, he scooped Pia's pet up with one hand. He could go now. He let Xander have a quick taste of the food, then sent the can flying down the long corridor, the other cats in hot pursuit. He was halfway through his incantation when Cleopatra came around the corner.

"Darius!" she cried, her pleasure at the sight of him obvious. "I thought you had vanished." She frowned. "Why, you're injured!"

"It's nothing. I just fell down some stairs."

"Then you never left the palace?"

"Well, sort of," he answered, clutching the wriggling Xander, who added fresh wounds to his already mangled body. "But I had to come back for something. I'm not staying, though."

Cleo glanced down the hallway at the mass of gluttonous felines. "Why have you charmed all my cats?"

"I didn't mean to bring all of them. I only wanted this one." Xander hissed at him ferociously.

"But I adore that cat. He's my favorite." Cleopatra reached

out for Xander and he tried to go into her arms, but Darius held him fast.

"I told you before, he belongs to a friend of mine. I have to take him home. I'm sorry, Cleopatra, but you won't miss him with all these others."

Cleo put her hands on her hips and stamped her foot. "Are you telling *me,* the Queen of Egypt, that I cannot have something I want?"

Darius chuckled. She sounded exactly like Pia.

Cleopatra had had her arms folded over her midsection while they talked. When she shifted that position, he got a good look at all of her for the first time. His gaze went directly to the swell of her belly. Judging her to be about six months gone, he nodded slightly toward her ample midsection. "Looks to me like you got what you wanted, Cleopatra. Caesar's I assume?"

She smiled and caressed her stomach. "You assume correctly. Little Caesar, the future emperor of Egypt and Rome. I am about to be the mother of the greatest ruler the world has ever known. Greater even than Alexander."

Darius felt a pang of sympathy for Cleopatra. She was absolutely glowing as she spoke of her unborn child. He knew in that moment why humans aren't allowed to know the future. Would she be so happy if she knew now that Caesar would never marry her officially, that they would never rule together, and that her bastard child would not live long enough to rule anything? If he told her the truth now, perhaps she could change things. But, no. Messing around with history was cheating.

"Tell me about the future," Cleopatra said as if she'd read his thoughts.

Darius shook his head, more tempted than she would ever guess to do just that. "I can't, Cleopatra," he answered softly.

"Not *all* the future, Darius. Only tell me if I am truly carrying Caesar's son. He longs for an heir so desperately.

I have slept little these past weeks worrying that I might bear him a daughter."

Darius thought for a minute. He smiled at her. "Rest easy, my queen," he whispered. "You carry the Roman's son."

Cleopatra glowed at his words. "Oh, Darius, I know now that I was not wrong to fish you from the sea. I loved you so much for so long. You know why I had to send you away. I want you to know, too, that I will love you as long as our spirits live. We'll be together again, I promise you. Not in this life, but someday, somewhere, we'll find each other again. We will be different people, but we will recognize each other. We will know, and we will fall in love all over again."

"I know you speak the truth, Cleopatra. I know it in my heart of hearts." He leaned down and kissed the tiny queen, the love of his life in this time just as she would be— through Pia—in the distant future. "Now I must go."

"One more question," she begged. "Only a wizard can tell me. For months I had the strangest experiences. It was as if another side of my soul had come alive. She had her own voice, her own being. She spoke to me. At times she chastised me. Yet she helped me, too. But now this voice, this other part of me is gone. I feel so very alone at times. What could account for this?"

Pia, of course, was to account for it, but Darius would have had a difficult time explaining time-travel to Cleopatra, so he answered her with a question. "Did this voice of yours vanish at about the same time you knew you were carrying your son?"

Cleo frowned in thought for a moment. She smiled. She glowed. "Why, yes!"

"I would guess that your son has filled you so that there is no room for this other being. The voice you heard has been silenced by your child. You have no further need of her advice or her prodding. You have accomplished your goal."

"Yes! That must be the answer!" she cried happily. "Surely, it is. And surely you are the wisest man on earth, Darius."

He grinned. *I told you, Pia!* he said to himself. To Cleopatra he said, "I hear you are planning a trip."

The queen's frown returned. She nodded. "Yes. I must keep Caesar here until his son is born and he can acknowledge him as his legal and rightful heir. His barren wife and the people of Rome would have him return immediately, but Caesar thirsts to see the glories of Egypt before he departs. I plan a long, leisurely cruise up the Nile to keep him amused. No Pharaoh ever possessed a royal ship like the *Thalameyos.* Caesar will have music, dancing girls, actors, banquets, anything his heart, his belly, or his lusty nature could desire. Anything to make him forget for the moment that I am not the lovely creature who once played in his bed. As much as Caesar longs for a son, I can tell that he finds Little Caesar's mother ponderous and unlovely at present."

Darius thought he saw tears in Cleopatra's beautiful Nile green eyes. He touched her cheek and lifted her gaze to his. "You could never be *unlovely,* my queen. You are the most beautiful woman in the world. The child you carry gives you a special glow—brighter even than the Pharos on a moonless night."

She smiled through her tears. "Was there ever another like you in my life, dear Darius?"

"I hope not," he whispered. "Think of me, won't you? Now, I must go before Caesar comes searching for his future bride."

It was only a small lie, Darius told himself. And it made Cleopatra happy. As he spoke the proper words over his crystal and was whisked away in time, his last vision of Cleopatra was her radiant, joyous smile.

Darius blew back in on the breeze at high tide. After over twenty-four hours at her computer, working at fever pitch while she waited for Darius to return, Pia was bent over Edgar Allan, neck cramped, shoulders aching. Finding her that way, Darius couldn't resist. As he had done the first time he came to her cottage, he sneaked up behind her and placed a hand on her shoulder.

She let out a yelp that could have been heard across the island. When she whirled around, her fear turned instantly to soul-deep relief.

"Darius, you scared the hell out of me!" Then she started to cry. "Oh, darling, I was so worried about you."

She was in his arms, kissing him instantly. Xander, ruffled and dusty from their flight, leaped out of his captor's arms and went to his favorite window sill to groom himself.

"I was *so* worried!" Pia repeated between quick, passionate kisses. "What took you so long? Look at you!" She stared at his battered face. "What on earth happened, darling?"

"A slight miscalculation. I ran into a pyramid. But don't worry. Nothing's broken. Nothing but the poor Sphinx's nose."

"What?"

He chuckled. "Never mind. I'll tell you all about it later. Come here! I missed you, sweetheart."

Pia didn't know why, but time-traveling always got Darius all hot and bothered. He did look mighty tempting in that short linen kilt and his leopard skin. But she had news to tell first. News that she was fairly bursting to share.

"Darius," she said, holding him at arm's length, "you'll never guess what's happened."

"Don't make me guess," he pleaded. "Just tell me, Pia."

IF YOU LOVE READING MORE OF TODAY'S BESTSELLING HISTORICAL ROMANCES.... WE HAVE AN OFFER FOR YOU!

*L*OOK INSIDE TO SEE HOW YOU CAN GET 4 FREE HISTORICAL ROMANCES BY TODAY'S LEADING ROMANCE AUTHORS!

4 BOOKS WORTH UP TO $23.96, ABSOLUTELY FREE!

4 BESTSELLING HISTORICAL ROMANCES BY YOUR FAVORITE AUTHORS CAN BE YOURS, FREE!

Kensington Choice, our newest book club now brings you historical romances by your favorite bestselling authors including Janelle Taylor, Shannon Drake, Rosanne Bittner, Jo Beverley, and Georgina Gentry, just to name a few! Each book is filled with passion, adventure and the excitement of bygone times!

To introduce you to this great new club which is part of Zebra Home Subscription Service, we'd like to send you your first 4 bestselling historical romances, absolutely free! And once you get these 4 free books to savor at home, we'll rush you the next 4 brand-new books at the lowest prices available, as soon as they are published.

The way the club works is that after your initial FREE shipment, you will get our 4 newest bestselling historical romances delivered to your doorstep each month at the preferred subscriber's rate of only $4.20 per book, a savings of up to $7.16 per month (since these titles sell in bookstores for $4.99-$5.99)! All books are sent on a 10-day free examination basis and there is no minimum number of books to buy. (And no charge for shipping.) Plus as a regular subscriber, you'll receive our FREE monthly newsletter, *Zebra/Pinnacle Romance News*, which features author profiles, contests, subscriber benefits, book previews and more!

So start today by returning the FREE BOOK CERTIFICATE provided. We'll send you 4 FREE BOOKS with no further obligation: A FREE gift offering you hours of reading pleasure with no obligation...how can you lose?

We have 4 FREE BOOKS for you as your introduction to KENSINGTON CHOICE! To get your FREE BOOKS, worth up to $23.96, mail the card below.

FREE BOOK CERTIFICATE

Yes! Please send me 4 Kensington Choice (the best of Zebra and Pinnacle Books) Historical Romances without cost or obligation (worth up to $23.96). As a Kensington Choice subscriber, I will then receive 4 brand-new romances to preview each month for 10 days FREE. I can return any books I decide not to keep and owe nothing. The publisher's prices for Kensington Choice romances range from $4.99-$5.99, but as a preferred subscriber I will get these books for only $4.20 per book or $16.80 for all four titles. There is no minimum number of books to buy and I may cancel my subscription at any time, plus there is no additional charge for postage and handling. No matter what I decide to do, my first 4 books are mine to keep, absolutely FREE!

KF0596

Name _____

Address _____ Apt. _____

City _____ State _____ Zip _____

Telephone (____) _____

Signature _____

(If under 18, parent or guardian must sign)

Subscription subject to acceptance. Terms and prices subject to change.

4 FREE
Historical Romances

*are waiting
for you to
claim them!*

(worth up to
$23.96)

*See details
inside....*

AFFIX
STAMP
HERE

KENSINGTON CHOICE
Zebra Home Subscription Service, Inc.
120 Brighton Road
P.O.Box 5214
Clifton, NJ 07015-5214

"Okay! *I'm pregnant!* Isn't that wonderful?"

He glanced at her flat stomach, encased in very tight shorts. "You're kidding!"

"No! I swear it! Cleo and I are going to have Caesar's baby."

He nodded, not the least surprised. "She is. You aren't."

"Of course I am! You told me yourself that I'm Cleo reincarnated. So if she's pregnant, I am, too."

He shook his head. "It doesn't work that way, Pia. If you were still inside her, then you would be pregnant, too. But from the size of her when I went back, I don't think she has room for you any longer."

Pia's eyes went wide. "You mean that much time had passed? She's showing?"

"She's *enormous!* Six months gone at least."

"Then I have to get back! Right away!"

"That's crazy, Pia! You can't go back there now."

"I'd like to know why not! I mean to be there when Caesarion is born."

"I don't think you'd enjoy that. Take a look at this." Darius walked over to Pia's bookcase and pulled out a shabby, old reference book, *Devils, Drugs, and Doctors*. He opened it to the very first page. "Feast your eyes on this, love."

Pia stared silently at the line-drawn illustration, captioned BIRTH OF CLEOPATRA'S CHILD. It showed six women and a baby. Cleopatra knelt in the middle of the group with one woman holding the queen's arms above her head. Three of the servants appeared to be lending only moral support while the sixth figure pulled the exceedingly large child out of the queen.

"Doesn't look like much fun to me," Darius observed. "No hospital, no doctor, no anesthesia. Just hang on for dear life and *do it!* And that's one *big* baby!"

"But you didn't read what it says," Pia accused. "His size denotes his royal personage. And they probably didn't do it that way. This is only an illustration, a bas-relief from the Temple of Esneh, it says. And look down here at the bottom of the page. It says, 'At the height of the Egyptian civilization and again at the height of the Greek and Roman civilizations the art of caring for the child-bearing woman was well developed.' Besides, Cleo has all that poppy juice and wine that she uses to dull pain."

"I still say you shouldn't go. What about your book? Besides, Cleo and Caesar are about to take off up the Nile."

"In the golden barge?" Pia cried excitedly. "Well, I certainly have to be there for that."

Darius accepted defeat, done in by his own big mouth. "When do you want to leave?" he asked resignedly.

Pia eased her arms up around his neck and snuggled close. "Not until after we've had our picnic supper on the beach, darling. It's the Fourth of July—time to celebrate. We'll watch the fireworks out over the water while we cuddle on a blanket. Tomorrow should be soon enough to go back, don't you think?"

Darius's spirits sank as he thought ahead to at least three months of celibacy. Cleopatra had made it clear that she was no longer sharing Caesar's bed, so she certainly wouldn't dare let Darius near her. And with Pia back inside the queen, he wouldn't be able to make love to her either.

"You'll come with me, won't you, darling?" Pia asked. "I'd be afraid to travel alone. You can be Cleo's wigmaker again."

"Oh, no! I'll go with you, but I think I'd better assume a less initimate position under the circumstances. Maybe I'll be an oarsman on the ship—work off some of my frustrations. You ready to hit the beach now?"

Pia giggled. "You can't go like that, Darius! What would people think?"

He'd forgotten he was still wearing his kilt and leopard skin. "I'll be right with you."

When Darius came out of the bathroom, Pia caught her breath. He was wearing the tiny, European-style bathing suit that he knew turned her on. Never taking her eyes from his body, Pia slipped off her shirt, then stepped out of her shorts. She, too, was bikini clad.

"I wanted to be ready for the beach when you got back," she whispered.

He wrapped one strong arm around her waist and drew her close, bare flesh to bare flesh. Pia sighed and gave a little shiver.

"God, you feel good!" she moaned.

His hands played over her breasts before sliding down her bare hips. He hooked one finger in the elastic low on her belly and teased the flesh beneath the stretchy, hot-pink fabric.

"You keep that up and we'll never make it to the beach," she warned.

He leaned down and kissed her ear. "You want fireworks, fireworks you get," he said in a rush of hot breath.

Clinging to each other, they headed for the beach. Pia knew a secluded spot in the dunes, sheltered all around by thick bay and palmetto scrubs. As starlike explosions of red, white, and blue fireworks lit the heavens, Pia and Darius created their own brilliant Fourth of July display on their blanket in the dunes.

Never had Darius made love to her so thoroughly, so hungrily, so magnificently. He needed no singing crystals to set her body on fire tonight. Each touch, each kiss was new and different and so exciting that tears came to her eyes.

When they finally reached the heights, then settled back to earth in a euphoric haze, Darius leaned down and kissed Pia softly. "Rest now," he said. "Then we'll go back to the house."

"Yes," Pia answered. "We need to get a good night's sleep before our trip tomorrow."

"No way," he answered in a voice husky with passionate intent. "I'm not nearly through with you yet."

And he certainly wasn't!

Chapter Twelve

Pia woke early after sleeping only two hours. She sat up in bed and rubbed her eyes, trying to think what was so important about this particular day. Surely there was something. She felt alive with excitement, her nerves zinging with anticipation.

Her gaze fell on her lover's face. "Darius," she murmured, not to wake him but simply because his name tasted so sweet on her lips. He lay partially covered by the sheet, his strong body gleaming golden in the first rays of the sun, his beautiful face relaxed, almost smiling.

"We're going back, my darling," she whispered. "Back to have a baby."

The full impact of her intentions hit her after she climbed out of bed. She would have to make plans and arrangements quickly. Her first order of business was to change the message on her answering machine. She had to say something that would placate her editor, keep her friends away, and satisfy her dad if he should call. After some thought, she spoke slowly and distinctly into the recorder. "This is Olympia Byrd. I'm sorry I can't take your call right now, but I'm racing a deadline on the great American novel. Try me again in a week."

She only hoped a week would be long enough to take a three-month cruise up the Nile, return to Alexandria, then bear Caesar's son. "Nothing to it!" she said. "Piece of cake!"

Xander-the-Cat posed a bigger problem. She was afraid to take him back to Egypt. Cleopatra had grown far too fond of Pia's pet. And besides, she kept remembering the sight of all those mummified cats on PBS.

I'll call Linda at Animal House, Pia decided. She'll look after Xander for me.

By the time Darius woke up, Linda had stopped by for Xander, breakfast was ready, and Pia was dressed and packed for her trip. She'd decided to take along a backpack this time with a few essentials. After some thought, she took out the carton of cigarettes. She'd gone without them last time. This time she didn't want to smoke because of the baby.

"Poor little fellow's going to have a hard enough time as it is."

"What did you say?" Darius called from the bathroom.

"Nothing, darling. Just talking to myself. Want some coffee?"

Darius sauntered out of the bathroom looking dewy-fresh from his shower. He was wearing the pleated linen kilt from Egypt. Pia gave him a wolf whistle.

He scowled at her. "You'd better cut that out. Fun time's over if you want to get back inside Cleo anytime today." Then he brightened. "Or have you changed your mind?"

Pia shook her head determinedly. "No, I haven't! I have to go back, Darius. The Nile cruise and Caesarion's birth are a major part of the story. I need to experience everything."

Pia carried a plate of muffins and the coffee pot out to the porch. The day was going to be a scorcher, but the tide was coming in so there was a stiff breeze. Darius followed her. He reached for a warm, poppyseed muffin as soon as she set them down.

"Tell me something," he said seriously. "What are you going to do for excitement after you finish this book? You won't need to go back to Egypt. What will you do with yourself?"

Pia shrugged. "Write another book, I guess. Maybe something a little less ambitious." She turned and smiled at him. "I'd like to have more time to myself. More time to spend with you. You will stay, won't you?"

"Is that a serious invitation, sweetheart?"

"About as serious as they come. If you haven't figured it out by now, I love you, Darius. I don't know how I'd go on without you."

He reached over and caressed her bare knee. "Do I even need to say that I feel the same way?" He gave her a slow, warm smile, his eyes sparking gold. Then his expression changed until he was almost frowning. "It's going to be hard, though."

"What do you mean? Love should make life easy for us."

"I'm a nobody here. I don't exist. No birth certificate, no Social Security number. How will I explain all that? You've got to have a number to be a real citizen in this day and age."

Pia thought hard, but couldn't come up with any quick answers. "Don't worry, darling. We'll cross that bridge when we come to it."

They held hands in silence as they finished their breakfast. The sound of the waves and the swaying of the sea oats hypnotized them both, as did the wonder of their feelings for each other, the perfect contentment of simply being in love.

Pia broke the spell at last. "I think we'd better get on with it, darling. You have the crystals?"

Darius produced the twin stones. They shared one final,

lingering kiss. When their lips parted, he said, "Ready, my love?"

She nodded and held her breath, gripping her backpack in one hand. Darius slipped his arm about her waist. They touched the crystals together. A great flash of sparks engulfed them. The next moment they found themselves hurtling through dark, empty space.

Pia landed with a whoosh and a plop, still clinging to her backpack and her half of the crystal pyramid. She shoved the stone inside the bag, then quickly dropped it to the floor and shoved it behind a wide column.

Cleopatra awoke with a start. She caressed her belly with her hands. "By all the gods, you are an active child, Little Caesar. That was quite a kick."

Pia knew immediately where she was by the tight fit of Cleo's petite form. Once more she had to suck in her body to make it fit. She took shallow breaths, trying to become acclimated again. Once she became accustomed to her tight confines, she realized that she could sense changes in Cleo's body. The queen's back ached, her ankles felt swollen, and the gentle rocking of the great, golden barge made her slightly ill. Yet there was a new softness to the queen's character. Now that Cleo was carrying Caesar's baby, Pia sensed a total, unselfish love that had not been a part of Cleo's nature before.

Mother love! she realized.

Gathering her wits, Pia looked about to see exactly where she was. She was lying on a wide golden bed in what appeared to be a Greek temple. Exquisite marble columns stood at intervals around the silk-covered walls of pearl-pale blue. The ceiling was painted with figures of gods all kneeling before Aphrodite, the goddess of love. Pia stared at the glowing face above her. The artist had copied Cleopatra's form and countenance exactly. And why not? After all, she was certainly Julius Caesar's love goddess.

Iras entered the chamber after knocking softly. "He is up and about already, my lady, bedeviling your scholars with questions only a wizard could answer."

The *he* the servant mentioned was obviously Julius Caesar. But Iras's mention of a wizard was what caught Pia's attention. She wondered where Darius was. She'd have to check out the oarsmen later and see if she could spot him.

Cleopatra sighed and struggled to rise. "I had hoped Caesar would relax and enjoy himself on this trip. Yet he keeps his mind and his body busy from dawn till long past dark. Help me up, Iras. I should join him."

"You need rest," the maid protested.

Cleopatra gave her a scorching look. "I need *Caesar!*" she snapped. "He will think me weak if I loll about in bed all day. Besides, this child needs exercise and fresh air if he is to be born strong and healthy."

Right on! Pia commented.

Cleopatra heard the voice inside her and smiled. "So, you have returned," she said softly. "I have missed you."

Well, I can't say I've exactly missed you, Pia answered, *but I wouldn't have missed this trip for the world. Nice boat!*

The queen smiled her pleasure at the compliment.

And I see we're pregnant. A boy, too. Caesar will be busting his buttons.

"I beg your pardon?" the queen said.

Just an expression. I mean he'll be proud.

"Already he struts like a cock."

Iras was watching Cleopatra closely, wondering who she could be talking to. Isis, no doubt. Or perhaps even the Greek goddess she had begun to worship. Knowing that it wouldn't do to interrupt her mistress's prayers, Iras kept silent and pretended not to hear.

Pia was relieved to find that now, so heavily pregnant,

Cleopatra had changed her wardrobe. No more bare belly and breasts. With Iras's help she donned a flowing, multilayered robe of sapphire silk that billowed like clouds about her ample figure. At her throat she wore a delicate, hammered gold necklace set with sparkling stones. To that magnificence she added rings, bracelets, and her asp crown.

"My people must be able to see me from the shore," she said. "When the sun lights my golden baubles, they will know who is passing on the Nile."

Moments later, Cleopatra swept out of the room and up on deck to a landscaped garden under a gold and purple-striped awning. Caesar sat at a low table, sipping wine and nibbling honeyed dates.

He rose as the queen approached. "My dear," he said brightly, "how is our son this morning?"

"Ready to climb the great pyramids at Giza, it seems. The boy has a healthy tread for one so young."

Motioning away a gaggle of eager servants, Caesar himself arranged the soft, silk cushions at Cleopatra's back and helped her settle on the couch beside his.

"May I pour you some wine?" he offered.

Oh, God! Not this early in the day, Pia moaned. *You shouldn't even be drinking while you're pregnant, you know.*

Ignoring Pia's complaints, Cleo accepted the large goblet Caesar offered. The drink was thick and sweet, giving Pia a kick like the Purple Jesus her friends mixed up at beach parties back on St. Simons. Before long she felt herself dropping off in a doze as Cleo and J.C. chatted about crops, flooding, irrigation canals, and the rising price of camels.

By the time Pia woke, the sun was directly overhead, a blazing eye in the sky. Pia gave herself a good shake. She needed to stay awake and alert. Find Darius! she told herself.

Cleopatra turned slightly to let the slave fanning her know that she was addressing him. "The sails have gone slack. Summon the oarsmen."

Passing the great peacock feather fan to another waiting slave, the giant Nubian dashed away to do the queen's bidding. Instantly, a line of muscled men, burned nearly black by the sun, marched up on deck carrying silver oars.

There he is! Pia cried excitedly.

Darius met Pia's gaze, offered the barest hint of a relieved smile, then quickly looked away. It would not do for a slave to be caught staring directly at the queen.

Pia's relief was so great that she didn't even fuss when Cleo quaffed down another cup of wine. What was one more drink when her head was already swimming? She allowed herself to relax and take in the sights.

The great barge, *Thalameyos,* which Pia knew from her research was three hundred feet long, forty-five feet at the beam, rising sixty feet above the water, was no less than a floating palace. Circling it and following it, a whole fleet of four hundred galleys and smaller boats carried entertainers, chefs, scholars, even men from Caesar's Roman legions. The watery gathering gave the appearance of an entire flotilla. Pia suddenly remembered stories she'd read in old movie magazines about Elizabeth Taylor's entourage when traveling to make a film version of the life of Cleopatra. Liz's trunks, pets, maids, and lovers couldn't hold a candle to the real Cleo's enormous assemblage.

They sailed grandly up the Nile while peasants gathered along the emerald-green shoreline to wave and bow, paying homage to their queen. In the brown distance of the desert beyond, Pia could make out faint outlines of ancient temples, tombs, and statues.

"This is an amazing land," Caesar said. "Your riches must be boundless."

Cleopatra laughed. "Hardly that," she said. "Rome has taken a toll in tribute."

He reached over and gripped her hand, his dark eyes glistening like polished obsidian. "But think about it, my love. Should we manage to combine the wealth of Egypt and Rome, we could easily gain all the riches of the world."

Cleo only smiled sweetly, but Pia felt the queen's heart leap with joy to hear Caesar voice her exact plans.

During the deadly midday heat of spring, the queen and her Roman retired to cooler quarters below decks. First they strolled to a dim, mosaic chapel dedicated to Aphrodite and Dionysos. There the two rulers made a small sacrifice of grain, honey, and wine. Assured of their protection by the gods for the rest of the day, they retired to Caesar's bedchamber, a virtual work of art, depicting friezes of scenes from the *Iliad.*

"Won't you lie for a time and rest, my dearest?" Caesar invited.

Oh, Lord! Pia exclaimed. *What's he up to now? We're too far along to be fooling around.*

Cleo intercepted Pia's message of concern before it escaped her smiling, painted lips. "Why, thank you, Caesar. I am a bit weary."

Cleopatra beached herself on the bed like a beautiful whale. Immediately, Caesar loosened his girdle and stretched out beside her, then leaned down and kissed her. One hand crept to her swollen breast.

"Ah, I do miss you so," he murmured between kisses. "At night my chamber is as dark and lonely as Hades without you, my little dove."

This brought a giggle from Pia that Cleo didn't quite catch in time. She did explain the amusement to the puzzled Roman. "Now I know you truly care for me. Only a lover could look on such a shape and still call me his 'little dove.' " She slipped her hand around his neck and brought his mouth down to her breast. Pia trembled as she felt his tongue slide over the layers of silk, teasing the taut nipple through her gown. But he went no further with his lovemaking. He seemed content to lie with the queen and hold her, kissing her parted lips from time to time before returning to her breasts.

"Soon our trip will be done and our son will arrive," Cleopatra said dreamily. "Will you claim him as your own, great Caesar? Or shall my poor child be only another royal bastard?"

He half rose and stared into her turquoise eyes. "You are my *wife!*" he declared in his most imperious tone.

The word sent a shiver of hope through the queen. Pia sensed it.

"By what authority, dear Caesar?"

"My own!" he assured her with some force. "For the good of the State, before I departed Rome to come here, I had my tribune, Helvius Cinna, draw up a decree to present to the people. It legitimizes my marriage to any woman or women of my choice for the procreation of children. So, you see, Cleopatra, we have been married since the first night I took you to my bed."

Pia could tell that Cleo felt like hopping up and dancing around the room. Only propriety and pregnancy kept her from doing so.

The queen trod carefully on the next ground she covered. "What of your Roman wife? Was she instantly divorced once you bedded me?"

"Of course not!" Caesar looked at her as if she'd gone mad. "What would the people think if I deserted my faithful Calpurnia to marry a foreign queen? As I said, the decree grants me the right to have more than one wife, if I choose. After all, you have another husband."

"My brat of a baby brother!" Cleo hissed, obviously as displeased with that match as she had been with the one with the older Ptolemy. "He is nothing to me but a bother."

"Yet useful in his way, Cleopatra. Never forget that. He is too young and sickly ever to threaten you. Still, he is your co-ruler as your father's will dictated, so no other can seek the position. When the time is right, he will be removed so that you and I can rule together without interference."

Pia knew instantly that those were exactly the promises Cleo had been trying to coax out of Caesar since the first time they made love. The queen kept a careful check on her outward expression, but inside she was glowing, doing cartwheels, flying high.

"This is a special occasion, my husband. Shall we celebrate our secret union with a grand feast and entertainment tonight?"

Caesar leaned down and kissed her tenderly. "Every moment with you is a special occasion, my wife. You are my love, my treasure, my life."

The bald guy was lying through his teeth, and Pia knew it. He loved himself first, power second, and the idea of having a son third. Cleo came somewhere farther down on his list. Still, he obviously found her alluring and amusing. And most important of all, he was awed by her power and her wealth. So it seemed everybody was telling a few fibs. But what the . . . Hay! Pia thought. As long as it's all in the family.

"Let's celebrate now!" Pia cried aloud. Cleo grinned at the unexpected words that came out of her mouth. "In grand style!" the queen added.

That night was made for love. A full moon turned the green verge of the Nile silver. A million stars twinkled overhead. Every few moments one of those brilliant heavenly bodies would fly across the sky, leaving a shining trail in its wake.

Cleopatra and Caesar, both dressed in cloth-of-gold banquet robes, reclined on their couches, a feast spread on the low ebony table between them. Torches blazed. Slaves stood in the shadows as silent as ghosts, fanning their masters, replenishing wine, removing platters to bring on more. All of Egypt seemed filled with perfume and music. Lovely, dark slave women dressed in scanty costumes made of leopard skin writhed and slithered around Caesar. One offered him more wine. A second dancer undraped her breast for him to fondle.

He glanced toward Cleopatra. She smiled and nodded. "Do as you will with them. They are for your pleasure now and later, if you wish."

The lusty Roman laughed heartily as he stroked the great, purple nipple.

A third dancer, feigning rage, threw the second girl aside, then tore off her own leopard skin to dance suggestively before Caesar in the buff. Still laughing, he made a grab for her. He caught her about the waist and pulled her down to his couch. For a moment Pia felt Cleo's jealousy flame. But Caesar only teased the sexy dancer a bit, then sent her on her way. A moment later, the three dancers performed a mock catfight, to Caesar's delight. They hissed and scratched and pulled one another's hair, putting on such a convincing performance that he finally ordered a jug of wine to be thrown on them to cool them down before they did real damage.

Jugglers followed, then fire-eaters, then actors in a comic play. All the while, musicians strolled the decks and singers filled the air with song. The best way Pia could describe all this was as an ancient, floating Disney World.

It was far into the night before Caesar and Cleopatra retired to their separate chambers. Neither Pia nor Cleo missed the Roman's signal to the naked, wine-spattered leopard-dancer. She smiled and tossed a look of triumph at the other two.

Both Pia and Cleo were exhausted by the time they reached the goddess chamber. Iras helped the queen bathe quickly, then assisted her into bed. She was asleep almost instantly. Pia had to force herself to stay awake, but she had to see Darius while she was in full control. Once Iras realized her mistress was fast asleep, she, too, went to her quarters, leaving Pia alone. Slowly, carefully, Pia rose from the bed.

Surely, Caesar must be sleeping by now, and no one else on the ship would dare question the queen if she wished to take a late-night stroll about her ship. At least, that was what Pia hoped.

Stealthily, she tiptoed out of the chamber. No one was about at this hour. She retraced the steps to the upper deck. Her heart sank when she saw that the ship was under sail again with no oarsmen at their posts.

Then I'll have to go below and find him, she told herself.

Clinging to the shadows, Pia made her way down deck after deck until she was in the very bowels of the ship. On the lowest level, she found a guard posted outside a locked door—no doubt where the galley slaves were kept. The place reeked of hard, sweaty bodies. She held a perfumed scarf to her nose.

"Halt!" the guard ordered when he saw someone coming toward him. Then he recognized the queen and bowed low before her. "My lady, forgive me."

"Rise!" she commanded. "Are the oarsmen kept here?"

"They are, my queen, under lock and constant guard. A dangerous lot, more animal than human. But you have nothing to fear. We drug them to keep them docile."

That's just great! Pia thought. Darius probably wouldn't even know who she was.

"There is a man named Darius who arrived on board today. He was to bring vital, secret information to me. I would speak with him." She used Cleo's most imperious tone on the flustered guard.

He bowed again. "Immediately, my queen. I know the man. I will bring him to you."

Pia backed down the passageway to get away from the

stench of the hold. She waited in the shadows for Darius to be brought out. Moments later, he emerged from the darkness. From the blank look on his face, she thought he must be heavily drugged.

"Come with me!" she ordered.

"But, my lady . . ." The guard tried to protest. She silenced him with a wave of her hand.

"I know this man. He will do me no harm."

Darius followed at a respectful distance, his head bowed low. Pia led the way up a narrow stairway to an empty temple-chamber she had noticed earlier.

The moment they entered, Darius rushed toward her and drew her into his arms, as close as he could with Cleo's bulging belly between them. He kissed her gently, not wanting to wake the queen.

"Thank God, you made it all right," he said. "I couldn't tell when I saw Cleo this afternoon. I was too far away to see the color of her eyes."

"I was there. I saw you, Darius. I wanted to do or say something to let you know, but Caesar was so close. Now that we're carrying his son, he watches us like a hawk."

"Damn that bloody Roman!" His temper flared with jealousy.

Pia shushed him. "Keep your voice down, Darius. You'll wake the whole ship."

He reined in his anger and stroked her cheek tenderly. "You were right to keep quiet, darling. But you'll never know how relieved I am to see you now. It's been one helluva night! For all I knew, you were still somewhere out there drifting in space."

"I'm fine, Darius. But what about you? That place stinks to high heaven, and the guard told me they drug all of you at night."

"They tried, but I knew about the poppy juice in the wine.

I gave my cup to another fellow. He's in happy oblivion now."

She drew him close, leaning her head against his chest. "How can you stand it, darling?"

He touched her cheek. "It's not so bad. Now that I know you're okay, I'll drink my poppy wine from now on. Can't hurt. Might help."

"You're sure?"

He nodded. "We've missed half the trip. Tomorrow we'll pass the Sphinx and the pyramids, then go as far as Aswan and the First Cataract. There's no way they can move this huge ship any farther. Besides, I hear Caesar's troops are getting restless. Seems Cleo forgot one little item—enough girls to keep the boys entertained. We'll be back to Alexandria in six weeks or so."

"Six weeks?" Pia cried, tears gathering in her eyes. "Darius, I won't let you do this. Get the crystals and let's get out of here."

"What about your research, darling?"

"To hell with my research!"

"If you're sure. Where's your crystal?"

Pia's heart sank. "Up in Cleo's bedroom. I hid it in my backpack behind a column."

"Damn!" Darius cursed. "I was hoping we might be able to get back with just one."

"What do you mean?" Pia asked, stricken.

"They searched me and took my belongings when I came aboard earlier. The guard said I won't get my stuff back till we return to Alexandria."

Pia's heart was racing so fast she was afraid its thumping might wake Cleopatra. "But they will give it back, even though you're a slave?"

"Well, we aren't exactly slaves. We get paid."

"How much?"

Darius squinted up at the ceiling, trying to convert ancient

Egyptian coinage into U.S. money. "Comes out to around two cents a day, I think."

"Good grief! That's less than romance writers make!"

Darius cupped her face in his blistered hands and gazed into her eyes. "Looks like we're stuck here, honey. At least for the time being. It would be tricky trying to travel on only half the crystal pyramid. You'd better go back now before Cleo wakes up. I'll be all right. Don't worry. Enjoy the cruise."

Pia tried a little laugh, but it died in her throat. "Sure! All the wine I can drink and naked dancing girls, to boot. Meanwhile, you're in that hellhole with a bunch of drugged thugs."

"Go on now. We don't want the guard getting suspicious."

They shared one last tender kiss before parting.

On sudden impulse, Pia followed Darius back down the stairs. When he reached the door to the hold, she said to the guard, "This man has served me well. See that he gets extra rations and all the poppy wine he wants."

"As you wish, my queen." The guard bowed low. When he rose, she was gone.

Back in Cleo's room, Pia checked quickly to make sure her backpack and the crystal were still safely hidden. Knowing that Darius no longer had his half of the stone made her feel utterly stranded, as if she were somewhere like Barrow, Alaska, with no way to get her back home.

She settled herself on the bed and tried to relax. She needed rest. It would be dawn soon and she'd had little or no sleep since the night before she left home. For now, she would simply go with the flow, let Cleo call the shots. What else could she do? The way things stood, she was in the game until the final whistle blew.

"Or until the final asp bite," she murmured drowsily.

For the rest of the night and part of the morning, Pia remained asleep, enduring horrible nightmares of serpents, large and small. There was little in life that frightened her, but the very sight of a snake made her hysterical. Over and over, she dreamed of the last scene of Cleopatra's life—the basket of figs, the slithering body with its poison fangs, and Cleo slumped in death upon her golden throne.

"No! Get away!"

It was mid morning when the terrified exclamations burst from Cleopatra's lips. She covered her mouth quickly and her eyes went wide with fear and embarrassment.

"Whatever is the matter, my dear?" Caesar asked solicitously.

"I'm sorry," she said. "Please forgive my outburst." She patted her stomach and smiled. "This morning he seems restless for some reason. Suddenly, out of nowhere, I saw a great serpent with blazing red eyes."

Caesar glanced about the small, luxurious boat that was carrying them ever nearer the shore, where the pyramids and the brooding Sphinx awaited his inspection. "There are no snakes here, Cleopatra."

She shook her head in puzzlement. "I know that. I have no fear of snakes, or never have before. As I said, it must have been caused by my present condition."

To Cleopatra's relief, Caesar dropped the subject in his eagerness to go ashore. Servants had gone ahead of them before dawn to set up a tent where the queen could rest. Caesar insisted on riding a camel to the ancient ruins. Cleopatra laughed softly at the noble Roman's clumsy efforts to mount his stubborn steed. But finally he seated himself properly. He waved a salute to her as he set off, with his entourage, for his goal.

Cleopatra waited until he was only a speck in the distance before she shooed the servants from her tent.

"I wish to be alone for a time to speak with the goddess," she lied. "Leave me!"

When everyone was out of earshot, Cleo addressed Pia directly. "What is this about a snake?" she demanded.

Pia hesitated, then finally said, *Are you talking to me?*

"Do you see anyone else about? I have no idea who you are or why I continue hearing your voice inside my head. However, I will not have you frightening my child. Was this vision of the red-eyed serpent meant to be some sort of warning? Will the child be threatened by such a creature?"

Not exactly, Pia hedged.

"Then tell me its meaning."

I can't, Pia said.

"You must. I order you to and I am the queen!"

Pia found herself squirming with discomfort. Worse, Little Caesar was kicking the hell out of both of them, making it hard to think. She knew she wasn't supposed to reveal the future to Cleo. Darius had warned her against doing or saying anything that might change the course of history.

"Well? I'm waiting!" Cleo prompted.

Let me just put it to you this way, Pia replied hesitantly, *keep a sharp eye out for snakes. Especially asps.*

Even talking about it made Pia shudder. She knew, though, that Cleo would keep pressing until she had the full truth. To distract her, Pia suggested, *Why don't we have some wine? It's awfully hot and dusty out here on the desert.*

The queen immediately struck the silver gong beside her to bring the servants back.

"Yes, my lady?"

"I wish some wine now."

"In a big cup," Pia added for the servant to hear, aloud in the queen's voice.

A short while later, Pia was blissfully oblivious to the threat of snakes. She lolled about inside Cleo on what seemed a river of cool, white wine from Crete. She would worry about asps when the time came. For now, she would just sip and drift.

Cleopatra's voice cut sharply through Pia's euphoric haze. "You may think I have forgotten all this. I have not! Sooner or later, you are going to tell me the truth about this snake. The *whole* truth, or else!"

With that, Cleo sucked in her breath giving Pia such a vicious squeeze that she all but passed out. Only then did she realize that she would have to be extra careful what she thought and dreamed now that the queen knew of her existence.

Chapter Thirteen

Things were looking up!

Cleo's floating palace approached Alexandria a few weeks later without mishap. For most of the return trip, the queen had been as quiet and docile as a kitten. She was so enormous there was little else she could do. Her time was very near. Pia could feel it.

Since Cleopatra spent so much time in her quarters napping through the unbearable heat of the day, Pia had more chances than she had anticipated to visit with Darius. It was easy enough for her to check the duty roster that came to the queen each morning to find out when the sentry she'd first spoken to would be at his post. Often during mid afternoon or late at night when everyone was sleeping, she would lumber down to the lower decks to be with Darius—"the queen's secret envoy," or so the guard believed.

The night before they arrived in Alexandria, Pia made one of her midnight visits. The moment she and Darius were alone, they went into each other's arms.

After they had embraced and kissed, Pia said, "Tomorrow's the day, darling. At last!"

"It can't come too soon for me," Darius whispered. He stretched his stiff arms and groaned. "I feel like I've rowed a million damn miles."

Pia caressed the rock-hard muscles of his arms. If he had looked strong and handsome before, he looked like a god now. His body had gone beyond golden to a deep, burnished bronze. His long hair and beard held the fire of sun-spun gold. And he had the build of a Greek wrestler. Just looking at him made Pia quiver all over.

"Poor darling," she whispered, resting her head against his hard chest. "I wish there was something I could do. We'll be away from here soon. I'll leave right after the baby comes."

"How about the minute we dock and I get my half of the crystal back?"

"Please, Darius. It won't be much longer. The baby's dropped already."

He narrowed his tiger-eyes at her. "What does that mean?"

"That he's positioning himself to be born."

"But Caesar and Cleopatra got together only eight months ago. Even if the first time was a take, isn't the normal pregnancy nine months?"

Pia laughed softly. Darius obviously wasn't sure how long a woman carried a child before its birth. That seemed a clear indication that he'd been a bachelor—no wife, no children—when she first saw him in Alexandria in 1979.

"Babies don't always take that long, darling. First babies in particular are unpredictable. They're often early or late. I give Cleo another week, max. We can stay that long, can't we?"

Darius shrugged. "I have to stay that long anyway. We were told tonight that after the ship arrives in port, we'll be detained on board to clean it from stem to stern."

"Oh!" Pia cried indignantly. "Can they make you do that?"

"We don't get our belongings returned unless we stay." He offered her a quick, insincere grin. "Nice, huh?"

"That's outrageous! If I were you, I'd protest to the oarsmen's union."

"That 'union' consists of one person—Cleopatra. As the saying goes down in the hold, 'Lodge a protest, lose your head.' "

"She wouldn't do that, would she?" Even as she voiced the question, Pia knew the answer. Cleo was as tough as nails when it came to discipline.

"I'd better get back, sweetheart. So had you. If Cleo wakes up, convince her that she's been sleepwalking."

Pia laughed. "I'm not sure she'll fall for that line again. I'll just tell her I needed to stretch our legs. Now that she knows I'm here and talks to me, things are a little easier. When she gives me trouble, I hint that I might be some sort of demon sent by Ra to keep an eye on her. That always cools her down."

Darius kissed her again—a long, deep kiss that made her think of warm days and starry nights back on St. Simons. "Be careful, darling," he warned. "No telling what you'll find when you get back to the palace tomorrow. Don't let your guard down for a minute. Promise?"

Pia smiled and touched his face. "I promise, Darius. You be careful, too."

It was not Pia or Cleopatra who had a shock the next day, but Caesar. A messenger had arrived with urgent dispatches from the East. King Pharnaces of Pontus had defeated one of Rome's generals in Asia Minor. Caesar meant to leave at once with his troops to quell the rebellion. Cleopatra, however, wouldn't hear of it.

"*Your son,* your *only* heir, is about to be born! How can

you even think of leaving at a time like this? What difference will a few days make? Must I take my own husband prisoner to make him stay for the birth of his child?"

Cleopatra's arguments and threats proved convincing—especially the one about taking him prisoner. Caesar knew she could—and would—do just that if he tried to leave. After giving it some thought, he decided he preferred that his son not see him for the first time in chains. He sent three legions ahead to Asia Minor, promising to join them soon.

His wait proved a short one. Only a few days later, in the first week of July, Cleopatra's water broke. Pia had heard many of her married friends talk endlessly about the pain of childbirth. She thought they exaggerated, taking gleeful pleasure in frightening the uninitiated. That was not so, she found. It seemed Caesarion was a bowling ball and she was the alley.

And he's not a very good bowler, she moaned through one contraction.

To add insult to injury, the line drawing in Dr. Haggard's *Devils, Drugs, and Doctors,* the reference book Darius had found in her library, turned out to be totally accurate. While Cleopatra knelt naked on the floor of her bedchamber, five women gathered around and one old man. At first, Pia thought he must be the physician. She was wrong. He was the head artist from the Museum, come to sketch the details of the birth so that it could later be recorded on a wall in the Temple of Esneh and eventually be reproduced in the research book that would be published in New York in 1929.

Cleopatra herself remained stoic through all the pain. Although Pia begged for poppy wine, the queen refused it, fearful that the drug might harm Caesar's son.

As the late afternoon sun turned its fiery bronze rays on the stifling room, Iras reached out and tugged the baby from Cleopatra. Pia sagged, exhausted, inside the queen as the women bathed the child and wrapped him in clean, white linen. Cleopatra, too, was helped to her bath for a long, refreshing soak before she dressed to receive her child's father.

"Shall I call Caesar now, my lady?" Iras asked, once the queen was in bed with her baby cradled in her arms.

"No, wait!" Cleopatra answered. "Hand me the jewel box from my ebony chest."

Iras did as instructed. Carefully, Cleopatra lifted out a miniature, gilt laurel wreath, an exact copy made by her goldsmiths of the one Caesar always wore. She placed it gently on her son's downy head.

"There," she said. "Now you are ready to meet your father."

Caesar entered the chamber a moment later. He paused at the door, glancing about uncertainly. Although Pia was done in from the ordeal, she remained alert enough to notice that the old Roman looked tired and worried, almost as if he himself had endured the long, painful labor.

"The babe came too early," Caesar said in the barest whisper. "Did he live?"

As if to answer his noble father, the boy-child gave a lusty cry. Caesar's whole countenance brightened. He squared his drooping shoulders. He was smiling as he strode across the room to Cleopatra's couch.

"I give you your son, my husband. Ptolemaeus Caesar, a fine strong heir, a born ruler."

Caesar reached out and fingered the tiny golden leaves encircling the infant's head. He looked at Cleopatra quizzically.

She smiled at him alluringly. "A sign from the gods, to be born with the laurel wreath."

"A sign, indeed!" Caesar proclaimed. "Before I depart for the East, we will appear together so that I may proclaim to all your subjects that this son is my rightful and legal heir, the future ruler of Egypt and Rome."

Caesar and Cleopatra talked on and on about ruling empires and having the priests proclaim their child the fruit of a divine union—a god come down to earth. Pia, on the other hand, saw only a baby. A sweet, small bundle of warmth with deep blue eyes in a face so beautiful it made her want to cry. She longed to hold Little Caesar forever, shelter him and protect him from the dangerous world outside the palace, outside the circle of her love.

Cradling him gently in Cleopatra's arms, Pia sang him a silent lullaby. She was so filled with a mother's love for the infant that she couldn't bear to think of leaving him. Not ever! The bond grew with each hour, each minute. While Caesarion seemed indifferent to his natural mother, he reacted immediately to the slightest word or thought from Pia.

As days passed, she came to feel like Caesarion's real mother. She knew she couldn't bear to leave him here in this foreign land. What would she tell Darius when he came to take her back through time? She didn't know. She only knew that she *must* make him understand.

Caesarion needed her. She couldn't abandon him.

Darius appeared at the palace a few days later, during the queen's regular napping hour, crystal in hand, ready to whisk them home.

"Good! She's sleeping, darling. This is the perfect time for our getaway."

Pia stared at him in shock. "I can't go!" she cried. "Not without my baby!"

"He's *Cleopatra's* baby, Pia," Darius corrected gently.

Pia bristled. "She'll only use him to get what *she* wants. What does she know about being a mother? What does she care about giving her baby the love he needs?"

"What do *you* know about any of that, Pia?" Darius stood

firm with her. "You know what's going to happen to him. It's all in your notes. You shouldn't have let yourself get so attached."

"Knowing his fate is all the more reason for me to stay and make sure he has a happy childhood. Just this morning Cleo threatened to give up nursing him. She's called one of her handmaidens to take over *'that loathsome task,'* as she called it. Poor little thing! He won't know who his mother is any longer."

"We don't have time to argue about this, Pia. Get your half of the crystal and let's go."

Pia was still wavering. She wanted to go home and be with Darius. Once they were back in her world they could get married and have their own baby. But when Caesarion reached up and touched his sleeping mother's cheek, such a strong flood of mother love swept through Pia that tears filled her eyes.

"Pia," Darius warned. "Don't start that. There's no time."

He was certainly right about that! Cleopatra woke up suddenly. She stared directly at her former lover, her turquoise eyes blazing. Then her look softened.

"Darius, my love! You've come back."

"To see your son," he said. "A handsome lad. Caesar is pleased?"

"Delirious with joy!" Cleo answered. "We have such plans now. Caesarion will someday rule the world." She lifted the baby as if she wanted to give Darius a better look. Instead she said, "Take him and put him in the cradle, won't you? He's wet again."

"Don't you want to call one of the maids to change him? I can hide behind the curtain."

Cleo shrugged. "Later, perhaps. Put him over there out of the way."

Caesarion whimpered hungrily when Darius took him.

It's feeding time! Pia screamed silently. *Nurse him, you bitch!*

Cleo only smiled. "Come to me, Darius. I have missed your arms, your touch, your kiss."

Now Pia was thumping mad. Not only was Cleo neglecting the baby, she was trying to seduce Darius, as well.

Darius sensed Pia's rage. "What about Caesar?"

"He's gone away. Some little war in Asia Minor and trouble in Rome as well. Only the gods know when he will return. I have dreamed of you, Darius, all these long months. I ache for you, my dearest."

"But it's too soon, Cleopatra. I don't want to hurt you or do you harm."

"What harm can a kiss do?" she insisted.

Darius was caught between a rock and a hard place. If he refused the queen, she could have him thrown into a dungeon or worse. If he kissed her, Pia was going to be mad as hell.

"What if we're caught?"

Cleopatra beckoned and smiled. "Who would question *my* actions now that Caesar has departed? This is *my* palace, *my* chamber, *my* bed. And *you* are *my* lover for all time."

"I guess I have no choice," he muttered under his breath for Pia's benefit.

He leaned down over Cleo's couch and kissed her on the cheek. She grabbed him around the neck, holding him fast.

"You call *that* a kiss?" she said with a throaty laugh. The queen stroked one hand up his hard thigh to his crotch. Darius moaned in spite of himself. Still fondling him, she traced his salty lips with the tip of her tongue.

"Now tell me you don't want me," she purred.

Darius's mind was getting foggy, but his thoughts remained on Pia. Surely she knew he had no choice in this.

"You are my queen, my only love, *my Olympia,*" he

whispered between kisses. "I want no other. Do you hear me? Do you understand, sweetheart?"

Pia understood. He had never called Cleo "sweetheart." Suddenly she realized how desperately she wanted him, too. And if her body had felt the queen's pain during childbirth, she would also share the pleasure when the queen and Darius made love.

She waited until Cleo parted her lips to give Darius a passionate kiss, then she said, "I do understand! I want you, too, Darius!"

He was smiling when Cleopatra's tongue darted into his mouth. He sucked at it gratefully, tasting Pia as well as Cleo. With nimble fingers, she removed the linen draped about his hips. There was no need for Darius to waste time undressing Cleopatra. Underneath the sky-colored silk of her bed linens, she was completely naked. He slipped the sheet down to uncover her breasts, magnificent in their fullness. She moaned as he kissed her, moving on the couch with sensual rhythm.

Every touch of his hands and lips was like a brand on Pia's flesh. She wanted him *now!* Yet Cleopatra stalled and teased, begging him to return her fondling. He stroked her breasts, her belly, her thighs. With his toes, he scraped the tender soles of her feet. He nibbled her earlobes, her chin, the tip of her nose.

Pia was going crazy! How much more of this could she take?

"Now, lover!" Cleopatra breathed heavily into his ear.

Pia had never felt anything like the sharp, hot pleasure that engulfed her with Darius's first, deep thrust. She begged Cleopatra to hold still. *Just feel him . . . so huge and hot and throbbing! Hold him, caress him, but don't you dare move!*

Uncharacteristically, Cleopatra heeded Pia's words. For long moments, she lay very still. Darius, too, stayed his actions, remaining buried deep inside. Then slowly, ever so slowly, he drew himself out. Cleopatra trembled with pleasure at the long, hot slide of him within her. Again, Darius paused, waiting, counting heartbeats, it seemed.

Cleopatra moaned his name. He covered her open mouth. At the same instant, he gave her a double thrust with tongue and staff. After that, there was no holding anyone back. The three of them climbed to the heights as one—panting, moaning, kissing, riding a winged steed through the sun-blanched heavens.

Pia flew over the rainbow first, followed a few moments later by Cleo. Darius surrendered to ecstasy only after he knew he'd pleased both his lovers.

They lay there for a few minutes, letting themselves drift back to earth, savoring the sweet release and the precious pleasure of the moment.

Darius was the first to speak, his question addressed to either woman who cared to answer. "So, what are we going to do now?"

"You will stay here with me, of course," the queen commanded.

"I thought you'd want me to vanish again."

"I wanted you out of sight while Caesar was here. But there's no reason for you to go now, my love. He's taken his soldiers with him to Asia Minor. Only a small guard is posted outside the palace. They will never know what goes on inside my private chambers."

"You're going to stay here, then?" Darius asked. Somewhere in the back of his mind lurked the knowledge that Caesar would order Cleopatra to Rome before long.

"He promised to send for me eventually," she said. "After he's put down the rebellion in the East, after he's taken care of the unrest in Rome." She laughed softly. "It could be years!"

"You don't mind that?" Darius asked, surprised.

"Why should I? I have his son and his promise to proclaim me his wife, queen of all the world. What more could I want from him?" She stared wide-eyed at Darius. "Surely you didn't imagine that I'd fallen in love with him."

"What if I stay and he returns and surprises us?" Darius was getting nervous.

"No one surprises *me,* Darius. I have runners posted all along Caesar's route of travel. Should there be any change in his plans, I will know long before he arrives in Alexandria. Really, my dearest, there is no cause to worry. We'll be perfectly free to do exactly as we please. Make love day or night. Make love day *and* night."

Darius groaned softly. He wasn't sure he was up to keeping two lovers happy around the clock. And another thing was bothering him. He needed to talk to Pia. But from the clear green of Cleo's eyes he knew that his blue-eyed sweetheart was fast asleep.

"How will you explain my presence?" he asked.

She shrugged. "I am queen! To whom must I explain it?"

"If you have spies to bring you news of Caesar, then he must have his own watching you."

Cleopatra propped her chin on one finger, deep in thought. Her face lit suddenly. "I know! I'll proclaim you my son's personal astrologer. Yes, Caesar would approve. He sets great store by the stars. And, of course, I'll need you near at all times to predict each hour of Caesarion's life."

"Do I have to wear one of those silly cone hats with the stars and moons all over it?"

"Heavens, no!" Cleopatra cried, laughing at such a thought. "And you needn't grow a long white beard and warts either. Where is it written that an astrologer must be old and ugly and wear a ridiculous hat?"

"Nowhere, unless you command it, my queen."

She nodded solemnly. "Very good, Darius. Your response pleases me."

"I'm bushed!" he said.

Cleo looked at him quizzically.

"Dead tired," he explained. "Mind if I take a nap?"

"I'll join you," she purred, snuggling close.

Darius closed his eyes and pretended to sleep.

"Ps-ss-st! Darius!" Pia whispered. "Are you asleep?"

"Just faking, but you weren't. You went out like a light as soon as—"

"I know. You wore me out . . . quite nicely, love."

He frowned and glanced away. "Then you don't know what's happened?"

"What?" She rose and glanced toward poor little Caesarion. He might be wet and hungry, but he had cried himself to sleep.

"It's not the baby. It's Cleopatra. She wants me to stay here now that Caesar's gone. We don't have to, though, Pia. We've got the crystals. We can leave right now, before she wakes."

Pia grinned excitedly. "Home!" she sighed. Just then the baby whimpered. Her smile faded as she glanced his way. "Poor little mite! His daddy gone off to war and his mama about to hand him over to a nursemaid." She turned back to Darius with a pleading look in her eyes. "I can't leave him. It wouldn't be right. He's as good as orphaned, Darius."

He gripped her hand. "Pia, don't you understand? *History* will take care of Caesarion. There's nothing you can do that will help him. His fate is sealed."

"I know there's nothing I can do to change the tragic outcome of his life. But I could be here for him for a time. I could make things better for him until he's old enough to look after himself." She rose and walked over to the beautifully carved cradle, then lifted the infant. He gurgled and flailed his fists. Without even thinking about it, Pia put him to Cleopatra's breast. He suckled greedily.

"She'll pitch a fit if she wakes up," Darius warned. "She

swore she wouldn't nurse him any longer now that Caesar's gone."

"Let her!" Pia said defiantly. "But as long as I'm here and Cleo has to sleep, this child is going to have what is rightfully his."

Pia settled on the edge of the bed, Little Caesar in her arms, nursing contentedly.

"You won't go then?" Darius said in defeat.

"I can't. Not yet. Soon, my darling!"

Pia's "soon" stretched into months and then a year. While she kept Cleopatra busy, raising Caesar's son properly, the great man himself was far away, engaged in forcing peace on Judea, then totally defeating Pharnaces in the battle of Zela about four hundred miles north of Ephesus. He sent word of his triumph in a message back to Rome. *"Veni, Vidi, Vici."*

Cleopatra would not have been pleased if she had known he considered her a major part of his conquest. On the other hand, she might have laughed and dismissed his remarks as Roman pomposity. Anyone who knew the exotic queen would have guessed that although Julius Caesar was the one who came and saw, she was the one who had conquered. Their son was the living evidence of her triumph.

Caesar went on to do battle in Sicily and North Africa in the winter of 47 B.C. The following spring he was finally ready to return to Rome to celebrate with the grandest triumphal the citizens were ever to witness. He sent for Cleopatra and Caesarion in the summer of 46. His message instructed her to bring along her eleven-year-old brother-"husband" in order to prevent any plots against the throne while she was away from Egypt. Her sister, Arsinoë, and Arsinoë's lover, Ganymede—Caesar's prisoners—were also in the entourage that sailed from Alexandria, along with courtiers, slaves, bodyguards, and eunuchs to see to the queen's every need. Caesarion's personal astrologer came along as well.

Every summer, in order to escape the heat and stench of Rome, the wealthy citizens emptied out of the city, retiring to their cool villas in the Alban foothills. This summer no one left. They would endure the sultry months of city life like ordinary plebeians in order not to miss a single tidbit of gossip and scandal. The "Whore Queen" was coming, with a bastard son she claimed was Caesar's own get. Everyone was dying to see Calpurnia's reaction—she who was Caesar's true wife and as such "above reproach." Would Calpurnia have henchmen murder her rival? Would she banish her husband from her house? Or would she simply remain above it all and igore the Egyptian harlot's existence?

Pia's nerves grew ragged as they sailed into the Roman port of Ostia. It had been a rough trip all the way. Everyone except Cleo had been seasick. Poor little Ptolemy, who was not a well lad in the best of times, seemed half dead by the time their journey ended. Pia herself was feeling none too well. She could hardly wait to set her feet on solid ground again. All the way across the Mediterranean she'd railed against her own stupidity at not packing some dramamine before she left St. Simons.

Cleopatra stood on deck as they entered the harbor, dressed in her most glittering royal finery: a gown of cloth-of-gold, magnificent jewels, and her Egyptian crown.

"I want them all to see *me* before they notice anyone else. These Romans must all know that a queen is arriving."

In spite of Cleopatra's wish to remain cool and aloof— a powerful queen, a living goddess in the eyes of Rome's citizens—Pia forced her to drop her regal facade in order to scramble across the deck in the nick of time to keep young Caesarion from tumbling over the side. The boy's mother might have spanked his royal backside, but Pia stayed her hand.

"Young Caesar, you will stand beside me and hold my hand," the queen said sharply. "You are dressed like your father, you will act accordingly."

Caesarion was indeed dressed like his father. Cleo had had her seamstresses make him what Pia referred to as a "little emperor suit." From the golden laurel wreath on his head to the Roman sandals on his feet, he was the image of his illustrious sire.

Pia couldn't stand it any longer. *What's Calpurnia going to say when she sees Caesarion?* she demanded silently.

The queen ignored her question.

I mean it, Cleo! We could be in for real trouble. I've heard these Roman women don't fool around. They're especially fond of poison.

"Hold your tongue!" Cleo snapped. "Caesar will protect me. I put my total trust in him."

As she spoke, the queen scanned the quay, hoping to spot Caesar in the crowd. Although it seemed that all of Rome had turned out to meet her ship, it seemed he had not come. She was less than pleased.

The nerve of the man! she fumed silently.

Then her gaze lit on a face she remembered from her childhood. Almost ten years had passed since the brash, hard-drinking cavalry officer had visited her father in Alexandria, an emissary from Julius Caesar. She had been only fourteen then and he twice her age. Still, he had flirted with her outrageously, praising her beauty and her wit, and warning her that he would find her again in a few years when she was "ripe." Had it not been for Darius, she might have allowed this handsome Roman to seduce her at the time. Clearly, that had been his intent.

Pia felt Cleo's anger cool when she spied the other Roman.

Who's that? Pia wanted to know.

Cleopatra laughed softly. "A charming brute of a Roman

I met once long ago. A handsome devil who drinks, curses, gambles, and uses women shamelessly."

But what's his name? Pia insisted.

At that moment, the huge, ruddy-faced, bull-necked Adonis strode on board and bowed before the Queen of Egypt. "Mark Antony, if you recall, my lady."

"How could I forget?"

His eyes played a passionate game with her before he spoke again. "Caesar sent me to welcome you to Rome. Dire matters of state detained him. He will come later to your villa for a private visit."

"Perhaps I will receive him. Perhaps not." Cleo's anger was showing again. Or was she simply putting on an act to impress Antony? Pia couldn't be sure; she felt too many emotions battling inside Cleopatra to understand clearly what the queen was feeling or thinking.

"Shall we go, my lady?"

Without asking permission, the big man leaned down and scooped Caesarion into his arms. The boy laughed and tugged at Antony's riotous locks.

"He's the image of his father, Cleopatra. No one could doubt it."

The queen smiled warmly at Mark Antony and took his arm. "Why should anyone doubt it?" she asked. "Caesar and I are wed, you know. He means to announce the news to all of Rome."

A dark look came over Antony's rough, handsome features, but he made no reply. Instead, he showed the foreign queen to his magnificent chariot, drawn by two tame lions.

"I thought you might fancy seeing some of Rome as we make our way to your villa. But if the heat and fragrance of our grand city are too much for you, I'll call for a closed litter, my lady."

Cleopatra was not about to show any weakness to this

cocky Roman. Putting a perfumed scarf to her nostrils, she said, "Order your beasts to proceed."

Pia could feel Cleo cringing inside. Compared to Alexandria, Rome was little more than a stinking bog. The streets were so narrow that wagons were not allowed about until after dark, yet still the thoroughfares were clogged with pedestrians and those borne on litters. The tall houses loomed dirty and stifling on every side, not allowing the smallest breath of air to stir around them. Lame beggars and starving children huddled along the way, crying pitifully for alms. Antony's lions roared, clearing a path through the teeming, sweltering streets for the royal entourage.

They crossed the Tiber River, from its right bank to its left. The transformation was staggering as they exited from the oppressive atmosphere of the city into a quarter of cool, lush gardens and stately marble villas. The air seemed to cool instantly. The urban stench was replaced by the delicate scents of lupine and oleander.

"Your house is there on the hill." Antony pointed with his whip.

Cleopatra gazed up at a palatial villa, gleaming blinding white in the afternoon sun. Tall colonnades framed the structure, which was set in acres of garden. The heady perfume of pine, cedar, and bay seemed to flow out from the place on a gentle breeze.

Wow! Pia exclaimed silently.

"Small, but quite lovely," Cleopatra said to Mark Antony.

"I'm afraid we have nothing to offer you here in Rome that can compare to your palace in Alexandria. I still wonder to this day if it is truly as grand as I remember or if I was simply so drunk with your beauty at the time that I've allowed my imagination to run wild."

Hm-m-m, Pia mused. *Coming on to you already, is he? Caesar won't like this. Neither will Darius.*

Cleo sucked in her breath and gave Pia a sharp jolt. *Be still!* she warned venomously.

"The sights you saw in Egypt are everything you remember, Antony," Cleo assured him.

He leaned close and whispered for her ears alone. "Oh, no, my queen. *You* are *more . . .* more beautiful, more fascinating, more enticing. I see now why Caesar dallied so long in your palace. Had I need to go to Alexandria again, I'm sure I would stay forever."

Girl, you're really asking for trouble, Pia hissed. *This man's not to be messed with.*

Cleopatra ignored her and went right on smiling into Mark Antony's dark, lust-bright eyes. She knew what she was doing, every step of the way. Granted, she had her own people around her, but she would need a Roman ally as well. Someone other than Julius Caesar, in case of emergency. Antony was obviously smitten with her. She could—and would—use that to her own advantage.

Pia picked up on this thought and decided to keep quiet. If ever there was a woman who didn't need help, it was Cleo. The queen was as wise as any general, as clever as any snake. No way would Antony get the upper hand. Cleopatra would play him like a fish on a line, knowing all the while that his loyalty to Caesar would force the lion-maned Roman to keep his distance as long as they were in Rome.

The villa was set up perfectly for Cleopatra's needs. Caesar had thought of everything. Quarters for her servants and the rest of her entourage were away from the main villa. That house would be for her, Caesar, and Caesarion alone. Even Darius was banished from their private domain. He had to bed down out back with two eunuchs and a chef.

Mark Antony escorted Cleopatra about the villa, beaming with pride even though he'd had no hand in the decorating.

Caesar had ordered his artisans to make the place as beautiful as the golden barge on which they'd sailed up the Nile. Each room was a new fantasy of gilded gods and goddesses, birds and flowers, saytrs and nymphs.

"Caesar melted down half the treasury to get all the gold needed to redecorate these rooms for you," Antony said in a gossipy tone. "I hear he even repossessed some of his wife's jewelry to add to the finery."

Cleopatra flashed the Roman a dark look. "*I* am Caesar's wife!" she snapped.

Antony cleared his throat and ran his long, blunt fingers through his rumpled, red-bronze hair. "Well, of course you are. I meant Calpurnia. His Roman wife . . . his . . ."

"His *barren* wife!" Cleo supplied. "And because of that fact, no wife at all to him."

Antony, blushing deeply, was still stumbling all over himself, trying to correct his blunder. "I'm sure he plans to divorce her now that you're here," he said pleasantly. "It's a simple enough procedure. All we have to do here in Rome is say, 'I divorce you. I divorce you. I divorce you.' Three times and it's all over. Free again! He won't stay with her. Why, I know for a fact that he hasn't slept with Calpurnia in years."

"I'll not have her name spoken again in my presence." Cleopatra's voice was level and calm, but her tone was deadly.

Flustered beyond words, Antony rang for the servants to bring food and wine.

Thank God! Pia moaned. *I'm half starved!*

She lost some of her appetite when the servants brought heavy platters of steamed eel, spiced hummingbird tongues, pickled doormice, strange-looking mushrooms that she guessed must be Roman toadstools, and tiny, pink squid with their purple eyes staring up at her. She was much relieved when Cleo opted for wine, cheese, grapes, and bread.

Caesarion, as adventurous as his father, tried some of everything, but made a face at most of it.

"Don't worry, my little darling," Cleo whispered to him, prompted by a suggestion from Pia. "We'll have our own chefs prepare our meals from now on."

Mark Antony didn't hear. He was too busy gorging himself on the Roman delicacies and quaffing down pints of wine at a swallow.

Their banquet finished, Antony took his leave so that Cleopatra could be alone to prepare for Caesar's arrival. But before he departed, he took the liberty of kissing the queen's hand. She allowed it, of course. She knew that sooner or later she would have need of this great, fiery-haired Roman buffoon.

By the time Antony left, Caesarion was curled up like a kitten, fast asleep on his dining couch.

"Put him to bed," the queen whispered to Iras. "He is exhausted. He must not be cranky when his father arrives."

What about me? Pia said. *I'm ready to drop. How about a nap, Cleo?*

Her pleading went ignored. The queen retired to her bath for a long soak in heavily perfumed water. The soak even revived Pia slightly. She could have stayed there all night long. In fact, she was nearly asleep in the cool marble bath when Cleo called for Iras to bring a drying cloth.

The massage with sweet oils that followed really did put Pia to sleep. Iras had knowing hands. She found every ache, every strained muscle, every twinge. But Pia was not meant to rest this night. It was time to dress for Caesar.

"One room is entirely filled with beautiful Roman gowns," Iras informed her mistress. "Would you like to come choose or shall I select for you?"

"I'll wear none of them," Cleo announced. "My rose-colored *mafortes,"* she ordered. "A golden girdle, and my best opals."

Oh, mercy! Not the mafortes, *that see-through thing!* Pia begged.

Iras, too, complained, shuddering slightly with embarrassment at the thought. "But, my lady, the women of Rome that I saw today never dress so immodestly. They cover themselves in a more than adequate fashion."

"All the more reason for me to dress as an Egyptian. I want Caesar to see the difference and appreciate it. Besides, he must learn this very night that I have regained my body after the birth of his child. When he saw me last, I was fat and flabby still. He must know that my beauty is ageless."

Pia could see her point. Even she was proud of the way Cleo had worked to get herself back into perfect shape after Little Caesar's birth. If anything, Cleopatra looked sexier than ever.

Damn right, Queenie! she chirped. *Show Caesar what you've got!*

To further the romance of their reunion, Cleopatra ordered her servants to bring wine and a light repast to a table in the garden. She would be waiting for Caesar when he climbed the marble steps from the dusty road below. She had torches set just so to create the effect of a goddess aglow in a garden grotto when he arrived.

Cleopatra's preparations impressed Pia. The queen didn't miss a trick. Pia wouldn't be surprised if Caesar fell on his lover the minute he saw her.

Boy, this marble bench is going to be an uncomfortable place to make love, Pia observed.

"Silly girl!" Cleo said with a laugh. "I won't allow him to remove my girdle until after he's seen his son and renewed all the promises he made before he left Alexandria. Then, if he wishes, I will grant my favors."

Pia laughed out loud. If he wishes! *Right! Like he's not going to come here with a hard-on as big as your arm!*

"Don't be crude!" Cleo snapped. "In fact, I wish you would simply go away and stop bedeviling me."

Not on your life, Queenie! I didn't take that long, rough trip to leave now. I mean to see Rome first.

"Feast your eyes on Rome, then, for even now he is climbing the stairs."

Pia looked through Cleo's eyes at the old man coming toward them. Battles had taken their toll on him over the past months. He looked every day of his fifty-six years and then some. But the light of lust still glistened in his black eyes when they lit on Cleopatra.

"Can this be my beloved?" he said the moment he reached her. "Or are you some pagan nymph hiding here in the garden to steal from me what is rightfully hers?"

"I am your *wife!*" Cleopatra reminded him in a sultry voice. "Everything you have, everything you are is mine. *Nobody* will ever steal that from me!"

Right on! Pia said silently. Suddenly, she was as excited about ruling the world with Caesar as Cleopatra was.

They kissed and touched and drank wine from each other's cup. Then, hand in hand, they walked together toward the great, white villa. As they passed a large cedar, Pia heard someone whisper her name. She couldn't see him, but she knew who it was.

"We've got to get out of here. Now!" came the voice from the darkness.

Pia's feelings caused Cleopatra's heart to race with strange anxiety for a moment, but she swept on without a word or a glance. Even Pia's frantic urging failed to dissuade the queen from her purpose.

Caesar woke his son to greet him, smiled at the boy's likeness to himself, then repeated all the promises Cleopatra longed to hear.

By the time the queen finally allowed him to remove her girdle, and strip away her transparent veil of rose-colored silk, the strong Roman wine had taken its toll on Pia. She was only vaguely aware when Caesar fell upon his goddess, making her writhe beneath him in the heat of pagan passion.

Her last thoughts before she slept were of Darius and his urgent plea to her in the garden.

Chapter Fourteen

Darius swore softly when Cleopatra ignored him in the garden. He knew she could do nothing else with Caesar at her side. Still, it galled him. She might at least have glanced his way. He only hoped that Pia had been awake and alert. They needed to talk, to make plans, *to leave.* Something here had gone amiss. Someone knew who he was and where he had come from. They could be in deep trouble!

The strange incident had taken place earlier in the day on the way from the port to the villa. Darius had been forced to walk with the rest of Cleopatra's entourage through the heat and the dust of Rome. Shortly before they crossed the bridge over the Tiber, a young woman—a slave, he presumed—had clutched his arm to keep from falling when she turned her ankle on a loose stone in the road. He had looked down at her, surprised when she grabbed him. The moment their eyes met, she'd cried in surprise, "Darius? Can it really be you? Thank God for a familiar face!"

He had nodded solemnly, trying not to betray his bewilder-

ment. He'd never seen this woman before—at least, not in
Alexandria.

"I am Darius," he acknowledged. "Astrologer to young
Ptolemaeus Caesar."

"But aren't you Pia's friend? The one from the conference
on St. Simons? She introduced us back in June on the beach
one day, remember?"

He looked hard at her, trying to recall. "Who are you?"

She giggled. "Goodness, I'm not sure I know any longer.
Everyone back at the palace in Alexandria called me Sudi,
but how I got there, I don't know. I'd barely arrived when
that pushy blonde named Iras hustled me on board that awful
boat and said we were going to Rome. I figured she meant
Rome, Georgia, and that was fine with me—a good deal
closer to home. I've been there; it's a nice place." She paused
and glanced around, taking in all of Rome's seven hills, her
eyes wide with amazement. "But somehow I don't think
we're in Georgia. Are we?"

Darius stared down at the tiny woman with flaming red
hair. She certainly didn't look like any palace servant he'd
ever seen before. But he did recall his brief meeting with
Pia's friend, Sudibeth Callahan, on the beach at St. Simons.

"How did you get here?" he asked.

"Beats me!" she said with a bewildered shrug. "Pia and I
talked on the phone a few days ago, after she got back to
the island from her research trip. She said she might be
leaving again for a week or so. I was on the beach a couple
of days later and decided I'd drop in on her for a visit.
Nobody was home, but I know where she keeps the key. I
meant to just slip in, make sure everything was all right,
and take a quick shower—get the sand off so it wouldn't
get in my car. When I got out of the shower, I heard her
computer clicking. I figured Pia had come home while I
was in the bathroom. But nobody was in the office. The
computer keys were typing up a storm all by themselves. I

wasn't too surprised. I know Pia's been having problems with that cranky, old machine. I sat down at the desk, meaning to turn it off. But I just had to read what was on the screen. That book's really coming along. It's—"

"Yes, I know, I know. But how did you get here?"

"I told you, I don't have any idea. One minute, I was staring at the screen, reading like crazy; the next thing I know, this big ugly lug is kicking me awake and ordering me to empty the palace slops. I gave him some lip and he threatened me with his long, black whip. I figured I'd better play along until I could find out where I was and what had happened to me. I thought I was dreaming until I realized that everything I'd read in Pia's book was real and I was right in the middle of it. It just about blew my mind!"

Darius frowned. He knew exactly what had happened. He'd opened a channel from ancient Egypt to a tiny space in Pia's office so that he could send work back to Edgar Allan. That window in time must have been open when Sudibeth sat down at the computer. If she was still there when Darius closed the channel, she would have been sucked into it and back through time like a twig in a whirlpool.

"I don't know how I got here," she said, "but this place sucks! I don't like the heat or the food, and I hate the guts of that big, ugly guy with the whip." Tears flooded her wide, soulful eyes. "I want to go home, Darius! How in the ever-lovin', blue-eyed world did this happen to me?"

Darius leaned down closer to Sudi. "Listen, you haven't told anybody else about this, have you?"

Tears rolled down her dusty cheeks making muddy trails. "I tried, but nobody seems to understand me. It's like I'm speaking a foreign language."

Darius nodded. English was definitely not spoken at the palace in Alexandria. Even if the language had been known that far back in time, Sudibeth's heavy Southern drawl would have made it difficult for the ancients to understand. That realization came as a relief to him.

"Don't try talking to anyone else, Sudi," he cautioned. "Keep up your act. I'll get us all out of here as soon as I can."

She brightened. "You mean Pia's here, too?"

"I'm afraid so."

Sudibeth glanced about. "Where? I haven't seen her."

"You won't," he confessed. "She's inside Cleopatra."

"Oh, my lord!" Sudi gasped. She glanced up ahead at the tiny woman beside the hulking Roman in the lion-drawn chariot. Then she looked back at Darius. *"Inside her?* You're sure?"

"I'm afraid there's no doubt."

"She always liked to get inside her characters. But how could this happen?"

"It's a long story," Darius answered. "Once we get back to St. Simons, we'll tell you all about it. But until I can get Pia to leave, we'll have to keep up this charade."

Sudibeth wrinkled her pert little nose. "You mean I have to keep on emptying slops? Yuck!"

"Look, I'll see what I can do. Maybe I can get you a better assignment."

"Like what?"

"I don't know," he answered. "Maybe kitchen maid or something."

"Double yuck! I hate cooking!" She looked up at Darius, a faint smile on her lips. "We're in the real Rome, aren't we? The one with baths and orgies and good-looking gladiators and emperors' love-slaves?"

Darius couldn't keep from smiling. "You could put it like that, I suppose."

"Well then, how about getting me a job as some rich guy's lover? It's been a while. He doesn't have to be gorgeous as long as he's got a big house and lots of slaves to do his dirty work."

He couldn't resist teasing her. "Why, Sudibeth, I was sure you were about to ask me to pull some strings to get you into the Vestal Virgins."

"God, no!" she cried in horror.

They had left it at that. Once they arrived moments later at the villa, the two of them got separated. As yet, Darius hadn't seen Sudibeth again. He had to find her. And he had to talk to Pia right away. They couldn't stay any longer, not with Sudibeth Callahan here. She was sure to blow her cover. Besides that danger, her absence back on the island would be noticed soon. Pia had been careful to cover her tracks before she left, but Sudibeth was simply there one minute and gone the next.

Darius wandered about the garden, trying to think how to get to Pia and how to get Sudibeth back home. They couldn't let her take the crystal pyramid—not even half of it—because then he and Pia would have no way back. He might try sending Sudibeth back alone through the open channel, but he wasn't sure that would work. She might end up simply as a character in Pia's novel, locked up forever in Edgar Allan's weird innards.

"Damn!" he swore. "To quote Sudibeth, 'This sucks!' "

"Ps-s-st! Darius? Is that you?"

When he turned, he saw a light silhouette in the shadows. "Pia? Thank God!"

"What's wrong?" she whispered, hurrying toward him.

He eyed Cleo's tousled hair, her bruised lips, the wine stains on her neck and shoulders, and his jealousy raged. "What could possibly be wrong? I'm in love with you and you've just come from having heavy sex with Julius Caesar. And you'll do it again and again, as often as he wants it, but you refuse to go back to St. Simons and marry me."

She ran to him and hugged him tightly. "Darius darling,

I'm so sorry. But you know I can't keep Cleo from doing whatever she wants to do. I didn't enjoy it."

"Sure!" he said in a pained voice. "Do you have any idea how it makes me feel to know you're in there with them when you haven't been with me since we left Alexandria? I could kill the bastard with my bare hands!"

"Hey, I haven't complained about you and Cleo, have I?" Pia spoke in a hurt tone, "Having to share you with *her*— it's not as good as when it's just the two of us. At least when I'm in bed with Cleo and Caesar it's research. What's *your* excuse?"

The whole argument sounded foolish, even to Darius. Finally, he grinned and pulled Pia into his arms. "Come here and kiss me, you sweet little baggage."

She did kiss him, long and deeply.

"Caesar and Cleo are dead to the world," she hinted. "The garden's dark. It's just the two of us now, darling."

Darius was way ahead of her. Already he was fumbling at her nightshift and spreading his cloak on the damp ground in the shelter of the cedar trees.

Pia thought she'd had all the lovemaking she could take for one evening, but when Darius kissed her neck, then stroked her breasts, she whimpered her desire for him. The danger of their tryst in the garden made the pleasure all the sweeter. There was something desperate and wonderfully passionate about making love under the midnight sky where they might be discovered at any moment. And they had to make love quietly—no moans or cries of ecstasy. That need for silence seemed to magnify their passion. Pia had never felt so transported by pleasure. For a long time after she reached the pinnacle, she drifted blissfully in a state of perfect euphoria.

Darius finally broke the magical silence. "Sweetheart, there's something I have to tell you."

"Don't waste your breath, darling. If I don't know by now that you love me, I never will."

He leaned down and kissed her. "That, too," he whispered. "But I meant something else, and it's good that you're still lying down."

Pia tensed in his arms. "What?" The question was only a thin thread of sound, like the sigh of the breeze in the tops of the cedars.

"Sudibeth's here."

Pia sat up like a shot. *Here?* In Rome? But how?"

Darius explained quickly and simply.

"She'll ruin everything!" Pia cried. "You've got to send her back, Darius. Right now!"

"It's not that easy," he said. "I don't know if I can."

"You brought her here!"

"No!" Darius shook his head. "It was an accident. She happened into the right place at the right time."

"You mean, don't you, the *wrong* place at the *wrong* time? Oh, Darius, what are we going to do?"

He caressed her shoulders and kissed her hair. "Take it easy, sweetheart. This may not be as terrible as it sounds. No one can understand her, so she can't tell anyone where she came from."

"You don't know Sudibeth. She'll find a way. She'll blab everything, and you know how the slaves love to gossip. You're both likely to wind up with royal Roman nooses around your necks." She clung to him tightly. "Darius, if anything happens to you, I'll never forgive myself."

He gave her a long, hard kiss. "Then come home with me, Pia. Now."

"We can't run off and leave Sudibeth! She's my best friend."

"Think about it, Pia. She's already asked me to find her a rich Roman who needs a mistress. I think she'd love it here if I set her up with the right man."

Pia stared through the darkness into his gleaming, amber eyes. "You can't be serious! She's got a family and a career and a life back home. Her folks must be worried sick if they've called and can't reach her. No, Darius," she said firmly. "I'm not going anywhere until you find a way to get Sudibeth back, too."

Suddenly Pia became aware that Cleopatra was waking up. "I've got to go. She mustn't find herself out here with you."

"But when can I see you again?"

"Don't worry, darling. I'll put a bug in Cleo's ear. I'll warn her about the Ides of March and suggest she check daily with Little Caesar's astrologer."

"But I'm not really an astrologer. She knows that."

"That won't matter," Pia assured him, already hurrying away. "She's been trying to think of a reason to spend more time with you. I'll suggest that you move into Caesarion's room to watch over him."

The next moment, Pia vanished into the darkness.

Darius wandered off through the shadowy garden, feeling more alone than before Pia came to him. What kind of life was this? Two women he loved with all his heart, in two different times, and he couldn't make either of them his.

He decided that instead of mulling it over and making himself more miserable, he'd try to do something about it. The first thing he had to do was find Sudibeth. Avoiding the guards, who were mostly sleeping at their posts anyway, he crept from building to building, whispering Sudi's name softly at the windows. He found her at the stable where the royal prisoners, Arsinoë and Ganymede, were being kept, along with their guards and a few slaves.

"Darius?" she whispered back.

"Can you slip out?"

"Yes. Everyone's sleeping."

"Hurry! And be quiet about it."

Suidbeth was beside him a couple of minutes later. "Are we going home?" she asked immediately.

"Not yet, but I talked to Pia."

"You mean Cleopatra, don't you?"

"No. The queen was sleeping at the time. She doesn't know anything about this, and we have to keep it a secret from her."

"You mean she doesn't know about Pia?"

"She knows she hears a voice at times, but she thinks it's her subconscious talking to her or maybe some demon who's trying to possess her."

Sudibeth giggled. "That's Pia all right. I always figured she'd make a good demon."

"This is serious, Sudibeth! We have to figure out what to do next. Pia's going to try to talk Cleo into moving me into the villa with her and Caesarion. You need to be there, too. But what post could you fill?"

"Hey, if you think I'm going to change the royal dirty diapers, forget it! I had my fill of that when I was growing up—all my little brothers. No way!"

Darius suddenly gripped her arm. "Don't you write children's stories?"

"I did. And, lordy, how I'd love to be back home doing that now. If I ever get back, I'm going to take my work a lot more seriously."

"Do you remember the stories you've written?"

"Of course!" Sudibeth answered sharply. "Every word of every one of them."

"That's it!" Darius exclaimed.

"That's what?"

"We'll create a post for you—royal storyteller."

"You mean, I won't get to entertain any rich guys?" Just the kid?" She sounded genuinely disappointed.

"You won't have to empty any more slops."

"I'll take it!" Sudibeth quickly agreed.

"Great! Go back to the stable and do what you're told until the queen sends for you. And have your best story ready to tell when you're brought to the villa."

"Why can't I go with you now? I hate that stable! It doesn't even have air conditioning."

"Sudibeth, this is 46 B.C.," he reminded her. "Nothing has air conditioning. Just do as I tell you. And try not to draw attention to yourself. Okay?"

He could see the brightness of her grin through the darkness. "That'll be hard, Darius. Guys just naturally notice me."

He gave her a little nudge to send on her way. "Try, Sudibeth! That's all I'm asking."

Pia managed to slip back into bed with Caesar before Cleo came fully awake. The queen stretched languidly, then hugged herself.

"Oh, these dreams!" she said softly. "They get better and better."

They won't last, Pia said softly.

"What?" Cleopatra sat up and glanced about the room. "Who said that?"

You know who's talking to you. Why won't you listen? I'm trying to warn you of a grave danger to you and Caesarion.

"What danger?" Cleo reached over and caressed Caesar's arm as if to assure herself that his very nearness would keep her and her son from harm.

I have had a vision. Pia assumed the tone of an ancient doomsayer. *Beware the Ides of March!*

"March?" Cleopatra snapped. "Why, that's months away! By then, Caesar will have divorced Calpurnia and he and I will share the throne of the world."

I see blood on the steps of the Senate. Pia closed her eyes, trying to remember all her research, but she could recall in detail only Marlon Brando calling out to the frightened citizens, " 'Friends, Romans, countrymen . . . ' "

"Whose blood?" the queen demanded.

Rome's blood, at the foot of Pompey's statue. Beware, Egypt! Beware, Rome! Beware the Ides of March!

That did the trick. Cleopatra was scared, shaking, murmuring to her goddess to protect her.

Only one person can protect you, Pia said ominously.

"Tell me! Who?"

The astrologer, Darius. He must be brought to the villa to watch over your son at all times and cast his star charts daily.

Cleopatra smiled. "So be it!" she murmured.

An hour before dawn, Caesar rose from the bed, kissed his sleeping queen goodbye, and left the villa.

Cleopatra waited until the sound of his chariot wheels died in the distance. Then she called for a guard to bring Darius to her. Dawn was coloring the hills of Rome gold and royal purple when the astrologer came to stand before the queen.

"What do you know of the Ides of March?" she demanded the moment he entered.

He bowed, then stared directly into her turquoise eyes and said, "A most dangerous time, my queen. The great Caesar's stars will be in chaos. All those near him will share the threat, especially anyone of his blood, for it will flow like the Nile at high flood."

Cleopatra clutched her throat and gasped. "Then my premonition is true. I dreamed last night that I should beware the Ides of March."

Darius nodded, his expression grave. "Your senses are alert and accurate, my queen."

"You will remain in the villa, Darius, with my son at all times. I will not have him harmed by this dark omen."

Darius controlled a pleased smile. "As you command, Queen Cleopatra. Might I make a suggestion."

"You may."

"In the stables there is a slave named Sudi from a far-off island. By reputation, she is the most gifted storyteller in all the world. Caesarion must not dwell upon his fate or this threatened danger. I suggest that you consider bringing her into the villa also, to tell the young ruler tales to ease his mind and to amuse and instruct him."

Cleopatra thought for a moment. Had anyone other than Darius made such a suggestion, she would have smelled a plot. But surely her own lover would not bring a spy into her household. Whatever his purpose, she saw no harm in bringing the slave woman under her roof. Storytellers by nature were old, ugly hags. She only hoped the creature wouldn't frighten Little Caesar with her ghastly appearance.

"Very well," she said. "Bring the woman to me at once, Darius."

Sudibeth couldn't have been happier to see Darius when he showed up at the stable. She had her hands full with a lusty, Roman guard who had caught her sneaking back in after their meeting. From her two years of high-school Latin, Sudibeth could understand enough of what he was saying to realize his intent. She had her choice: Let him tumble her in the hay or be turned in for sneaking about the queen's property like a thief in the night.

Sudibeth, of course, opted for the tumble. He wasn't exactly handsome, but the Roman was big and strong and looked like he'd had a lot of practice. Besides, she hadn't sampled any Roman goods yet.

"No time like the present," she told the eager fellow.

He didn't understand what she said, but the inviting smile

on her face was universally understood. He tossed her down and fell upon her, nearly knocking the breath out of her.

"No! No! No!" she told him. "Take off that metal breast-plate and those shin guards first. You're hurting me! Get off me!"

Darius arrived in time to find Sudibeth fighting the huge barbarian——he wasn't even a Roman——who tried to hold her still long enough to take his best shot. Darius grabbed him by his long, dirty hair and hauled him up.

Sudibeth lay in the pile of straw, her shift torn and her legs wide, staring up in a daze.

"Darius?" she muttered. "Bless you!"

The mean-tempered guard took a swing at Darius. Obviously, he wasn't very good at hand-to-hand combat. Darius put him away with one shot, a right cross to the jaw.

"Are you all right, Sudi?"

She looked down at herself and quickly covered her bare breasts with a shred of torn fabric. "I think so. You got here in the nick of time. Thanks!"

"You can't tease these guys, Sudibeth. They're barbarians."

"So I noticed," she snapped. "And for your information, Mr. Know-It-All, I wasn't teasing him. It was just a bit of payola to keep myself out of the joint. He caught me when I came back inside and was going to put me away. Unless I . . . you know." She glanced at her attacker and made a face. "He's hardly my type. He smells like he's been bathing in horse piss."

"Forget about him. Get yourself together. We're going to see the queen."

"Cleopatra?" Sudibeth's eyes got as big as moons in her face.

"The very one," Darius assured her. "You're about to become the royal storyteller."

"Boy, do I have a story to tell after tonight!"

"You'd better keep that one to yourself. Come on, now. Cleopatra doesn't like to be kept waiting."

Sudibeth combed through her rampant red curls with her fingers. She wiped a corner of her ruined shift over her face, trying to rub away some of the dirt. "Doesn't anyone ever bathe in this place?"

She got her answer to that question the minute she was ushered into the queen's presence. Cleopatra was in her bath, a sunken marble tub large enough to qualify as a swimming pool. The water was purple and was scented with heliotrope. Large golden lily pads floated on the surface.

"Bow!" Darius ordered in a stage whisper from the doorway.

Sudibeth did as instructed, but kept her eyes on Cleopatra all the while. She ached with envy. How could one woman have so much? The bath chamber was huge, the size of some of the temples she'd seen as they passed through Rome. The walls of pale pink marble were covered with tapestries woven in gold and silver. Enormous white fur rugs covered most of the floor. A dozen or more gorgeous slave women hovered about, ready to do Cleopatra's bidding. One of them, an especially beautiful blonde, sat at a stringed instrument that resembled a harp, plucking it and singing softly.

The queen had yet to notice Sudibeth. She lay in the water, her head supported by a floating pillow, her eyes closed. She looked totally relaxed.

"My queen?" Darius called softly.

Cleopatra's turquoise eyes fluttered open and she smiled at him. Then she spotted Sudibeth and her expression changed to outrage. "Who is this filthy, ragged creature? How dare you bring her here! Away with her at once!"

"But, Cleopatra, this is the storyteller I promised to bring to you."

"I'll not have this ragged beggar woman near my son. Away with her!"

Sudibeth didn't need to understand the words; the woman's tone was insult enough. She was thoroughly offended. "Listen, here, Queenie, you just watch your damn mouth!"

Fortunately, Cleopatra couldn't understand a word of Sudibeth's drawling threat. Pia did, however, and flinched inside the queen.

"What's the wretch mumbling about?" Cleo demanded. "Is she too witless to speak Caesar's Latin?"

"She says what an honor it is to meet you and how eager she is to tell her stories to Caesarion," Darius improvised quickly. "Believe me, my queen, her appearance is not her fault. One of Caesar's barbarian guards fell upon her a short time ago. Had I not come along when I did, the poor young woman would have lost her virginity to the brute."

Sudibeth didn't understand what he was saying, but Pia groaned silently, *Oh, come on, Darius. Where'd you come up with that line?*

"I swear to you, Cleopatra, Sudi is of royal blood, a princess in her own land. And her stories weave magic spells to protect those who hear them. She has the power to ward off evil."

Only this final remark moved Cleopatra to soften her attitude toward Sudibeth.

"Very well, then, but she must be bathed."

Sudibeth turned and looked at Darius. "What's she saying?"

"That you need a bath."

"Ah-h-h!" Sudibeth closed her eyes and sighed with ecstasy, imagining herself sharing the wonderful-smelling, purple waters with the queen. "Tell her thanks for me, Darius. I'd love to join her."

Sudibeth began stripping off her tattered rags right then,

ready to dive into the marble bath. But Darius put his hand on her shoulder to stop her. "Not in there, you little fool!"

Cleopatra clapped her hands. Immediately, two plump, hairless eunuchs hurried into the chamber.

"Scrub the skin off her, if you must, but get her clean," Cleo ordered the two men.

Sudibeth looked to Darius for translation. "Go with them," he told her simply.

Sudibeth stared in horror at the pair of dull-eyed men. She didn't have to be told that they were eunuchs. Her bare breasts were clearly visible through her torn shift, yet neither of them even bothered to look.

"I'm not going anywhere with anybody!" she yelled.

The pair ignored her protests, gripped her arms, and hauled her out of the queen's bath, into the open yard where they dumped her into a hollowed-out wooden horse trough. She came up sputtering and cursing, but the rinse washed some of the filth from her. The eunuchs then took her to a back room of the villa where a great metal pot simmered over the low-burning fire.

"Help!" Sudibeth screamed when she saw that they meant to put her into what looked like a huge cookpot. "Darius, don't let them boil me!"

The silent men wrestled her into the hot water, then went at her with stiff brushes and pumice stones. An hour later, the bath Sudibeth had so longed for ended with a cold shower of melted snow brought down from the mountains. At last, Sudibeth, the "Queen of Kiddy Lit," stood naked before her pair of torturers, her flesh scoured red, but clean.

One of them wiped her dry with a rough piece of cloth. Finished with that task, he motioned toward a marble slab at the back of the dim room.

"No more," Sudibeth begged. "I can't take it. You fat little bastards have scrubbed me practically down to the bone already."

She kicked, screamed, and fought. It was no use. They finally subdued her. Right before she decided to send the fatter of the two flying across the room with a swift kick to his midsection, she went limp on the table.

"Ah, that feels good," she sighed.

They worked on her—both of them at once—massaging soothing oils into her raw skin. She tried to stay awake to enjoy it, but it felt too good. Within minutes, Sudibeth, exhausted from the ordeal of her bath, drifted off to sleep.

She woke up in another chamber, a normal-sized room with a bed, a chest, a table, and a tall mirror. She smiled. "Not bad digs!"

She realized that she was still naked, but at least she was between clean, soft sheets. She was about to go back to sleep when she heard a knock at the door.

"Who is it?" she asked, dreading the answer, hoping it wasn't the fat guys again.

"It's Darius, Sudibeth. May I come in?"

"Sure. Everybody else does whatever they want to around this place. Why not?"

Darius looked worried when he slipped into the room.

Sudibeth sat up in bed, his expression of fear clutching at her heart. "What's wrong? They aren't coming for me again, are they?"

"No, Sudibeth. It's all right."

"Then why do you look so worried?"

"I was worried about you. They didn't hurt you, did they?"

"Oh, no," she answered, sarcasm dripping from her words. "Not if you don't count boiling me alive then scraping the skin off, bit by bit. It was lovely, Darius. *Thanks a bunch!*"

"Hey, keep your voice down!" he snapped. "All they did was give you a bath. But, if you wake that baby, you'll really be in for it. I wish you'd get out of the bed so I can talk to you. It's very distracting with you lying there like that."

Sudibeth grinned. If there was anything she loved, it was for a man to find her distracting. "Whatever you say, Darius." She swung her bare legs to the floor and let the sheet drop to her waist.

"For God's sake, don't you have any clothes on?"

Sudibeth held the sheet out and peered down at herself, then grinned playfully at him. "Not so's you'd notice."

"I'll turn my back while you get dressed."

"In what?" she asked.

"The chest." He pointed. "Look in there."

Sudibeth walked over to the armoire-type chest that smelled of warm cedar. She opened the doors and gave a cry of delight. "Oh, my wor-r-rd! I never . . . I mean, this is like heaven. Will you look at all this great stuff?"

"Not until you're wearing some of it. Hurry up, Sudibeth. Get dressed!"

When she signaled all clear a few minutes later, Darius turned to find her wearing a gorgeously revealing gown. The wisp of lime green cloud lay in soft folds over her breasts. Rosettes of gold stitching hid her nipples. A gold cord crossed over the bodice and wound around her tiny waist. She had golden flowers in her hair and golden sandals on her feet. She was truly a vision.

Darius closed his mouth and forced his gaze away. "I'm to take you to Cleopatra at once," he said. Then he added nervously, "Now that you're presentable."

"Oh, is that what I am?" She hadn't missed that look in his eyes when he first turned and saw her. Sudibeth wasn't above flirting with any man—not even Pia's guy.

"You'll do," he said stiffly. "Now, come on. You don't want to make her mad again."

"Wait a damn minute!" She caught his arm and stopped him. "Do you mind explaining to me how I'm supposed to tell her kid stories when he's not going to understand a word I say?"

Darius smiled, then chuckled, pleased with himself. "I've already taken care of that. I told Cleopatra that the language you speak is magical, that only those who are meant to understand will know the meaning of the words you speak. She'll never admit that she can't understand you. It would be beneath her, especially since she's so good at linguistics. And since the queen won't admit it, none of her subjects will either. You tell your stories to Caesarion in English—he'll be amused by any attention—and don't worry about anybody else."

"You think this will work?"

"Trust me."

Sudibeth flounced past him. "Hell! I *trusted* you when you sent me off with those fat guys and said I was just going to get a bath."

"You got one, didn't you?"

"You can bet your family jewels on that!" she snapped. "I'm so clean, I squeak when I walk."

"Well then, quit bitching and come on!"

The queen was being dressed for the evening when they arrived at her chamber. "Show them in," she told Iras.

On the way down the corridor, they'd passed several Roman guards, not barbarians like the joker in the stable, but members of the Tenth Legion, Caesar's elite. Each man had given Sudibeth the once-over as she passed, so by the time they reached the queen's quarters, Sudibeth had herself convinced that she would outshine even Cleopatra. That notion died the moment they walked in.

Cleo was wearing one of those cutwork bras like the sexy little numbers Sudibeth ordered from Frederick's of Hollywood. Thin, gold chains held the whole works together and lifted her breasts high so that her bare, scarlet-painted nipples seemed aimed right at Darius's eyes when he looked at her. Her skirt, which clung to her shapely hips, dipped low in front and back. It was some filmy, blood-red fabric that glimmered with gold threads. Her hair—a wig, although Sudibeth didn't know that—was dressed in hundreds of perfectly even cornrows and shone with gold and ruby beads. Sudibeth felt another deep stab of envy. The queen was a knockout!

Cleopatra stood for a moment, looking at Darius and Sudibeth. Then, without a word, she turned her back on them and stared at her face in the looking glass. She frowned slightly, sat down at her dressing table, and motioned to one of her servants. "The swan's feather again. My right eye needs more kohl."

Darius and Sudibeth waited in silence, watching the pretty maid draw an even line over the queen's closed eyelid with the dark-tipped feather. If there had been a clock in the chamber, it would have ticked on and on. Finally, without turning, Cleopatra ordered, "Tell me a story. *Now!*"

Sudibeth jumped, shocked senseless by the queen's abrupt command. She couldn't think of a thing. Darius nudged her. "Quick!" he whispered. "Just a short one."

Her mind was a total blank. Nothing came to her with the queen's eyes blazing at her in the mirror.

"Well? Get on with it!" Cleopatra slammed a scent bottle down on her table, making Sudibeth jump again.

Sudi blurted out the first story that came to mind, something she'd heard in a bar a few weeks back. "What do you do when a pit bull starts humping your leg? Don't know, do you, Queenie? Well, I'll just tell you then, sugar. You fake an orgasm *fast!*"

Pia hadn't heard that one before. When Sudibeth finished the short joke, Cleo had her mouth wide open while Iras touched up her lip paint. Pia roared with laughter, which poured out of the queen's open mouth. Cleo looked startled at first, but soon joined in. All the servants laughed. The guards laughed. Sudibeth laughed.

Only Darius remained solemn. "You're a wise one all right, Sudi."

"She is, indeed!" Cleopatra said. "I will allow her to spin her fantastic tales for my son. I find much knowledge and much magic in her words."

"I've got a million more where that came from, Queenie. Have you heard the one about the old man and the three-legged pig?"

Darius glared her to silence.

"What was that she said?" Cleo asked. "Another jewel from her lips?"

Oh, that one's a jewel for sure! Pia said silently, between giggles.

Darius remained straight-faced. "She thanks you, my queen, and asks the gods to give her the right words to amuse and protect your son."

At that moment, Caesar's trumpeters announced his arrival at the gates below.

"Leave me, all of you," the queen commanded. "I shall receive my husband alone."

"Geeze!" Sudibeth fumed. "I wanted to see Julius Caesar."

"You get yourself on into the nursery and tell Little Caesar a nice, *clean* bedtime story. One with bunnies and lambs in it," Darius ordered.

"No pit bulls?" Sudibeth asked through a gale of giggles. "She liked that one. Did you hear how she laughed?"

"That was Pia laughing, not Cleopatra. The queen didn't understand a word you said. Remember?"

"Oh!" Sudibeth's mouth drew down in disappointment. "Shoot! I thought she really liked me."

"Don't worry, Sudi, you'll know when she *doesn't* like you."

"How?"

"She'll poison you and throw your body in the Tiber."

"Let's see," Sudibeth said, thinking quickly. "I could tell the kid about Tiny Tommy Tottle or Merry Mistress Muffin."

"Whatever!" Darius snapped. "Just get on with it!"

He listened in for a few minutes to make sure Sudibeth was keeping it clean. He couldn't stay, however. He had to get back to the queen's chamber. He meant to hang around outside until Cleopatra went to sleep. One thing was sure, they had to get out of here and back to St. Simons. Otherwise, Sudibeth was bound to give them away. Then they'd all three be floating in the Tiber!

Chapter Fifteen

Pia forced herself to stay awake and keep quiet during the long evening Cleopatra spent with Caesar. It was the usual ho-hum. They ate exotic foods, drank exotic wines, made exotic love.

Something new was added tonight, however. Caesar was bubbling over with plans for his great triumphal parade through the streets of Rome. He wanted desperately for Cleopatra to be in the spectacle, to ride in a golden chariot as if she were just another glittering treasure he'd brought back from his foray into the East. The queen, of course, flatly refused. She was not one of his conquered rulers to be hauled through leering, jeering mobs. To force her point home, she refused to make love until Caesar promised that she would have a place of honor in the viewing stands between him and their son. She wanted all of Rome, and especially Calpurnia, to see them as the royal family.

Eager to remove the golden chains that bound her breasts, Caesar gave in to all her demands. He went further than that. He promised to have a new Temple of Venus erected in her honor. A statue of Cleo herself, as the goddess of love, would be displayed inside. Pleased with his generous offer, she came out of her chains and her scarlet silks. She allowed him to make love to her at last, pretending that she really was a goddess and he a mere mortal worshipper.

At least nobody's yanked down any bed curtain ropes. Pia sighed silently as she endured Caesar's painstaking worship.

Pia almost shouted for joy when Caesar said he couldn't stay all night, that he had an important speech to write before the next morning's meeting of the Senate. That meant Cleo could sleep undisturbed and Pia could slip out to find Darius. She was going crazy, not knowing what was happening now that Sudibeth was here. Cleo was highly suspicious of the red-haired foreigner despite Darius's reassurances.

Earlier in the day, Pia had awakened from a short nap to find the queen scribbling notes on a piece of papyrus, trying to decipher and understand the storyteller's bizarre speech. If Cleo cracked the code of the English language, they'd all be in deep trouble. And it was only a matter of time. She had never met a language she couldn't conquer.

Moments after Caesar left, Cleo went to sleep. Pia hastily put on her gold chains and scarlet skirt. When she hurried into the hall, she found Darius waiting. But the Roman guards were on duty and alert. It wasn't safe to talk in front of them.

Imitating the queen's voice, Pia commanded, "Come into my chamber at once. I must confer with you on the night's astrological charts. From my window as I waved goodbye to Caesar, I saw something strange in the heavens. I demand an explanation."

Darius bowed. "Yes, my queen. I have been waiting to confer with you on that very matter. There is a disturbance in the universe."

The stoic guards obviously dismissed the midnight conference as nothing out of the ordinary.

Once they were alone in the queen's chamber, Darius embraced Pia and kissed her. "Are you all right?" he asked in a worried tone. "I know you didn't really see anything strange, but you might as well have. We've got trouble."

"Sudibeth!" Pia said at once. She didn't have to ask. "Cleo's already working on figuring out her 'magical language.'"

"I was afraid of that. Are you willing to leave now? I have my half of the crystal right here. Say the word and we're out of here."

He produced the glowing pryamid. For a time Pia stared at it, transfixed by its shifting colors. It seemed that she could see her cottage on St. Simons deep inside. A sharp pang of homesickness stabbed at her.

"But how will we get Sudibeth back?"

A deep frown etched Darius's brow. "I could send the two of you back, sweetheart."

"You expect me to leave you here?" she cried. "No! I won't go without you, Darius!" She clung to him fiercely.

"Maybe the crystals are strong enough to carry all three of us," he suggested.

Pia stared up into his worried face. "But you don't know that for sure, do you? What would happen if something went wrong?"

He looked away from her demanding gaze. "I can't say," he admitted. "Most likely, one of us would get left behind. Or, worse yet, we could all get stranded in some other century along the way. But it *might* work."

"*Might* isn't good enough. I have to know we'll all get back safely." She stared at the stone in silence for a time, then shook her head. "No! It's too risky. We'll have to stay until we can figure out a better plan."

Darius kissed her again . . . tenderly, sweetly. When he spoke to her, his voice was no more than a whisper. "Pia, you know what's ahead for Cleopatra. The Ides of March, remember? Caesar's going to be murdered. Then she'll barely escape with her life. Then *Mark Antony!*" He said the name as if it tasted bad in his mouth. "You don't want to have to put up with that brute."

"Why, darling, you're jealous, aren't you?" She sounded more sympathetic than accusing.

He gave his head a quick nod. "Yes! I'm *damn* jealous! It's bad enough knowing you're with Caesar, but that Antony character is a first-class bastard! Do you know how many women he's slept with?"

"How many?"

"Don't ask!"

Pia slipped her arms around his waist and hugged him close, kissing his bare chest. "All right, Darius. I'll go back."

He moaned with relief—short-lived.

"Just as soon as you figure out a way to get Sudibeth home safely, too."

But Darius couldn't do that. He'd discovered how to send words through time—back to the computer in Pia's office— but the same formula clearly would not work for sending solid objects. He tested his theory first with a feather from the brilliant-colored tail of one of the peacocks that strutted through the garden. His hopes rose when he saw the feather flutter down to the cluttered floor of Pia's office. To make certain he had his calculations right, he took a wax tablet and scribbled a note on it for Pia, then signed his name, followed by *X*'s and *O*'s for kisses and hugs. That, too, made a safe flight, landing on the desk beside Edgar Allan's glowing face. At that point, he almost told Pia his promising news.

It was good that he waited.

When he experimented with a larger object, a golden chair, its weight slowed its flight and sent it off course. To the delight of an elderly widow in a poor section of nineteenth-century Dublin, the lovely chair landed in her sorry flat. Never one to look a gift horse in the mouth, she attributed her landfall to the work of fairies and put this ancient treasure to good use in her parlor.

Disappointed, but not yet discouraged beyond all hope, Darius calculated that the heavy, gold chair had weighed more than Sudibeth. Besides, he'd missed by only one century and the width of one ocean. Undaunted, he decided to try sending something live back to see if it survived the trip. For this test, he went to the garden and caught an electric-blue salamander.

He swore loudly a short time later when the animal was discovered in a London gutter by an early twentieth-century scientist walking home for tea. The next day, the *Times* carried the headline, "CREATURE THOUGHT EXTINCT SINCE THE RULE OF NERO FOUND IN LONDON STREET."

Darius went back to the drawing board, so to speak.

While he continued sending ancient Roman and Egyptian treasures all over the world in failed attempts to work the kinks out of his equation, Cleopatra and Caesar were keeping Pia busy. When she was not sitting for the Greek sculptor, Archelaus, for her likeness that would be installed in the newly constructed Temple of Venus, she was holding court in her gardens with the noble ladies, who came not to admire her, but to gather tidbits of gossip about Caesar's royal mistress. These busybodies might have driven Cleopatra to mass murder if it hadn't been for Pia's calming influence. Pia had her hands full keeping the hot-tempered queen in check. When any spare moment presented itself, plans were made for Cleopatra and Caesarion's appearance at Caesar's great victory celebration, which was fast approaching.

Caesar's triumphs, which lasted for four days, were the most lavish Rome had ever seen. The citizens turned out in jubilant hordes for the celebration. By Caesar's decree, free food was served at every street corner. The filthy streets were washed down so that wine could flow through the gutters. The entire city was decorated with garlands of flowers, colorful banners, and gilded branches of bay.

On the first day, Caesar celebrated his conquest over Gaul. Dressed in full battle regalia, he rode through the streets in a golden chariot drawn by matched white horses. His legions followed, singing their titillating verses about the "bald adulterer." Forty elephants amazed and frightened the citizens, They had never seen such huge beasts or heard such tramping and trumpeting.

After his ride through the city, Caesar joined Cleopatra and Caesarion on the viewing stand to watch the day's parade. All eyes focused on the great leader when he gazed at the foreign queen with a look of tender love and burning passion. A murmur of awe went through their ranks.

But soon their attention was diverted. The citizens seemed to share Pia's sympathy for the conquered Gallic general, Vercingetorix. He had surrendered to Caesar to save his people from more suffering at the hands and swords of the Roman legions. Now the brave hero of Gaul walked in chains, head down on this final day of his mortal life. Even Caesar commented to Cleopatra that it seemed a shame to execute such a worthy foe. But the law was the law.

Caesar's Egyptian triumph provided a lavish spectacle on the second day. Cleopatra was dressed all in gold, looking like a glittering goddess as she stood between her lover and her son, who were dressed alike in Roman fashion. The parade wound on for hours and hours. A statue of the Nile god watching over a replica of the whole river, a scale model of the great Pharos lighthouse, models of Cleopatra's palace, the great pyramids, and the Sphinx. Cleopatra smiled in triumph when the portraits of the long-dead allies of her brother Ptolemy came into view. The Romans went wild at the sight of the queen's beautiful slaves in their scant shifts, dancing and swaying through the streets. Then came the exotic animals from the East—long-necked giraffes, pretty zebras led by silken ribbons, chattering monkeys, bright jungle birds, hippopotami, and the fierce-looking crocodiles that made the Romans gasp aloud in fear.

Cleopatra's scheming younger sister, Arsinoë, was paraded nearly naked, in golden chains, along with her lover and fellow conspirator, Ganymede. Caesar decided it would be bad politics to execute the queen's sister, so, after her humiliation in the streets of Rome, she was exiled to live out the rest of her life in the Temple of Artemis at Ephesus. Ganymede received no such royal anmesty. He could not be allowed to live on to hatch other plots against Egypt and Rome. As further punishment, Caesar forced Arsinoë to watch her lover's execution.

On the third day, the Queen of Egypt opted to rest and prepare herself for the fourth and final extravaganza. She missed all the celebration of Caesar's triumph over Pharnaces and his conquest of Pontus. She missed the great banner that proclaimed, Veni, Vidi, Vici. She missed the riotous celebration that night when Caesar presented lavish gifts to his soldiers, then fed the people of Rome, en masse, at the Circus Maximus. The plebeians lounged on twenty thousand dining couches for their feast while Caesar provided them with gladiatorial spectacles and naval battles in the flooded arena.

Cleopatra couldn't sleep that evening. She paced her chamber, on edge, her nerves ragged. From her window she could see the whole city across the Tiber. It glowed with thousands of torches. She could hear the shouts and cheers from the Circus. Rome itself seem to moan with one great, drunken roar.

"Think of tomorrow," she kept telling herself. "That day of days!"

She stopped short of saying the rest aloud, afraid she might make the gods jealous. But Pia heard her thoughts: *Tomorrow Rome and the world will be mine!*

Pia knew from studying history that Cleo was about to get the biggest disappointment of her life. Caesar was going to present Cleopatra and Caesarion to Rome, all right. He was going to dedicate the new Temple of Venus Genetrix, Venus the Mother of All. He was going to unveil the statue of the goddess that was a likeness of Cleopatra. It would be *her* day—all to her glorification. He even meant to proclaim her a divine being, the incarnation of the Egyptian goddess Isis, the counterpart of the Roman Venus.

But the one thing Cleopatra most longed for she wouldn't get. Caesar had yet to divorce Calpurnia. And he was not, as the queen hoped, going to marry her publicly and proclaim their joint rule.

Why don't you settle down? Pia said finally. *You're making me edgy.*

Cleopatra jumped at again hearing her long-silent inner voice. "So, you have returned," she snapped.

I never went anywhere. I figured you were too busy to be bothered these past few days.

"So why are you bothering me now?" the queen demanded.

Because you're driving me crazy. Why don't you have some poppy wine? You're jumping out of your skin.

Cleo stared down at herself. "I am in my skin. Why do you talk in riddles? What do you want of me?"

Pia sighed. *All I want is for you to take it easy. What will be, will be. Your worrying about things won't change them.*

"He *must* marry me tomorrow!" Cleopatra spoke through clenched teeth as if she could will it so.

And if he doesn't? So what? It won't kill you. You'll still be the Queen of Egypt, Caesarion's mother, the most beautiful woman in the world. That should be enough for any person.

Pia's reasoning only made Cleopatra more agitated. "You know something, don't you? Why won't you tell me? At least I could prepare myself."

Pia was tempted, but she knew that if Cleo learned the bad news in advance, she might do something drastic to change history.

I have an idea, Pia said. *Caesar's going to be out there partying with that mob all night. Why don't you call your astrologer, have a consultation? Maybe he could tell you more than I can.* Pia shrugged and grinned. Her smile spread over the queen's face. *If not, well, he's good company anyway. You'll feel better. Trust me!*

"Darius," Cleo breathed. The hint of a smile betrayed a shift in her thoughts. "Yes, it's been so long."

Pia felt a moment of hot jealousy. She didn't like sharing Darius with another woman, but sharing him was better than not having him at all.

Cleopatra hurried through the corridor to Caesarion's chamber. She found Sudibeth sprawled in a chair where she'd dozed off in the middle of a bedtime story. Darius, however, was nowhere to be found.

"Where could he be?" Cleopatra fumed.

Why don't you try the little temple out at the edge of the garden? He sometimes goes there at night. Better view of the heavens, Pia suggested quickly, afraid that she'd given away one of the places she and Darius often met.

Sure enough, Cleopatra asked suspiciously, "How do you know that?"

Pia chuckled. *Oh, I get around.*

* * *

Darius stood at a window at the back of the circular temple, trying to catch a breeze from the river. Even though it was September, the air was stifling, and his frame of mind didn't help any. He'd just tried sending one of the Forum's scrawny, long-legged cats forward in time. He'd pondered the humane side of such a project before deciding that the ebony-furred feline would make out far better in some other place than here, where it might be killed and eaten by a hungry Roman. He saved the cat, all right, but missed his mark by farther than ever. He also managed to get some poor innocent in Salem convicted of witchcraft. The black cat had landed right in the middle of the Massachusetts courtroom where her trial was in progress. Due to the cat's unorthodox arrival—out of thin air—it was immediately pronounced the woman's familiar and consort in evil. The cat got away; the "witch" got burned.

Darius was mad as hell—at himself—when he heard someone whisper his name at the temple door. He turned, about to snarl at whomever dared disturb him. The angry words died in his throat when he saw her there.

"Cleopatra?" he murmured.

He'd never seen her like this before. She looked younger, more innocent and more troubled than she had the day she'd fished him out of the sea. Under her plain blue cloak, she wore a simple, white shift, very like a child's garment. No jewels, no chains, no crown. Her face was washed of all paints and kohl. Her dark hair was brushed out straight and long, falling to her waist. She looked clean and soft and honest. More beautiful than he had ever imagined she could be.

"There's no sleeping tonight with all that going on." She waved a slender arm toward Rome, blazing with torches, roaring with the cheers of her drunken citizens.

Darius gazed out over the seven hills. "Caesar's throwing quite a party. Rome's never seen anything like it. You weren't invited?"

"I didn't want to go," she explained with a shiver of revulsion. "Rome depresses me, Darius. It's so different from Alexandria. I thought Caesar's city would be clean and new and elegant. But the Romans build instant ruins. Someday this whole place is going to go up in flames."

Not until Nero starts fiddling around, Pia put in silently.

"You're homesick for your own country. That's all, Cleopatra." He reached out and brushed her cheek with his fingertips.

"Darius, hold me," she begged.

He slipped the light cloak from her shoulders. For several moments, he stood looking at her in silence, letting his gaze admire the womanly figure beneath the sheer gown.

"What's wrong?" she asked breathlessly.

He shook his head and smiled. "Not a thing! It's only that you amaze me. You grow more beautiful with the years." His eyes met the turquoise gleam of hers. "Tomorrow Caesar will proclaim you the incarnation of Venus. But tonight you truly are that goddess come to life."

Darius reached out to her. Gripping her bare shoulders gently, he drew her to him. He held her close, murmuring her name. She trembled in his arms. Inside the queen, Pia was trembling as well.

"Something else is bothering you. Can you tell me what it is?" he asked softly.

"I'm worried about tomorrow," she confessed. "If Caesar fails to make me his legal wife, what's going to happen to me, Darius? What's going to happen to Caesarion? Mark Antony told me that Roman divorce is such a simple matter. Why hasn't Caesar said the words to Calpurnia to free himself to marry me?"

She was suffering, so Darius felt he had to give her some

hope. "Perhaps he plans to do that tomorrow, as part of the ceremony."

"Do you think he would shame her so? Public divorce seems harsh for a ruler's wife. I doubt he would do it that way."

"Calpurnia is barren. You have given him a son. He may want the citizens to see his divorce and marriage for themselves so that there can be no questions, no doubts."

Stop coddling her! Pia chided. *You know that's not going to happen, Darius.*

He didn't hear, of course, and went right on trying to soothe Cleo's fears. But it was obvious that words were not enough.

Leaning down, he kissed her gently. Then harder, deeper. She clutched at him and moaned.

Pia was trying not to let Cleo's desires influence her own. She wanted Darius—oh, yes! But the longer she could ignore the things Darius was doing to the queen, the better off she'd be. She had to get her eyes off him. To keep from looking at him and wanting him so, she let her gaze travel to the tiny temple. Now, where on earth were they going to make love? The desanctified structure had been stripped of everything when its goddess went—the furniture, the tapestries, even the sheets of gold had been pulled down from its columns. Near the front of the round room a stone altar still stood in place.

Darius spotted it at the same time Pia did. Still holding Cleopatra, he whispered, "This was once the Temple of Venus, wasn't it?"

"So I've been told," she answered breathlessly.

"The Goddess of Love brought you here tonight, my queen."

She was dizzy from his kisses, from his hands caressing her breasts. "Do you think that's true, my love?"

"I know it for a fact," he vowed. "She has brought you

to her altar to be sacrificed to love." He edged closer to the marble table, drawing Cleopatra along with him. "Tomorrow you become the goddess. Tonight you must pay her tribute."

A great cheer rose from the hills of Rome as if the city's citizens were urging Darius on.

He lifted her in his arms and placed her on the cool marble slab. For a time, he stood over her, staring down into her eyes, making love to her with his gaze.

"Oh, Darius," she moaned. "Make me *your* goddess!"

She placed her palms flat on his chest and rubbed circles against his hard flesh. She rose and kissed his nipples, teasing them with the tip of her tongue.

Darius groaned. He stood erect and turned from her.

"What's wrong?" she gasped.

"Too bright."

He moved about the room, snuffing oil lamps until only an eerie glow remained—a glow that seemed to turn Cleopatra's flesh to polished marble. The reflection of the single flame danced in her eyes.

"I have something to show you," he said. "Something magical."

Transfixed by the dark fire in his voice, Cleopatra remained silent, her eyes wide, her body tense.

"You've seen it before. Remember?"

Out of the semidarkness, he produced his half of the crystal pyramid. He held it so that the light from the single lamp seemed to glow inside the stone.

Cleopatra caught her breath. "Why, it's the fragment I broke from Alexander's sarcophagus so long ago! You've kept it all these years?"

"It saved my life. It brought us together. I treasure it. And I respect its magic."

Darius rubbed the stone between his hands until it began to hum with its own erotic melody. Then he held it to the light once more. Cleopatra gave a soft cry of surprise.

"What's that inside?" she asked.

"Look closer," he invited with a cunning smile. "Tell me what you see."

She didn't have to tell him. She would see what she wanted to see. That was the magic of the stone. She would see Darius making love to her, their bodies writhing together in a timeless sea of liquid heat and light. That was what Pia saw, too, only she was the woman, not Cleopatra. She squirmed with pleasure inside the queen.

"Darius?" There was pleading in Cleo's voice. She was no more immune to the crystal pyramid than Pia was.

He came to her and kissed her, holding her with his lips as he stripped away her gown. He rubbed the stone between his palms until it sang. When he touched it to Cleopatra's breast, she cried out with pleasure as waves of vibration raced through her whole body.

"I can't hold on," Pia said in a squeaky little voice through Cleo's open mouth. But she managed.

By the time Darius finally put the stone aside and "sacrificed" his goddess on the altar of love, both women were limp with desire. Even Cleopatra was no match for the crystal pyramid. She and Pia both reached the heights at the same time. Their magical lover joined them in the flight through the starry heavens.

The next morning Pia slept late. Cleopatra, however, was up with the sun, preparing for her day as a goddess. She smiled, thinking how her night as a goddess had calmed her nerves and given her strength.

For the first time, the Egyptian queen consented to wear traditional Roman garb. It would be difficult, if not impossible, for the citizens of Rome to accept the fact that the Egyptian Queen, looking as alien as she truly was, could become the embodiment of their goddess Venus.

Before the dressing was done, Pia decided that Cleopatra had the patience of a saint. Even in the sweltering, September heat, the Romans wore layers upon complicated layers of clothes. Since Iras was confounded by all the garments, Caesar sent a Roman servant to Cleopatra's villa to help. Both Cleo and Pia suspected that the stolid, efficient servant had been borrowed from Caesar's wife.

The square-built, heavy-framed maid named Lucretia proved to be as efficient and as humorless as a head nurse. She marched into the royal chamber without so much as a bow to the tiny Egyptian queen.

"Remove the robe!" She barked the order at Iras, who quickly complied, leaving the queen stark naked before the stranger's penetrating, black eyes.

The woman walked around, measuring Cleopatra's lush figure with a specialist's gaze. "For a small woman, she is heavily endowed. She must wear a *mamillare* as well as a *strophium* to support her breasts."

She rummaged through a pile of garments Iras had brought from the chest, tossing things aside, until she found the two things she needed. First, Lucretia took a length of linen and wound it around Cleopatra's breasts. Next a longer piece, the *strophium*, was wrapped around the *mamillare* and down over the queen's hips.

"I feel as if I'm being prepared for mummification," Cleopatra snapped.

Lucretia ignored her, going back to the pile of clothes for more. She brought ungainly looking briefs for Cleopatra to step into. After a quick, satisfied nod, the Roman servant slipped two short wool tunics over the queen's head.

"This is hot," Cleopatra complained. "And not at all lovely."

Lucretia looked to Iras, never speaking directly to the queen. "She should be happy she had regained her figure after childbirth so that she will not be forced to wear a stomach-band as well."

The next garment the servant chose from the pile brought a hint of a smile to Cleopatra's face. The *stola*, very much like the Greek *chiton* that the queen had always favored, was silk, as pure and white as new-fallen snow. Full and pleated, the garment was fringed in gold, with elaborate embroidery on its edges. Pleased with the slither of cool silk against her flesh, Cleopatra almost forgot her uncomfortable, unlovely undergarments. She turned this way and that, admiring her image in the looking glass—the way the pleated train trailed the marble floor, the flattering length of the sleeves, the flash of gold as she moved.

"You look lovely, my lady," said Iras.

"I am not yet finished with the task," Lucretia announced.

She lumbered over to the heavy jewel trunk that Caesar had ordered brought to the queen's chamber. Her back to the other two women, she raised the lid. The clink of gold filled the silent room as she rummaged through Rome's treasures.

"Ah!" she cried at last. "Fit for a goddess!"

She turned, raising the elaborately embroidered and bejeweled girdle for Cleopatra and Iras to see. They caught their breath as one. The morning sun flashed off rubies, emeralds, sapphires, and fire opals all set in gold stitching as delicate as a cobweb.

"The *cingulum!*" Lucretia announced.

She bound Cleopatra's waist with the shining girdle. Silence again filled the chamber as all three woman stood back to admire the effect in the long mirror.

"Now the *palla*," Lucretia said, "and she will be ready."

With a flourish, the servant produced a large rectangle of fine, purple wool, again embroidered and deeply fringed in gold. This she draped loosely about Cleopatra's shoulders and over her head.

"My queen, you are a vision," Iras whispered, almost breathless.

"She should please the gods, if not the Romans," Lucretia said almost sarcastically. Obviously, she was a servant with some standing in Calpurnia's household. A lesser maid would surely have been whipped for such insolence, Cleopatra thought.

Pia sagged inside Cleo. She had never worn this many clothes in her life. They'd be lucky if they both didn't faint before the ceremony was over. If she felt this uncomfortable, the queen must be dying—all that tight linen wrapped around her and woolen tunics rubbing her raw. It amazed Pia that she caught no thoughts of Cleo's misery. Instead, the queen was excited and nervous. Most of all, she seemed curious once more, anxious to find out if Caesar would make her his wife as well as his goddess of love on this day.

Moments after Lucretia left, her mission accomplished, the trumpeter sounded his horn at the gate, announcing Caesar's arrival.

"At last!" Cleopatra said. "Iras, go and bring Caesarion. We are ready to leave for the Temple of Venus Genetrix."

Once Iras left, Pia felt the full impact of Cleopatra's nerves. Had they been in the twentieth century, the queen's nervous state would have been termed a "panic attack." Her heart raced, her palms went sweaty, her mouth felt dry. Suddenly, she didn't want to see anyone, especially not Caesar, not all those screaming, cheering, drunken Romans. She felt the urge to hide in her clothes chest or, at the very least, pull her purple *palla* up to cover her face and close out the world.

Hey, take it easy, Pia said. *It won't be so bad. I promise. Nobody's going to get killed today. You just go to the temple, look and act like a goddess, and it's all over. You'll be back here before you know it, peeling out of all that uncomfortable underwear.*

"If you know so much, tell me if Caesar plans to make me his wife," Cleo snapped.

Now it was Pia who panicked. She'd said too much already. She didn't dare tell Cleo what she wanted to know. Better, she figured, to clam up for the time being.

"Well? Why don't you say something? Where are you?"

"I'm here, my love," Caesar answered from the door. "And look at you. Venus incarnate. All Rome will adore you."

She accepted his kiss on her cheek, a bit more coolly than usual. "That's not what I hear," she snapped. "That woman who dressed me hinted that Rome cares nothing for me. I thought at first of having her whipped for such insolence. Then I decided she might be trying to warn me."

Caesar chuckled. "Pay no mind to Lucretia. The old baggage has served my indulgent wife far too long. I'm afraid she's too old either to be whipped or to be trained. But she is a master at what she does." He stepped back, spread his arms, and gazed at her worshipfully. "Just look at you! There was never a goddess so breathtaking. No one will be able to resist you, Cleopatra."

Unimpressed by his flattery, she accused, "Caesar, however, manages to resist me quite well."

He frowned so deeply that his black, deep-set eyes almost closed. "Whatever are you talking about, my love? Why, I've been your foremost admirer since the moment we met, your *slave* since we first made love."

"But you still aren't willing to be my husband, are you, Caesar?" Her voice was cold and regal.

He came quickly to her and took her hand, kissed her fingers. "I *am* your husband! Caesarion is our proof. Could anyone doubt that he is my son?"

"Caesarion is the proof of our love, not the proof of our marriage. Only by divorcing Calpurnia and marrying me legally will I become more than your royal whore."

Give him hell, Cleo! Pia couldn't resist. The old bastard deserved that and more.

"We'll talk about this later, Cleopatra. We must not keep the priests and the people waiting. Come!"

Pia had thought the queen would be crushed by Caesar's admission that he had no plans for a wedding ceremony today at the temple. Instead, Cleopatra gained strength from that knowledge and even from her own disappointment.

I don't get it, Pia commented silently as Caesar escorted them to his waiting litter.

Cleo answered silently, smiling. *To know one's fate is to conquer it, often to change it. Caesar will soon learn that I am a strong woman, much stronger than he suspects. I have given him the son he longed for. My duties are at an end. If he wishes to bed me, he will wed me first. Here, in his city, before his people.*

You're riding for a fall, Queenie, Pia retorted.

Cleopatra ignored her comment; she didn't understand it anyway. Instead of worrying about the future, she concentrated on the present. She put on her best "goddess face," the very one she used back in Egypt on feast days when her subjects worshipped her as Isis. She accepted the Romans' cheers and adulation with the same cool reserve that she offered Caesar when he whispered love words in her ear.

From the glow of Caesar's countenance, Cleopatra could tell that his power to proclaim her a goddess made him feel even more godlike. The man was drunk on his own power. He confessed to her softly during the ceremony, as they stood in the temple before her likeness in marble, that he had a god's urge to sacrifice her on the altar of love.

Pia giggled silently. *We already did that, J.C., last night. To bad you missed it!*

Cleopatra had to stifle the urge to laugh when she heard

Pia's taunt. *Wicked voice!* she shot back. *Mind he doesn't hear you.*

There was no fear of that. Pia was careful to make sure that her words didn't escape the queen. The two women were almost like conspirators now, flashing unspoken messages back and forth.

As for Caesar, the man didn't know it yet, but he was out in the cold. He'd marry Cleopatra or else!

All the way back to the villa after the ceremony at the temple, Caesar tried his best to get Cleopatra in the mood. The lavish, closed litter afforded ample opportunity for his work. With the heavy gold curtains drawn, they might even have made love in perfect privacy on their ride back through the city. The randy conqueror would have welcomed such a novel tryst.

"Please, no, Caesar," she begged. "It's too hot. And the motion of the litter makes me almost faint." She widened her eyes until she wore a childlike expression. "If I swoon, will you take care of me?"

God, what an actress! Pia mused. Even as Cleo was refusing his advances, she was doing everything in her power to turn him on. That helpless female act got to Caesar every time.

"I *will* take care of you, my love," he promised. "I'll carry you in my own arms into your chamber. I'll send your servants away and I'll undress you myself. I'll strip away all this Roman finery until I find Egypt beneath. Egypt with her honey-flavored breasts, her cool as silk flesh, her passion as hot as the fiery chariot that passes through her heavens."

"Oh, thank you, Caesar!" Her voice sounded like that of a frightened child. "I feared, if I swooned, that you might do as you once threatened."

His plucked brows drew together. "I *never* threatened you, Cleopatra!"

"Yes, once when we first met. You said you would bring

some brutish soldier from your legion to watch as you made love to me."

A slow smile curved Caesar's lips. He remembered. And he guessed that Cleopatra was teasing him. If he was correct, she was disappointed that he had never carried through with that threat. Perhaps today would be the perfect time. The nearer they drew to the villa, the more excited he became. By the time they crossed the bridge, he was nearly bursting with anticipation.

As he helped her out of the litter, he leaned close and whispered, "I've decided on the perfect man to join us this afternoon, Cleopatra. Mark Antony!" His eyes glittered with excitement, sure that the queen would be most grateful.

He was in for a disappointment.

"Some other time, perhaps." She drew the back of her hand languidly across her brow. "I have a headache now."

The queen stood in the garden and waved as Caesar rode off in the litter, his plans for the afternoon dashed, his amorous mood turned sour. Both Cleo and Pia chuckled.

"See how he likes that!" the queen said.

Want to visit the other temple? Pia suggested.

Cleopatra laughed brightly. "At times you amaze me with your clever ideas."

They wandered off through the garden, in search of Darius. In search of love.

Chapter Sixteen

Cleopatra didn't have long to work her feminine wiles on Caesar. Only weeks after the dedication of the Temple of Venus Genetrix, he received an urgent message to hurry to Spain. His old enemies, the sons of Pompey the Great, were rising up against him in a civil war that was taking on all the aspects of a recurring nightmare. In November of 46 B.C. he set out with his legions, promising a speedy victory and a prompt return.

Still in a godlike mood, Caesar never considered the possibility that he might not return at all. That thought, however, haunted Cleopatra through all the long months that he was away. She had yet to convince him to marry her; if he didn't return, she would never be his wife and empress. She would never get her chance to rule the world.

In fact, Julius Caesar was nearly killed in March of 45. Later he told Cleopatra, "I have often fought for victory, but this was the first time I had to fight for my very life."

Caesar, now fifty-six but looking older than his years, returned to Rome in the late spring, the unchallenged ruler of an empire that spread from Britain far to the east, to Asia Minor.

If the noble Roman had any further doubts that he was truly a god, those misgivings fled following his return from the war. After a long absence of the malady, he was once more struck down with the "falling sickness"—epileptic fits that told him for certain his body was inhabited by a divine being. Cleopatra pampered him and let him think that she believed the same, but she knew better. The more refined medical community in Alexandria attributed these seizures, not to visitations by the gods, but to overwork and advancing age.

While he was recovering from one such attack, Cleopatra urged him gently, "Caesar, the gods are trying to give you a sign. Don't you see it?"

They were sitting in the garden of her villa on an especially clear and fragrant spring day. Down the hill, Caesarion and his storyteller were playing a riotous game of tag. The breeze off the seven hills of the city fluttered the violet silk of the queen's light gown. Caesar stared at her, his eyes dull with the poppy juice she had slipped into his wine. But it was clear that the potion—meant to calm him—had not dulled his desire for her in the least.

He reached for her hand and brought it to his lips. "What is it the gods would have me know, my dear?"

She inclined her head toward Caesarion. "You have only to gaze on our son for your answer. See how fast he grows? Already he has the look of a ruler, a young god." She turned dewy eyes on Caesar. "Yet, poor lad, he has no father."

"I am his father!" Caesar snapped, half rising from the lounge in his anger. "Let no man dispute that!"

Cleopatra pressed him back down. "I don't want to upset you, dearest, but *every* man disputes that. As long as I am your mistress, nothing more, Rome will see our son as fatherless."

She paused, waiting for his reaction. He only stared off in the distance, his gaze following the boy at play.

"It would be so simple," Cleopatra prodded gently. "Divorce Calpurnia. Marry me. Legitimize Caesarion. Already you and I have established a dynasty. Use your unlimited power to force the people to accept that fact."

Pia was holding her breath inside the queen. At any minute she expected to see Caesar fall off his couch in another of his fits—not a pretty sight!

Cleopatra waited. Pia waited. Caesar remained silent. He brought his golden goblet to his mouth. He sipped. He set it down. Finally he turned toward the queen.

"I intend to do exactly that," he said quietly. "Even now plans for the ceremony are in progress."

Pia felt Cleo's triumphant reaction. Even though the queen retained a calm facade, mentally she was singing, dancing, and doing cartwheels.

"*When*, Caesar?" she prompted gently.

Again, Pia held her breath, waiting for his answer.

He chuckled softly. "Ah, the young are always so impatient. Important matters such as this take some preparation."

"We need no lavish ceremony. I'm quite bored with all the triumphs, feasts, and games. What sort of preparation must we make?"

"I have a plan, my dear." For the first time since before his spell, his black eyes glittered with excitement. "A grand master plan for all of Rome. These civil wars have left the very fabric of Roman life in tatters. I must do some reconstruction before we wed. The city has gone to seed. Unemployment is rampant."

Cleopatra's mouth was slightly open. Pia took advantage of her opportunity to say, "It's the bread-dole. If you give free food to the citizens once a week, that's no better than welfare. They won't work if you encourage their laziness.

Take away the handouts, then see how fast they all find employment."

The queen clamped her mouth shut and gave Pia a shot in the ribs.

He turned and looked at her, his eyes wide. "How wise you are for your years!" he exclaimed. "But I've always known that. You are exactly correct, Cleopatra. I have encouraged indigence. I will discontinue the dole immediately. In its place, I will encourage colonization. I'm planning new colonies in Carthage, Corinth, and Hispalis in Spain. I plan to send eighty thousand Romans out to build new towns and make new lives for themselves. That will reduce the overcrowding and make more jobs for those who remain here. I mean to make a law, too, that men between the ages of twenty and forty cannot leave Rome for more than three years at a time and remain citizens. That way, we won't be left with an aging population. I have changes to make in the Criminal Code and the Civil Law. I also want to encourage the arts and medicine. I'll grant citizenship to all artists and doctors who wish to come to Rome.

Cleopatra gasped. "Caesar, stop! You make me dizzy with all these plans. If I were your co-ruler, I could help."

He chuckled at her suggestion. Not that he thought she was incapable of helping, he simply recognized the fact that she wanted their marriage *now.*

She knew what he was thinking. To cover her blunder, she said, "At least let Sosigenes, the brilliant mathematician and astronomer I summoned from Alexandria assist you in these endeavors."

Caesar's eyes flashed with pleasure. "By all means. Having your man to help will speed up the rebuilding of the city, the erection of new temples and of the grand theater I've always wanted at the foot of the Tarpeian Rock. I intend to reclaim the Pontine Marshes as well, make more room for expansion."

Cleopatra sagged in her chair. Caesar was correct. Rome needed much work. Compared to Alexandria, the city was a crowded, dirty, unplanned mess of winding streets, crumbling buildings, and squalid squares. However, to put it to rights could take years, decades. Caesarion might not live to see the reconstruction's finish. Certainly Caesar would never survive that long.

Her dark thoughts were interrupted when the eighteen-month-old Caesarion came running up the hill to throw himself into his mother's arms. The beautiful boy, with his tousled gold curls and sapphire-bright eyes, hugged Cleopatra and began babbling excitedly in a combination of Latin and Sudi's mystical language, English.

"What's that he's saying?" Caesar asked.

"I believe he's telling us that it's a shame he hasn't a real father to teach him to speak properly." Cleopatra rose, took Caesarion by the hand, and retired to the villa, leaving Caesar to ponder her words.

During the months after Caesar's return, Pia spent as much time with Darius as possible. Cleopatra often slept alone. Caesar almost seemed to be avoiding her. Maybe, Pia thought, he didn't want her to witness another of his epileptic fits. Or it could be that he was tired of her harping about their marriage. For whatever reason, he was still holding back on that one detail, while he plunged into all his new programs.

One cold night in early 44, when Caesar had been absent from the villa for nearly a week, Pia slipped out of the queen's chamber once Cleo fell asleep. She darted through the gardens to the old temple. Darius was still trying, and failing at, his experiments to return Sudibeth to St. Simons. He'd become almost obsessed with this open window to the future that led back to Pia's beach cottage—but with many stops along the way. When Pia walked in on him, he was grinning like a kid.

"I just sent an ancient Roman parchment into the twenty-first century," he said. "Think about it, Pia! Won't some future historian go out of his skull when he finds *that!*"

"I hope it wasn't one of Caesar's important papers," she said, frowning.

"Naw!" He grinned and winked at her. "Just one of those fancy invitations to the Lupercalia next month. You know, the Romans' celebration that's sort of like your Mardi Gras."

"You mean the old Etruscan fertility festival?"

"Yep! Sounds like it'll be fun. Antony promised to make me an honorary member of the Order of Lupercus so I can be one of the Faun-men that day."

Knowing Mark Antony's reputation, Pia gave Darius a suspicious look. "I thought you two didn't get along."

"He's not such a bad guy. The way he struts around all the time put me off at first. Then I realized he uses all that posturing to hide his insecurities. I can identify with that."

Pia's eyes went wide and she chuckled. *"You? Insecure?* Come on, Darius!"

"Hey, scratch any man and underneath you'll find a little boy. I'm no different." He laughed and winked at her. "If you don't believe me, just watch my antics as a Faun-man."

"What do they do?"

"Run around and act crazy and touch women with these little whips. It's supposed to guarantee that they'll get pregnant."

Pia stared at him. "That's a new way of doing it. What are the whips dipped in?"

"Come on, Pia. You remember the story from your research."

"Oh, yes. My book." She looked away quickly, but not before Darius saw tears spring to her eyes.

He wrapped her in his arms. "What's the matter, sweetheart?"

Sympathy was the last thing she needed. She immediately burst into tears, then had to choke out her answer through fitful sobs. "I don't know what we're going to do, Darius. We've been here so long, and I've got a deadline. We may never get back. Everything's just so messed up. Cleo's the worst mother I've ever seen. Poor little Caesarion breaks my heart, he yearns so to be loved. He clings to Sudibeth, and she's teaching him stuff he shouldn't know—stuff that's going to get him into trouble, I'm afraid."

"Like what, Pia?"

She shrugged in his arms. "English, for one thing. His own mother can hardly understand him any longer. And Sudi's showed him how to draw happy faces. He's already learning to write the hieroglyphics that stand for his name, but now he insists on putting a happy face in with the other figures. Lord only knows what that spells in ancient Egyptian."

Darius threw back his head and laughed. "Can't you just see come archaeologist centuries from now coming across young Caesarion's signature? I'd love to be there for that." When Pia kept on crying, Darius kissed her and said, "That's not so terrible, is it, sweetheart?"

"Not really," she admitted, half smiling. Then her face turned troubled again. "But bad times are coming, Darius. We both know that. And now Cassius and Brutus are sneaking around, plotting against Caesar. Isn't there *anything* we can do?"

Darius turned up her face with his hands and stared down into her eyes. His expression was deadly serious as he brushed away her tears. "Yes, you could probably do something, Pia. You could tell Cleopatra everything you know. You could finger the guys who are planning to kill Caesar. I'm sure before the Ides of March she'd send some of her goons to waste that whole bunch of conspirators. Or I could tell Antony, and he'd kill them all with his bare hands. But then what?"

Pia had stopped crying. She had a hopeful gleam in her eyes. A smile twitched her lips. "Then Caesar wouldn't be killed!" she cried excitedly. "We *can* save him! Oh, Darius!" She hugged him tightly, kissing his bare chest.

He unwrapped her arms from around his waist and took a step away. "Okay! Let me see if I have this right? You want to save Caesar's life."

"Yes!" Pia cried.

He nodded, unsmiling. "So that means he and Cleopatra will probably get married."

Pia nodded enthusiastically. She'd been inside Cleo so long it seemed like the queen's wishes were her own.

"All right, let's look at the big picture here. They get married. They declare themselves Emperor and Empress of all Roman holdings and Egyptian lands. They can do that." He nodded, still looking thoughtful. "And together they and their dynasty will have enough power to rule the whole planet for eons to come. Of course that means Londoners, when the city comes of age, will all speak Latin. Hell, the whole world will! And instead of the Capitol in Washington, D.C., only looking Roman, it will be. Your dollar bills won't read In God We Trust, but instead, In Caesar We Trust. If we do happen to get organized enough to elect a president, he'll have to wear a tunic or a toga at press conferences."

Pia's eyes got wider and wider while Darius talked on, painting his odd pictures with words. Finally, she giggled, then she laughed.

"I give!" she said. "We shouldn't change history. You're right. I hate to think of scantily clad dancing girls at White House receptions. And from what I've seen of the president, his knees aren't good enough to be displayed in public. But what about my book?"

"Don't worry about that, sweetheart. You told everybody you'd be back in a week. You know how time goes all whacko on these trips. My guess is you'll be home in time to make your deadline, no matter how long we stay here." He turned to a pile of papers—figures, formulas, calculations—and frowned. "If I can ever figure out this damn window and how to get Sudibeth out of here."

The minute he said her name, the pert redhead appeared at the temple door. "Am I interrupting anything?" she asked.

"No." They both answered at once.

She wrinkled her nose in a grin. "Too bad! I was just out for a stroll and I heard your voices. I figured I'd pop in and catch up on the latest gossip. What's up? Any progress with your window, Darius?"

He shook his head and shrugged. "I'm sorry, Sudibeth."

"Oh, no problem! I've met this great guy from Gaul."

Pia and Darius exchanged glances.

Sudibeth failed to notice their reactions. "Lord, is he something! Big, gorgeous, sexy as hell! And he's been off in the wars so long, he's all but forgotten what it's like to be with a woman."

"Right!" Pia said sarcastically. "Like he hasn't done his share of pillaging and raping."

"No, honest, Pia! This guy's just starved for female flesh. He probably took some sort of oath or something. So I just wanted to tell you, Darius, not to hurry. I'm having a ball. Even taking care of the kid isn't bad. He's a corker! I've been teaching him some English, and as he learns Latin I'm picking it up, too. He's smart as a whip. Makes me wish he was mine."

"He's *mine!*" Pia snapped.

Both Darius and Sudibeth stared at her.

"Caesarion belongs to Cleopatra," Darius reminded her evenly.

Pia brushed a hand over her eyes. "I know. It's just that

she doesn't care that much for kids. I'm the one who loves him and looks out for him. He's just one of her pets—like her cats and her monkeys and her peacocks. When we go back, I think I'll take him with me."

"Pia, I thought we got all that settled a while ago," Darius said.

"Well, I know we can't change history. But what difference would it make if I took Caesarion home? I could say I'd adopted him. We could raise him as our own."

"No, Pia!" Darius used a sharp tone with her this time.

"If we leave him here, he's going to die, Darius. I can't stand thinking about it. Shoot, Cleo probably wouldn't notice he was gone for days. If it weren't for me, she'd never pay any attention to him. And he's so sweet and dear." Her eyes sparkled as she went on. "I could fix up my office as a nursery—move Edgar Allan into my bedroom. Caesarion would just love the beach. We could collect sand dollars and starfish and shells."

"Darius, I think you'd better get her out of here," Sudibeth whispered. "She's about to go right off the deep end."

He went to Pia and took her into his arms again. "Darling, listen to me. You know you can't take Caesarion home. He has to stay here with his natural mother. He's part of history, part of the past."

Pia whimpered against his chest, still muttering about taking Caesarion to the playground at Neptune Park and to Fort Frederica and to the yogurt shop near the pier on Mallory Street.

Sudibeth made a sign over Pia's head and mouthed that she was leaving. Darius nodded gravely, still trying to calm Pia.

He'd hoped that they could make love tonight. It had been a week. But Pia was too upset. Finally, when he got her calmed down enough so the guards in the villa wouldn't think anything odd, he led her back to Cleopatra's chamber. He stayed with her until she finally fell asleep.

Despite the winter damp that chilled to the marrow, all of Rome turned out on February 15 for the foolish feast of Lupercalia. Although Lupercus had been an ancient Etruscan god, the Romans kept him on after they ran Rome's early settlers off the land. They identified him with their own nature god, Faunus, the Greek god Pan, and celebrated his day in order to make plants grow and animals and humans reproduce. The ceremony, Cleopatra mused, was not unlike an ancient rite of Egypt to the old god Min-Amon, who made all things fecund with his whip of braided jackal hides.

Caesar had proclaimed himself the god Lupercus for the day. He presided over the festivities from a throne in the Forum.

"Wear a cloak, at least," Cleopatra had urged him before they left her villa.

Caesar, in his royal purple toga, refused. "Gods know no cold," he insisted haughtily, obviously taking his role quite seriously.

In the windswept Forum, Cleopatra huddled inside her furs and Pia huddled inside Cleopatra. It was truly a bitter day, the perfect setting for the cold events about to take place.

The Queen of Egypt was a master of decorum. Never once did she wince or turn away as the priests sacrificed a goat and a dog to the old god. Her gaze remained steady on the gruesome scene as the animals were skinned and their coats sliced and plaited into bloody whips for the Faunmen.

Pia, sickened, closed her eyes, refusing to watch. Only when she heard cheers from the crowd, then the riotous laughter of Mark Antony, Darius, and the others did she once more allow her gaze to sweep the Forum.

She shivered at the sight of Darius and the whip-men. They were all but naked in the cold, codpieces and short capes of fur their only covering.

Caesar, in Roman terms, "threw out the first ball." His speech was brief and rather lewd, as befitted the tone of the day. Bawdy shouts followed his words. Darius and the others streaked through the crowds, whipping barren women who put themselves in the way.

Drinking, dancing, singing, and laughter followed. But beneath all this frivolity, Cleopatra sensed an undercurrent of malevolence. Pia watched through the queen's ever-shifting eyes to see what—or more properly, *who*—had set her nerves on edge. For a time, she gazed surreptitiously at Calpurnia, Caesar's Roman wife. The woman was older. She held herself erect at all times, seeming to peer out at something above and beyond Caesar's subjects. A yellow wig woven with pearls covered her natural hair. Ropes of pearls wrapped her neck and wrists. In fact, neither Cleo nor Pia had ever seen any one woman wear so many pearls. But then, they were Caesar's passion. He collected them, played with them, hoarded them. Some of the senators whispered that he had invaded Britain only for the fabled pearls to be found there. Pia felt a twinge of jealousy from Cleopatra as she stared at Calpurnia, not so much for her pearls as for her title—*wife*. A moment later, the Egyptian queen turned away abruptly, putting all thoughts of Calpurnia far from her mind.

Their turquoise gaze fell next upon a number of high-born Romans—nobles and tribunes. Cassius, Trebonius, the two Casca brothers, Tillius Cimber, Servus Galba. Cleopatra's suspicious stare remained for a long time on Caesar's illegitimate son Brutus. Of course, Cleo had no idea why the sight of these men, huddled together, whispering furtively, made the hair at the back of her neck bristle. But Pia knew and shuddered with her knowledge of the future. All these men were among the conspirators. Each of them would plunge a dagger into Caesar a month from this very day. Pia felt cold, miserable, and desperately homesick. More than anything, she longed to leave this doomed queen's body. It was tearing her apart, knowing that she *could* change things, yet realizing that she didn't dare.

The Faun-men burst suddenly through the crowd, running straight for Caesar's throne, laughing and shouting. Before they reached him, several noblemen's wives stepped into their path for a flick of the whip. Calpurnia herself, still solemn and regal, bared her shoulder for Mark Antony's whip. He hesitated, turned, and gave Cleopatra the lash instead. In a rare moment of feminine weakness, the Egyptian Queen offered Caesar's wife a smile of triumph.

That moment of cattiness was lost on the crowd, however. All eyes turned to Mark Antony and then to Caesar. From beneath his cloak, Antony produced a crown and offered it to the ruler of Rome.

"You are our Imperator, our Dictator for life, and our god, Caesar," Antony cried for all to hear. "Allow me to crown you king as well!"

Caesar smiled and inclined his head slightly, ready to accept until he realized the throngs had gone dead silent. Both Cleopatra and Pia sensed the tension in Caesar's body. He ached to accept. He had wanted this forever. Yet what was that angry whisper flowing from Roman to Roman? The last king of Rome had been an Etruscan, dethroned and vanquished nearly five hundred years before. Still, every Roman remembered the stories of the struggles of their ancestors to rid the land of that *Rex*. The title, along with the race, had been banished. No king should ever rule Rome again, so the people had decreed long ago.

A few cheers rang out, but the overall tone was one of

disapproval at the very thought of Caesar accepting the crown of a king. The moment of decision was at hand.

"Take back your crown!" Caesar shouted, shoving away the handsome diadem. "I'll not be king. Not ever!"

Cheers from all sides.

Antony waved his arm toward the crowds. "Take the crown, Caesar. Hear how your people desire a king."

The second time proved even more difficult for Caesar. Cleopatra watched him closely as he reconsidered. She knew what was at stake. If he accepted, there would be no limit to his power. They could be married immediately and create the dynasty for which they both longed. But should he accept, the old guard of Rome would rebel. Once more he would face civil war. He *might* win, if he lived that long. But the chances were slim at best.

Caesar shook his head almost imperceptibly. With a sigh, he said, "No. Rome has endured her last king. Let it be written that on this day, acting on the wishes of the people, Mark Antony offered Caesar the royal crown, but the Dictator refused to accept it."

Pia experienced Cleopatra's relief mingled with regret at Caesar's final words. But overlaying both those feelings, she realized a sense of hope on the queen's part. Perhaps Caesar's gesture would put an end to all the whispering and plotting in the city. Perhaps now all the citizens, high and low, would trust him. And if they trusted him, they would eventually accept his plans to divorce his Roman wife and take an Egyptian Queen instead.

Such was not to be and Pia knew it. She felt deeply depressed as the royal party made their way out of the Forum late that afternoon. She knew this was the beginning of the end. Before long, Cleopatra, Caesar, and even Calpurnia would know it, too.

* * *

Immediately after Lupercalia, Caesar announced his intentions to leave for the East. He meant to expand the Empire's boundaries by taking Dacia. Then he would head south through Armenia to go against the Parthians. He advised Cleopatra that she should ready her entourage to return to Alexandria.

"I'll be gone at least three years," he said with his old swagger. "You'll find yourself bored here alone. Besides, you need to look out for our interests in Egypt."

Pia felt Cleopatra bristle when he said *"our interests."* "*I* am Egypt's ruler. You have no interests there until we are properly wed."

Cleopatra's sharp tone caused Caesar to raise an eyebrow. For a moment, they did battle with their eyes. Then he threw back his head and laughed. Pia sensed murder in Cleo's heart.

Before the angry queen could react, Caesar popped his surprise. "I have a secret to tell you, my love. When I ride out of Rome, I will be wearing the crown as its king—ruler of all Rome's conquests."

"But you refused the crown. And wisely so."

A merry light danced in his dark eyes. "Ah, but things have changed since then. Who am I to refuse the age-old pronouncement found by the priests in the *Sibylline Books?* I commanded the wise ones to consult those texts for any prophecy concerning the Parthians. Long ago in her cave at Cumae the sacred oracle recorded these very words. 'No war can succeed against the Parthians unless the Roman armies are led by a king.' "

He finished with a self-satisfied smirk.

"But the priests' words are only interpretations of the ancient writings." Cleopatra was horrified. It was clear Caesar had been tampering with the sacred oracle, perhaps bribing the priests, to suit his own desires.

"Nevertheless—"

"Caesar, you can't do this!" Cleopatra was panic stricken. "Only ill can come from such a sacrilegious action."

"It is done!" he said emphatically. "On the Ides of March, I go to discuss with the Senate a proposal that will insure the success of my Parthian campaign."

"You mean insure your own doom!" Cleopatra cried. "You saw how the people reacted when Antony offered you the crown. They fear a king, Caesar. You mustn't think of doing this!"

He sighed wearily. "How you and Calpurnia do go on! Women!"

Cleopatra's fear was suddenly overlaind by a veneer of raw anger. How dare he mention his wife's name in the same breath with her own? How dare he classify her simply as a woman?

"It seems Calpurnia has been having dreadful dreams— murder, mayhem, disaster." Again he smiled at Cleopatra and this time drew her into his arms. "Perhaps she guesses that once I am king, my first act will be to divorce her and marry the mother of my son," he whispered. "I have changed our plans. You will accompany me when I leave Rome. We can be wed on the ancient site of Troy, with the ghosts of many heroes to witness our triumph and our power."

Pia felt Cleo's dream come alive once more. The Queen of Egypt closed her eyes and saw the plains of Troy, the gold of Agamemnon, her husband at her side and the whole wide world at her feet.

"Yes, Caesar," she whispered. "Yes."

The night before the Ides of March, the queen slept little and Pia less. Since the evening when Caesar had told Cleopatra of his plans, rumors had run rampant as the city was shocked by one omen of doom after another. Cleopatra, like Calpurnia, experienced dreadful dreams of blood and betrayal. Strange lights were seen in the sky over Rome. A lone raven cried out in the Forum each midnight. A sacrificial animal was found to have no heart. Cleopatra herself had seen a flock of birds carry a laurel branch into the Hall of Pompey, the very place where Caesar was to meet with the Senators the following morning.

Cleopatra stood alone at the window of her villa, packed and ready to leave Rome with Caesar, but feeling no joy in her heart. Even the tramping of thousands of troops through the city toward the port seemed an ill omen. Nervous, upset, and frightened, she hurried out to seek Darius.

Her search took only moments. She found him down the corridor, coming to her.

"Darius!" she cried. "We must talk. I need a promise from you before I can rest."

"Anything, my queen." He looked at her through troubled eyes. Tomorrow was the day that would change the world— that would shatter Cleopatra's dreams.

She gripped his arm, hurrying him back to her room. Once they were alone, she said, "You must promise to go with Caesar tomorrow, to stay by his side."

"He may not allow that."

She tossed her head impatiently. "Disguise yourself as a Senator. Do whatever you must, but stay with him. I have a terrible sense of dread."

"Where is he tonight?" Darius knew, but he wondered if she did.

"With Calpurnia," she snapped. "But, the gods willing, this will be their *last* night together. By this time tomorrow, we will be gone from this stinking city and his simpering wife." She turned an anxious gaze on him. "Promise me, Darius!" she commanded.

He nodded, his face grim. "I promise, Cleopatra. I swear it on the love we once shared."

"The love we still share," she whispered.

She went up on tiptoe to kiss him softly.

"I'll leave you now, my queen."

"No!" Her cry was frantic. "Stay until I sleep. *Please!*"

He nodded and took a seat, stretching out his long legs before him. He watched as she climbed into bed and pulled the silken sheets over her lithe, young body. He still marveled at her beauty. Was there ever a man born who could resist her?

Moments later, he heard her quiet, even breathing. The queen slept. He waited. He listened. He watched.

"Darius?" The whisper was so low it sounded like a gentle breeze passing through the room.

"Pia?"

"Thank God!" she said. "I thought I'd never get a moment alone with you again. Cleopatra's hardly slept for a week. She knows something's going to happen tomorrow. Honest, Darius, I didn't tell her. She just feels it. It's like a dark cloud closing around her heart."

She rose from the bed and went to him. He drew her down on his lap and cradled her gently, kissed her tenderly.

"How are you holding up, sweetheart?"

"I'm a wreck, if you really want to know." Pia tried to laugh, but the effort died on her lips. She hugged Darius tighter. "Oh, darling, I thought life back on St. Simons was complicated. Racing deadlines, counting pennies. So much pressure. So much stress." Now she did laugh softly, but the sound was pure irony. "I didn't know how good I had it. Poor Cleo! What's going to become of her?"

"You know as well as I do, sweetheart. There's no way we can change the outcome."

Pia sighed and clung to him. "I know," she whispered. "I'll just be so glad when it's over tomorrow."

"We could leave right now," he suggested. "Sudibeth told me she wanted to stay. She's got a real thing going with that soldier. She says they want to get married."

Pia made an angry sound. "Sudibeth's crazy! I refuse to leave her here, I don't care what she says."

"All right," he answered. "Whatever you say. I'll keep testing the window."

For a long time, they sat together—kissing, touching, imagining what it would be like when they could finally be alone together. All the while, they concentrated on trying to forget about what the morning would bring.

It was no use. The Ides of March overshadowed all else.

Dawn broke blood-red. Cleopatra rose early and out of sorts. She had dreamed again of death. Pia shuddered at the queen's deep sense of doom.

Across the river in the city, Caesar's wife had suffered through her own nightmares. Calpurnia begged and pleaded until her husband finally agreed not to go to the Hall of Pompey. And he would have stayed, if Brutus hadn't come for him, insisting that the Senators were all waiting to confer a great honor on their heroic leader.

Caesar, beaming at the thought of the crown awaiting him, gave Calpurnia a peck on the cheek. "Be brave, old girl. What could happen on such a fine day?"

Brutus saw Caesar to his waiting litter, then signaled for the entourage to move out. It wouldn't do for the Emperor to have a last-minute change of heart.

Darius, dressed as a member of Caesar's elite guard, marched behind the royal vehicle. As they passed through the streets, he noted that the citizens of Rome seemed especially argumentative and on edge this morning. There were quarrels all along the way, fist fights, shouted curses. The city itself seemed caught up in some strange, dark tumult of emotions.

Mark Antony rode his horse beside Caesar's litter. The big consul looked grim. His head jerked back and forth, his eyes darting over the restless crowds. When a servant hurried to the litter and thrust a rolled parchment into Caesar's hand, Antony kicked the man away. "Be gone with you!" he roared.

Darius knew what was written on the parchment. A friend had uncovered the Senators' plot and written every detail to warn Caesar. The parchment, still rolled and tied, would be found later beside Caesar's bloody body. Darius was tempted to call out to Caesar to read the message. He held his tongue. The will of the gods, he reminded himself.

As they neared the Hall of Pompey, the ancient soothsayer, Spurrina, approached Caesar. The man had warned time and again against the danger of this day. Seeing him, Caesar called out jovially, "Well, the Ides of March have arrived, my friend!"

Spurrina, his rough cloak pulled close against his bearded face, answered, "Yes, Caesar, but they are not yet past."

Outside the Hall of Pompey, Caesar and Mark Antony held a brief conference. Darius moved close enough to hear their words.

"I don't like this," Antony said. "There's a bad feel in the air."

Caesar laughed. "You act like a woman! What could happen on this day of days, my friend?"

"I don't know. But I mean to stay here, outside the entrance. Should any assassin try to enter the hall, I'll make short work of him."

Caesar was obviously disappointed. "Stay here and miss seeing me crowned king? Antony, come with me."

Mark Antony refused. He took up his watchful post as Caesar mounted the wide, marble stairs. Brutus, Darius noted, rushed ahead of him to join the other conspirators.

What happened at the top of those stairs is written in blood in all history books. The Senators—eighty in all—

awaited Caesar, their weapons hidden inside their togas or concealed in their stylus cases.

First the priests made sacrifices. Caesar hurried them along, eager to receive his crown. When he entered the chamber, the Senators rose as one to their feet to greet him. Caesar took his throne, ready to begin the session. The conspirators drew close, all begging at once for their ruler's attention. Tillius Cimber asked a favor. Caesar denied it. Cimber pleaded, gripping Caesar's purple robe in his agitation, ripping it off his shoulder.

Caesar realized at that moment that no crown awaited him. "But this is violence!" he cried, trying to thrust Cimber away.

Casca struck the first blow, then they set on him like a pack of jackals. A few gruesome minutes later, Caesar collapsed from twenty-three stab wounds at the foot of Pompey's statue. His last vision was the face of Brutus as he struck the killing blow.

"And you, too, my child?" Caesar spoke the words in Greek, with his final breath.

Across the river, Cleopatra was one of the first to receive the dreadful news. A runner sprinted to her villa the moment the word spread.

Pia had felt sorry for herself many times, but never had she felt as sorry for anyone as she did for Cleopatra in those awful moments. It would have been easier for the queen if the conspirators' daggers had torn her own flesh. Caesar was dead, and in the wake of his death all was chaos.

The queen's first thoughts were of Caesarion's safety. If all Rome had gone mad, he would likely be their next target. She hurried into his room, scooped the child into her arms, and wept. For hours, Cleopatra allowed herself to be simply a woman. She huddled in the dark, bolted chamber with

Caesar's son, cringing at every sound and wondering where to turn now.

Alexandria, Pia urged. *Go home! Get Caesarion away from this awful place.*

"Yes," Cleopatra agreed. "We'll leave as soon as possible."

When Darius pounded on the door and called to her, Cleopatra finally snapped out of it. She was a queen, after all, with a queen's duties to be done. She dried her eyes and unbolted the door.

"Cleopatra?" Darius said. Quickly, he took in her red eyes and disheveled appearance. "You've heard?"

She gave a firm nod, her face like carved marble. "I have. *The filthy butchers!*" she spat. "I'm taking Caesarion home, Darius. I want you to accompany us."

"Of course," he answered. He ached to reach out and comfort her, but he knew that was the last thing she wanted right now.

Cleopatra knew she must leave Rome soon. She would stay only long enough to witness Caesar's funeral and to hear the contents of Caesar's will from his closest friend, Mark Antony, the only Roman she felt she could trust now.

Before Caesar's body even went to its pyre, Antony and Cleopatra learned the awful truth from the dead Dictator's will. He had made no changes to include either Cleopatra or their son. In fact, he had written that should a natural son be born to him after his death, three of the men who had murdered him would be the child's guardians until he came of age. Cleopatra shuddered at the thought.

The villa and gardens Caesar had provided for his Egyptian lover now belonged to the people of Rome, who also inherited three hundred sesterces each. The only codicil to the will proved most disturbing of all. Caesar had declared his nineteen-year-old great-nephew, Octavian, his adopted son. Furthermore, Caesar named Antony and Octavian to rule jointly in his stead. The two despised each other.

Cleopatra stayed on in Rome only long enough to see Caesar's body consumed by funeral flames five days after his murder. Mark Antony delivered a moving eulogy. Women wailed and soldiers banged their shields. At the end of his plainspoken, but poetic speech, Antony whipped the mourners to hysteria by raising Caesar's blood-stained, dagger-pierced robe upon a spear for all to see. The Roman citizens, worked into a frenzy of grief, refused to carry their dead leader's body to the Campus Martius for a proper ceremony, but burned it there in the Forum. The Romans stripped furniture and woodwork from nearby buildings for the pyre. Noblemen cast their costly robes into the flames and women their exquisite jewels. The smoke filled the March sky, drifting in a dark column to the heavens.

"And so it ends." Cleopatra, with no more tears to shed, watched from the gardens across the Tiber.

Think of Caesarion, Pia told her, *Think of Alexandria.*

Cleopatra smiled for the first time in days. "Home!" she murmured.

That one word set Pia's tears flowing. When would she ever see her house on the beach again? She was overwhelmed suddenly with a homesickness that wrenched her soul.

A strong arm clamped around Cleopatra's shoulders—comforting the queen, comforting Pia.

"Are you ready to leave?" Darius asked.

"More than ready!" they both answered.

Chapter Seventeen

The nerve of the man! Pia exclaimed after she and Cleopatra had read Mark Antony's curt message. *You aren't going, are you?*

The queen smiled and thoughtfully stroked a perfumed peacock feather across her cheek. "But of course I will. I hear Tarsus in the autumn is quite lovely."

You're going to let him order you around—snap his fingers and bring you running? He's only trying to prove he's as strong as Caesar was and that he can have any woman Caesar had.

"What makes you think he can't?"

That shut Pia up.

Cleopatra fanned herself with Antony's letter and stared out her window. The sunset had turned the smooth waters of the Mediterranean to vermilion silk. She rose from her couch and went to stand before her looking glass. Pia knew at once what she was doing. The queen was giving herself a good once-over, trying to detect any signs of age that might have marred her looks in the three years since she'd left Rome, the three years since she'd last seen Mark Antony.

Not bad for a gal pushing thirty. Don't worry. You've still got it, Pia told her. *You'll have that Roman brute eating out of your hand the minute he sees you.*

"Exactly what I was planning," Cleo said with a sensual smirk, pulling her sheer gown tight to check the span of her hips, still enticingly youthful even after Caesarion's birth.

A moment later, Pia became aware that an alien emotion stirred in the queen. For some reason, she was feeling guilty about something. What? Pia wondered.

"Iras," Cleopatra said, "find Darius and bring him to me. At once!"

Ah, so that was it! Pia realized Darius was about to receive his pink slip from the queen. With no Roman on the scene, Cleopatra had once more taken Darius as her lover over the past three years. Pia had been none too happy about this arrangement at first. She had to admit she'd enjoyed their strange *ménage à trois,* but the idea of sharing the man she loved still irked her, even if the other woman was an earlier incarnation of Pia herself. As the months and years had slipped away, however, she had come to look upon this bizarre love affair as the normal course of events. Darius had been careful to keep reminding Pia at every opportunity that *she* was the real love of his life now, the woman he meant to marry. His reassurances went a long way toward soothing her jealous feelings.

But how would Darius take this latest turn of events?

He strode into the chamber looking confident, virile, and heart-stoppingly handsome in his short kilt and gold sandals, his broad chest gleaming with fragrant cedar oil. Without so much as a bow, he stalked straight to the queen, gripped her shoulders, and bent her into his arms. He kissed her slowly, deeply, until she trembled against him.

With a sigh of regret, Cleo pushed him away. "No more," she whispered.

By way of explanation, she handed him the letter from Antony. As Darius scanned the sheet of papyrus, she said, "I plan to go, of course. This is the opportunity I've been waiting for. You know I have no other choice."

His face was grave when he nodded. "I'll accompany you?"

She smiled. "Most definitely. But *only* as Caesarion's astrologer."

"I understand." His voice was bleak.

Cleopatra felt a need to explain her actions. "I have kept close watch on the Triumvirate these past three years as they struggled to gain control. Of Rome's trio of leaders, only Antony holds any hope of final triumph. Old Lepidus has never been more than a figurehead, a buffer to keep Antony and Octavius from each other's throats. For a time, I considered casting my lot with young Octavius even though I despise him." She shivered slightly at the mere thought of the man. "His youth and sickliness remind me of my two dead brother-kings. But Mark Antony, even with his boorish nature, is bound to win out over Octavius, especially if I take his side." She reached out and touched Darius's shoulder, her eyes shining with new hope. "There's still a chance for Caesar's dynasty. Antony loved Caesar; he will love Caesarion. I can make him love me. Even more to my advantage, I can make him *need* me."

Darius nodded. What was there for him to say? He knew, just as Pia did, that this was the beginning of the end for Cleopatra and her long-dreamed-of dynasty. But telling her such a thing was out of the question.

"I will be ready whenever you wish to leave, my queen."

She smiled a little sadly at the very proper tone of his words. "That won't be for some weeks yet. First, I must prepare for my grand entrance up the river Cydnus to Antony's headquarters at Tarsus. He styles himself the descendant of Hercules, the New Dionysus. I mean to match his claims and more by presenting myself to him as a goddess incarnate—Venus Anadyomene, Venus risen from the waves. For generations, the citizens of Cilicia will tell and retell the story of my coming. The news will quickly spread to Rome. Soon the whole world will know of my alliance with Mark Antony. They will know and they will honor us." She laughed softly. "Better still, they will fear us!"

"As you say, my queen." Darius bowed and left the chamber, some of the swagger gone from his stride.

Even before Darius departed, Pia felt the queen's mind swirling with plans and ideas. She would need a great barge, even larger and more extravagant than the ship on which she and Caesar had sailed up the Nile. Exquisite gifts to dazzle the greedy Romans. Exotic slaves to lure them. Feats of magic to astound them. And her son Caesarian to remind them of whose lover and consort she had been.

Twice more the Roman leader sent his summons to the Egyptian queen. Cleopatra kept Antony cooling his heels for several weeks before she sent her messenger to Tarsus to announce her imminent arrival. While she kept Antony waiting, she guessed that he would spend his time drinking, whoring, and bleeding tax money from the Cilicians. Rome's strongest general had indulged himself in one long debauch over the past months, according to Cleopatra's spies. He was said to surround himself with more musicians, dancers, actors, whores, and mountebanks than with soldiers. In Ephesus he had reigned like an Oriental potentate, existing for pleasure alone. A greedy, naughty boy who demanded a new toy every hour of every day.

One story Caesar had told Cleopatra about Antony years ago came back to mind now. The tale amused the queen as much as it shocked Pia. It seemed that, like Caesar, Antony, the notorious womanizer, had enjoyed a homosexual fling in his youthful years. He had taken a younger lover named Curio. According to Caesar, the two lads had been deeply in love. Curio's father finally bought Antony off and quickly married his son to a flamboyant woman named Fulvia, a widow who was described as "one of the most profligate characters of a profligate age." Later, after Curio's untimely death, Antony took Fulvia as his second wife, claiming that to make love to the widow of his former lover was almost as good as having his dear Curio once more in his arms.

Mark Antony was still married to Fulvia, but rumors from Rome had it that she was now enjoying a fling with Antony's own brother. Cleopatra relished the thought of stealing the profligate's powerful husband away. In the process, she also intended to make him forget once and for all his lost lover, Curio. The challenge fired her spirit, prompting her to spare no expense on this hunting expedition.

Twelve treasure-laden triremes formed Cleopatra's opulent fleet as it approached the river Cydnus. The queen's own ship with purple sails, golden decks, and silver oars provided the centerpiece of the miniature armada. As Cleopatra had planned, it was nearly sunset when her floating palace entered the narrow river. The blood-red rays of the sun made her fantastic vessel blaze like fire upon the water. Pastel-colored clouds of perfume swirled on the soft breeze, wafting in to shore. The music of flute and harp filled the air. Instead of sailors and oarsmen, the queen's ship was manned by scantily clad slave girls. Beautiful little boys dressed as Cupids fanned the queen—Venus herself, who reclined in a great, gleaming shell beneath a canopy of gold.

Before her ship neared the Cydnus, Cleopatra had soaked for hours in a tub of almond milk and honey, so that her skin looked dewy. She glowed in the glimmering light. Beneath a clinging drape of gossamer silk, shot through with golden threads, she wore only pearls—hundreds of pearls from the Red Sea. Twin shells made of pearls cupped her breasts. Swinging ropes of pearls circled low on her hips. Her hair, swept up in a Greek knot, was twined round with them as well. Rings on her fingers, rings on her toes. More pearls at her ears. She wore a fortune next to her gleaming flesh. The largest pearl of all—the size of her own fist—enticingly suspended on a thin chain of gold about her waist, dangled between her upper thighs. The bauble was sure to draw Antony's attention, to fire his imagination and his lust.

Progress proved slow through the reed- and papyrus-choked channel. That was fine, too, Cleopatra assured herself. It would give the natives time to gather. The word quickly spread on shore of the fantastic goddess-queen sailing toward Tarsus. Soon the banks on both sides were filled with awestruck spectators, among them Antony's own troops.

It seemed Antony was the only person who had not come down to see the queen. As soon as her ship sailed into the small lake at the head of the river, a boat was rowed out to summon Cleopatra into town for her audience with the powerful Roman.

She read between the lines and chuckled. "The fool!" she muttered only to herself and Pia. "He thinks that I will parade through those dusty streets to bow before him—do him homage. I will go him one better!"

Shifting to give the bug-eyed messenger an even better view of her luscious body, Cleopatra stroked her breast and sighed. In a breathy voice, she said, "Please tell your general that I do appreciate his offer. But it is my wish that he allow me to entertain him tonight." She smiled at the man and plucked a pearl from her hair. "For your trouble," she said.

Once the messenger had backed away, bowing repeatedly to the queen, Pia commented, *That was a pretty cool move.*

If your invitation doesn't budge Antony, the sight of that pearl will.

Cleopatra laughed softly. "Exactly my thoughts. The Romans are such fools for pearls. In Egypt they are common things. The Red Sea is filled with them."

At that moment, six-year-old Caesarion marched up to his mother's shell-throne. He was dressed in a miniature version of his dead father's finest tunic and golden armor. A small laurel wreath gleamed through his fair curls.

"Is the Roman coming?" he demanded, sounding very much like Caesar.

Cleopatra might have struck the boy for his insolent tone, but Pia stayed her hand. "Do not call him 'the Roman.' It is disrespectful, Caesarion."

"He *is* a Roman," the child argued, testing his mother's will.

The queen nodded, holding her temper in check. "Mark Antony is a very special Roman. In time, this Roman will make you king, my son. I intend to make him my husband, your father. I demand that you show him respect. I gave birth to you for one reason and one reason alone—to perpetuate and share Julius Caesar's power. He is gone now, but I have another chance at my goal. I won't have you ruining my plans. Do you understand me, boy?"

Caesarion's pretty face remained unreadable. But Pia was certain she saw tears in his great, blue-black eyes.

When Caesarion turned and strode away, Pia said sharply, *How could you do that to him? He's just a little kid. A poor fatherless boy who desperately wants your affection. Sometimes, Cleopatra, you're a real bitch!*

Pia felt the queen simmer at her words. She fully expected one of Cleo's sharp jabs. Instead, she got a reasonable answer. "I am a queen," was said evenly. "And sometimes a queen must be a bitch in order to save her child and her country. Antony must come to love Caesarion, if my plans are to work. His affection could never grow for a pampered, insolent child. Antony must see Caesar in Caesarion."

Further discussion proved impossible. A blast of trumpets announced Mark Antony's arrival. Pia caught her breath at the sight of the man. She had forgotten what a hunk he was. He looked like a wrestler with his bulging muscles and bull-like neck. He was tall, heavily built, but without an ounce of fat on his body. His florid face had none of the aristocratic planes and angles that had attested to Caesar's noble heritage. Instead he looked rugged, battle-scarred, yet sensual with his deep-set eyes, wide mouth, and flaring nostrils. The thought of making love with him was unsettling to Pia. It would be like mating with some wild beast from the forest.

Cleopatra heard that thought and smiled. "Even the wildest beast can be tamed by the proper handler," she whispered.

He was dressed outrageously—half Hercules, half Diony-sus. The vine leaves twined through his curling hair and beard honored the God of Wine. But he wore a coarse animal skin clasped at his shoulder, and his body was nearly as bare as the great statue of Hercules in the Museum. Overall, the effect was pagan, earthy, and outrageously sexy.

He strode directly to Cleopatra and went down on one knee. When she offered her delicate hand, he crushed it in his fingers and kissed it with a good deal of enthusiasm.

"It's good to see you again, Antony." She made her voice as sweet and musical as the flutes playing in the night.

He gazed into her eyes, his own glowing with the tawny glitter of smoky topaz. He seemed stunned speechless by the sight of her. Finally, he found his tongue, although it was thick with wine. "A happier occasion, my queen, than when we parted."

She sighed, letting him know she remembered every detail of that horror. After a moment, she brightened. "You've been well?"

"Tolerable," he said, then threw back his head and laughed. She was joking, of course. He was never ill.

"And your wife Fulvia?" The tiny jab was meant to sting.

He growled like one of his lions. "Screwing my brother the last I heard. We'll not speak of her."

Cleopatra smiled and inclined her head. "As you wish. I have had my servants set tables below and lay a small repast for you and your officers. I must apologize in advance for its inadequacy. We hurried to leave and have been at sea . . ." She let her words trail off and covered her cunning smile with her fan.

"Well, of course, we don't require anything lavish." In spite of his words, his disappointment was evident. "We're soldiers, used to rough rations."

"Will you help me rise?" Cleopatra's voice was now child-like, slightly flirtatious.

Antony took her hand, kissed it once more, then let his hungry gaze travel the queen's lithe body as she rose from her shell. He spotted the large, dangling pearl and fixed his eyes upon it. He licked his lips. Beads of perspiration popped out on his wide forehead.

"Lovely, isn't it?" Cleopatra said. "Its value is small, but if you like it, you may have it."

Antony's eyes widened with desire—desire for the pearl and for its wearer. Yet he dared not reach out to take it. His hands were large and clumsy. He might grope the queen by accident.

Seeing his quandary, Cleopatra leaned close and whispered, "You may take it later, when we're alone."

He looked at her with stark joy in his eyes. Her promise that they would be together later was a far better gift than the huge pearl. He could hardly believe his good fortune.

Cleopatra smiled, noting how his codpiece rose.

"Shall we go down?" she suggested.

Antony frowned, but his face changed quickly into a lecherous grin. "Now? Before dinner?"

He had misunderstood; the queen had hoped he would. She laughed aloud and stabbed playfully at his shoulder with a long fingernail. "How eager you are, Antony! That's *not* what I meant. I have wine from Lesbos chilled in snow from the mountains. The day has been long and hot. I thought it might clear the dust from your throat."

After a flicker of disappointment in his eyes, he threw back his head and laughed. "You know me well, Cleopatra. I'm a man who thinks with his prick. Speak to me of hunger, I hunger for the taste of a woman. Speak to me of thirst, I thirst to drink the sweet wine from a woman's lips. Speak to me of sleep, and I say, 'Not before I've had a woman beneath me on my couch.'" Again, he roared with laughter.

Pia felt Cleopatra cringe, but the queen showed no sign of it outwardly. Mark Antony was big and crude, an oversexed, alcoholic peasant.

"Very well," Pia heard Cleo whisper. "I can play that role. I can outdrink you, outlove you, and outwit you, General Marcus Antonius! And I will!"

Oh, lord! Pia thought. We're in for it now!

The poor repast Cleopatra had hinted at turned out to be anything but. The dining chamber below glowed with lights—oil lamps reflected in hundreds of mirrors. Purple tapestries embroidered with spun gold shimmered on the walls. Twelve golden couches received the diners. Each table was set with gold plates encrusted with emeralds, rubies, and sapphires. Blood red Persian rose petals lay a foot deep on the floor. Each step they took released the intoxicating scent.

Antony was struck dumb by the richness of the setting.

"I hope this will suit," Cleopatra said demurely.

"By the gods, I never saw anything like it! Did you empty the entire treasury of Egypt, woman?"

Cleopatra bristled, but forced herself to continue smiling. "A thousand such banquets could not empty Egypt's brimming coffers."

Once again, Antony's gaze went to the large pearl. The hunger in his eyes delighted the queen.

He'll be an easy mark, Pia said. *A piece of cake!*

"Child's play," Cleo agreed.

"What's that about a child?" Antony asked absently. He was too busy trying to calculate the value of the plates to listen to what she said.

"I'd like you to meet Caesar's child," she quickly covered. "Caesarion, come here, my darling."

Caesarion had heard his mother's words to him earlier. He knew what was expected of him. Forcing an aristocratic smile, he strode toward the big Roman. He bowed slightly before them. "My queen? You wished to see me?"

She leaned down and hugged him, an uncharacteristic gesture for Cleopatra. "General Mark Antony, I wish to present my son."

The big man offered an enormous mock bow. "Young Caesar, this is a great honor. You are your father through and through." He stood straight and fished in a leather pouch at his waist. "I have something for you, Caesarion. It's a coin struck with your father's image."

He pressed the gold piece into Caesarion's small palm. The boy glowed. "It's my father! It's really him!"

When Caesarion looked up at Mark Antony, who now seemed like a giant towering above him, he was grinning. "I thank you, my Roman friend. It's the best present I ever received."

Cleopatra broke the spell between the boy and the man. "Run along with Sudi now, Caesarion. It's time for your story and then bed."

"Will I see you again, Mark Antony?"

"You can bet on it, young man. I'll take you fishing one of these days."

"Hot doggies!" Caesarion yelped.

Antony looked to Cleopatra for translation. She shrugged and smiled. "He learns these strange words from his story-teller. She came to us from some far-off land. Try as I might to break the code of her language, it still mystifies me. Caesarion has had her with him for so long that he seems to understand her."

All through the long meal of many courses and much wine, Cleopatra went out of her way to amuse Antony. He hung on her every word, laughing whether it was appropriate or not, having such a good time that the queen found herself enjoying his coarse company and the otherwise dull evening. He reminded her of one of her pets back at the palace, a huge lion-hound that would rather share her couch and have his ears scratched than take to the plains for the hunt. The pampered dog had the run of the palace and regularly broke statues, chased slaves, and tracked Nile mud onto the queen's best bed-silks. Still, she loved the beast for his lack of cunning. She could make the great animal do her will with the slightest look or word. And so, it seemed, it would be with Mark Antony.

"More wine?" she offered. His eyes were glazed already with the amount he had consumed. Cleopatra wore her ame-thyst ring, swearing not to take it off as long as she was in this Roman's company. "Would you prefer Falernian or Pramnian?"

He gripped both golden ewers by their delicate necks and poured them together into his bowl. "Hades! Let's mix them and see how they taste." He roared with laughter, shaking the couch, spilling the wine. "But I'll only drink it from your lips, my queen."

At Antony's words, silence fell over the other couches.

All eyes turned to the couple. What would the queen say? What would she do? Tense moments passed.

"Then *drink*, Roman!" Laughing almost as loud as Antony, Cleopatra gripped his great, golden wine bowl with both hands and put it to her lips. Some of the purple liquid dribbled down her chin, her neck, and stained the pearls at her breasts. She leaned toward him, offering him a drink from her lips.

Antony stopped laughing. He eyed her suspiciously for long moments, wondering if he dared. Then, openmouthed, he covered her lips. Gasps and murmurs filled the room. For a long time, he held the back of her head with one huge hand and drank the sweet, burning wine from her mouth. When he'd sucked the last drops from her tongue, he licked her chin, her neck, and the pearls at her breasts. He lifted his head. His eyes met hers. They both knew in that instant what the night would bring.

Pia, meanwhile, was fuzzy with wine. Sloshing in wine. Drowning in it. But, mercy, did she feel the heat of Antony's kiss! She knew as well as everyone else in the room that an explosion was imminent.

Darius? she whimpered.

Silence! Cleopatra ordered.

Darius had seen enough. He'd slipped into the dining chamber moments before, posing as a server. He'd wanted to make sure that both Cleopatra and Pia were doing all right. He didn't trust this brutish Roman. He knew the queen planned to take Antony as her lover, but he didn't want any kinky stuff going on. What could he do, though? Only bide his time and hope that later tonight he could convince Pia to leave for good.

Shortly after the wine-kiss, the banquet portion of the evening came to an end. Cleopatra invited all the guests on deck for entertainment. She had another surprise for them. The servants had strung the ship's rigging and the branches of trees on the shore with brightly colored lanterns. The whole vessel looked like a fairyland. While the others shuffled about, staring up at the marvelous display, Cleopatra led Antony to a wide couch where Venus's shell had been before.

Once they were settled side by side, the queen pulled a cord that brought silken curtains down to conceal them from the other guests.

"This will be more private," she whispered.

Clearly, Antony could hardly believe his good fortune. For a moment, he remained silent, motionless, breathing heavily.

"You may take your pearl now," Cleopatra offered. She did not, however, offer to help him find it.

He fumbled at her gauzy gown, stripping it at last from her body. The pearls gleamed like phosphorus in the soft glow from the lanterns. He leaned back on one elbow and stared at her.

"You are more beautiful than I remember."

She laughed softly. "I should hope so. I was only fourteen when we first met."

"You made me hungry even then," he confessed, stroking her bare hip with his fingers. "Hungrier still when you came to Rome."

"You hardly gave me a glance in Rome. I wondered why."

"You belonged to Caesar then. I'm a foolish man at times, but I'm not crazy. He would have had me killed and my body thrown into the Tiber like any common criminal's." He flattened his wide palm against her belly. "That was a difficult time for me. I have no control over my desires when it comes to a beautiful woman."

Cleopatra's laughter was drowned out by the music and bawdy songs from her preformers at the far end of the deck. "So I have heard, Dionysus. Does it strike you as odd to think that Venus has desires, too?"

His hand suddenly swooped downward to Cleo's thigh. His grip jolted Pia awake just in time to hear the queen's taunting question.

Don't egg him on! Pia begged. *He's about to bust his codpiece as it is.*

Ignoring her inner voice, Cleopatra guided his hand toward the pearl between her legs. He clutched it in his fist. She tightened the muscles in her upper thighs, holding his hand prisoner. She rocked her hips slowly, sensually.

"You mean to drive me wild," he accused in a throaty whisper.

She gripped the leather band of his swollen codpiece, testing it gently. "You are big . . . for a Roman."

This remark brought another guffaw from Antony. "For a Roman, eh? *Huge* by any standards, my little queen. My inheritance from Hercules."

"Do you mean to make me tremble?"

"Not with words," he answered, still gripping the pearl, rubbing it against her now.

Pia, hot as a pistol, didn't know how Cleo could keep her cool. While the big guy was teasing her with one pearl, he was plucking the others from her breasts. When he'd uncovered her nipples, he leaned down and kissed them thoroughly. Pia wriggled inside Cleo, but the queen just lay there and took it.

"More wine?" she offered while he was still suckling her.

He let go and grinned at her. "If you'll drink it first."

Cleopatra took a swig, then placed her mouth on his. Once more, he drank from her lips, but this time the kiss didn't end when the wine was all gone. They went on and on and on. Cleo outlasted Antony. Suddenly, he couldn't wait any longer. Still kissing her, he ripped off his codpiece and unleashed his hugeness upon her. He tore at her pearls; they scattered everywhere. When he mounted her, ready to force entry if need be, Cleopatra opened for him eagerly.

The couch heaved with their motion. Pia nearly got seasick, but Cleo was more than holding her own. This guy might be big, but he had a short fuse. It was over for him before either Cleo or Pia hit the jackpot.

As soon as he reached his grunting climax, Antony rolled off, grinning. "Best I've had today!" he exclaimed. "Best you *ever* had, I'd wager." He looked down at Cleopatra for confirmation.

She gave him a cool smile. "It will be better as we grow used to each other, learn each other's needs."

He shrugged. "You don't need to thank me. I know you've been alone all these years since Caesar. It takes a woman a while to get the feel for it again. But you probably haven't lost it. Don't worry."

Cleopatra was seething, and Pia would have liked nothing better than to punch the guy out. Of all the stupid, patronizing things to say to a woman he'd just disappointed! The thoughts of both women turned to Darius.

"I'd better be going now," Antony said, adjusting his codpiece. It wasn't such a tight fit now. "You said we could bear away the plates and the tables and the couches from dinner. Right?"

"Why, of course," Cleopatra answered evenly, a smile frozen on her lips.

"And tomorrow night I want you to come into Tarsus so I can repay your hospitality. You haven't lived till you've been to one of my feasts."

Cleopatra saw Antony and his men off, wondering if perhaps she'd made a mistake by not siding with Octavian. Then she remembered her lion-hound again. He might not be a hunter, but he had been easily trained to simple tasks.

"And so it is with you, Antony my love." She waved and blew him a kiss as he trudged back toward town, carrying a golden couch over his shoulder and twirling her pearl on its long chain.

"Man, that was the pits!" Pia complained aloud as Cleopatra opened her mouth to yawn.

Darius was near enough to overhear her remark. He took heart. Maybe *now* she would be willing to leave for home.

However, later when he slipped into the queen's bedchamber, he found both women fast asleep. He shook his head. "Pia, you shouldn't drink so much wine."

But in the next few weeks in Tarsus, Pia, thanks to Cleo, consumed more wine than she had ever thought possible. Each night, the queen and the Roman feasted, drank, and made love. The two of them tried to outdo each other with lavish banquets, expensive gifts, and interesting positions. Cleo won hands down in all categories. Her greatest coup came the night she named a fantastic sum and bet Antony— a sucker for any wager—that she could consume that amount of money in one night's feasting. Antony brought along his accountant, a mealy-faced man named Plancus, to tally the expense. At the end of the evening, Antony's man said Cleopatra had fallen short of her goal.

She laughed, because Antony was very drunk by now, and called for a cup of vinegar.

"Vinegar's cheap," Antony mumbled. "That won't do it."

"But this will," Cleopatra answered. Her eyes gleaming devilishly, she removed one of her large pearl earrings and dropped it into the cup. As Antony watched, bug-eyed, she drank it down, pearl and all.

Plancus scribbled furiously on his wax tablet with his stylus. "Yes! That more than covers the shortage. You have most definitely won the wager, Queen Cleopatra."

Antony let loose a stream of inordinately crude oaths, and later that night he was intentionally rough in bed to punish Cleopatra for tricking him. She had the last laugh the next morning when he woke with a raging hangover. She had one of her women mix a curative concoction for him to drink. When he had half of the thick, red liquid down already and the rest of it in his mouth, she said brightly, "That potion always cures the aftereffects of too much wine. Crocodile blood, snake eggs, and horse piss."

Antony immediately threw up the cure and spent the rest of the day in bed, cursing Dionysus, the God of Wine.

Drinking, parties, and rough jokes became the day-to-day fare for the Roman and his Egyptian lover. Bit by careful bit, Cleopatra trained Antony to her needs and desires. And after a time, she convinced him that the only place for him was by her side in Alexandria.

Two nights before Cleopatra's ships were to set sail at dawn for Egypt, Darius slipped into her chamber. Since Mark Antony liked to spend every night with the queen, it had been weeks since Darius had had a chance to talk to Pia.

He leaned down and whispered her name into Cleopatra's ear. Her eyes fluttered open immediately and she lifted her arms to hug him.

"Oh, Darius, I thought I'd never get to be with you again."

"Same here," he whispered. "Antony's a real pain."

"Tell me about it," Pia whimpered.

"He hasn't hurt you, has he?"

"Not intentionally, since the night Cleo tricked him with the pearl. But he's so *big!*"

"I don't want to hear about it!" Darius snapped.

"Don't worry," Pia mumbled. "He's a jerk in bed." She looked up at him with teary eyes. "To tell the truth, Cleo misses you almost as much as I do. I shouldn't tell you, but she thinks about you all the time, even when she's in bed with Antony. It helps her climax."

"Pia, please!" he groaned. "I *really* don't even want to think about what's been going on with the three of you. I only want to get you out of here." He pulled her gently from the bed. "Now, come on. I have the crystals. Sudibeth says she's not ever going back. She's found this guy in Tarsus . . ."

Pia rolled her eyes.

"Well, you know how she is," Darius pointed out. "The way she goes through lovers, I guess she's better off here than back where she has to worry about AIDS."

"Sudibeth isn't the problem right now," Pia said.

"Then *what?*" Darius sounded exasperated. "I know you don't want to stick around all winter while Cleo and the bull continue their sacred mating ritual."

"She's pregnant, Darius."

"What?"

Pia shrugged. "It was bound to happen, they spend so much time in the sack."

"So? What does that have to do with us? We can still leave."

Pia shook her head. "Can't," she muttered. "It's twins this time. She's not going to have an easy delivery. I need to be here to help."

"My god, Pia! What next?"

"Please don't be mad, Darius."

"I'm not," he said, drawing her into his arms. "I just miss you so much. Why couldn't we have stayed on your island instead of coming here? Then we'd be the ones expecting a baby."

He kissed her so tenderly that Pia almost changed her mind. But she was so close now. It was too late to turn back. She had to see Cleopatra's life through to the end. Well, almost! She didn't plan to stick around once the guy with the basket of figs showed up with the asp. No way!

"It won't be much longer, Darius," she whispered. "And I've noticed something. The time goes by a lot faster when Cleo's alone."

"But she's *not* alone! Antony means to hang around for a long time. He knows a good thing when he finds it."

"Yes, but after the winter in Alexandria, he'll leave. He won't come back until almost the end. We'll be home before you know it. I might still make my deadline, if you help me."

"I will, if you'll help me, darling." Darius's voice sounded different—husky. He drew Pia away from the bed, to a couch in a far corner of the room.

Understanding his intentions, Pia hugged him tightly and sighed. "Darius, I've missed you so."

They eased down to the couch and made slow, tender, delicious love until the rising sun threatened to expose their secret rendezvous. After Antony's brutish ways and rough fumbling, making love to Darius was the sweetest pleasure Pia had ever known.

"The next time somebody makes a baby around here, I want it to be us," Darius whispered as he held Pia afterward.

"Do you think we could get married first, darling?"

Darius kissed her one last time. "I know a priest in Alexandria," he promised.

"Wonderful!" Pia answered. But deep in her heart, she knew that they couldn't really be husband and wife until they returned to their own time.

Whenever . . . wherever . . . that was.

Chapter Eighteen

On a spectacularly starlit night, Cleopatra's last in Tarsus before her return to Egypt, she and Antony were making love on the open deck of her ship. The Roman was in an expansive mood, trying everything in his power to please his lover, to bind her to him.

He picked up an unlighted lamp of gold and rubbed its smooth surface. "Do you know what I'd like, Cleopatra?"

She stared at Antony, suspicious as she watched him caress the lamp. "I have no idea," she said.

He leaned close and kissed her, rubbing the cool gold against her breast. "I'd like to be a genie in this lamp. If I were, I could grant you three wishes. But what could you possibly wish for? You have more treasure than all of Rome. You have your own throne. And you have the most accomplished lover in the world—me."

He gave a great laugh and crushed her in his huge arms. She pulled free and lay back on her cushions, smiling up at him.

"I can think of three wishes. But I don't need a genie

from a lamp. *You,* Antony, could grant all my wishes with ease."

"Honestly?" His deep voice trembled with excitement. He was eager as always to please. "Tell me, then."

Plucking at his curling beard, she smiled into his eyes. "First, I would like two lives. Execute my sister Arsinoë, who even now lives in luxury in the temple at Ephesus. Caesar should have executed her long ago. Also, I'd like the head of a certain Phoenician who claims to be my long-dead brother Ptolemy the Thirteenth, a pretender to my throne. If he wishes to play the role of a dead man, let it be so."

Mark Antony remained silent, watching her every move, hanging on her every word.

"My second wish would be to have the island of Cyprus returned so that I could once more rule all of the old Ptolemaic empire."

Antony nodded.

Cleopatra slipped her hands over his broad, oiled chest, locked them behind his neck, and drew his mouth down to hers. She gave him a lingering kiss.

"Last of all, I want your promise that you will come and spend the winter with me at my palace in Alexandria. After your coming trip to Syria, forget war for a time. Think only of passion."

He kissed her three times, quickly. "Done! Done! And done, my queen!"

When Cleopatra sailed for home the next morning, she was glowing with satisfaction. Mark Antony had promised to sweep away all the immediate problems in her life. She meant to reward him handsomely once he settled some disputes in Syria and Judea, then joined her in Alexandria.

"Yes, Mark Antony, you will be well pleased by your reception at my palace. And why not? Soon you and I will rule together."

Pia had stayed out of it the night before, but she couldn't hold her tongue any longer. *Is he really going to kill Arsinoë?*

"I commanded it, didn't I?"

But she's your sister!

"Only my *half* sister. Still, it is difficult to kill half a person. At any rate, she's hatched her last plot against me. Once she's gone, I will be the only one left of the Flute Player's five children. The only one who can claim the throne."

Pia didn't answer. She couldn't think of a thing to say. How could the throne mean more to Cleopatra than her own family? This was a side of the queen that disturbed her deeply. She had discussed it with Darius. He'd only shrugged and told her that things were different when kings and queens ruled, and that Cleopatra did only what she had to do to stay on the throne.

As if she sensed Pia's questions, Cleo answered, "Caesarion is my only family now, at least until Antony and I are wed and have a child of our own."

Again Pia remembered that Cleopatra was pregnant already, although she didn't realize it yet. Maybe that was what caused her to be so out of sorts these days.

But Cleopatra seemed calm this morning. Her nagging inner voice forgotten, she gazed out over the sea toward Alexandria. "Yes," she murmured, "Antony will be happy with me. I will see to that!"

Cleopatra was as good as her word, catering to Antony's every whim once he joined her in Alexandria. He loved The City. He gloried in its luxurious lifestyle, its bawdy night life, and its brassy pageantry. Most of all, he enjoyed being with Cleopatra, having her as his partner in crime. She was ever game for his pranks and schemes, ever forgiving of his mishaps. She was his lover, his drinking buddy, his sensual sidekick.

One particularly pleasant night, Antony was left to his own devices while the queen held a dull business banquet. The palace guard apologized profusely to Cleopatra when he interrupted her dinner to drag a bloody drunk before her.

Cleopatra abruptly dismissed the other diners—Darius and several mathematicians and scientists.

"I'm so sorry, my queen, but this fellow insisted he be brought before you when I broke up the fight down at the taverna by the docks. I was all for taking him straight to the dungeon, and I will if you wish. A sorry sight he is!"

"A sorry sight, indeed!" Cleopatra agreed.

The ruffian was covered in filth and blood. One eye was swollen shut. His clothes were in tatters. He had lost his sandals. Cleopatra hid a smile behind her fingertips.

"Leave him!" she ordered. "I've been needing a prisoner upon whom I could test a new poison. This one will do."

When the guard released his hold on the man's arm, he slumped to a bloody heap on the polished marble floor. The queen walked around him, nudged him with her toe. He groaned.

"You may leave now," she said without looking at the guard.

"Are you sure, my lady? He's a mean one. He could be dangerous."

"Only to himself," she said with a chuckle.

Once they were alone, she addressed her prisoner directly. "Well, Antony, it seems you've been out at play again. Why did you go alone? You know it's safer when I accompany you."

"You were busy," he mumbled through a groan. "Business! Always business."

"I'm never too busy to sport with you, my love." Her voice was as cool and melodious as a tinkling fountain.

"What was it this time? A drunken brawl with the fishermen? Or have you been out banging on doors again, rousing decent citizens from their sleep? From the looks of you, you chose the wrong door tonight."

Antony struggled to a sitting position and wiped the blood from his one good eye. He grinned up at Cleopatra through split and swollen lips. "You should have been there," he said. "There were twenty of them. They all jumped me at once. I put up a good fight."

"Not from the looks of you. You started it, of course."

He shied away from her gaze, hoping against all hope that she wouldn't suspect the truth. He'd started it, all right. He'd tried to steal a soldier's girl. She'd been more than willing, but the Roman had paid for her services already. The disgruntled man had taken serious exception to sharing her.

"I was just having fun," Antony said. "A few laughs, a bit of sport."

"At someone else's expense, I'll wager."

He tried his best to look repentant. Cleopatra tugged at his arm, trying to get him to his feet.

"Come along. I'll get you to the bath. A good soak will help your cuts and bruises. You'll be yourself again in a few days."

She rolled her eyes at her own words. Mark Antony being himself was exactly what she had on her hands tonight. She had never seen any man, especially not a general and a ruler, act with such childish disregard for appearances. At forty, it seemed he was going through his second childhood— brawling in the streets, cheating at dice in the taverns, chasing every woman who dared to cross his path. But he seemed to be enjoying every minute of it, every black eye and broken rib. Sometimes she felt that his love affair was not with her, but with The City. Mark Antony had made Alexandria his own personal playground. He was finding out, however, that the other kids were as rough and tumble as he was. So ordinarily, when he skulked out into the night dressed as a peasant, Cleopatra disguised herself, too, going along to protect him.

While Antony soaked in Cleopatra's great bath, Pia had a thing or two to say to her hostess.

He's such a schmuck! *Why on earth do you put up with him, Cleo?*

"Because he is the one man *on earth* who can give me Rome! Don't you realize *yet* that I have planned and lived my entire life with only one goal in sight. I will do *anything* to reach that goal." She paused, pulling nervously at the string of lapis lazuli beads around her neck. "Besides, it's too late to switch to the other team. Octavian would never accept me now that I'm carrying Antony's child."

Shouldn't you send him back to Rome? Pia asked. *You know that his wife Fulvia and his brother—*

"Her lover!" Cleopatra interrupted in a passionate outburst.

Well, yes, Pia mumbled. *The two of them are plotting Octavian's downfall. If Antony were to rush back to Rome with his men, he could help them and then all this fighting would be over. Antony would be the sole ruler of Rome.*

"Don't you think I've tried to convince him to go? The timing is perfect. And while he's in Rome he could divorce Fulvia, if she's not murdered first by one of Octavian's henchmen." She sighed deeply and shook her head. "He won't go! He says he doesn't want to leave me. But it's actually The City he doesn't want to leave."

Can't you make him go, Cleopatra?

"Have you ever tried to push a stubborn bull when it doesn't want to move?"

No, I can't say as I—"

"Well, are we going or aren't we?" Antony roared from the doorway.

Cleopatra turned toward the boom of his voice. He was still mangled but clean, dressed in a fresh Greek tunic.

"I thought you said you'd go with me next time, Cleopatra? Well, I'm ready!"

He can't be serious! Pia silently told the queen.

Cleopatra shrugged. "I won't be long, Antony. Just a moment to change. Have some wine while you wait."

For the rest of the night, Mark Antony dragged Cleopatra and Pia through the dark alleys of Alexandria. They drank the foulest wine Pia had ever tasted. They staggered from door to door, banging and cursing until someone answered. Then Antony would beg for bread, money, sex, anything that came to mind in his mindless state of drunkenness. Finally, just before dawn, Antony forced the queen to make love on the dirty straw in a stable in the poorest part of The City. Cleo and Pia were *not* amused. Antony, however, seemed inordinately fired by the rank smell of the place and the eyes of the animals watching them.

When he had finished with her, Cleopatra quickly pulled on her clothes. She shook her lover roughly. "Antony!" she hissed. "Antony, don't you dare go to sleep. It's almost dawn. We have to get back to the palace. You need to leave for Rome."

But he didn't leave. He stayed and fought and gambled and made drunken love to his queen even as she grew larger and larger with his child. She began to think she would never convince him to go.

At long last, after a day of fishing, when Cleopatra had paid a diver to attach a large salted fish to Antony's line, a joke at his expense that brought riotous laughter from all their friends, the queen said to him, "Leave the fishing rod to another, General. Your game lies in cities, provinces, and kingdoms."

Cleopatra's words snapped Antony out of his extended debauch. Almost overnight it seemed that he realized his kingdom was crumbling around him. In February of 40 B.C., his brother surrendered to Octavian. Fulvia fled for her life to Athens. She sent urgent word for her husband to meet her there. Antony was less than eager to rejoin Fulvia. He took his time after leaving Alexandria, traveling to Athens by way of Tyre, Cyprus, and Rhodes. He was right to be wary. Fulvia gave him hell about his months of frolic with Cleopatra. In turn he yelled at her for losing to Octavian's army. There was no love lost between the two. Finally, Antony realized that there was nothing left for him to do but go back home and either fight Octavian or join him.

He had yet to arrive in Rome when word reached him that Fulvia was dead. Of "natural causes," or so the messenger said. Never one to pass up a fortunate opportunity, Antony told Octavian that his dead wife was at the root of the plot against Rome. The tale satisfied Octavian, who quickly arranged another marriage for Mark Antony.

Even as Cleopatra was laboring to present Antony with twins back in Egypt, he was honeymooning with Octavian's beautiful sister Octavia far away in Rome.

Shortly before Cleopatra went into labor, her spies informed her of Antony's untimely state of widowerhood and his even more untimely remarriage. Through all her hours of agony she cursed him soundly. Pia helped.

"May the gods of Rome and Egypt give you boils and sour your wine, Antony!" the queen yelled.

Come on, you can do better than that, Pia urged. *May your lions crap in your sandals, Roman!*

"May your balls turn to worm fodder!"

Hey, yeah! Now you're getting the hang of it. Give him what for!

Both women went silent except for a final shared groan as the twins made their way into the world, one immediately followed by the other. A boy and a girl, Alexander Helios

and Cleopatra Selene for the sun god and moon goddess of
ancient Greece.

At that moment, as Cleopatra stared at her two fatherless
infants, it seemed that her world was about to fall apart. But
Pia felt none of the queen's dark fears. Overwhelmed with
love for the beautiful babies, she could only coo and sigh
with pleasure.

Three years passed before Mark Antony finally returned
to Alexandria to see his children. Cleopatra had spent the
time well—putting her government in order, strengthening
her fleet, adding gold to her treasury. Pia had spent *her* time
falling in love with the twins. She doted on them. They were
almost as wonderful as Caesarion. Darius kept warning her
not to get too attached, but it was no use. Pia missed her
own mother so much that she wanted Caesarion, Helios,
and Selene to know the mother's love she had missed.

Early in the year 37, the Triumvirate had signed a pact
for another five years. At that time, the two major players,
Antony and Octavian, drew up their individual master plans.
Octavian would build a vast fleet and rid the Mediterranean
of pirates, securing the waterways for Roman vessels.
Antony would go East against the Parthians, who had been
bedeviling Rome since before Caesar's death. But Antony
had his own secret master plan. At Corfu, he made his
pregnant wife Octavia return to Rome, a sign to her family
and to Cleopatra of where his devotions and his alliances
lay. It was time to cement his relationship with the Queen
of Egypt, even marry her, if need be. She could finance his
conquest of Parthia, giving him total control in the East.
Then, the two of them could go against Octavian together
and win control of the West as well. Besides, he was bored

with his upstanding Roman wife, who lectured him constantly on his drinking, his health, and his women. He was more than ready for a good romp with Cleopatra.

In the fall of 37, Antony once more requested an audience with Cleopatra. This time he sent his trusted friend, Fonteius Capito, as messenger to Alexandria. Instead of commanding, Antony begged the queen to join him in Antioch. This note had an entirely different tone from the one he'd dispatched to her from Tarsus nearly four years before.

> *My Queen, my love,*
> *Our time has come! I—WE, if you agree—will soon go against the Parthians. Having done with them, we shall put down our OTHER enemy once and for all. Marry me and I will make you my Empress and give you the world as a wedding gift. Kiss my sweet children for me and tell them that they shall soon meet their father, who intends to be the Absolute Ruler of the World.*

Cleopatra smiled and hugged the letter to her breast when she saw the way he signed it: "Mark Antony, *Autocrator.*"

"Ruler Absolute," she whispered happily.

Can he do that? Pia wanted to know.

"Do what?" Cleo asked dreamily.

Make himself ruler of everything like that? Isn't there supposed to be a vote or something?

Cleopatra tossed her long hair over her shoulder, her face lit with a sublime smile. "Mark Antony can do anything he sets out to accomplish, when he is sober—or when he is drunk, as long as I'm with him to guide the course of events." To Iras and her cousin Charmion, who had recently returned to the palace after a long exile, she ordered, "Get the children packed and order my royal barge made ready. We'll take only six ships and a small entourage of three hundred. We're off to Syria, to Antioch, to Antony."

It was late that night before Cleopatra slept, before Pia could slip away to find Darius. He was not sleeping either. Pia found him in his chamber, pacing; naked except for a length of linen draped low on his hips.

"Darling?" she whispered from the doorway.

He shook himself slightly before turning, as if trying to cast off heavy thoughts. "Pia, thank goodness you've come. I've been concentrating, trying to summon you with my mind."

He covered the distance between them quickly and silently, on bare feet. Drawing her into his arms, he kissed her deeply.

"I heard the news from Capito himself," Darius said. "Antioch! Dammit! If we can't go back to St. Simons, why can't we just stay here in Egypt? What's she thinking, running off to meet Antony this way?"

Pia kissed his neck, his shoulder, his chest. "She's thinking that all her prayers to her goddess are about to be answered, darling. Can you blame her for going? She's fought and suffered all her life for this."

"But *Antony!* God, I hate the thought of you being with him again."

"It won't be for long," Pia reminded him.

"One night is too long when I know you're with another man. Especially *that* man!"

"It's almost over," she whispered. "She doesn't have much more time."

"We don't seem to have much time either. Never *enough* time."

Darius kissed her again. Holding her close, he tugged her diaphanous gown from her shoulders. The silky fabric slithered down her body. She clung to him, glorying in the heat of his bare flesh that sent shivers of pleasure blazing through her.

She smoothed her palms over his hips, undraping his linen. They stood together, naked in the moonlight, feeling the night breeze from the Mediterranean cool the love-sweat on their bodies.

Darius caressed her breasts, her hips, her back. She trembled in his arms—loving him so, needing him so.

"We might wake her," Pia cautioned.

"Who gives a damn? I want you!"

He had her, there in the moonlight, on a deep bed of pillows on the cool, mosaic floor. Knowing that this might be their last chance together for weeks or months made their loving all the sweeter. When the sweetest moment of all came in a star-shower of sensations and passions, Darius gripped her tightly, murmuring her name over and over. For a long time afterward, he held her in his arms.

"I wish we could stay like this forever," Darius whispered between kisses.

"Forever and ever and ever," Pia answered.

But dawn was coming. Cleopatra would surely wake soon. One last kiss and then they parted, not knowing when or where they would hold each other again.

The capital of Syria was a beautiful city, almost as noble as those two jewels of the world, Alexandria and Athens. Antioch's imposing buildings and exquisite works of art gleamed in a setting of woodlands and streams. Its port was a forest of sails from many lands. The smells of woodsmoke and tar filled Cleopatra's nostrils as oarsmen rowed her vessel toward the dock in the red-gold light of late afternoon.

The queen and Pia both scanned the shore. No sign of Mark Antony.

The nerve of him, Pia fumed, *not even coming to meet*

you. I guess he plans on sending for you like he did in Tarsus.

The queen laughed. "He won't have to send for me this time. I plan to ride to his headquarters immediately. Surprise him!"

Pia didn't comment. She only hoped that when Cleo surprised Antony, she wouldn't be in for a surprise herself. No telling what harlot she'd find in his bed.

Within the hour, the queen was regally gowned and upon her white Arabian stallion, sidesaddle to accommodate her flowing skirts. Caesarion, in a Roman tunic and gilded armor, rode at her side, his head high, his dark eyes trained on the road ahead. He looked far older than his ten years. A man almost, with his father's grace and elegance.

As the entourage approached Antony's headquarters, guards came out to meet them. Before the soldiers reached their horses, Cleopatra said to her son, "You will wait here. I want to greet Antony alone. I'll send for you shortly."

"Shortly?" Caesarion responded with a smirk. He obviously thought he knew why his mother wanted to be alone with the man.

"You've a smart mouth on you, Caesarion!" She all but snapped his head off. "For your information, I have a plan. I said *shortly,* and so it will be!"

After his mother's scolding, Caesarion looked more child than man. Pia longed to force Cleo to say something soothing to her son, but the queen had already dismissed Caesarion from her thoughts. All her concentration was now on Mark Antony. As for her plan, she meant to keep the lusty Roman at arm's length until he married her. She meant to remain cool, aloof, and untouchable until she was his wife.

Good luck! Pia told her with more than a touch of sarcasm.

Cleopatra ignored her inner voice as she glided down from her horse and into Antony's stronghold.

Pia sighed with relief when she saw Antony. He was drunk as a lord, but there wasn't a woman in sight.

"Autocrator Antony, I greet you!" The queen's voice was as formal and cool as if she were simply any visiting dignitary arriving for a meeting on state matters.

"Cleopatra?" Antony stumbled to his feet and crossed the room. He reached for her, meaning to give her one of his bone-crushing hugs. She sidestepped quickly.

"I have come to join you," she said. "We will be married immediately."

He grinned at her and squinted his eyes, trying to focus. "Well, sure!" he roared. "But all in a good time. First, come here. I've been a long time without the feel of a woman's warmth."

If warmth was what he was looking for, he wouldn't get it from Cleo, Pia mused. A bit of mild punishment would pay him back for marrying Octavia and for all the pain she'd endured bearing his twins.

"I'll dine with you tonight. No more than that," she answered. "We have much business to discuss. The fate of an empire."

And that's what they did that first night in Antioch. They dined. Cleopatra discussed. As for Antony, he drank and smoldered. By the time the queen left to return to her ship, the Autocrator had passed out on the floor.

On the ride back, Cleopatra spoke in a hushed whisper to Caesarion, "I want you to understand that although I intend to marry Antony and he will be *called* 'emperor,' you will rule Egypt with me. It was your father's wish."

For the first time, Pia realized that Cleopatra had seen the hieroglyphics on the wall. It was all too clear that Antony's lifestyle had taken its toll over the past years. Even sober, he was now bound to be impaired by his heavy drinking and disregard for his health. With Cleopatra's help he might defeat Octavian, but he would not live long enough to enjoy his conquest.

"A pity he is not more like my father," Caesarion answered.

Cleopatra let that pass. She had had the same thought.

Two days passed and Cleopatra kept to her plan. She had not allowed Antony so much as a kiss. Not even a caress. Angry, frustrated, and still drunk, he hastily planned their wedding.

"But first," she said when he announced that the ceremony was set, "we will come to terms on your wedding gift to me. Spread your maps, Autocrator."

Antony jumped to comply with the queen's order.

With a wide sweep of her hand, she indicated all the territories that had been ruled by the ancient Pharaohs fifteen hundred years before. "I want the Sinai peninsula, a portion of Arabia, Petra, Chalcis, part of the Jordan valley, Jericho, the Phoenician coasts, Samaria and Galilee, Lebanon, half of Crete, and the tin mines on the slopes of Tarsus, also the cedar forests on the hills to the west."

Antony's brow beaded with sweat. "We will rule it all— *together.*"

"I want it for Egypt. These lands once belonged to us. Make your decision, Antony. What will it be?"

"Cleopatra, be reasonable," he begged. "I know you hate Herod. Still, I've recently named him King of Judea. He'll war against us if I take Jericho from him. We'll have a similar problem if I make King Malchos surrender the Sinai. Perhaps we can work out a lease to satisfy all parties." He gazed at her with pleading in his bloodshot eyes.

A long, tense silence followed while Cleopatra thought over his proposal.

Who wants those places? Pia mused. They're going to be battlegrounds for the rest of time anyway.

Whether Cleo took Pia's advice or made her own decision, she finally nodded and said, "Agreed! Let the wedding begin."

Both dressed in the old Greek style, the Egyptian queen and the Roman Autocrator stood before the people of Antioch, the priests, and their numerous gods to be joined as man and wife. Antony ordered a coin to be struck with both their likenesses upon it. They feasted, they drank, and at long last they made love. Their honeymoon lasted all winter.

By the time Antony set out from Antioch with his legions to do battle against Parthia, Cleopatra was carrying her fourth child. Although she wanted to go to war with Antony, her husband insisted she return to Alexandria. The battlefield was no place for birthing babies. Ptolemy Philadelphus was born late in the year 36.

Those months while Cleopatra awaited the birth of her new son were some of her calmest and happiest ever. She was sure that Antony's troop of one hundred thousand men—legionaries, horsemen, mercenaries, archers—would be more than a match for the Parthian forces. She dreamed of his triumphant return, when he would take her and their children to Rome for great victory parades. While they were there, he could divorce Octavia and send her brother running for his life. She dreamed of a Roman wedding in the Forum with all the citizens cheering for their hero—their Ruler Absolute—and his beautiful and cunning bride.

Pia and Darius, too, had a pleasant time. Sudibeth sometimes joined them when Cleopatra was napping in the afternoons during her confinement. They would get together on one of the balconies overlooking Pharos and the two harbors to talk of home, of a normal life again.

"I'd give just about anything for a Bloody Mary at the Binnacle on Mallory Street," Sudibeth said with a sigh. "And

I miss my guy from Miami. Shoot, I even get homesick thinking about Bubba from Hahira. When can we go home?"

Pia and Darius exchanged glances. That was the sixty-four-thousand-dollar question! *When?*

"I'm working on it, Sudibeth," Darius assured her.

"I thought you wanted to stay," Pia said.

"I thought I did, too. But I miss hairspray and television and writers' conferences and hotdogs. Hell, I even miss my agent!"

A shudder went through Pia. "I wonder how much time has passed back home. If I don't make that deadline, I'm a dead duck."

"I'll stay," Darius offered, "if you two want to go back right now. You can use the crystals."

"No!" Pia cried. "I told you before, I'm not going back without you, Darius."

"I'm still working on that window I opened back to your computer. If I can just get the bugs worked out of it—"

"While the bugs stay, we all stay!" Pia said emphatically.

"I guess I'd better go check on the twins," Sudibeth said glumly. "They'll be waking up from their naps soon. I promised to take them on a camel ride this afternoon."

"Have fun," Pia said.

"Yeah, sure." Sudibeth's face was as long as the Nile.

Pia and Darius fell silent after she left. They sat on the balcony, holding hands, both staring out over the water, thinking that if they looked hard enough, they might catch a glimpse of the lighthouse on St. Simons.

"Don't worry, sweetheart." Darius leaned over and gave Cleo's lips such a tender kiss it made Pia warm through and through. "I'll get us home—all of us."

But the three time-travelers were still in the palace at Alexandria when news reached the queen that Antony's assault on the Parthians had met with disaster.

Antony's message told of his sorry state. In full retreat,

his army was without money, was running out of food, wore uniforms in tatters with winter fast approaching, and most of their weapons and equipment had been lost to the enemy. He begged her for help. He could go no farther. She must bring her ships and meet him north of Sidon at a fort called "White Hair."

Cleopatra noticed with displeasure and a creeping sense of dread that Antony's handwriting was barely legible and the papyrus was stained with wine.

The queen clutched the note to her breasts, feeling his pain mingle with her own. "I must be strong for him now."

Pia experienced Cleopatra's disappointment. She also experienced the queen's renewed determination to win. Cleopatra had come too far to give up now.

Within hours, her triremes were loaded to go to Antony. No brocade couches, gold plates, or dancing girls this time. Her fleet carried food, clothing, and supplies for her husband's battered troops.

When she arrived, Mark Antony was waiting. He stood on the beach, his eyes red from the sun's glare off the water. He had kept watch there for hours, days. The beaten warrior gathered his wife—his savior—into his arms.

"You came," he whispered, "thank the gods!"

He looked terrible. Battle-scarred, but worse than that. He had lost weight. He was pale, with a sickly pallor. His hands shook. His lion's eyes look glazed and dull. He seemed a smaller man than he had been.

"Cleopatra," he began, sounding apologetic as he spoke her name.

She touched his lips with her fingertips to silence him. "I've come to take you home."

"But the battle!"

"The battle is over for now."

"The battle is *lost,*" he said in a trembling voice.

"Not lost! Never lost," Cleopatra assured him.

Restocked and rested, Antony wanted to return to Parthia for another round. Cleopatra refused to allow it. Over the next weeks, they ranted and raved, shouted and screamed, and when their passionate struggles reached a fever pitch, they dropped their fighting to make love. Their lovemaking during this tumultuous period all but exhausted Pia. They did battle by day and by night. Once more Mark Antony lost.

When they sailed back into the harbor at Alexandria, Darius, like Antony before him, was waiting on the shore for his lover. Pia had never been so happy to see anyone in her whole life.

"The window?" she whispered hopefully as Cleopatra brushed past Darius.

He looked away and shook his head sadly.

Chapter Nineteen

Even Pia was shocked when Octavian, fresh from victories in North Africa and Sicily, sent Antony a patronizing message, supposedly meant to bolster his morale after the defeat by the Parthians. Antony's reaction to this was no surprise to anyone. He set about, in black despair, trying to drink all of Egypt dry.

"That Octavian's a bastard!" Pia said to Darius after the queen had fallen asleep next to her snoring husband late one night.

"It's all in the game of war," Darius explained.

"I *thought* Octavian and Antony were fighting on the same side—that's what the reference books say. That's what I've written in my book."

"Then you'd better do some rewrite, Pia. Their alliance is only for the sake of appearances. They've been against each other since the minute Antony read Caesar's will, maybe even before that. The whole world is like a chessboard to those two guys, and Octavian is about to attack with his queen."

"Who do you mean? Cleopatra?"

Even in the shadowy lamplight of Darius's bedchamber, Pia could see the grim look on his face. "No. I mean Antony's *other* wife, Octavia. A couple of hours ago, around midnight, a Roman nobleman named Niger showed up here at the palace, unannounced. He's brought a letter from Octavia for Antony. Antony had already passed out by the time Niger got here, so he said he'd rest until daylight. He plans to deliver Octavia's message first thing in the morning. Antony's reaction to her letter will seal his fate . . . Cleopatra's fate . . . the fate of the world."

His words made Pia nervous. She inched closer in his arms. "The ancient world, you mean."

"No, the *whole* world, even ours, far ahead in time. Your government's future peace talks at Camp David will never be necessary if Antony reacts properly tomorrow to Octavia's letter. A few diplomatic words to his brother-in-law via his wife, a visit to Athens to spend some time with her, smooth things over, and all would be well."

"But Antony's no diplomat, Darius."

"You've got that right! That's why Camp David is going to come in handy in the twentieth century. This whole section of the planet is going to erupt soon, and upheavals will continue throughout history."

"Can't we do anything?"

"Nope! Just sit by and watch. Can't change history. Remember? But think about it. You told me Cleopatra's worried about Antony's health, that she doesn't think he'll live long enough to rule with her. She's right. Of course, you and I know he's going to kill himself before long. But even if he didn't fall on his sword, his liver's about to blow sky-high."

Pia shivered. "You could have spared me that picture."

Darius shrugged and kissed her forehead. "I'm sorry, but you know it's the truth. On the other hand, what if Antony did make peace with Octavia by going to Athens? Then he and Cleo might be able to wrest control from Octavian?

She's trained Caesarion to rule with her, and that boy's even smarter than his daddy was. So if Antony died and Cleopatra and the kid ruled the world, what a place it would be! Cleopatra's still young. She could sit on the throne for another fifty years. And you can bet she wouldn't put up with all these petty squabbles among minor rulers. She might be a little thing, but she's tough and smart and she can be vicious when she needs to be. She'd have this ole world whipped into shape in a few years."

Pia chuckled.

"What's funny?"

"I was just thinking. If all that happened, there wouldn't be any women's liberation movement in the twentieth century. It would be men's lib. No 'good ole boys.' 'Good ole gals' instead. You're right, Darius. It sure would be a different world."

"One that was never meant to be, I'm afraid. I don't know who holds the blueprint for history—Rome's gods, Egypt's gods, or your God—but whoever's calling the shots doesn't seem to want world peace." He looked at her with a melancholy smile. "I guess the powers-that-be figure we'd get fat and lazy just lying around on the beach, drinking beer and making love."

Pia started to cry. "Oh, Darius, what's going to become of us?"

"Shhh, honey. Everything will be all right."

"No, it won't," she whimpered. "Not ever! Not for any of us! Why don't we steal that letter from Octavia and tear it up before Antony gets a chance to read it?"

"No chance," Darius said with a twinge of sadness. He pulled her down into his arms. "But we could make a little history of our own," he whispered, brushing away her tears. "Just you and me, right here in this silvery spot of ancient moonlight, in the palace of Alexandria, during the final days of its glory."

His words only made Pia cry harder. But Darius knew how to stop her weeping. Soon she was whimpering for another reason. When she moaned after a time, it was with perfect, blissful pleasure.

Octavia's letter to Antony began without salutation:

> *I send you greetings from Rome, my husband. My brother has given his consent for me to sail to Athens, bringing you ships, supplies, and arms. We know of your recent misfortune although Octavian has kept the news from the people of Rome. Better they should imagine you still their hero. Your children and I look forward to the day when we can have you with us. We miss you desperately. Come to us in Athens posthaste or we shall come to you.*

Bleary-eyed from his recent bout with Bacchus, Antony made the mistake of asking Cleopatra to read the note to him. "My eyesight fails me this morning," he said.

"Your *senses* fail you!" she hissed under her breath so that only Pia heard.

As Cleopatra read the letter aloud, her voice went cold, then colder. When she finished, she turned on Antony, her eyes blazing. "Well?" she demanded.

He held his head and groaned. "Please, Cleopatra. Don't shout."

In a deadly whisper, she asked, "Do you intend to accept this woman's invitation?"

"She has ships for me. Besides, I love Athens, above all places. Except for Alexandria," he added too late.

If he didn't want her to shout, he certainly gave her the wrong answer. "I forbid you to go!" she yelled. Slaves cowered, her great lion-hound whimpered, and Antony groaned in agony.

"Then I won't," he said in a helpless, injured tone. "Never mind about my children, my wife."

"*Your children? Your wife?*" She slapped him hard across the face.

He fell back, more startled than hurt by the blow. His head, however, reverberated like a belfry.

Cleopatra leaned so close that her hot breath scorched his face. "*I* am your *wife!* Helios, Selene, Philadelphus, and the great Caesar's son are your *children!*"

"Of course," he stammered. "But, of course, Cleopatra. You are my wife, my queen, my only love."

"Then send this bitch your regrets. *Immediately!*"

Antony sagged on the bed. Pia sagged inside the angry queen.

At Cleopatra's urging, Antony hastily scribbled a response to Octavia, requesting that she send the ships and supplies to Alexandria, but remain in Athens where she was. He told her also that he would be leaving in a few days to meet the Parthians again, this time in Armenia. He said he would be gone for a long time, possibly years. As an afterthought, he instructed her to give his three children greetings from their father.

Peering over his shoulder, Cleopatra scowled deeply when she read that line, but she said no more. She had made her point and won this round. Now, if she could only whip Antony into proper physical shape during the winter months before his planned spring campaign in Armenia.

In the spring of 34, it seemed that all Mark Antony's stars must be in their proper spots in the heavens. His fortunes turned suddenly. He could do no wrong. He soundly defeated the portion of the Parthian army that was assigned to Armenia, after which he took King Artavasdes and all his family as prisoners, looted their country, stole their treasury, and declared Armenia the newest Roman province.

In a second coup, he made a new alliance with the King of Media by betrothing young Alexander Helios to one of the king's daughters. Then he sent glorious dispatches to Rome, telling of his fantastic triumphs.

All of Rome was a-buzz with tales of Mark Antony's great victories. Surely the Senate would decree a Triumph for Antony. He would ride in his lion-drawn war chariot from the Capitol to the Forum, making a grand show for the Senate and the people as was the age-old tradition. The citizens dreamed of his return to the city, his triumphal procession with the royal family of Armenia in chains and their captured treasures on display. Free banquets. Gladiatorial exhibitions. Wine flowing in the gutters. It would be just like the old days, when Caesar still lived.

Antony fooled them. Going against all Roman law and tradition, he decreed his own Triumph in Alexandria. He had no desire to return to Rome. Why should he share his hour of glory with Octavian? Besides, Cleopatra was much more fun to be with at a party than prim and proper Octavia.

"That will show the Romans!" Cleopatra told Pia shortly after she heard Antony's plans.

Show them what?

"That Alexandria, not Rome, is now the center of the Roman Empire. Caesar had hoped to move his seat of power here. Now Antony has accomplished that feat."

Octavian's going to be royally pissed, Pia warned.

Cleopatra threw back her head and laughed. "How nice!"

Pia was correct. Octavian was pissed! The day of Mark Antony's Alexandrian Triumph became the true beginning of the end.

The palace bustled with excited activity that morning. Not only would Cleopatra and Antony appear before the people, but all four children as well, right down to two-year-old Philadelphus. As for the citizens of The City, they had been lining the route from the palace on Lochias promontory all through the streets to the Temple of Serapis since well before dark the night before. Everyone wanted a good seat for this first Roman Triumph ever to be held in Alexandria.

"It looks like one giant tailgate party," Pia told Darius as they gazed from the queen's balcony during the wee hours. "No one's sleeping. Everyone's eating and drinking."

"That's because all the wineshops and eateries are open all night for the occasion. And everything's free, billed to the queen."

"They all seem to be having a great time," Pia observed.

"They don't know what's coming."

"What?" Pia asked.

"Rome!" Darius answered darkly.

Pia shivered. He was right. Octavian would never stand still for this. Antony's plans were an insult to all of Rome. How could Cleopatra and Antony not see it?

Pia kissed Darius good night and slipped back into Cleo's bed. In spite of her troubled thoughts, sleep came instantly.

Cleopatra and Pia were still sleeping when Antony rushed in not long after dawn. His face was florid with excitement, his tawny eyes glittering like gold. "I can't get this damn snake-brooch fastened," he roared.

"My darling Dionysus," Cleo purred drowsily, "come, let me help."

Antony leaned close, his gaze locked on her lovely, bare breasts. Any other morning, he would have said, "To hell with it!" and climbed into bed with her. But not today. Not this day of all days!

"There!" she said. "You look wonderful, dear. You made

a wise choice, deciding to appear as Dionysus instead of dressing as a Roman general. The people will adore you."

"As I adore you." He couldn't resist. He dipped his head quickly and suckled her nipple for a moment.

She sighed with pleasure, but pushed him away. "You'll be late," she warned. "Don't forget the ivy garland for your hair and your god's thyrsus."

He grinned at her, looking more like a big boy than a middle-aged man. "The pine cone came off the top of the thyrsus, but your Cousin Charmion is mending it for me."

"You had better hurry." The queen sat up in bed and let the silk sheet fall to her waist.

Antony tarried a moment more, gazing at her longingly.

She smiled back and blew him a kiss. "After your Triumph, my love. There will be plenty of time then."

"See you at the Serapeum," he said. Then he was gone.

Cleopatra rose slowly. What a delicious morning this was! She wanted to savor every moment so she could relive this celebration in memories for the rest of her life.

She bathed, had a massage, drank a bit of watered wine, and nibbled at figs and cheese. Finally, Iras and Charmion insisted that she must dress. Already cheers were going up from the streets below. The procession was about to begin.

Cleopatra went to her balcony and looked out. She could see Antony's entourage, moving slowly like a great, glittering snake toward the broad thoroughfare of Canopus. First the Roman legions, carrying on their shining shields a *C* for Cleopatra and for Caesar. They were followed by her own Egyptian army and troops from other lands. She spied the royal prisoners—King Artavasdes, his wife, and children— all bound in chains of gold. And then the great litters, piled high with the spoils of war—gold, silver, and foreign crowns. Brightly robed dignitaries walked behind the treasure. At the very end of the long procession, she spied

Antony, standing tall, proud, and arrogant in his golden chariot of war. His lions roared. The people cheered.

"Hurry, Iras!" Cleopatra called breathlessly. "I mustn't be late!"

A short while later, the Queen of Egypt, costumed as Venus to match Antony's Dionysus, sat upon a high throne before the entrance to the sacred Serapeum. A shaft of sunlight fell through the doorway of the dark temple, lighting the golden face of the Greek god of Alexandria, making his jeweled eyes gleam as if with pleasure. The idol seemed almost alive.

Cleopatra focused her gaze straight ahead, down the Street of Serapis. The procession came slowly nearer, stretching as far as she could see. Finally, the multitudes parted for Antony. With more swagger than he had ever before displayed, the conqueror swung down from his chariot and climbed the sacred steps up the hill to the temple. With the aid of priests, he made sacrifices to Serapis while his queen looked on.

Next, the captives paid tribute to Cleopatra and Antony. King Artavasdes, a learned poet and playwright, refused to kneel before the Egyptian Queen. Antony was enraged. He threatened to strike the man dead on the spot, but Cleopatra stayed his swordhand and gazed into his eyes.

"Under these circumstances, what would Octavian do?" she whispered.

"Octavian, 'the Executioner'? Why, he'd torture the king long and hard until the prisoner begged for death. Then he'd crucify the surly wretch."

Cleopatra smiled. "Then let us do the opposite. Send Octavian and all Rome a message that we are above such scandalous behavior."

His sword still raised above the king's head, Antony bellowed a laugh. "Let it be told that the great Antony is not only brave, but merciful. Keep your miserable life, Artavasdes. But you remain my prisoner. Your sentence——write poetry and plays to amuse the queen."

Cleopatra smiled and Pia knew why. She was thinking of Octavian's reaction when word reached him that Antony had spared an enemy of Rome. Octavian detested his nickname, "the Executioner." He would hate it even more once the word was passed that Antony was to be called "the Merciful."

Following the formal ceremonies, Cleopatra rode beside Antony in his chariot back to the palace. All along the way, the people cheered and threw flowers and garlands of ivy. Although the lions moved slowly, Antony kept an arm firmly about Cleopatra's waist. To anyone who happened to notice, this looked like no more than a gentlemanly gesture to keep the queen steady on her feet. But the grip was wholly for Antony's pleasure. He loved the feel of her body pressed close to his side. He enjoyed having the people see his hold on the most beautiful, most powerful woman in the world.

As they drove slowly along, he whispered bold words in her ear. "Remember this morning when I came to your bed? Your breast tasted of milk and honey. I've drunk no wine since then. I wanted to savor your sweetness on my tongue. But it is fading with the hours, my love. Shall I taste you again? Here for all our people to see? They would enjoy the spectacle."

When he bent toward her thinly clad breasts, Cleopatra pulled away. "Antony, you'll make me blush. You wouldn't dare suckle me here!"

His laugh was like the roar of one of his lions. "You think not?"

"Please, no!" she cried in feigned horror. Pia knew that his lurid suggestions were secretly fanning Cleo's flames.

"Ah, *now* you beg 'no.' Later, I'll wager you beg 'yes.' When I have you alone. When I've stripped you and teased you properly. You'll beg, all right."

Cleopatra was truly blushing now, thinking about his words and what would come later. Antony might be an unrefined drunkard, but he had been a quick study of the queen's oriental lessons on the art of love. In fact, he had taken her instructions and refined them to exquisite, passionate perfection.

He sure knows how to turn you on, Pia said silently to Cleo.

You should know! the queen answered, and inside her it was Pia's turn to blush.

"It's good that the robes of Dionysus are full and flowing," Antony said in a hoarse whisper. "Otherwise, all of Alexandria would see for themselves how you fire my blood, woman."

Calling Cleopatra "woman" was dangerous business, and Antony knew it. But she could hardly react with a slap or a kick with all her citizens watching. Instead, she played it another way. Let him suffer, she mused.

"Do you know what Caesar once proposed, Antony? He suggested that he bring you to my villa in Rome. He had threatened when we first met to have a soldier come in and undress me, then make the man watch while Caesar took me. In Rome, he suggested that we summon you for that purpose."

She glanced up. His face had gone almost as purple as his cloak.

"Would you have enjoyed that, my love?" she asked playfully.

Without a word, he removed his arm from around Cleopatra. He smoothed his hand down the front of his robe, obviously making some adjustment.

"I told Caesar that I would agree only if you were allowed to join us after you had stripped me naked. He said he thought that might be most amusing."

"Hush!" Antony whispered violently. "Do you mean to drive me wild?"

"Why, yes," she answered demurely. "What else would you expect of a mere woman?"

Antony fell silent until they reached the palace. At the foot of the wide marble steps, he tossed his lions' reins to a servant and commanded one of his guards to keep everyone away from the queen's chamber for the rest of the day. Then he swooped Cleopatra into his arms, and dashed with her for the bedchamber.

"You'll pay dearly for taunting me so," he warned.

Tossing her on the bed, he shoved up her skirts, ripped away her linens, and fell upon her instantly, diving deeper and deeper until his frenzied lust was spent in one great gorge.

"How dare you?" she spat, clawing his face in her disappointment and frustration.

Antony soon had his Egyptian cat purring. With his own needs momentarily satisfied, he could take his time with her. First he stole away her amethyst ring and put it on his little finger.

"Let the God of Wine keep *me* from drunkenness for once," he said with a grin. Then he put the cup to Cleopatra's lips, urging her to drink time and again. Before long, her senses were as fuzzy as Pia's. For the first time in her life, the Queen of Egypt was tipsy, and made all the more passionate by the lack of her magical ring and the practiced skill of her lover.

He had a way of undressing her that made her quiver inside. He wouldn't simply take her clothes off. He would slide the silky garments over her flesh until she could barely keep her wits. And all the while that he was undressing her, she never knew where he might kiss her next. One moment he'd be suckling her breast, then in an instant she'd feel his hungry mouth at her thighs or her toes. He knew her too well—well enough to drive her wild. And he clearly relished her descent into passionate madness.

"I mean for this day to be my Triumph in every way. I have conquered Armenia. Now I mean to conquer Egypt."

His mouth locked to hers, his tongue probing deeply, he reached up and grasped the silken ropes of the bed curtains. Cleopatra's eyes flickered open when the cords brushed her face. Caesar had often threatened her with this sweet form of torture, but he had never carried through. She could only moan at Antony's obvious intent. It was the first of many moans as he bound her wrists and ankles to the posts, then spent a long, lazy afternoon teasing her trembling flesh and listening to his conquered queen beg, "Yes, please! Yes, now! Please, Antony. Yes!"

No one could have guessed what the Queen of Egypt and her Roman Autocrator had been up to that day behind Cleopatra's bedroom doors. Only Pia knew, and she still blushed at the thought.

But this was no time to think of the past, only the future. Two days later, at a solemn ceremony in the *Gymnasion* close to the tomb of Alexander the Great, Cleopatra and Antony sat on two towering, golden thrones resting upon a platform of hammered silver. Next to them, on four smaller thrones, sat the children—Caesarion, who was now thirteen and already wore his father's old uniform well; the six-year-old twins, Helios and Selene; and the baby Philadelphus, a robust toddler of two. This was a show of glittering solidarity for all of Egypt and the world. Most especially for Rome.

Antony was once more dressed as Dionysus, while Cleopatra presided next to him in the guise of Isis. Their very appearance proclaimed them the sole rulers of Rome's Eastern Empire.

To drive this point home, should anyone fail to understand,

in a solemn speech Antony proclaimed Cleopatra Queen of Egypt, Cyprus, Libya, and southern Syria, naming Caesarion as her co-regent. Young Caesar also received the title King of Kings. Antony's children were named queen and king of other Roman holdings. Each child was dressed in the costume of the country he or she would someday rule. Even little Philadelphus wore boots from Macedonia, a purple cloak, and a native cap with a crown upon it.

To commemorate this grand occasion, coins were struck with Cleopatra's head on one side and the words "Cleopatra, Queen of Kings, and of her sons the Kings." The reverse side showed Antony's strong profile above the legend, "Armenia is conquered." Just in case Octavian didn't get the word in Rome, Antony had detailed dispatches sent directly to him.

As Pia would have said, "Octavian was pissed! *Big time!*"

Cleopatra and Antony became known in Rome as that "African Problem." The lands they had stripped from the Roman Empire would soon be called "The Donations," always spoken with a sarcastic sneer.

Late that night, Darius and Pia met in one of the palace gardens. Both were tense, nervous, wary.

"I can't remember my research," Pia said after they'd embraced and kissed. "How much time do they have before Octavian attacks?"

"A few months. It will be January of 33 before Octavian speaks before the Senate on the State of the Republic. That's when he'll blast Antony and turn the people against him. All of Rome will be crying out for Antony's blood, as if Octavian needed any encouragement."

"I remember now," Pia said, her voice gloomy. "As soon as Antony hears about Octavian's speech, he'll fire off that stupid letter to Rome."

Darius nodded. "Bad move," he agreed.

"I remember writing it in my notes. God, that seems like

a lifetime ago! I was sitting on the beach, thumbing through an old paperback copy of *The Lives of the Caesars* by Suetonius. I just about flipped out when I read it. Imagine Antony writing such a thing to Octavian!" She glanced overhead, concentrating to recall the words. "I remember now. It went something like, 'Why this change of attitude toward me? Because I sleep with the queen? She's my wife. Haven't I been with her nine years? Do you sleep only with Livy? My sincere compliments, if, by the time you receive this letter, you haven't been fooling around with Tertulla, Terentilla, Rufilla, or Salvia Titisenia, or all of them together. What does it matter with whom one fucks?' "

In spite of the dire situation, Darius chuckled. "I'm not sure that's Suetonius word for word, but you remembered the gist of it, sweetheart. And you're right. It's going to push Octavian right to the brink. He probably has been fooling around behind his wife's back. And nothing makes a guilty man madder than being accused of his secret crimes."

Pia hugged Darius and laid Cleo's head upon his chest. "I don't want to put the rest of this in my book. Why can't I just quit with that wonderful ceremony this morning? The kids all looked so cute in their foreign costumes. Well, not Caesarion. He looked very dignified. And Cleopatra was a knockout. Everything was so nice and civilized. Why can't my story stop right there, with everyone smiling and the sun flashing off all their crowns?"

"Because Cleopatra's story doesn't end there. Octavian's going to come with a huge fleet. Cleopatra's going to fight by Antony's side, but there's no way they can win. The war's going to rage for more than a year. The skies will be black with smoke and the waters red with blood. Don't you see, darling? This is a battle to see who gets the whole ancient world. It's going to be bigger than *Star Wars*. You'd better keep your half of the crystal pryamid with you at all times. No telling when it might come in handy."

"I have it," Pia said. Then she gripped him tightly. "Make love to me, Darius!" she begged desperately. "I don't want to think about the war. I don't want to have to live through it. Make me forget, Darius. Make me happy!"

One of those odd miracles of time-travel occurred while Pia and Darius made love: When Pia floated back to earth again, months had passed. She found herself standing on the queen's balcony, watching a horrifying sight. Antony, at the head of his vast Roman legions, charged straight for Octavian's forces just outside the walls of Alexandria. Suddenly, the lines became ragged and blurred. Something was wrong. Chaos reigned. Realization came like a dagger through Cleopatra's heart. Antony's army was deserting, going over to join Octavian. All was lost.

"At least Caesarion is safe," Cleopatra murmured. Pia read her thoughts. She had sent Caesar's son from The City. Even now he would be at the port of Berenice, boarding his ship to flee. "Yes, he'll live even if Octavian kills all of us."

Pia felt numb, disoriented. She tried to figure out what had happened. She had been making love to Darius in the garden. The year had been 34 B.C. Now, if she remembered her research accurately, it must be August of the following year. Octavian was ready to storm Alexandria's gates, ready to take the Queen of Egypt back to Rome, to parade her through the streets in golden chains.

"Iras!" Cleopatra yelled. "Hide the children in the secret room, then you and Charmion come with me. Quickly! There's not much time. Thank the goddess I sent Caesarion away. He'll be safe, no matter what happens here."

Pia felt the queen's words like a physical blow. If Cleopatra was headed with her serving women to the great funeral chamber she had ordered built by the Temple of Isis, she was about to kill herself. That meant Caesarion would soon be dead, too, tricked by a message from Octavian into staying at Berenice until his henchman could hurry there to strangle the trusting young man.

Pia shivered at the thought. She loved Caesarion as if he were her own son. She had been there at this conception and at his birth, she had protected him from the wrath of his natural mother, she had adored the baby, the child, the young adult. And now he was lost to her. She'd never see him again. She tried not to think about it, not to cry. Cleopatra had too much else on her mind to deal with Pia's emotional state.

As the women raced for the mausoleum, Cleopatra shouted to a servant, "Take a message to Mark Antony. Tell him that the queen is hiding or she might be killed." Not certain that the first message would reach him, she told a second slave to urge Antony to join her in her fortresslike tomb from which they would fight on against Octavian.

The first slave, a slow-witted fellow, did as he was instructed, but bungled the job. He found Antony rushing into the palace in a rage.

"Please, General," the man begged. "I bring you news of the queen. She may be killed."

"You mean, the queen may be *dead?*"

Faced with such an awesome, angry figure, the frightened servant dared not dispute his word. He nodded vigorously, then hurried out of Antony's way.

"Cleopatra!" Antony's grief-stricken wail echoed through the silent halls of the palace, echoing even over the sounds of battle from The City. He slumped and hung his head. "If my love is gone, then fate has taken away my last reason to live."

He immediately unsheathed his sword and fell upon it. But he did a bad job of the suicide, inflicting a deep belly wound that would allow him to live on in agony for hours.

The second messenger from Cleopatra found Antony

semiconscious on the floor, his blood turning the marble red. "General Antony, the queen wishes you to join her in her tomb."

"I tried," he gasped. "But I have failed her even in death. Take my body to lie by hers."

The man looked at him oddly. "The queen lives. She asks you to come immediately."

Meanwhile, Cleopatra and her two serving women were busily piling rubbish and wood about the treasure room of the mausoleum, preparing a surprise for Octavian.

"The bastard thinks he'll loot the treasury of Egypt, then haul me back to Rome for his Triumph." Cleopatra laughed bitterly. "When he comes, he'll find me gone on to the next life and my gold burned to ashes."

Just then, she heard shouts from below and banging on the heavy, bolted door of the temple-tomb.

"We have brought Mark Antony," came the call. "He is dying."

"It's a trick!" Iras warned.

"Perhaps. Perhaps not," Cleopatra said. She and Antony had long discussed the merits of death over dishonor. "I refuse to open for them in any case."

She hurried to a high window on the upper floor of the tomb. Staring out, she saw a group of slaves carrying Antony's bloody body. Pia felt Cleopatra's stomach turn at the gory sight.

"I will throw down ropes to bring him up. You men, get ladders to ease his way."

It took a long time to raise Antony with the three women tugging the ropes, straining and sweating. Finally, Cleopatra, Iras, and Charmion pulled him through the window. He collapsed on the floor at their feet.

With trembling, rope-blistered fingers, Cleopatra reached out and wiped blood from his wound, then rubbed it on her cheeks. She began the mourning process, wailing loudly, tearing at her clothes, beating her breasts.

"He is dead!" she screamed. "Gone forever!"

But Antony roused and asked for wine. "Don't grieve for me, my queen. Let us share a cup while there is still time."

While he drank, he begged her to make terms with Octavian. "Take him as your lover, if you must. But keep our Eastern Empire at all costs."

"Antony," she whispered, "don't try to talk. Rest, my love."

He shook his head. "No time. No time left. Do not pity me for my fate. Better this than to return to Rome disgraced. Be happy with me that I will die. Remember the good times we shared." He smiled into her eyes, his own glazed with the shadow of death. "I have been the most powerful and illustrious of men. Now I am not conquered, but a Roman by another Roman overthrown."

Cleopatra cradled his head to her breasts. He died with her kiss on his lips.

Chapter Twenty

Time was running out and Pia knew it. She was frantic.
Where was Darius? And where was the crystal pyramid?
She must have left it in the garden the night they made love.

Cleopatra was still grieving over the loss of Antony and
the loss of Egypt. She seemed to have no plan for the
moment. Only worry over her children kept her from joining
Antony in suicide. This concern, however, was fired not by
motherly affection but by her desire to see them live to rule.
Before she took her life, she wanted some promise from
Octavian that her sons and daughter would retain their lives
and their crowns.

Before long, Octavian sent one of his generals to make
overtures to the queen. While he engaged Cleopatra in discussion through the bolted door, his men scaled the wall to
the high window.

One of her women screamed from above, "Unhappy Cleopatra, you are now Rome's prisoner!"

The queen snatched a dagger from her girdle, meaning
to drive it through her heart. She was not quick enough.

One of the soldiers tackled her. She watched with angry, outraged eyes as her blade flew across the marble floor out of reach.

After a body search by the rough-handed soldiers for poisons or other weapons, Cleopatra and her women were herded to the upper floor, where Antony's body still lay.

Play for time! Pia urged. She needn't have bothered. Cleopatra was way ahead of her.

When the soldiers lifted Antony's inert form, the queen threw herself upon it, weeping and begging to be allowed to prepare the body for burial. "It is my right as his wife," she wailed.

Her plea was carried to Octavian. He sent his permission. Under close guard, she took as much time as possible readying Antony for the grave. Finally, Octavian's patience ran out. He ordered the burial accomplished without further delay.

On the day of the funeral, Cleopatra played her part well, beating herself bloody as she walked with his cortege to the burying crypt below her mausoleum where Alexander The Great still slept.

Pia, by this time, was frantic. She was also exhausted by Cleopatra's rigorous mourning and fasting. Hopelessness had set in. She'd never see Darius or St. Simons again. But in an instant, all changed. Along the route she chanced to glimpse a familiar face in the crowd. He reached out a hand to the queen, but his words were for Pia.

"The crystal pyramid," Darius whispered, holding out Pia's half. "I found this. Keep it close. I'll be there when you need me."

Cleopatra in her frenzied state wasn't sure she'd heard her lover correctly. But Pia heard and understood. Relief flooded her with such force that she all but fainted inside the queen.

Following the funeral ceremony, Octavian ordered Cleopatra returned to her old chamber at the palace, to be kept under heavy guard. Now, Pia realized, the queen had only two things on her mind—to save her children and to do away with herself. Making use of a secret cache of poisonous herbs hidden in her chamber, she soon induced an illness and a high fever. Using her sickness as an excuse, she stopped eating, determined to starve herself to death rather than return to Rome in Octavian's chains.

For Pia, this was the worst period of all. *I can't stand it!* she told the queen. *I'm dying in here. Eat something! Drink something! Even some wine! God, I'd kill for a Big Mac!*

Cleopatra ignored her inner voice. She had too much strength to be tempted. A curt message from Octavian put an abrupt end to her fast. "I have your children. Stop this nonsense and eat or I will kill Selene and Philadelphus."

Pia was in ecstasy when Cleopatra agreed to have a bit of bread and cheese with a cup of watered wine. It tasted better than any Big Mac she'd ever eaten.

The next day Cleopatra was resting when she got a surprise visitor. Octavian strode into her bedchamber without so much as a knock. The queen, gowned only in a thin shift, was lying on her couch, staring vacantly out at the Mediterranean, wishing she were one of the seabirds gliding on the breeze.

Octavian gazed at her with cold, luminous eyes. He had not seen her since his arrival in The City. In fact, it had been many years since they last came face to face. In Rome she had been young and breathtakingly beautiful. Now, at thirty-nine, having starved herself and bruised her body in mourning, she looked far different. He had thought he might allow her to seduce him. Another trophy for his spear. But that notion quickly left him when he saw her.

As if she were reading his mind, Cleopatra smiled slightly, slithered off her bed, and prostrated herself at his feet.

"Great Caesar, you have come at last!" Only Pia felt the sarcasm dripping from her words.

She gained what she wanted. Octavian raised her from the floor and led her back to her bed. They talked. She begged mercy for her children. She showed him letters from Julius Caesar, conferring the crown of Egypt upon her and her children after her.

Pia felt a new scheme bubbling inside Cleopatra. What was she up to now? She rose from the bed and went to her jewel chest. Choosing several choice pieces, she laid them before Octavian. "Gifts," she said with a faint smile. "For your wife Livia and your sister Octavia. Perhaps they will be moved to intercede with you on my behalf."

The queen's ploy did the trick. By trying to bribe him, she convinced Octavian that she meant to live. Once more the cunning Cleopatra had outwitted a noble Roman. He let his guard down just enough to give her the chance she needed for her ultimate plan.

Cleopatra had one friend left at court, an old nobleman by the name of Dolabella. He kept her informed at all times as to what Octavian was up to. When he came to her with the news that the Roman ruler planned to ship her and her children back to Rome in three days where they would be imprisoned until his Egyptian Triumph, Cleopatra knew that her time had run out.

What are you going to do? Pia asked, frantic.

"I'm going to join Antony, of course," the queen replied in a casual tone.

She sat down immediately and wrote a note to Octavian, begging him to allow her to visit Antony's grave to make offerings and place a wreath. After making her wait for more than a day, he finally agreed to honor her wishes.

On a sultry afternoon in late August, Cleopatra, Iras, Charmion, and Sudibeth, guarded on all sides by heavily armed soldiers, made their way to Mark Antony's crypt. Once inside the gloomy place, Cleopatra again worked herself into a frenzy of grief.

Throwing herself on his tomb, she sobbed to him, "Oh, my darling husband, when I buried you I was a free woman. Today I come to you as a slave. I am watched closely every minute, night and day, so that Octavian can take me back to Rome to be shamed in his victor's Triumph. I will come no more to you, my love. Nothing could part us in life. Now we have changed places—you, a Roman, lying in Egyptian soil, while I, the Egyptian, go to be executed and buried in Rome."

She put on a wonderful show for the soldiers, knowing that her every word would be reported to Octavian. There was hardly a dry eye in the crypt. It took little effort on the weeping queen's part to convince her escorts to allow her and her women a moment alone in the temple-tomb where she had planned to be buried. She needed to pray to her goddess, she explained.

The minute the women stepped inside, they bolted the mausoleum door. The duped soldiers shouted, then battered the strong wood with their shoulders. It was no use. She was locked in and she wasn't coming out.

The mausoleum had been stripped of all its treasures by the Romans. They didn't know, however, of Cleopatra's secret vault. There she had stored her emergency provisions—her finest royal robes and crown, a golden couch, some superb old wine, and enough food for a royal banquet. Alas, she hadn't thought to conceal a weapon for her own destruction. Not even the tiniest vial of poison.

"I will think of a way," she told the others. "Prepare me now, for soon I go to join Antony, Caesar, and Alexander The Great."

Oh, God! Pia thought. What am I going to do? Darius is out there somewhere, but I can't leave unless he's here. I don't know how to make the crystal work.

While Iras and Charmion prepared the queen, bathing her, dressing her, styling her hair, Sudibeth sat slumped in a corner, whimpering. "I didn't want to come here in the first place. I want to go home! Pia, if you can hear me, do something! Get us out of this place!"

Cleopatra turned suddenly toward the miserable redhead and said in perfect English, "It'll be okay, Sudibeth. Don't worry."

"My queen?" Iras said, astonished by Cleopatra's strange words.

She was no more surprised than the queen herself, who explained, "Death must be speaking to me and through me. Death is near now. Let him come! I welcome his cold caress."

Fully prepared, Cleopatra reclined on the golden couch and drank wine with her women. They ate quietly, each thinking her own grim thoughts.

"How will you meet your death?" Iras asked at length.

"A way will come. Trust me!"

Down in the street, Darius milled about with the throngs of people who had gathered once the news spread of Cleopatra's escape. He was dressed as a farmer in baggy pants, a hat pulled low over his eyes. He waited and watched. At last he spotted the man he'd been looking for.

"You brought the figs?" Darius asked.

The real farmer uncovered his basket. "I have them."

"Nice ripe ones," Darius said.

The dusky man nodded gravely. "They have flavor and bite, as you requested," he answered, handing the basket to Darius.

Darius dropped several coins in the fellow's open palm, then he vanished into the crowd.

Guards surrounded the base of the mausoleum. A ladder had been placed at the high window, but Cleopatra had closed its bars so that no one could surprise her again. Darius sauntered over to the young soldier posted at the foot of the ladder.

"I've brought something for Queen Cleopatra," he said.

"Show me!" the guard ordered.

"Only figs," Darius answered. "Have one, if you like."

The soldier took one of the ripe, purple-brown fruits and bit into it. He grinned and juice ran down his chin. "They're good!" he said. "Go on up to the window. The queen will like these. She won't get their equal in Rome."

Carefully balancing the basket, Darius climbed the ladder. At the window, he called to Cleopatra. "I've brought fresh figs, my queen. They'll end your pain."

Recognizing Darius's voice, Cleopatra said to her women, "Open the bars for him. Take the basket. He's brought an answer to our prayers—poison figs." She gripped Charmion's arm. "Wait!" she said. "Give him this in payment, in thanks, and to remind him of the love we've shared."

She dropped the token into Charmion's open palm.

"Darius!" Pia cried aloud. "Get us out of this place!"

"Get the crystal ready," he called.

Charmion unbarred the window and quickly took the basket from Darius and handed him the queen's gift in exchange.

Darius was still struggling to hoist himself through the opening when Cleopatra discovered the surprise hidden under a napkin beneath the figs. Pia shivered with revulsion when Cleo grasped the asp in her hand.

Snake! Pia screamed silently. *Get him away from me! I'm going to faint!*

"Hold on, Pia, I'm coming," Darius called.

Cleopatra was playing with the slithery thing, petting it, rubbing it against her breasts, begging it to bite her. She wrapped it around her arm like a bracelet. Pia shuddered. She screamed.

"The crystal, Pia!" Darius yelled. "Forget the asp. Don't look at it. Concentrate on the crystal pyramid!"

Cleopatra's free hand fumbled in the folds of her robe until she drew out the shining half of the crystal pyramid. Darius grabbed Sudibeth's hand and hurried to the throne. He touched his portion of the stone to Pia's. Closing his eyes, he mumbled strange incantations.

Pia heard his words, but she couldn't concentrate. All she could see was that damn asp. Even though it was a tiny snake, it looked a mile long, crawling all over her, driving her crazy.

"Ah, you like my breast," Cleopatra whispered to the thing as if she were seducing a lover. "Sink your fangs there, where my flesh is tender."

"Darius!" Pia screamed.

Too late! She felt the sting of the asp, then swirling colors exploded in her brain. Blackness closed around her. She heard a roar in her ears that gradually softened to the gentle murmur of waves.

"My God!" Sudibeth gasped, staggering across Pia's office on shaky legs. "What the hell was *that?*"

She couldn't see Pia sprawled motionless on the front porch. She didn't remember anything that had happened to her since she'd turned on her friend's computer.

Sudibeth glared at the machine. "Damn you, Edgar Allan! You must have given me a shock. When Pia gets back, I'm going to tell on you. She'll have a technician over here so fast it'll make your screen spin."

Pia heard her friend's voice through a haze of chimes ringing in her ears and swirling clouds of color drifting before her eyes. She shook her head and looked around. It was high tide. The surf was pounding the beach. The sky boiled with gray clouds and rain spattered through the screen, wetting her face.

"A Nor'easter," she mumbled. Then she grinned and

hugged herself. "I'm home! It's storming on St. Simons Island. Isn't that wonderful!"

She dragged herself to a standing position and checked to see if anything was broken. "Nope! Everything works." Then she stretched. "Oh, it feels good to stand up. I was getting a cramp all squashed up inside Cleo."

"Pia-bird? Is that you I hear out there?" Sudibeth sauntered to the front door and smiled. "Well, I'm sure glad you're home. Your damn, ornery computer just knocked me flat on my tush. You've got to get that thing fixed."

Pia thought it was odd that Sudibeth's first words to her were about Edgar Allan instead of all they had been through together back in time. She decided to play it cool, test the waters.

"How long have you been here, Sudibeth?"

"I don't know exactly. A couple of hours, maybe. I was down on the beach, but then it started raining. I figured I'd stop by and check on the place for you. I turned on the computer to see how your book was coming, and I don't remember anything after that. Damn machine must have knocked me cold."

"It'll do that in a storm," Pia answered innocently. "I'm sorry. Are you all right?"

Sudibeth looked herself over. "I guess so. But I'll bet the shock frizzed my hair."

"Your hair's fine." Pia grinned. "Have you seen Darius?"

"Nope. I thought he went with you on your research trip."

"He did," Pia answered, a cold, sickening lump forming in the pit of her stomach. "But we didn't come home together."

She had a hard time getting the words out when the full weight of the truth sank in: Darius was still back there, still in ancient Egypt, watching Cleopatra die. The two halves of the crystal pyramid, as Darius had suspected all along, weren't strong enough to transport three people through time. Tears welled in her eyes.

"Something wrong, honey?"

"No, Sudibeth. I'm just real tired."

"Well, you go rest. I was about to leave anyway. I'll call you later."

"Thanks for checking on the house while I was gone."

"Sure thing!" Sudibeth answered. "Anytime!"

Once Pia was alone, she dashed from room to room, calling Darius. She even checked the attic and the yard. Nothing!

She went back inside, feeling lost and alone. She switched on the television for some background noise. The news was coming on. The date! She listened intently. Sure enough, only one week had passed in the real world while she'd spent years back in time.

"I'll make my deadline," she said with relief. That relief was short-lived. What did it matter? Sure, the book would be great. She had details of Cleopatra's life that no other living writer would ever know. She'd probably sell a million copies, make the bestseller list, get rich and famous. But that thought didn't make her jump up and down and click her heels.

"What do I care about fame?" she muttered miserably. "It doesn't mean a damn thing without love. I don't want money. I just want Darius."

She sank down at her computer, staring at nothing, her mind a hopeless blank. She felt numb, as if she'd misplaced a part of herself. After a time, she tried to shake off her gloom.

"I can't do this. I've got to stay busy, figure a way to make myself go on. Surely, Darius will find his way back. Someday . . ."

When she reached for the computer's switch, her hand brushed something soft. "A peacock feather?" she said, puzzled. She picked it up and rubbed it against her cheek. It smelled like the garden in Rome, like a thousand memories from back in time.

Then her eyes fixed on something else on her desk. It was a small wax tablet with a message incised on its face. "Pia, my darling, I love you," she read aloud. "I always have and I always will. Whatever happens, sweetheart, I'll find you again. It will never be over between us." Pia's eyes filled with tears when she saw Darius's signature and the XOXOXO that followed his name.

She put her head down on her arms and moaned. How long she stayed there, clutching the tablet, she couldn't guess. It was getting dark by the time she rose from her chair. For a time, she wandered aimlessly about the empty house. Finally, she got a beer from the refrigerator and went out on the porch. She slumped down in the rocker in which she'd been sitting when they'd first touched their crystals and flown off to the palace in Alexandria.

"Darius," she called into the wind, "I'm home. I'm waiting for you. If you can hear me, I mean to keep waiting. Forever, if it takes that long. See, I love you, and that's the way love works. And love's all that matters."

She leaned forward in her chair and listened. No answer. Only the boom of the waves and the howl of the wind.

"I've got cold beers ready," she cried, holding up her frosty bottle as if he might see it and be lured back to her through the gulf of hundreds of years.

When nothing happened, she couldn't hold back the tears any longer. She sobbed and sobbed until she had cried herself out. Until she was all used up. Worn out, wrung out. For the first time, she could identify with Cleopatra's longing to just lie down and die.

She set her empty bottle on the floor. It tipped over. When she reached for it, her fingers touched the crystal pyramid, lying where she'd dropped it when she'd landed after her flight through time. She brought the stone close and stared at it. Even though the sky had gone dark, the crystal glowed brightly with its inner light.

"Darius?" she whispered, feeling a small ray of hope. "Can you hear me, sweetheart?"

The colors shifted from green to pink to gold. Deep inside the stone, she saw something move. As she watched, the figure grew larger, more distinct. Finally, she could see what it was.

"Darius! she whooped. "You're coming, aren't you? That's why I can see you in the stone. Hurry, darling! Hurry home to me. I love you so much!"

For the next weeks Pia kept the crystal pyramid always with her. When she went to pick up Xander from Animal House, it was in her pocket. When she went to the grocery store, it was in her purse. In bed, it was under her pillow. And always, Darius was there, too, swimming inside the chunk of colored crystal like a fish in an aquarium.

With Darius beside her computer, Pia whipped out the final draft of her book. She made her deadline. She received calls of glowing praise from her editor. Her book would have a special cover. It was being passed around in Hollywood. It was sure to make the bestseller list. Her publisher was planning a big promotion tour that would wind up in New York with her autographing copies at a fancy bookstore on Fifth Avenue, followed by a party at the Plaza in her honor. An advance review called it "A masterpiece! Lusty, touching, insightful—written with the skill of a true master."

Life should be good! Life should be *wonderful!*

But Pia was miserable.

"It's okay," she said, staring at Darius in the crystal pyramid. "I can live with miserable as long as I can see you. As long as I know there's still a chance you'll find your way back to me, darling."

It was a beautiful morning in spring when tragedy struck. Pia bounded out of bed, ready to grab a shower and then hit the beach in her new bikini. When Darius did show up, she meant to have a tan that would knock his eyes out.

All ready—a new bottle of Hawaiian Tropic and a good book tucked in her beach bag—she reached for the crystal pyramid. The minute she touched it, she knew something was wrong. It felt cool instead of warm. Tears welled in her eyes when she looked at it.

The glow was gone.

Chapter Twenty-one

Pia's hand had gone numb forty-five minutes ago. She'd given up signing her books "Olympia Byrd," and was now writing simply "Pia." She glanced up. She'd been doing this two hours already, but the line still stretched through the store and out onto Fifth Avenue. The autograph party was a huge success.

"Isn't this *marvelous!*" her editor cooed into her ear. "You're a hit, Pia! They love you. And that curious dedication you wrote has everyone mystified and guessing who the man in your life could be. You've made yourself a cult figure."

Pia glanced at the dedication in a copy of the book. "For the man in the crystal pyramid, the man who owns my heart." She wiped at her eyes. It wouldn't do to start crying now.

Giving her next fan a quick smile, Pia took the woman's book to autograph it. She no longer saw faces, only hands. The hands before her at the moment were tipped with long, violet-lacquered nails, the fingers circled with more gold rings than even Cleo had worn.

"I simply adored this book, Ms. Byrd," said the husky voice that belonged to the violet nails. "I read the part where Mark Antony tied Cleopatra to the bed aloud to my husband. Afterward . . . well, suffice it to say, we hadn't had sex like that in *years!*"

Pia mumbled her thanks, blushing as she recalled that tawdry night with Antony.

Squared-off, work-callused, blue-collar hands reached out toward her next. They could have been Mark Antony's, if Cleo's lover had been a construction worker instead of a Roman ruler. "What happened to the kids? Me and the wife have five of our own. We love 'em all. You should have told what happened to Cleopatra's."

She gave the man an extra warm smile. She'd loved those kids, too. "It's in the 'Author's Note' at the end of the book. Octavian took them all back to Rome and paraded them in golden cages at his Triumph in 29 B.C."

"Sorry bastard!" the man muttered under his breath.

"He didn't treat them too badly. In fact, he raised Helios, Selene, and Philadelphus with his own children."

"What happened to 'em?"

Pia shook her head, wishing that she knew. "There's no record of the boys in later years. Selene married King Juba of Numidia. They had a son, but he was murdered by Caligula. He was probably the last of the Ptolemy line."

The man thanked her, then moved aside for the next pair of hands clutching Pia's bestseller.

"Pia." The pretty, blond bookstore manager touched her shoulder. "Someone left this note at the counter for you earlier. I almost forgot in all this excitement."

"Who?"

The woman shrugged and smiled. "I don't know. With this mob you've lured in, I never saw the man."

"A man?" Pia frowned. She didn't know any men in New York City.

"He probably signed it," the woman suggested.

While her waiting fan tapped impatiently with a pen, Pia unfolded the note and glanced at the signature. "Dr. D. Starbuck." She frowned. It didn't ring any bells. She scanned the note quickly.

Dear Ms. Byrd,

I'm sorry to approach you so mysteriously, but I couldn't get through the line to you. Your book, by the way, is most interesting. Reading it made me feel as if I had actually been there in Egypt with Cleopatra. I am an Egyptologist, and I would like to speak with you about an ancient artifact that has recently been unearthed in Alexandria by my young associate. I know this is an odd request, but could you please meet me later? Central Park, five o'clock, at Cleopatra's Needle. I think you will find what I have to show you of great interest. My thanks in advance for your time.

Pia tugged her editor's sleeve. "Where's Cleopatra's Needle?" she asked.

The woman, a born and bred New Yorker, looked blank. "Oh, you mean that little cafe? I think it's up in the Nineties somewhere."

"It's not in Central Park?" Pia glanced back at the note.

"Oh, *that* Cleopatra's Needle! Why didn't you say so? It's an obelisk from ancient Egypt. There were two of them originally. The other one is in London."

"But how do I find the one in Central Park?"

"I'll get you a map."

An hour later, map in hand and well over two hundred books sold and signed, Pia caught a cab and headed for her mysterious rendezvous with Dr. Starbuck, whoever he was.

As the taxi alternately zipped through rush-hour traffic or sat immobile with horn blasting, Pia tried to clear her mind of the afternoon's tension. Autograph parties were always tiring and a little scary. She almost laughed at the thought. If she wanted *scary,* she was sure on the right track—meeting a total stranger with dark coming on and in Central Park, of all places! But somehow she found the idea intriguing rather than frightening.

She reached into her purse to get out money to pay the driver. Her hand touched something warm. "What in the world?" She drew out the crystal pyramid. It was glowing, changing colors, almost pulsing in her hand. She stared at it, transfixed. Deep down inside, she saw movement, a figure swimming toward the surface.

"That'll be four bucks, lady."

The cab driver's gruff voice jolted her. She shoved the crystal back in her purse, then counted out the money, plus tip.

After the taxi sped away into traffic, Pia felt very alone. The park was in shadows. Thoughts came to mind of stories she'd seen on TV—muggings, rapes, murders.

"What the hell am I doing here?" she said. She turned to hail another cab, but spied the tall obelisk, dark against the gold-and-purple sky. She dropped her hand just as a cab screeched to a halt beside her. When she motioned him away with a "Never mind," he peeled rubber angrily.

As if she were in a trance, Pia walked slowly toward Cleopatra's Needle. The tall monument was obviously centuries old, with hieroglyphics on all four sides. At its base, it rested on four metal crabs. Pia smoothed her hand over the cool stone.

"I don't remember this being in Alexandria," she said aloud, trying to place the towering stone in her memories of Cleopatra's Egypt.

A deep voice answered from the shadows beyond the

Needle. "That's because it wasn't taken to Alexandria until 12 B.C. The Romans moved it from its original site where Thothmes the Third had it quarried in the fifteenth century B.C. It seemed right to me that I meet you here because of the name."

The man had yet to show himself. Pia knew she should feel nervous, but she didn't. She laughed softly. "I'm glad it's not something I missed on my research trip."

"I don't think you missed much, Ms. Byrd." He came toward her then, tall and golden in the glare of a streetlight. "I'm Dr. Starbuck. Thank you for coming."

When he pressed her hand, Pia's knees went weak. She realized that she was trembling.

A sudden need to make small talk came over her. She couldn't stand the silence, the electric zing of tension between them. "How did the obelisk wind up here, in Central Park?" she asked.

He chuckled, a deep, very male sound. "That's quite a story in itself. It was brought to this country—a gift from Egypt—in 1880. With much difficulty, I might add. It was unloaded at Staten Island and towed up the Hudson to Ninety-sixth Street, then unloaded again and rolled to this site on cannon balls." He stared up at the top of the Needle, and Pia could see his white smile in the shadows. "Can you imagine? Two hundred tons of granite being hauled over hill and dale on a creaking sledge."

"Amazing!" Pia answered, gazing up and up and up.

"Forgive me," he said. "I shouldn't ramble on so. I'm taking too much of your time."

"I do have a party to attend tonight." She'd all but forgotten the big bash at the Plaza later.

"Then I'll get right to the point." He took her arm, as casually as if they had known each other forever, and started walking her toward the museum. "I have a young protégé, John Caesar, who for the past few months has been on a work/study program in Egypt. While on a dig at the presumed site of Cleopatra's palace, he uncovered a most fascinating artifact. I had been working on discovering its origin and its purpose for weeks—without luck—when I read your book. You told the story of Cleopatra as a child, chipping a corner from the sarcophagus of Alexander The Great."

"Yes?" Pia said, her heart thundering.

"You called it 'the crystal pyramid.' Was that your own name for the object or does it have some historical basis?"

Pia had to think before she could answer. After all she'd been through, it was hard to sort out what was true historical fact from what wasn't. "Let's see. I got the crystal pyramid from a vendor in Alexandria back in 1979. Well, my half of it, that is. A Greek sailor bought it from the peddler. He broke it in half and gave me one part of it. I guess I must have named the thing."

"None of that really matters, except that you say it was broken into two pieces. Do you still have your half?"

Pia patted her purse; the leather was hot to the touch. "Yes! I always carry it with me. Sort of a good-luck charm."

"What happened to the other half?" he asked.

Pia thought for a minute then shook her head. "I don't really know." How could she confess to this stranger that the other half—Darius's half—was back in ancient Egypt, probably crushed to dust by now?

At a back door to the museum, Dr. Starbuck used his key to let them in. It was after hours; the vast halls were empty except for a few guards. In the dim light it looked like a dream world.

"Come with me to my office. Young Caesar is waiting there. He'd like to meet you, and I'm sure you'll be interested in his find."

"Well, yes, of course," Pia stammered. "But I don't have much time."

"This won't take long, I assure you."

Inside the museum, she got her first good look at Dr. Starbuck. He was deeply tanned with longish hair the color of old gold. She could see that behind his glasses, his eyes were amber. Her heart all but stopped when she realized how much he looked like Darius.

She was about to ask him his first name when they walked into his brightly lighted office. A young man rose to greet them. Pia couldn't help herself. She gasped.

"Ms. Byrd, this is John Caesar, my associate."

"Caesar?" Pia whispered. She knew her mouth was open, but she couldn't close it. The young man was tall and lean, with eyes that were like black sapphires, a Roman nose, a regal bearing.

When they shook hands, a warm river of mother love flowed through Pia's veins. She glanced down at the pad in his hand. He'd been doodling while he waited, making cartouches with ancient hieroglyphics and drawing a happy face in the middle of each one. Tears flooded her eyes.

"I'm so happy to meet you, Mr. Caesar." She murmured the words in a trembling voice.

"John, Ms. Byrd would like to see your artifact."

The young man, in his mid twenties, grinned at her with Caesarion's open, heartbreaking smile. "Sure, Dr. Starbuck. Right this way."

They left the office and entered the dark, mysterious cavern of the dimly lit, empty museum. Their footsteps echoed on the floors like drumbeats. When they turned in at the Egyptian exhibit—rooms and rooms of relics from Cleopatra's age and before—Pia felt that she was once more traveling back through time.

She stopped suddenly. Her breath caught in her throat. Beneath a light shining directly down from above, Darius's half of the crystal pyramid rested under glass on a pillar draped in black velvet. Its inner colors swirled and intensified as she drew near.

"Do you recognize it?" Dr. Starbuck asked.

Pia couldn't answer. She had no voice. She stood silent, mesmerized, staring at the crystal. By way of an answer, she reached into her purse and drew out her half. She held it close to the glass that shielded its mate. The colors in both stones grew brighter, more fluid.

"So," she heard Starbuck breathe out beside her. "The mystery is solved."

Not by a long shot! Pia thought.

"If you don't need me any longer, Dr. Starbuck, I'd better run. Hot date tonight, sir."

"That's fine, Caesar. Thank you."

"Yes, thank you, John," Pia answered. "You don't know what a wonderful discovery you've made. I hope I'll see you again."

"Sure thing, Ms. Byrd. Nice meeting you."

A moment later, they were alone. Just Pia, Dr. D. Starbuck, and the two glowing crystals."

"Your book had an unusual effect on me, Pia."

She noted that he'd dropped the formalities. She also remembered the woman with the violet nails and wondered, in sudden panic, if Starbuck was referring to that same scene, the hot night starring Antony and Cleopatra.

"In what way?" she asked cautiously.

"I've led an unusual life. I have no recollection of my early years. I woke up from what seemed like a long sleep several years ago in Alexandria. I was dressed as a peasant, but I realized quickly that I had a vast knowledge of ancient times. In dreams, I see things. I see myself actually back in Cleopatra's Egypt, in Rome, and on a modern island I haven't been able to identify. When I read your book, some of the scenes you wrote were identical to dreams I've had. And the crystal you described, was so similar to the one John brought back from Egypt, I knew that I must contact you."

He paused, staring deeply into her eyes. "Do you know me, Pia Byrd? Have you ever seen me before?"

At that moment, Pia was tingling all over. After several deep breaths, she said, "Yes, I know you, Darius. I've been waiting for you."

He arched one golden brow. "How long?"

She thought before she answered. "Since Cleopatra's death. Forever. Over two years. Lifetimes. Eternities."

"We were lovers, you and I." It wasn't a question. In that moment, he knew. His voice was soft now, caressing.

"Oh, yes. Repeatedly."

He frowned. "How could I not remember?"

"There was an accident."

"I guessed as much." His gaze flickered over her face. "When?"

"The day Cleopatra died. You were there. You brought the figs ... the asp."

He looked shocked. "I killed the great Queen of Egypt?"

Pia touched his face. "No, love. You saved her from a fate worse than death at Octavian's hands."

He covered her hand with his. A thousand starbursts exploded in Pia's heart.

"I wish I could remember," he said sadly.

Pia glanced toward the crystals. "May I hold the other one?"

He nodded, then removed the relic from its case.

She held one piece in each hand, bringing them closer and closer as he watched. They flashed rainbows around the room.

"Would you please kiss me, Dr. Starbuck?"

"If you wish," he answered awkwardly.

But there was nothing awkward about that kiss. At the moment their lips met, Pia pressed the stones together. The release of energy and cosmic memory sent passionate electricity through both. Darius pulled her into his arms, kissing her deeply, thoroughly, the same way they had kissed many times before, many centuries ago.

Pia's body was rejoicing. There was no stopping now.

"Pia, my darling," he moaned, tugging at her blouse, unzipping her skirt. "I've been searching all this time, trying to find you, not knowing who I was looking for."

"Oh, Darius, I was so miserable when I got home and you weren't there." She wrestled with his tie and then his belt.

Moments later, they were making love on an ancient couch that had once graced Cleopatra's bedchamber, a couch that felt familiar to them, as did the body of the other. It seemed they could smell the sandalwood and the lotus blossoms of Egypt. At the same time, they heard the waves crashing on the beach at St. Simons. When their moment came—their New York Triumph—they needed no golden chariot to carry them through the starry heavens. They flew, together at last, in each other's arms.

Afterward, still holding her, Darius drew a ring from his pocket. "I think this belongs to you," he said, slipping it onto Pia's finger.

She gasped when she saw it. "Why, that's Cleopatra's amethyst! Where did you get it?"

"She gave it to me during those final moments, after I brought the figs." He kissed her and smiled. "Now you won't have to worry about drinking too much champagne at our wedding, sweetheart."

Pia was late for the party that night, but she had a good excuse.

"I'm engaged!" she cried as she burst into the room, her eyes flashing almost as brightly as her electric-blue sequin dress.

"Your man in the crystal pyramid?" her editor asked.

"One and the same," Pia answered. "I'd like you all to meet Dr. Darius Starbuck."

Darius looked good enough to eat in his midnight blue tux, his long burnished-gold hair tied back to show his single gold earring.

"Girl, he never looked better!" Sudibeth cooed appreciatively. She'd flown to New York for the party—"To check out the Big Apple action," she'd told Pia.

"Glad you made it okay," Darius said, his eyes twinkling at Sudibeth.

"Well, it was a rough flight," she said, "but I'm here."

"A rough flight, indeed," Pia whispered. "Don't worry. She doesn't remember a thing."

Pia and Darius exchanged secretive glances, then smiled for the cameras.

"Give her a kiss!" one of the photographers called.

"Happy to oblige," Darius answered.

As he took Pia into his arms, Darius touched his half of the crystal to hers. Once more, sparks flew, hearts raced, and love was born anew, to last forevermore.

Here is an excerpt from
Becky Lee Weyrich's
next paranormal novel

SAVANNAH SCARLETT

Coming from Zebra Books in 1997

Prologue

Mary Scarlett could hear her parents fighting downstairs in the parlor, the very room where the shiny cherrywood coffin had lain on its bier until noon. The cloyingly funereal perfume of gladioli, chrysanthemums, and carnations still hung in the air in the tall rooms of the old house on Bull Street. Granny Boo wasn't even cold in the ground, yet already they were at it again. Big Dick's voice boomed through the house like cannon shot, out-blasting her mother Lucy's shrill protests and shrieked accusations.

Their hysterical racket brought an alarming change over Mary Scarlett Lamar, reducing the recent, poised graduate of Sweet Briar College to a weeping, fearful child again.

"Make the yelling go away," she moaned, covering her head with her pillow, shivering with terror and revulsion. "Please, Granny Boo, make them stop it."

Of course there was no answer. Except for the angry voices coming from the ground floor, the house seemed unaccountably still to Mary Scarlett. She had never realized before what comfort she had drawn from the sound of her great-grandmother's footsteps overhead in the attic. Now only silence eminated from that dark hideaway under the eaves.

From the time of her birth twenty-one years ago, Mary Scarlett had drawn solice and succor from the knowledge that her Granny Boo was always there—always ready to soothe tears, tell stories, chase away the ghosts. Now a young woman, on the very brink of her new adult life, Mary Scarlett knew she should be stronger. She should haul herself out of bed, march down the stairs, and confront her parents, demand that they put a stop to their ridiculous behavior. They should at least call a moratorium out of respect for the dead.

"But what good would that do? It *never* ends." Mary Scarlett turned onto her back and stared up at the dark, silent ceiling, feeling tears of frustration slide down both sides of her face.

A crash, then the sound of shattering china, made her jump and set her trembling all the more. She dug her nails into a pillow, holding it hard against her chest like a shield.

"Granny Boo, where *are* you?"

It was a foolish question. Mary Scarlett knew exactly where her great-grandmother was. The dear old woman had simply given out after a hundred-and-three years. Now, at last, she could have some peace and quiet, sleeping under the moss-draped oaks of Bonaventure Cemetery. It was difficult, though, for Mary Scarlett to imagine her prim and petite granny, embraced by quilted-satin and lead-lined cherrywood, lying far below the flowering azaleas. The mental picture made her shiver again.

"You're not really there, are you, Granny Boo? You're off flying with angels by now."

A stiff breeze blew in through the open window, bringing with it the delicious smells of springtime Savannah—Confederate jasmine, wisteria, honeysuckle, and the river, always

the river. The lace curtains fluttered for a moment like butter-
fly wings. Mary Scarlett breathed in the sweet air. She sat
bolt upright when she recognized another scent. Not flowers,
but Pond's facepowder, the kind Granny Boo had always
used.

Despite her over-wrought state, Mary Scarlett smiled.
"No. You're not buried deep in the ground. I knew it!"

"Indeed not!" came a thin but distinct voice.

Mary Scarlett jumped at the sound. "Granny Boo?"

"You called?"

She rubbed her eyes, then glanced about the bedroom.
"I'm imagining things."

From below she could still hear the quarrel in progress,
but the noise seemed muted now, as if she were suddenly
protected from the drunken brawl by some invisible, other-
worldy wall.

"The only thing you're imagining, young lady, is that you
can stay here and know any peace. Why do you think I
moved to the attic?"

Mary Scarlett scanned the room again. She was all alone.
So where was the voice coming from? Was she asking questions, then answering them herself? If so, she must be as
crazy as Granny Boo had been.

"I was *never* crazy!" the voice replied emphatically. "I was
simply eccentric, a Southern lady's prerogative." A familiar
high-pitched chuckle followed the statement. "It suited my
purposes to have most of Savannah *think* I was crazy. As
crazy as the rest of them. Truth be told, all the sane folks
died years ago. I was about the only one left with a grain
of sense."

Convinced now that she was truly hearing her great-grandmother's voice, Mary Scarlett climbed out of bed and
removed the black bunting from her vanity mirror. Granny
had always been fascinated by mirrors. Maybe that's where
she was hiding.

"If you're really here, why can't I see you?"

"You can, dear. All you had to do was ask."

A strange lilac-colored light glowed suddenly in the mirror right above Mary Scarlett's reflection. Still staring, she reached up to see if she could feel anything, maybe a warm spot above her head. Nothing. When she glanced up, she realized the glow reflected nothing in the room, but existed only in the mirror.

She stared as the circle of light slowly widened and intensified. Two eyes and a familiar thin-lipped smile materialized. Gradually, her great-grandmother's face took shape around the smiling eyes and mouth.

"There, dear. Wasn't that clever? I learned it from a cat I met here. Claims he came from Cheshire." The ghostly face turned thoughtful. "Isn't that in Effingham County? I believe I had some kin there a long time ago."

Another loud crash from below made Mary Scarlett jump back into bed. The image in the mirror wavered and all but disappeared.

"Don't go!" Mary Scarlett begged. "Don't leave me alone with them, Granny Boo."

"I'll try to stay, but they make it difficult. We're not allowed to remain where we aren't wanted. It was different in life."

"They always wanted you here."

"I wouldn't be too sure of that. I'd heard whispers about a nursing home in the past weeks. That was enough to send me packing. But, actually, they were getting on my nerves, so I decided that it was time to go."

"You *decided?*" Mary Scarlett cried. "Granny Boo, how could you do that to me?"

"It's a free country, my dear. You don't have to stay either, you know."

Thoughts of the funeral service in the front parlor and the interment at Bonaventure Cemetery flashed through Mary

Scarlett's mind. She shuddered. "I don't think I'm ready to go yet."

"Heavens, child!" Again the lavender image in the mirror wavered dangerously. "I didn't mean for a minute that you should join me. You have your whole lovely life ahead of you."

"Lovely? I doubt it," Mary Scarlett mumbled, thinking of the probable cause of her parents' combat. The major reason for their endless fights in recent months was Mary Scarlett's stalled marriage plans. The two men in her life, Bolton Conrad and Allen Overman, had both proposed. She had given neither man an answer. Her stubborn indecision had set her parents one against the other. Not that they needed her for that.

"It's not *their* choice, you know." Granny Boo seemed tuned into Mary Scarlett's every thought and worry, just as she had been during her lifetime.

"Then I have to decide," Mary Scarlett replied in utter frustration.

"No, you don't."

"Yes, I do. I can't leave both Bolt and Allen hanging forever."

"Why not? At least until you know what you want from life and with whom you wish to spend it. Might I mention a small matter called *love?*"

"Mama says marrying for love is only for foolish women and white trash."

"Poppycock! Your mama should have her mouth washed out with soap. *She* is the foolish one in the family—marrying Richard Habersham Lamar because he could support her in style. Some style! Just listen to them. If she'd minded what I'd told her, she wouldn't have married any man until she could see his face in my mirror."

"Mama says that's just an old wives' tale!"

"Ah, I see. And her method of choosing a husband has

proved so much sounder than mine." Granny Boo's word
reeked with scorn and her image went from lilac to fluores
cent purple. "Have you taken a peek in my mirror lately
Mary Scarlett?"

"Yes," she confessed.

"And which of your beaus did you see?"

"Neither. That's the problem."

Granny Boo's ghost frowned thoughtfully. "Hm-m-m
That *is* a problem."

"So what do I do now?"

After a moment's silent thought, Granny Boo said, "
suggest you simply disappear for a time. Leave Savannah
Maybe neither man is the love of your life."

"I'm not even sure I know what love is, Granny Boo
How am I supposed to recognize it if I ever find the rea
thing?"

"Ah, *love!*" The thin lips in the mirror caressed the wor
as if it were a kiss. "Believe me, child, you'll know it. Let'
see now. How can I put this? When you fall in love, he
won't be someone you can live with, but the one and only
man you can't live without. Does that make sense?"

Mary Scarlett thought for a moment, then shook her head
"Not really."

"Mark my words, it will make sense when the time comes
Yes, I think it best that you go away until you know you
heart for sure."

"Daddy would never allow it. He'd be furious and Mam
would have one of her spells for sure. She's made all thes
wedding plans, even bought my gown. Now if only I knev
who I'm supposed to marry."

"Is this *your* life or *theirs* we're talking about?"

"Mine, but . . ."

"No, buts, my dear! There have been too many broker
hearts and broken lives in this family because the womer
gave in to pressure instead of following their own desires

If you only knew. I won't have you added to that sorry list. I named you and I raised you and I mean to see that you have a good and happy life."

Mary Scarlett was tired of arguing with her mirror, and beyond weariness from worrying over her dilemma. She decided to change the subject. "What's it like where you are now, Granny Boo?"

The old shadow giggled like a girl. "Oh, simply delightful! I was at a party tonight until I heard you calling. Such a grand soiree!"

"A party?" Mary Scarlett asked skeptically.

"Indeed! Why don't you come with me now? See for yourself."

"I don't think that would be appropriate, do you?"

"Oh, I see your point entirely. Nothing to wear. That skimpy black nightie certainly would never do."

"Well, clothes were not exactly my main concern. Actually, I'm not sure I'd fit in. Where is this party anyway?"

"Right here at Bonaventure, the Tattnall plantation. The house is all decorated for the holidays—cedar, bay, and shiny magnolia leaves everywhere. All the folks from plantations up and down the river are coming in by boat. You can tell who's arriving by the songs their slaves sing as they row. Close your eyes, dear. I'll show you."

Wary, but trusting her granny, Mary Scarlett stretched out on the bed and shut her eyes tight. The minute she did, all sounds of the escalating fight downstairs vanished, replaced by the deep, melodic voices of black boatmen, singing their songs as they plied the darkly gleaming ribbon of the Wilmington River.

When Mary Scarlett opened her eyes, she found herself with a group of partygoers waiting near the plantation dock. She wasn't really herself any longer, however. The handsome, dark-haired young gentleman standing next to her—a Tattnall cousin—called her "Miss Lou."

When a new boatload of guests from Ceylon Plantation walked up from the landing, her companion introduced her to a stranger as Miss Louise Manigault Robillard. "But we all call her 'Lou,' " he added.

The new arrival, a tall, dark-haired Adonis with sherry-brown eyes, bowed over Miss Lou's hand. Mary Scarlett felt the warmth of his breath through her lace glove.

"*Enchanté,* Mademoiselle Robillard." He had a New Orleans accent that curled her toes inside her satin slippers.

Thanks to her French mother, Louise spoke the language. She answered the young man, Jacque St. Julian, in kind. Mary Scarlett felt immediate intimacy flowering between them. Every other young man at the party vanished from her mind and her heart at the instant her eyes met Jacque's.

For the rest of the evening, Lou and Jacque were never apart. He swept her over the polished floor of the gold-and-blue ballroom of the Tattnall mansion while slave musicians filled the scented night air with songs of love. Only her heart felt lighter than her feet as the folds of her Savannah-silk gown swirled around her.

They found themselves seated together at dinner, side by side at the long table in the fabulous dining room of the Tattnall home. An unimaginable array of low country dishes was offered. As silent as ghosts, the servants passed silver platters piled with roasted venison, wild turkey, pink prawns, oysters on the half shell, and every manner of vegetable from Bonaventure Plantation's kitchen gardens.

Midway through the meal, the butler hurried into the room and whispered something quietly to Mr. Tattnall. The man's face went grim for a moment, then he smiled at his guests.

"If you please," he said, "I believe we must move our feast out of doors. We have a slight problem, it seems."

Amidst excited murmurs, the guests filed out through the wide front door. Jacque held Lou's arm as they descended the veranda stairs. If he clung a bit too tightly, no one noticed but the young lady herself.

A general gasp went up as soon as they all reached the lawn and saw flames, vivid orange, leaping through the roof of the beautiful mansion.

"No need for alarm," their host announced calmly. "We're all safely out. Shall we resume our dinner by the light of the fire?"

The servants scurried this way and that, setting up tables, spreading damask, and resuming service. As the great plantation house turned into a massive bonfire, their host proposed a toast to his dying home, then smashed his crystal goblet against one of the ancient oaks under which they now dined. The guests followed suit.

No one noticed when Jacque St. Julian brought Mademoiselle Robillard's ungloved hand to his lips to kiss her fingers. No one, but Lou herself. Flames hotter than any fire licked at her heart. Only the smoky black curls that draped her cheeks hid her blush.

Later, as the house burned to nothing, Jacque led his new love through the dark garden. They stopped by the burying ground where the moss-darkened stones stood enclosed in a spear fence of wrought-iron. The silent dead seemed to welcome the young lovers.

Jacque bent low to kiss Lou's bow-shaped lips. This was her first kiss, and with it he captured her tender young heart.

"Forgive my boldness," he whispered. "But, you see, I believe I love you, Mademoiselle Robillard."

She blushed, her heart hammering, her joy boundless. "Will you be stopping long in Savannah, sir?" she asked breathlessly.

"Alas, no. I must leave for New Orleans with the dawn. But I shall return, my darling Miss Lou. And when that time comes, I mean to ask your father for your hand in marriage. Would that displease you?"

Feeling another, stronger blush of happiness, Louise lowered her lashes. "By no means, Jacque. I do believe you've won me with one kiss."

Mary Scarlett found herself back in her room as quickly as she'd left it. Her heart was still pounding and her whole body burned with excitement and joy. Her lips tingled from Jacque St. Julian's kiss.

"There, you see," Granny Boo said proudly from her mirror perch. "*That,* my girl, is love!"

"But it wasn't real." Mary Scarlett argued. "It was all a dream, wasn't it?"

"My goodness, no. Mary Scarlett! That party took place long before my time. November of 1800, if memory serves. But every detail you experienced was exactly as it happened on that night. The dashing Jacque St. Julian made his promises to my own Great-Grandmother Louise."

"And did Jacque come back to Savannah to make Miss Lou his wife?" Mary Scarlett asked hopefully, sure that they must have married and lived happily ever after.

"No," the ghost said with a sad sigh. "Upon his return to New Orleans, he lost his life saving a woman and her child when their carriage plunged off the levee. Poor Lou grieved for him the rest of her life. A suitable marriage for her was arranged to an older man."

"How sad," Mary Scarlett sighed, feeling tears sting her eyes.

"But the party goes on," Granny Boo said in a cheery and surprisingly youthful voice. "Each night here at Bonaventure you can hear music and the tinkle of smashing crystal. I expect my own long lost love will turn up one of these nights."

"I never knew Great-Grandpa Horace."

"Doesn't matter. He was a good enough husband, but not the man I loved."

"Granny Boo!"

"Don't sound so shocked. I'm in Heaven after all. You get your wishes up here, all the good things that were denied you during life. But now to business. Where's my mirror?"

Mary Scarlett reached to the floor beside the bed. "I brought it to my room. I was afraid they might smash it."

"Good girl! From the sound of things down in the parlor, you're probably right. Now I want you to close your eyes, hold the mirror before your face, then look to see who the love of your life truly is. We'll settle the matter this minute."

Gripping the guilt-framed antique, Mary Scarlett did as instructed. When she opened her eyes, she gasped.

"So! You know at last," Granny Boo said smugly. "I told you it would work. Which man is it—Bolton Conrad or Allen Overman? Tell me quickly, dear."

"It's neither," Mary Scarlett whispered.

"Who then?"

"Jacque St. Julian." She glanced up at the other mirror where her granny's violet image still glowed. "What does it mean?"

"It means that you must never marry until you love a man the way Louise loved Jacque St. Julian. Obviously, he has come back, looking for his own lost love in *you*, Mary Scarlett."

The thought of such a thing was staggering. "How will I ever find him?"

"Your heart will know. Give it time."

"There *is* no time! Bolt's building me a house. Allen has already shown Mama the antique sapphire and diamond ring that all the brides in his family have worn for generations."

"Which man's kisses make your heart flutter the way Jacque's did?"

"Both . . . *neither!*" Mary Scarlett stammered. "I don't

know. Bolt keeps pushing so hard to get married. He wants
to put me in a house closed in by a picket fence. Allen just
keeps *pushing*. I'm not sure he cares about marriage so much
as just getting me in his bed. It's *my* life, *my* decision! I
wish they'd all leave me be!"

Granny Boo laughed heartily. "That's what I wanted to
hear—a bit of piss and vinegar from my girl. You have
your answer, Mary Scarlett. Go, child. Now!" Granny Boo's
familiar voice began to fade along with her image. "Don't
you marry a soul until you see him in my mirror."

"But I can't just run away, leave Bolton and Allen hanging.
What would Mama say? And, oh, how Savannah would
gossip about me! If I go, it will cause a terrible scandal."

"Go, go-o, go-o-o-o . . ." The single word swooped and
surged through the dark room like a hurricane wind.

An hour later, the sound of the train on its tracks seemed
to echo Granny Boo's final admonition. For better or worse,
Mary Scarlett Lamar was leaving Savannah, fleeing north
through the night into the unknown.

Only one thing did she regret leaving behind—Granny
Boo's magic mirror. Without the mirror, how on earth was
she supposed to find her man?

About the Author

SANDS OF DESTINY is Becky Lee Weyrich's twentieth novel. She is also the author of four novellas. Since she began publishing fiction in 1978, she has written for various publishers in a variety of genres, including historical romance, fantasy, saga, Gothic, horror/mystery, contemporary, and time-travel. Her first novel, *Through Caverns Infinite,* is now a collectors' item among New Age aficionados.

In 1991, Weyrich won *Romantic Times* magazine's Lifetime Achievement Award for New Age Fiction. Several of her books have won Reviewers' Choice awards, and ALMOST HEAVEN (Zebra, May 1995) is nominated for the same award. Her books have been translated into ten foreign languages and produced on tape.

Beginning as a non-fiction writer in 1960, Becky Lee Weyrich did freelance work for magazines while her byline was seen in newspapers in Maine, Maryland, and Georgia. She also wrote and illustrated two chapbooks of poetry before turning to a full time career in fiction.

A member of Romance Writers of America, Novelists Inc., and a board member of Southeastern Writers' Association,

Weyrich is the originator of the Becky Lee Weyrich Fiction Award, presented annually at the Southeastern Writers' Workshop on St. Simons Island, Georgia. She established the cash award to aid and encourage new writers.

After roaming the world as a Navy wife, residing in such diverse locations as Maine, Florida, California, and Italy, the Georgia-born author now lives on St. Simons Island with her husband of thirty-six years, several cats, and a Beagle named Barnacle.

If you would like to receive Becky Lee Weyrich's newsletter, please send a self-addressed, stamped envelope to P.O. Box 24374, St. Simons Island, GA 31522.